New Rain

This is a work of fiction. All of the characters, organizations, and events portrayed are either products of the author's imagination, or are used fictitiously.

ISBN 978-1-7338478-0-3

Trade Paperback 2019

Published by:

FALCON WEST BOOKS

Cover design by Eve West Bessier

Printed in the United States of America

Also by Eve West Bessier

Roots Music: Listening to Jazz
Exposures: Tripod Poems
Pink Cadillacs: Short Stories
Poems Before Breakfast: Poetic Micro Essays

New Rain

Eve West Bessier

FALCON WEST BOOKS

For Elisabeth and Patrick
with all my love

Book One

Tionpin: Arrival

(Translation courtesy of the IDS Caifanii database)

Chapter 1

Day One (morning)
Huin: Zero

Sola glanced at her pilot, Colby, who was wearing a mischievous grin and his favorite old Stetson.

"Ready?" he asked.

"You're on!" she said.

Colby activated the ionic shield that protected the ship from entry burn, and guided their Orion-class shuttle, Minerva, expertly into the planet Caifanii's atmosphere. His ingenious enhancements to the shield added an entertaining side effect, a light-spectrum resembling an aurora borealis. Long plumes of chartreuse, ice blue, and magenta light filled the view screen.

"Hoowee!" Colby yelped, like a cowboy in an old-time Western.

They sat transfixed. It was a one-minute extravaganza and worth every nanosecond. Colby's psychedelic light show was one of his better tricks, perfectly safe but certainly not protocol. When the boss is light years away, things can get creative.

As they passed out of the ionosphere, Colby shut down the field and continued their descent into the blue-green expanse of the Caifanii sky.

"That sky will take some getting used to," Sola said.

In the daily grind of interstellar sales, everything took some getting used to. Sola liked the challenge.

Colby scanned her from head to toe with a smirk on his face. "That is some outfit Protocol came up with."

"I know. Can you believe this? They really outdid themselves. It looks like a potato sack!"

"Very haute couture!"

"More like *oat* couture!"

The appearance of an official looking spacecraft on the view screen interrupted their jovial banter.

"What the Crobustian Creepers do we have here?" Colby said. "Was there anything about a welcoming committee in your briefs?"

"No, and they'd better stay out of my briefs!"

"Woman, you crack me up." He activated the communications system. Nothing happened. "What the heck?" He frowned.

"What's wrong?"

"Some sort of a system glitch." He turned the com on and off a few times. "Hold on. Okay. I've got them now."

Sola switched on the console translator. "This is Representative Sola Alturas of IDS, Interstellar Data Systems. I have official clearance by invitation of the High Council for Trade and Commerce: Permit 83-A."

The vessel took position alongside their shuttle, to starboard.

A gruff voice responded in Caifanii, the translation following in its consistently pleasant, feminine tone.

"Welcome to Caifanii, Representative Alturas. This is Haikon Port Authority. We are ready to assist your vessel into the landing bay."

Sola muted the com and gave Colby a goofy look, crossing her blue eyes. She wondered what other surprises might be in store.

"Sheee-it," Colby swore under his breath. "I can land this thing on the edge of a tin cup."

"In a category 10 solar storm," Sola agreed, "but I guess we're stuck with the escort." She gave Colby a conciliatory pat on the back. "I do think they meant 'escort' not 'assist.'"

"Still insulting," he said, lowering his head in mock shame. His soft tawny curls falling over his eyes in a coquettish manner. Colby had a Texan tan, athletic body, big feet and hands, and a bounding, optimistic attitude. He reminded Sola of her childhood pal, Sam, a golden retriever with whom she had shared many adventures.

She unmuted the com. "Awaiting instructions," she said. Bureaucracy at its best was a pain in the ass. The vessel did not look like port authority. It looked more like a police or military craft: clean and expensive, with an ostentatious seal on its hull.

The Caifanii were potential new clients for IDS. They should be showing their first date face right now.

Maybe they thought sending the escort was a courtesy. Maybe this spaceport always sent an escort. Hard to know, she had heard stories floating around at local galactic trading stations about the Caifanii, stories of underhanded dealings, but every culture had its seedy underbelly.

That didn't mean the official channels of government were corrupt. Then again, politics was a dirty business. Getting to the top usually required sleeping with the dark side, or at least engaging in some heavy flirting.

Ever since the corporate buy out of her company, six months ago, IDS seemed to have a new credo: profit above integrity. The newly installed corporate leadership wasn't particular about whom they invited to play the game, and they certainly weren't playing by the old rules of fair trade and honorable protocol.

Up until recently, IDS had a policy of working only with societies who were United Planets members. She respected that. It made smart business sense. It made her work a lot safer.

The Caifanii were not members of the UP. Sola wasn't onboard with her company's new modus operandi, but she'd weighed the balance and decided she'd get through this assignment before jumping ship. Her assignment was a first contact situation for humans on this planet. She was an unofficial diplomat, and had the needed skill set.

Some newbie from corporate could botch the job, not have the practical understanding gained by her twelve years of experience.

She still felt badly about not bailing as soon as she'd found out IDS was no longer the company she'd respected and had been proud to represent, but to complicate her ethical concerns, there was the commission to be considered.

This assignment would allow her to retire and live full-time in Hawaii. She was good at door-to-door sales, but the doors were light-years apart. Space travel was a brutal physical marathon. She was 34, and in great shape, but the lifestyle was getting old, and she wanted out before she started getting prematurely old from living it.

Docking took only fifteen minutes. The skyport was all but deserted. That was odd. Haikon was the commercial center of the Northern Continent.

"Wonder why it's so dead around here?" Sola said, walking to the back of the shuttle with Colby.

She went into the airlock chamber, deep in thought.

She pulled herself out of her ruminations and took a decontamination suit out of the locker.

"Maybe it's a religious holiday or something?" Colby suggested, standing behind the airlock command console.

She looked at him through the small window.

"According to my materials, religion is an unpopular topic on this planet," she said. "I think someone is paying a little too much attention to our arrival." She stepped into the decon suit.

"Maybe so, then again, maybe Tuesdays are just a little slow. Beats our last arrival!"

Their docking at Luko Station had been a bit hairy. The Poaz, the station's political majority party, misidentified Minerva as belonging to one of their current enemies, and directed weapons fire across their nose.

"Now, *that* was a warm welcome!" Sola said.

She was up to her thighs in the decon suit. She was wearing a long, traditional Caifanii dress called a tjong. It was a dark grey, thanks to the bad fashion sense of the Protocol Department.

She stuck her arms into the decon suit, pulled it up over her shoulders, fluffed her auburn curls out from under the collar, and stuffed the excess folds of the tjong in over her belly and closed the suit.

"When's the baby due?" Colby asked, chuckling at her.

"It's a boy," Sola responded, rubbing her round, lumpy belly with feigned affection. "Gonna look just like his Daddy!"

"Really? And who might that be?"

She smiled at him, suddenly feeling self-conscious. A few years ago, it might have been Colby, if they had decided to make that happen. Did she want that now, to settle down, live some sort of normal adult life with him?

She's envisioned her dream life being alone, living on Maui, writing, hiking, swimming, being free and safe from further emotional loss?

She and Colby had logged over two-dozen assignments together since he started working for the company seven years ago. They were romantic partners for several months, five years ago, shortly after over-zealous authorities killed Sola's younger brother, Ramon, during a peaceful university demonstration. Colby was there for her in that moment when her life contracted into a white dwarf of rage. He was her rock, helped her survive an un-survivable loss.

Tragedy opens you to intimacy in unexpected ways, but intimacy born of tragedy can be a temporary balm, difficult to sustain, too intrinsically linked with that tragedy.

Sola felt that she was in the relationship for the wrong reason, out of need in crisis. She wasn't sure she loved Colby the way he obviously loved her. She felt terrible about it, but had to be truthful with him. She needed to return to being best friends. He respected her decision and managed to make the transition, but she knew it hurt him deeply.

Colby was her truest friend, but he was also in love with her. Sometimes, she wondered how he could keep working so closely with her under those circumstances. Sometimes, she wondered if he had managed to fall out of love in order to do it. She didn't want to risk hurting him again, but sometimes she missed what they shared as lovers. Sometimes, in the wide emptiness of space, and the isolation of the shuttle, they needed the physical intimacy to stay sane. It was always good in the moment. They each understood that their lovemaking did not mean they were once again a couple, but it always left an awkward tension for them both. She felt his desire to make the reconnection permanent, clashing with her own resistance for reasons not fully understood. Why was life so damned complicated?

Not just complicated, cruel. Two years ago, Sola's mother died from an outbreak of Lynga's disease at a remote research station on Galone. She was devastated. Lynga's disease was now curable with the right treatment and medications. The research station was delinquent in not having those meds in supply. Funding cuts had killed her mom. Life was relentlessly painful.

She was still raw from losing Ramon. Sola and her mother, Anuhea, had always been ultra-close. They had talked daily whenever communication links were available.

Sola felt utterly lost in the Universe without her mom. It was more than she could process or accept.

She took a month leave from work to stay with her maternal grandmother on Maui, after attending the funeral there.

When she returned to work, Sola was a mere shell of her former self. She was unable to feel anything but sad, unable to access anything but grief and anger. She poured that anger into her job, becoming a complete workaholic for the next year. She broke all sales records for her company, and raked in enough commissions to put 40% down on her one-bedroom condominium on the Maui coast. She hadn't even moved in yet.

No time, but this assignment, along with the royalties from her cookbook, would allow her to cover the monthly payments in early retirement.

That was why, three months ago, despite her misgivings about the new corporate environment, Sola agreed to take this assignment, the biggest assignment of her career to date.

The irony of the situation did not escape her. The new management, impressed by her aggressive, goal-focused, effective sales approach, put her on this assignment because they thought she was tough.

It made her cringe. Everything they assumed to be a sign of her prowess was actually a veneer of bravado, a thin armor keeping her safe from the complete vulnerability she felt inside of her. They judged her as "tough" based on the external scaffolding she built to support the crumbling structure of her internal life She just had to fortify that scaffolding one more time, make it hold long enough to complete this job. She did not feel tough, but she could act tough.

She told Colby in confidence before they left Earth that she planned to quit working for IDS right after this assignment. He told her he planned to do the same. He hated the new company politics and leadership.

That conversation made Sola wonder what might happen to their relationship. Would she even see him once he was no longer her pilot? Their relationship might be rooted in their mutual uprootedness. She was moving into her condo in Wailea, no question. She wasn't so sure Hawaii would suit Colby. He was a Texan to the core, loved the land, almost as much as the open range of space, not that he spent much time on his Dad's ranch anymore. Sure, there were still a few cowboys in the islands, but they were weary old souls plucking their ukuleles with arthritic hands and singing the old songs with thin voices. Not exactly Colby's style.

"Sola?" Colby's voice pulled her out of her ruminations. "You okay?"

She looked at him looking at her with such genuine concern. Damn. That man really knew how to be himself. She envied that.

He was so forthright, so clear, so 100% Colby. She herself felt murky, not even 50% Sola.

She was healing though, coming back into her own skin, her truer self.

She smiled at Colby and gave him the go ahead to close the hatch on the inner hull. It slid into place and locked with a hiss. She listened to the automated countdown.

"Ten, nine, eight, seven ..."

Standing in the amber light of the narrow airlock, Sola closed her eyes and slipped into the threshold place in her mind. It always came at this exact moment, the feeling of suspension between past and future, a momentary disconnection from time.

She could feel the tingle of the bio-decontaminant moving through her decon suit. She waited for the outer hatch to slide away and reveal to her the colors of another alien world. Sometimes she felt as if it would open and reveal only a vast blackness. She imagined she could step out into the void and become something undefined, something new.

The computer's even voice continued. "Three, two, one, zero."

Zero. The fulcrum of possibility.

In her mind, Sola heard an unfamiliar woman's voice as if it had spoken aloud.

In a warm, gentle tone it said, "E komo mai."

She was startled.

She was used to hearing her incessant inner critic blab on in her head, and often still heard the remembered voice of her mother giving sage life advice, but this was a completely unknown voice.

It had welcomed her in Hawaiian, a language now rarely spoken, even in her native Hawaii.

She experienced a tingling sensation. It was very different from the usual bio-decon reaction. What just happened?

"Aloha?" she whispered.

She kept her eyes closed, listening intently.

There was no response.

She waited in the silence, then heard the hermetic seals on the compression lock release, letting local air hiss into the airlock.

Sola opened her eyes. She stood for a moment, just breathing deeply, dazed.

That was seriously weird, she thought, a side effect of the environmental stabilizers? Aural hallucinations were not included in the long list of possible side effects.

Whoever had spoken to her knew she was Hawaiian. How was that possible?

She snapped out of her reverie, and convinced herself it was just her brain having a drug-induced synaptic misfire. She dreamt about being on Maui last night. That probably sparked this. She was nervous about this assignment. Stress could wig you out.

She unclasped the helmet buckles of the decon suit and pulled off its bulbous dome. She gave her hair a good shaking out.

She looked at Colby through the window. He was busy with something on the console. As her lungs filled with rich Caifanii oxygen, she began to feel drowsy, a side effect of the heavily ionized air. One more time, she coached herself. You can do this!

Caifanii was a more massive planet than Earth. Therefore, its gravitational field was greater. According to her materials, the field here was 10.83N/kg at the altitude of a shuttle in near orbit as compared to 7.83N/kg for Earth. The surface effect of Earth's gravity on a human being was 1 g force. On Caifanii, the g-force was to 1.25. That made everything heavier, including the fluids in her body. Pumping heavier blood was a strain on the heart muscle.

Sola had just spent six months on Danuba IV, the nearest IDS client planet, where walking unaided by a weight belt was like maneuvering on a trampoline. She had grown fond of being temporarily light.

Now, she would have to adjust to being temporarily heavy.

During the three-week of travel time to Caifanii, Sola spent hours running in the holoscape at simulated high altitudes to increase her lung capacity and muscle strength in preparation. It helped that she currently lived at 2200 meters in Evergreen, Colorado, in the Rockies above Denver, though she spent little time there.

Her favorite holoscape programs were Trails in the Santa Fe National Forest, starting at 2200 meters working up to 3400; and Trails in the Chilean Andes, starting at 2200 meters and working up to 3700. Despite her rigorous workouts, this was still going to be a challenging assignment.

The only life-hospitable planet in this six-planet star system, Caifanii was on the interstellar commerce radar because of its participation in a trade conference on Denuba IV a year ago.

She and Colby met the two Caifanii delegates at the conference. Colby called them the "little green men from Mars," though not to their faces. Colby was always coming up with perfect snippets from his historical pop-culture obsession. There were, of course, no "little green men" on Mars, just crazy Earthlings living in nasty domed cities.

The Caifanii however, were actually green. They had light-green skin, almost round heads, no hair, and were short in stature.

They fit Earth's pre First Contact stereotype of the alien perfectly. They were alone in that distinction. Sola had never seen any other "little green men." As an outcome of that conference, networking support for the Caifanii was new territory for IDS, and that territory was hers for the first five years of royalties.

Even if she terminated her employment, her contract still gave her legal rights to those royalties. Whenever a client made a trade deal based on their networking connections through IDS, Sola received a royalty. Not a lot, but it added up nicely. Passive income streams were the best kind of bonus.

Her Caifanii clients were eager to become IDS affiliates by purchasing the *Encyclopedia Interstellar* database system, and having their own information included in future editions. IDS was a Super Club in the trade arena. Being a member had its privileges. If nothing went awry, it was going to be a quick, smooth ride to a completed contract.

The Caifanii's main objective in becoming associated with IDS, according to their High Council for Trade and Commerce, was finding an interstellar market for their mineral resources. Their planet was rich in minerals used in technology manufacturing, including quartz (the source for silicon), chalcopyrite, coronate, and cuprite, (all sources of the now rare copper). These minerals were worth gold to a plethora of potential trade partners, including Earth.

Now, here she was, ready to negotiate with the High Council.

Sola bent down to compress the stabilizers on each ankle strap and released the remaining air pressure from the decon suit. The suit was manufactured to accommodate a wide variety of body types, that ubiquitous "one size fits all," which ultimately doesn't fit anyone.

The suit was a tremendous improvement over sitting naked in a decontamination chamber. Nonetheless, it still worried her. You were isolated in a layer of synthetic skin and blasted with antiseptic gasses that smelled of seaweed and green apples. There were always side effects, next morning headaches, digestive upset, one time she had a painful rash. In her line of work, chemical manipulations were a routine fact of life.

For this assignment, Doc Mirn had prescribed two environmental stabilizers for her and Colby. They were conveniently melded into one small pill called the PI-33. She took the first dose an hour ago. It contained a muscle strength booster to cope with the extra g-force, and a stimulant to keep them awake in this hot, humid sea of negative ions.

On planets like this, you had to resign yourself to feeling slower than a galactic freighter and limit your stay to 60 Earth days. They were only staying as long as it took her to close the deal, probably four or five days max.

The PI-33 pills, nicknamed peppers, were bright red and had a reputation for making you irritable. According to the PDR, 5% of users also experienced increased libido, dry mouth, mild to severe intestinal discomfort, dizziness, lack of mental focus, and an increased susceptibility to fungal infection. No mention of aural hallucinations.

Lucky her! She was the first to experience that side effect. She wasn't looking forward to being chemically altered for the next few days.

She was looking forward to exploring some new dishes for

her upcoming publication, *Cuisines of the Cosmos, The Encore*.

Sola was a gourmet. Not trained, just good at food. Her first cookbook, published by IDS, was so popular that she received offers from several other publishers for a second edition. She hadn't decided whether to remain with IDS for the sequel, or snag one of the more generous advances.

Sola loosened the pressure seals on the front and sides of the decon suit, unzipped the inner layer and carefully stepped out of its silver folds.

She pulled her translation unit out of the tjong's pocket.

On this trip, she was using the latest model Translation Linguistics Computer by Solvex, nicknamed the TLC. The update provided better idiomatic translations, a smaller earpiece, and an ultra-thin strand microphone/speaker unit.

It was still odd to hear the translation of her English into the local language in that computerized, androgynous voice, but this unit's speaker packed a punch compared to its predecessor. At least she didn't sound like she was whispering all the time, and the delay was minimized.

"Ready Freddy?" Colby asked.

She pulled on a pair of mustard-colored gloves. They clashed badly with the tjong.

"All set," she said, giving Colby a queenly wave.

"See you when the satellites come home!" He blew her a kiss.

She smiled back.

He was a nutcase, and she loved that about him.

She suddenly remembered her orchids.

"Hey Buddy, do me a favor will you? I forgot to switch my plants to auto-water."

"I'll take care of it. Oh, and I'll get that data processor unit through customs and take it over to the hotel with me later."

"Oh, thanks. That thing is ridiculously heavy. I swear those guys in engineering put bricks inside just as a joke."

"Wouldn't put it past 'em. Hey, I need to move Minerva into long-term parking. Then, I want to run some diagnostics before I join up with you. See what might have caused that glitch in the com system. Had trouble with the airlock console too. Something's up with the rig. I'll give'er a good shake down."

"Okay. Keep me posted."

"Sure thing. It'll be a while. I'll need to stay put until the diagnostics are complete. If you need to reach me, call my PCU. The main system will be offline during the diagnostic."

"Okey-dokey!" she said. "Hope you can make it to the hotel for dinner."

"Should be no problem, but I won't be there by their check-in time, so could you check me into my room?"

"Sure."

"Gracias."

"De nada!"

"I'll get the key, or code thingy, from you at dinner."

"See you then!"

Sola swung her ukulele case over her shoulder, picked up her travel bag and briefcase. These were her must-have items.

She descended the shuttle gangway and walked into a narrow hallway leading to the terminal.

It was low ceilinged, dimly lit and humid. At its termination, she passed through a set of slow automatic doors.

While she was here, she would deal with substandard technology, and do so graciously.

Nothing was more detrimental to sales negotiations than letting on you thought your clients were living in the Dark Ages, even if they were.

"Here we go trooper!" she told herself.

Chapter 2

Day One (morning)
Tatjin: Introduction

Sola reached the end of the hallway and entered the main terminal where the air was refreshingly cooler. It was disappointingly standard: the glare of artificial light, the faint smell of industrial cleansers, the stark metallic décor, and the feeling that you could be just about anywhere in any universe. Then again, standard was acceptable. Standard was good. In this particular case, the more standard, the better.

She passed through the Caifanii customs inspection without a hitch, a good sign as nit picky customs inspectors were always a good indicator of nit picky sales clients.

As promised, an attendant sent by her hotel awaited her beyond the customs gate.

"Esteemed greetings," the attendant said, giving her a wide smile with ultra-white teeth, no canines.

The Caifanii were vegetarians. No ceremonial consumption of squirming Rotchak worms on this trip! That was a blessing. The Caifanii tiat, a popular tuber, and the houbob, a vitamin rich legume, were tough and difficult to digest. She would avoid them. Just about everything else should be manageable.

She followed the attendant, who wore a powder-pink tjing. The traditional female attire was the only clue to the attendant's gender.

The Caifanii were members of the Archaldian species, all of whom were androgynous in physical appearance, sexual differences being subtle and difficult to detect. The Caifanii had lean, muscular bodies. Their green skin was glossy with a silvery sheen. Through its semitransparent surface, you could see the delicate patterns of veins that looked like lace. Their skin color reminded Sola of pale jade, that rare Earth gemstone. For her thirteenth birthday, her mother gave her a small piece of jade, in the shape of a whale, carved in the nation of China in the late nineteenth century. Sola treasured it not only for its beauty but because it was passed down to her through her matriarchal lineage from her Great, Great, Great Grandmother, Mana'olana. She kept it in a carved monkey pod box in her bedroom at home.

The Caifanii had large, round heads and inquisitive eyes which, according to her briefing materials, came in shades ranging from pale gray to icy blue, and quite rarely, light amber. They had no hair, not on their heads, faces, or bodies. The attedant's eyes were a light gray. She was a lovely young female, whose elegant tjong and matching gloves made Sola feel embarrassed about her own dowdy attire. She looked forward to buying nicer clothing as soon as possible.

Gloves were a statement of respectable modesty on Caifanii. Showing your bare hands in public was promiscuous. Touching hands, without wearing gloves, was equivalent to an intimate kiss. No handshakes on this trip, even with gloves on! The preferred Caifanii greeting was a simple bow of the head with hands placed modestly behind your back.

Alien sexual behaviors were often fascinating, sometimes unpalatable, and in this case, a bit of a mystery as there was little information available on the Caifanii. Her work here would open up informational trade.

The attendant was walking quickly. Sola had a difficult time keeping up. The greater g-force made walking a strenuous workout.

She looked up through the skydome. The brilliance and color of the Caifanii sky reminded her of Napili Bay, a favorite snorkeling spot. Seen from the planet's surface, the sky was azure. The color made her want to dive in and swim, made everything look like it was underwater. That was almost true. Here on the Northern Continent, it rained abundantly every afternoon.

Only 30% of the planet's surface was landmass. There were two large continents: one in the western hemisphere, slightly north of the equator, the other in the eastern hemisphere, slightly south of the equator and crowned with archipelagos. A single global government ruled both continents, with the primary seat located in the capitol city of Haikon. There was a secondary, and much less empowered, seat on the southern continent in the capitol, Djintu City.

The attendant looked back at Sola and kindly slowed down. "Your accommodations are prepared. May I assist you with your bags?" The attendant spoke with marked pronunciation. The TLC did its job perfectly, almost no lag time.

Sola declined politely. She preferred to keep her essentials under her own control, though the bag and case felt like bowling balls. Even her light travel uke felt cumbersome. She left her precious tenor ukulele safely on the shuttle. It was handmade by her mother's younger brother, Taavi, her makua kāne 'ōpio. He gave it to her after the funeral service for her mom. It was his favorite, so she cherished it. It was made of traditional koa wood, very hard to find these days, with mother of pearl inlays on the neck and rosette. It was a work of art with an amazingly warm yet clear voice. She'd bought the smaller, soprano uke so she could play daily even while on assignment without jeopardizing her family heirloom. Playing kept her fingers agile, calmed her mind, and made her feel more at home in the succession of alien worlds that made up her day-to-day life.

"We will be at *The Hotel Final Rest* quite soon," the attendant assured her, using an English translation for the name of the hotel, and with impressively accurate pronunciation. Sola smiled. "Final" was an interesting choice for the Caifanii word meaning, "planned destination." The "Hotel Planned Destination for Gentle Resting," was the full Caifanii name, according to her briefing materials. The hotel had two of its suites remodeled to accommodate human needs. She was curious as to exactly what that might mean.

As they exited the terminal building, Sola noticed two officials in dark gray uniforms standing guard by the doors. Their weapons holstered but menacing nonetheless. They fell in behind her at a distance of about twenty-five meters. Her stomach muscles tightened. She could hear the steady step of their heavy boots. It tapped into her vein of anger, her Ramon trigger as she called it.

There was no mention in her briefing materials of an armed escort. IDS had strict guidelines about such things. It was a serious omission, a breach of interstellar directives. She would definitely report it.

Her attendant seemed unconcerned and brought her to a small transport vehicle waiting at the end of the walkway. Sola glanced over her shoulder. The guards were boarding a small, gray transport with an official insignia on the hatch, the same seal as the one on the craft that had guided them into the port. Sola followed her escort into the transport. The palms of her hands were moist and warm inside the gloves.

The small hovercraft lifted and pulled away from the terminal. She glanced through the rear window and could see that the other vehicle was following. The ride into the city took almost twenty minutes.

The heat lulled Sola to the edge of sleep, though she tried to stay alert.

Suddenly, the hovercraft came to an abrupt halt. Sola felt her head jerk forward. She must have nodded off. She pulled her thoughts together like scattered puka shells from a broken necklace.

The attendant was quickly outside, and waiting politely.

Sola looked for the other vehicle. It was gone, a relief.

In the hotel lobby, she thanked the attendant with the proper Caifanii decorum, avoided tipping as this culture considered it an insult to the employee's personal work ethic. She went to the front desk to register.

"Greetings, I am Sola Alturas," she said. "I am checking in."

Sola used her mother's maiden name, Alturas. Her legal documentation included both her mother and father's family names: Alturas and MacGregor, even though the practice of using family names was outdated. Most people chose their own secondary ID according to their individual preference. Sola wanted to honor her parents in the classic fashion, and now that her mother was gone, it brought her solace to carry the Alturas family name as her own. Solace was in fact her first name, but she much preferred the shortened version. She loved her maternal grandfather, Juan Alturas, whose Mayan genetics informed her high cheekbones and fiery passion for life. Her mix of her Mayan, Hawaiian and Scottish ancestry came together as an arresting combination of light brown skin, blue eyes and auburn hair.

She received her room code. "Thank you. I would also like to check in for my business partner, Colby Stanton. He will not be here by your 3:00 check in time. Is that possible?"

"How do you spell his name?"

Sola spelled Colby's full name.

"Yes. We have him listed as paid in full. That will be no problem. One moment and I will get you his code as well."

"Excellent. Thank you."

Sola let a young Caifanii male employee of the hotel carry her bags to her suite.

She was vigilant about her gear, but not a control freak. Nice to have a *bellhop*, she thought. *Bellhop* was a term she learned from Colby, taken from an old novel he had dug up on some database. He was addicted to twentieth and twenty-first century pop culture.

She was a thoroughly twenty-third century woman.

The bellhop graciously opened the door to her suite, deposited her bags in a corner. She thanked him graciously before he left.

The suite was invitingly cool and spacious. There was a huge bed piled high with fat, round pillows. She chuckled softly to herself. There were enough pillows to accommodate a Girl Scout Troop in the mood for a good pillow fight.

She remembered those giggle-fit pillow fights at summer camp, her troop housed in musty wooden cabins near Seven Pools on the Hana coast.

There was a small metal closet in the suite's bathroom with a narrow door. A shower!

She needed that in this sticky climate. In fact, she needed it right now.

She preferred a shower to a tub any day, but showers were oddly hard to come by on foreign planets. Three Brownie Points for the Hotel Final Rest!

Sola locked the suite door, placed the uke case on the bed, slipped off her clothes and shoes and got in the shower. The cool stream of water felt like spring rain against her shoulders and back. It quickly revitalized her, and the peppers were kicking in. She stayed in the shower a long time, until her skin was deeply chilled. The hotel towel was more like a blanket. She wrapped it around her to dry off, but it was too cumbersome to wear. She discarded it, and put on her own lightweight batik robe. She hopped up onto the bed. It was so ridiculously high, her legs dangled like a child's, nowhere near the floor. She smiled at the charming misconceptions alien species had of human comfort needs.

She pulled her uke from its case and played through a few songs she knew by heart, singing along softly in a warm, low register. Two were traditional Hawaiian pieces, *Henehene Kou, Aka*, and *I Ali'i Nō' Oe*. The third was a recently learned favorite, *I Kona* by George Kelepolo. Hotel suites were so impersonal. The old tunes brought the spirit of aloha into the sterile space.

She reluctantly put away the uke, and brought her briefcase over to the bed.

She let her mind run through her scheduled agenda. She received notice only yesterday that her sales meeting with the

High Council, which was supposed to be tomorrow, was set back by three days. That was a major annoyance, but she was a firm believer in making the best of things, and seeing the glass half-full.

She decided to see the delay as a luxury. She now had the next two days to stabilize, get some contact with the culture, and do additional preparation for the meeting. A few centuries ago on Earth, people flew around in air buses, sitting crammed together in rows of seats for hours in order to get from one side of the planet to the other. They crossed time zones and threw their biological clocks off rhythm for days. She could hop planets and near-Earth solar systems and feel almost no ill effects, but traveling from one end of the galaxy to another, that was a different story. The hyperspace transports were comfortable and spacious. She could maintain a normal work routine, sleep, eat, work out in the holoscapes, catch some live jazz at one of the clubs in the evening, and access the shuttle's computer systems while it was in the storage bay. Still, there was a nagging fatigue from the lack of direct sunlight and from gravitational simulation. She always felt *jet lagged*, as Colby called it.

She decided not to wait for Colby. She wanted to go do a little exploring and purchase something to replace the hideous grey tjong. She pulled it on over her cool skin with reluctance.

Haikon was the largest city on the heavily populated Northern Continent. The sparsely populated southern continent was the source of the planet's mineral wealth. Aside from the industrial areas, where mining meant employment, the southern continent's population lived in village-sized, agricultural communities on the shorelines and at the edges of the vast rainforests.

Djintu City, the Southern Capitol, was the only large metropolis. She would not be going south. The Caifanii government databases would provide IDS with all the information they needed.

That was fine with Sola. Surface travel on less technologically advanced planets was arduous.

Chapter 3

Day One (afternoon)
Saviantu: To meet with destiny

Sola strolled the maze of pedestrian pathways in Haikon's City Center, where her hotel was conveniently located. She felt like a giant among the throng of Caifanii who passed in both directions. The Caifanii walked fast for such short-legged folk.

She stopped to get a better look at the ornate facades of the buildings. They reminded her of the storefronts and residences in the historic Chinatown district in Honolulu.

The Caifanii language and culture also seemed Asian, reserved and of high etiquette, ambitious yet unassuming. It sounded a little like Cantonese, nasal and with a singsong quality.

Then there were the odd clicks and chirping sounds of the Caifanii equivalents of consonants. Walking in the midst of a crowd with her translator switched off was like walking through an aviary.

She was enjoying herself. She was also attracting considerable attention from the Caifanii. A few openly stared at her abundant hair blowing in the warm breeze as she walked by them. She was used to gawking alien fascination. As she ambled toward the city center, she thought about the Caifanii language. The meaning of words altered drastically with subtle changes of inflection and emphasis. The word tchenjo, when pronounced with the emphasis on the tchen, meant to ratify or accept the terms of a contract.

However, with the emphasis placed on the jo, it meant to fertilize or inseminate. She hoped the translator would be accurate in its pronunciation when the time came to close this deal.

Sola recalled her last translator mishap on Faruzk. Faruzkian was another language in which the meaning of words drastically altered with slight changes in inflection. One evening, at a social event, Sola excused herself politely saying that she needed to get up early to attend a business meeting. The computer voice simulation inflected the word for 'meeting' incorrectly. She had told them she needed to get up early to attend a *rauihck*, a political practice of mudslinging, with real mud. In ceremonial dress, the political opponents start flinging the filth at each other until one or both "break stature" and succumb to laughter. The practice is a proper christening of political candidates and precedes formal debates and campaigning.

She had learned these details days later, after the story had gotten around. Her comment had been good for a healthy laugh, and probably helped her negotiations, as the Faruzk were famous for their robust sense of humor. She liked the Faruzk. They were honest, straightforward folk, and damned good cooks. Their spicy bean pies made your eyes water.

Sola found a shop displaying brightly colored tjongs in the window. She stepped inside. A small number of customers milled around the bins and display racks filled with clothing. The Caifanii females stared openly at her. She brought a teal gown and a pair of gloves in a silky blue material into a dressing room. Luckily, the Caifanii had five digits on each hand. Their fingers were smaller. Her hands barely fit into an extra-large size. The tjong only reached to her mid-calf, but would do, bare calves and ankles were not taboo, just hands. She kept on the new clothes, and paid the shopkeeper, who put her old clothes in a red net bag for her.

She ambled a while, then noticed a small cheese shop. Her culinary instincts were aroused. She went inside to explore.

"Hello," she greeted the shopkeeper.

The air was filled with fantastic aromas.

"What a wonderful shop," Sola said.

"Thank you," the shopkeeper replied, at first a little confused by the translator.

She smiled that wide Caifanii smile. "All of these cheeses are made with yamma milk from Honshai Province. Yamma produce rich milk, high in protein. I have several varieties here, all with different herbal infusions."

"Could I taste a sample?" she asked.

"Of course!" The shopkeeper pulled three cheese triangles from the case, obviously meant for sampling, carved off three slices placed them on a small plate and offered them to Sola.

"Here you are."

"Thank you," Sola said. She took a bite. The flavor was sublime, woodsy with an edge on it, but not too sharp. "This is delicious!"

"Thank you. I sell only the finest cheeses."

"Are all Caifanii cheeses made from yamma milk?"

"No," the shopkeeper shook her head. "Most cheeses come from the common granif. Those cheeses are not nearly as flavorful, but are cheaper to make, not long-aged, so cheaper to buy. Unfortunately, most people prefer cheaper."

"That's the way it is where I come from as well, but I'll take good taste over cheap prices any time." Sola said.

"I am glad to hear that! Would you like to buy a bit of these cheeses?"

"Yes, I would." she returned with enthusiasm.

Sola purchased a small triangle of each of the three cheeses for herself, plus a sample pack of twelve cheeses to offer her clients at their first meeting. The samples whetted her appetite. It was time for lunch.

"Could you recommend a good restaurant nearby," she said, "one that serves high quality local foods?"

"The Fuiga Nakaii is my favorite," said the shopkeeper. "It is only a few minutes from here." She gave Sola directions.

Sola was always looking for new recipes and hoped her lunch would offer some interesting explorations. She found the restaurant without any trouble. The atmosphere inside was friendly but subdued. Candle lanterns at each table created a charming ambiance. She sat far in the back, facing the wall for optimum privacy. The service was quick and polite. She ordered the special of the day, a sweet and spicy bean pie served hot. It was excellent. She closed her eyes and savored another bite.

The sound of an unexpected voice broke her culinary reverie. "Esteemed greetings, Representative Alturas. May I join you?" Sola looked up. A tallish Caifanii male was hovering over her table like a hummingbird seeking nectar. "You are looking exceptionally ravishing," he said, and then flashed a toothy smile.

Sola awkwardly chewed and quickly swallowing the bite of bean pie she had in her mouth. Who was this? Sola wondered, and where had he found that line? Exceptionally ravishing? He needed to update his cross-cultural communications resources in a desperate way. There currently were no resources for Caifanii/Terran interactions, so she couldn't fault him. She thought for an instant he might be one of the delegates she met on Denuba IV; but no, they were considerably older and he was considerably more handsome, in an alien sort of way.

To her surprise, her unexpected guest took a seat across the table, as if invited. She was not particularly in the mood to chitchat, she was in the mood to savor her meal, but she usually enjoyed her interactions with aliens, once she got into conversation with them, so she decided to see what this one had to offer.

"Pardon my lack of manners," her visitor said. "Let me introduce myself. My name is Jaitain I'lliana." He looked over her shoulder into the dining area, and seemed on edge. "I heard from a friend that you are here on business, and when I came in to have my midday meal, I chanced to see you back here. Good luck, yes?"

"Uh, yes," she said, though his explanation was a bit odd. He acted as if she was an old school mate and was pleased to run into her again after all these years. It made her feel tempted to play along, to pretend to recognize him and say something ridiculous like, "Jaitain, you rascal! You don't look a day older!" The friend he mentioned must be on the High Council, or maybe an employee at her hotel. Who else would know about her being here? What did he want from her?

"You will be staying in Haikon for some time?" he asked. He looked at her intensely.

His eyes were light silver with a hint of blue. His candid gaze affected her in an unexpected way. She felt herself blush and lowered her eyes.

She noticed her hands resting next to the plate of bean pie. They were naked. Crap! She quickly slipped her hands under the table and pulled on the gloves lying on her lap. She hoped Jaitain had not noticed, but was sure he had.

They sat in an uncomfortable silence for several moments. Sola became acutely aware that the remaining bean pie was getting cold, but as he had nothing to eat, she felt awkward about eating in front of him. Something about him made her feel awkward altogether, a little jittery.

"I wonder if you have plans for the evening," he said. "There is a concert in the Pavilion if you would like to join me. I think you will enjoy it."

She stared, perhaps too directly at his anxious face. He seemed to grow more agitated, scanning the room behind her again.

"I think you will find the program very stimulating," he continued. "Traditional Caifanii with a postmodern twist."

She looked at his round, bald, green head and wondered what his scalp would feel like to the touch. She was immediately annoyed with herself for the thought and pushed it aside. She did not want to spend the evening listening to atonal clanging of gongs while trying to make light conversation with this nervous, oddly spectacular Caifanii who had seen her hands naked.

"That is a very considerate offer, Tcelli I'lliani," she used the formal salutation, deliberately putting distance between them, "but I must decline. I have much work to do before the morning."

Poor fellow. Now he looked quite miserable. "So, how long have you lived in Haikon?" she asked, trying to steer the conversation in a new direction.

"Not long," he said. "Actually, I do not live here. I am from Djintu."

"The Southern Continent," she said. "Well, then you are far from home."

"Yes, but certainly not as far as you!" he replied, with a hint of humor that she found interesting.

"What brings you to Haikon?" she asked.

"That topic is of great importance to me," he said, "the motivation for my seeking to speak with you."

Here comes the sales pitch, Sola thought. IDS did not allow her to do side business while on company time, and all of her time here was company time. She often received business offers from locals who wanted to cash in on some lucrative interstellar trade. She was not in the mood to be schmoozed. She wanted to graciously excuse herself from the conversation, and eat the rest of her bean pie. Jaitain's presence was making her feel self-conscious.

He was looking past her again, in the direction of the restaurant entrance. He suddenly grabbed the menu and held it up to cover his face.

"I really need to be going," he said, from behind the menu. "I will contact you again soon."

He got up abruptly, walked rapidly towards the kitchen, and disappeared through the swinging double doors. Presumable there was a back exit. She glanced over her shoulder to see what might have disturbed him. There were just a few people waiting for open tables. Jaitain was quite a character. She didn't know what to make of him.

She finished her bean pie and ordered a cold Ylatua melon drink for dessert. She wondered what Jaitain wanted from her? Now she might never know. Maybe he was just another alien interested in sexual exploration. It seemed alien races either found your appearance utterly disgusting, or they wanted to "get to know you better" with a passion.

This was not her first restaurant meal interrupted by an uninvited guest. Sometimes the deal offered was not business but pleasure. Mostly those offers came from males, on some planets from females.

Despite his smarmy opening line, she doubted Jaitain was looking for a sexual encounter. He seemed too formal and serious, though there was that brief sparkle of something intriguing in his eyes. The man had amazing eyes! She hoped he was okay. Maybe an ex-wife or girlfriend had showed up, or someone to whom he owed money. Such speculations were entertaining, but obviously a waste of her time.

She was relieved to be alone again. His nervousness had made her nervous for him. She also felt a surprising physical attraction to him that turned her into a bumbling adolescent in his presence. Not a feeling she enjoyed.

She left the restaurant. The heat outside was intense. The silky material of her new tjong clung to her damp shoulders and back. She checked the PCU on her wrist, 43 C with 75% humidity. That was about equivalent to a topnotch Scandinavian steam bath.

She planned to take a stroll through the pavilions after lunch, but now she just wanted to get back to her suite, take another cool shower, unpack and organize. She moved through the crowded pavilions, dodging shoppers with packages and parents with children. The Caifanii all looked cool as cucumbers. She was melting faster than butter on a corncob. By the time she got back to her suite, she felt like she'd run ten miles, even though she'd only walked about ten city blocks.

In the quiet suite, she undressed and showered for a long time, leaning her back against the chilly metal of the shower wall and letting the water cascade over her forehead, nose, lips, and chin; drinking its coolness into her mind.

She shut off the water, dried with a fresh blanket towel and pulled on a sleeveless tunic. Its deep, cobalt blue enveloped her with a sense of calm, and the pure silk fell like a soft breeze over her cooled skin. She hung her fresh clothes and Protocol's two tjongs in the closet, and hung her new, now damp tjong by the open window to give it air. She sat on the bed and played her ukelele, too tired to sing, just strumming lightly through the chords of *Lei Nani*.

About halfway through the song her PCU beeped.

"Colby!" she said into the unit.

"Heydi-howdy-hodi!" he returned.

"How goes it?"

"Well," he said, "not exactly hunky-dory."

"Okay. What's the scoop?"

"You know that glitch in the communications system while we were coming into port?"

"Yeah."

"This is embarrassing. Okay. I'll start with what's up now and work backwards to what might have caused it."

"I'm all ears." At moments like this Sola felt the uncomfortable tension of being both Colby's best friend and, technically, his boss.

"While I was running the diagnostic, Minerva's database systems went into a cascading security lockdown."

"That sounds bad."

"It is, but it doesn't make any sense. Only three things can cause that kind of lockdown. You or I can instigate it. Obviously, that was not the case. Minerva's AI program can instigate it, if there is unauthorized access to the central data core. Update at 11:00 on that one. Last scenario: the system was damaged in some way."

"Oh, crap. You mean like by the field generator during our little light show?" Sola asked.

He sighed loudly, making the mic overload. "I thought of that too. This planet's ionosphere may have enough variance in its electro-magnetic field to have caused a charged spike, which might have caused damage to the core, but that's so unlikely, it's barely worth considering. There is one other possibility. It could be a software issue. Our new District Manager insisted I install an update to the operating system just before we left."

"Well, that sounds like the culprit to me! When has an OS update ever worked correctly straight out of the gate?"

"I know, but I should have noticed that much sooner. It's been running for three weeks without a hitch. Why cause a problem now, and I'm talking a BIG problem, a problem with some serious hair on its chest?"

"Oh, gross, Colby."

"I'm just sayin' not a petite kinda problem here. It's not just that the core data drives went into a security lockdown. That lockdown triggered a cascade of system failures including the com system, and pretty much everything except the environmental systems."

"Well thank goodness for small miracles."

"Yeah. I'm partial to breathing. I think the only reasonable scenario here is that someone tried to rustle our long horns."

"Do you think that Port Authority craft scanned us?"

"I think they tried to download our databases. They had the opportunity during our communications exchange, though I'm surprised they'd have the technology to do it. It's a pretty sophisticated maneuver, and as far as I can tell, nothing was actually downloaded. So, I've got no hard evidence that there was foul play."

"Well, if our friendly, neighborhood escort tried to pirate our systems, that certainly doesn't bode well, but as
we have no proof, we can't make that assumption."

"But wait, there's more!"

"For only 9.99 I can also get the handy dandy slicer-dicer?" she said, not actually feeling jovial.

"We're temporarily out of stock on those," he returned. "Okay. I'm trying to remedy the situation. This has never happened in the seven years I've been flyin' Minerva. I know the protocol for terminating the lockdown and reactivating the systems in reverse order of the cascade. It's tedious but relatively simple. I just need to key in the security code manually for each system."

"Yet, something in your tone tells me that isn't going to be so easy."

"It would be a slice of pie, except that the security code, which was so very nicely provided to me seven years ago, is currently missing in action. I can't find the damned thing anywhere."

"Oh, shit!"

"Something like that, yes. I've been in a pile of it for hours."

She laughed.

"It's not funny, Sola. We are seriously hosed. It's not like I can just call the Geek Squad and have them do a house call."

"I know. I know. It's just so typical! I've had this exact thing happen to me so many times! I hate passwords and access codes. I can never remember them, and then when I authorize a new code, because I've forgotten the old one, inevitably the next time I need the code, I end up remembering the old one, and not the new one!"

"Yeah, it's the old adage, 'technology is great when it works.'"

"It's even better when it lets you in the door! Now what?"

"Luckily, I moved Minerva into the long-term docking bay we rented before I ran the diagnostics. Doubt I could've moved her after the cascade started."

"Wow. This is sounding worse and worse."

"Agreed. Here's what I'm thinking. Since there's a chance that we can't trust the Port Authority, or whoever those guys really are, I think it's best that I stayed in the shuttle tonight. I actually think you should stay here too, just until we know more."

"Hmm," Sola said, thinking it over. "Here's something else to chew on. Two armed guards wearing uniforms with the same insignia as that Port Authority craft followed me from the skyport. By the time I got out of my transport at the hotel, their vehicle was gone, but I don't know if they followed me all the way to the hotel or not. I fell asleep in the cab. You won't believe how hard it is to stay awake on this planet!"

"Sola, that's seriously creepy, and all the more reason for you to come back here tonight."

"I hear you, Colby, but I need to stay put here. We don't have anything solid. I just settled in. I don't think it's time to go to an orange alert. Not yet."

"I defrosted two ribeyes? Does that sweeten the deal?"

"The steaks sound great, but I'm going to have to go with the local vegetarian fare."

"All right then," he said, disappointed. "You're the boss. I do think I should stay on the shuttle though. Keep Minerva safe. She's our only pony home."

"I agree. Keep looking for that code, and keep me apprised. If need be, we'll contact IDS."

"Well we can't do that until the com system is back online. The PCU signal isn't strong enough."

"Well, it's not like I want to contact IDS." Sola said.

There were benefits to having your superiors light years away, no opportunity for them to micro-manage your work. She much preferred to keep this under wraps for now.

"Colby, you'll figure something out. You always do. I'm going to go to a decent little restaurant I found today, and see what's on their dinner menu. I'll call ya later."

"Okay. Use caution."

"I will. Don't worry." She signed off.

Sola pulled her new tjong from the hanger by the window. It wasn't exactly dry, but it would have to do. She was used to wearing damp clothing. Nothing ever dried completely on Maui.

She headed back to the shopping district. She ate her meal in leisure. No one interrupted her savoring of the minced baka tort, and a creamed soup that reminded her of butternut squash, except the waiter offering to refill her glass with iced herbal tea.

After her meal, she wandered along the now cooler pavilions as the shops were closing.

When she got back to her suite, she checked in with Colby. Nothing had changed.

"Why don't you call it a night, Colby? Get some rest. Pick it up in the morning when you're fresh."

"I won't argue with that. I'll call you mañana."

"Great. You'll work it out."

She had every confidence that he would.

She hoped it was the field generator during their light show, or the OS update that caused the cascade, and not the other, disturbing scenario.

She selected one pillow from the collection on the bed, and hurled the others onto the floor, one at a time. Throwing them relieved some of her tension. She laughed, sighed, and felt fatigue fill her senses with a longing for oblivion. She sank her head into the plush texture of the remaining pillow and found sleep ready to welcome her, a familiar threshold. She crossed over.

Chapter 4

Sola knew she was asleep and dreaming, yet she felt as present in the dream as if she were awake. Her father spent years cultivating his ability to experience lucid dreaming as often as possible. For Sola, this was the first such experience.

In her dream, she walked through a rain forest. The ground was soft, moist and springy beneath her bare feet. She wore only a loose tunic of an almost weightless, white material. It was sleeveless and fell just above her knees.

There were flowering plants everywhere around her. Some were familiar. Hibiscus, orchids, plumeria. Some were unfamiliar. Their sweet perfumes mingled and filled the warm humid air. The foliage was lush and diverse. She was walking in a painting made of a thousand brush strokes, no two greens exactly the same hue. The rain forest was vibrant with the sounds of a thousand hidden creatures. Some chirped, sounding like small birds. Others rustled in the underbrush. Some made haunting calls, high up in the branches and among the arboreal vines that created a canopy of life above her. Although she could not see the sky, it was not dark. The plants themselves were glowing with an emerald luminescence.

The path was barely visible in the thick jungle of growth around her feet, yet she felt she had a specific destination.

After a short walk, she came to a clearing. Flowering moss covered the ground. Tiny magenta flowers created a thick carpet. It began to rain lightly. Droplets of water fell as a fine, cool mist on her face, arms and legs.

Through the misty rain, she could see that there was a cottage at the opposite edge of the clearing.

She walked towards it, over the flowering moss. The cool, soft flower petals caressed the soles of her feet and the bottoms of her toes, making her feel tickled and giddy. She laughed. The sound of her own voice startled her. She felt happy. She wished her father could see this, could share this lucid dream.

A Caifanii woman appeared in the doorway of the cottage and waved at her, smiling. Sola waved back. The woman wore sky-blue robes of that flowed over her body like waterfalls. Sola stood at the edge of the flowering moss where a stone path led towards the cottage door.

The woman moved slowly down the path toward her. The rain fell, creating a veil of moist light all around them.

The woman seemed very old. Her slow, laborious movements, her posture, the lines of her face, and her air of wisdom all spoke of age; but her energy was somehow youthful, spirited, filled with joy.

The woman reached out to Sola, speaking to her in a language so similar to Hawaiian that Sola understood her perfectly.

"Welcome," the woman said, in rich, lyrical voice full of compassion. "Our waiting has brought forth its fruit. Your journey begins. Let your heart be radiant."

The tone of the woman's voice made Sola feel calm and safe. The voice was oddly familiar to her, as if she had heard it before. She realized she had, and where. In the airlock!

She felt simultaneously stunned and enchanted. She moved closer to the woman, wanting to know more, but suddenly found herself awake in the hotel suite, with the sheet twisted around her legs.

She lay sideways on the bed, sunlight on her face. To her amazement, she had slept through the entire night and much of the morning.

Chapter 5

Sola listened to the cool air hissing through the vents in the ceiling above her head. Her heartbeat labored and her head ached.

She lay still for a few moments, keeping the details of the dream in full focus. It felt like remembering something that actually happened in her waking life. She sighed and stretched. She slept too long, several hours past her pepper medication time. It was hot in the room despite the air-conditioning. Interstellar travel only looks glamorous from the outside, she thought.

She rolled out of bed, remembering the height of the mattress a second too late. She landed hard on the carpet, got up with a moan and dragged herself into the shower stall, forgetting to remove her shirt. The water was shockingly cold. She needed that wake-up call right now. She stood in the invigorating flow until she shivered, and then turned the water off.

Her drenched shirt clung to her like a second skin. She was a wet, cobalt lizard on a hot, foreign rock.

"This is nuts," she mumbled to herself, then sighed.

She combed her fingers through her wet hair. How was she going to function through several days of this? She felt like going right back to bed, but knew better.

She started to pull off the clinging shirt. It became stuck halfway, with her arms up over her head, and her mouth breathing through blue silk.

In an exasperated frenzy, she freed herself and threw the wet shirt behind her into the corner of the shower stall.

Her PCU started beeping, each beep a little louder than the last. Not her favorite feature. Had to be Colby. She stumbled over to the nightstand, dripping a trail of water onto the carpet. She switched the PCU to audio only.

"Colby?" she said.

"What, no visual?"

"Just got out of the shower," she said.

"Don't tease me, woman! I've been trying to get through to you for hours."

"I'm sorry. I seriously overslept. My PCU was on. Can't believe I slept through that obnoxious beeping, seriously. I must have been comatose! So what's the status?"

"Well, I haven't managed to get the systems back on line, but I may have found a way to get the security code. Remember that software engineer who joined us for dinner on Danuba IV, Moses Fukahula?"

"You don't forget a name like that!"

"Especially on a Tongan built like a linebacker!"

"Love that guy!"

"Yeah, I thought he was rather nifty too. Anyway, he's on a virtual team with Alan Soroni in our Denver office. I remembered that useful piece of information at about four this morning. I also remembered the name of the company Moses works with on Denuba IV, so I was able to find a number for him."

"That's impressive!"

"It gets better. I wired some serious signal boosters to the PCU and was able to reach him."

"Holy crap! You're amazing."

"I talked with him a long time, some static, a few echo issues, but all in all a damned good connection, considering. He tried talking me through getting into the system by the backdoor, but we kept hitting firewalls. So, he's gonna contact Alan to see if I can get or reset the security code. As soon as I hear back from Moses, I'll let you know. Oh, crap!"

"What?"

"I totally forgot about your data processor yesterday. Do you need it today?"

"I won't need it until after the sales meeting tomorrow, and who knows what will go down there, so just stay put. I have all the SDI data sets I need for the demos on my portable."

"Okay. Back to Moses. I asked him what he thought about OS 220. He updated to it about three months ago. Says it's got lots of bad code issues. He doubts those issues could cause a cascading lockdown, but in combination with a possible electrical spike resulting from the field generator, there's a small chance the update was the culprit."

"You told him about your light show? Dude! You must really trust this guy!"

"He's salt of the earth, I'll tell ya. We're invited to his place for BBQ any time. He says he does it luau style, buries the whole pig in the ground with the fire."

"Love luau. Doubt we'll be in his neighborhood any time soon."

"Especially after we step off the SDI gravy train."

"So, we have nothing definite. What's your take?"

"Bad code issues notwithstanding, I'm sticking with the data pirating scheme. Maybe the Port Authority craft, maybe from somewhere on the surface while we were in descent."

"That's my gut feeling too. Maybe the High Council authorized it. Wouldn't be the first time. Why pay for what you can get for free? Right? At least it looks like they didn't get anything. Can we be sure of that?"

"Darn near sure, yes."

"I suppose if it was the Council, and they were successful, I'd have received a courteous cancellation call by now. That happened to me once, before you were onboard, before IDS put more armor around their intelligence. It's also possible the Council wasn't involved. We don't know who the players are here. If the scan came from the surface, our list of suspects could include everyone in Haikon. Sorry, I'm just thinking out loud here."

"I'm with ya. I still think the Port Authority craft is our number one suspect. The only one with a mug shot anyway."

"There's definitely a police or military connection there. Usually, Port Authority doesn't have any authority outside the port. That armed guard unit followed me into the city. They could be working for the government. Then again, they could be working for just about anyone, if they're getting paid enough."

"What? No faith in the Men in Blue?"

"Their uniforms were grey, and a little too upscale, and their guns were a lot too outsized."

"Minerva may have some clues, if I can get to them, residual energy signatures that could identify the source of the security breach, if there was one, but I'll need the system up and running in order to look for those residuals. The longer it's down the more faded they will be. We're just going to have to wait."

"Okay."

"Hey, listen, can you stay under the radar? I mean, don't ask too many questions out there."

"The only questions I am going to ask today are for the cook at that place where I ate last night. Unbelievably delicious."

"Glad to hear it. I'll be happy with that second steak and some of my four-alarm chili."

That reminded Sola to reach for her bag, look for the red pills and take one. It was hard to swallow without water and the coating left a metallic taste in her dry mouth.

"Colby, I'll just move forward as planned, but with caution. While you're waiting on Moses, just relax. You deserve it. Read some Louis L'Amour. Just hang out."

"Thanks, boss, but I don't feel much like relaxing. Do me a favor will you? Stay close to the hotel, just in case we need to make a quick getaway."

"I'll take the PCU with me if I go out. But we can't go anywhere until our systems are back online, right?"

"Right."

"Okay, and Colby?"

"Si, Senorita?"

"I'm sorry you're stuck on the shuttle. It's no picnic on this planet, take my word for that, but you deserve some shore leave."

"Thanks. I'll get a bunch once we quit this puppet show. Miss ya, Missy!"

"Miss you too, Bud! See you real soon, promise!"

Sola switched off the unit, strapped it to her wrist, got dressed, and decided breakfast was a necessity. She'd stay at the hotel for now.

That meant she was stuck with hotel food, probably some soggy, scrambled bean curd, or worse.

The lobby was quiet, just one elderly-looking man sitting by the window, intent on the view screen in his lap. He looked Alkorian, or maybe Misan, two bony ridges across the forehead. He was first non-Caifanii she encountered here. The clerk at the registry desk smiled at her, looking bored.

The Hotel restaurant too was nearly empty. It was too late for breakfast, too early for lunch. She hoped they would be serving something fresh. The host approached her. "Please sit anywhere," he said, motioning to the tables. "The current courses are listed at each table."

He had a pleasant voice. The place looked clean and cheerful. She sat down in a corner booth and perused the menu. She decided to have the grain cakes and fruit, local stuff. She ordered a glass of cooled tea, and hoped it had some caffeine.

It was very muggy and not even eleven. Maybe the afternoon rain would cool things down a little. The restaurant hosts were talking quickly and quietly in the far corner. One of them seemed agitated, or perhaps angry with the other. He kept raising his voice and then checking himself and bringing it down to a whisper. She couldn't catch what they were saying. They were outside of the TLC's range.

The food arrived quickly. The grain cakes tasted nutty and had a crisp texture. The pale blue fruit reminded her of sliced cantaloupe, slightly sweet, very juicy and served delightfully chilled. She finished her meal, paid, and wandered over to the windows at the far end of the lobby which, like her suite on the fourth floor above, faced the hotel's beautifully landscaped gardens. There was a profusion of foliage, large bushes, small trees, and meandering pathways. A walk in the gardens was a perfect plan. She was technically still at the hotel.

She stepped out into the bright heat, squinting into the glare. Even with eyeshades, the light was intense. She walked down one of the paths. There were no flowering plants, no splashes of color to offset the solid wall of green. After wandering a while in the direct sun, she needed shade. She felt fatigued, despite the medications. It always took a couple of days for the dosage to build up to its full strength. The sun was high, no shade in sight. There was no one else around.

She stepped off the path and pushed her arms through the vegetation hoping for a shady spot under the thicker foliage. Just through the bushes, there was a small area with short grassy vegetation and deep shade under the taller trees. She pushed through the soft, damp leaves. The clearing was just large enough for her to lie down. The plants felt moist and refreshing against her back, legs and arms. Caifanii had no mosquitoes or biting flies. That was a pleasure. There were no birds either, genetically speaking. There were other small flying creatures with multi-colored, feathered arms, but they were winged reptiles that had not evolved into singing.

She placed her hands behind her head and closed her eyes. She could hear the scurrying of small creatures in the underbrush. They made a humorous noise a little like the chatter of squirrels or keiloos. She took a deep breath and sighed, then heard the sound of approaching voices. Two Caifaniis were clicking and chirping, out of translator range.

They were on the path, coming from the side away from The Hotel. They stopped directly in front of the bushes that hid her from their view. She rolled over onto her side, as quietly as possible, and could see their legs through the brush. Her spot had become a secret hiding place. It would be awkward to make her presence known now. What was she supposed to do, jump up and introduce herself? She just happened to be there. It wasn't like she'd planned to spy on them.

Nonetheless, curiosity got the better of her. She switched on her TLC. She turned it down as low as it would go. It whispered their dialogue into her ear.

They kept talking, unaware of her presence. It felt sinister and a little embarrassing to be eavesdropping on strangers. She assumed they would quickly pass on down the path, but they stayed a long while, talking in low tones. She listened.

They stood very close to the shrubs that hid her from them. If she reached out between the branches, she could touch their dusty shoes. She started to get a little worried that they would discover her. Then what? She could pretend to be asleep. She was stuck, in any case. She couldn't leave until they did. She had to wait for them to walk away. She could feel the tension between the two Caifaniis. There was a sense of urgency about their interaction.

"Did anyone see you?" asked one of them, a male judging by his shoes.

"I was very careful," said his companion, also male. Similar shoes, but a few sizes smaller.

"Can we trust him?" Larger Shoes said.

"Yes. Completely!" Smaller Shoes replied. "He's Jaitain's brother."

Sola felt suddenly wide awake and alert.

Jaitain was a common Caifanii first name, but could this be *the* Jaitain, the one she'd met?

"How do you feel?" Larger Shoes asked, in a whisper.

"It is not deep. I will be fine in a few days."

"I want to get you to a doctor," Larger Shoes insisted.

"No need, I am not seriously injured."

"I know someone who will help us, a sympathizer."

What were they talking about? Sola wondered.

Slices of conversation, overheard out of context, were often spicy, while in their actual context, they might be quite bland.

This was probably just some ordinary business.

Yet, she sensed that this was a clandestine conversation, not meant to be heard by anyone else's ears, or translators. This was getting spooky.

She felt like the heroine in some archaic mystery story, like the ones her dad had found for her in an old bookstore when she was seven. The Nancy Drew Mysteries, in which young Nancy spied on unscrupulous villains, with her heart beating out of her chest, and her mind bent on unraveling the twisted plot. The thought almost made Sola laugh aloud. She bit her lip and tried to breathe very quietly.

"This place makes me nervous," Smaller Shoes said.

She wasn't sure if he meant Haikon or that particular spot in the garden.

"Can we get going?" he continued.

"Fine," Larger Shoes replied. "I will be in touch with Jaitain later. It is unfortunate things did not go as he had planned with her."

They were moving away now.

"He gave those concert tickets to me," Larger Shoes said. "I went, but it was too loud. Why do they always play too loud?"

Jaitain? Concert! Her mind was suddenly full of quarreling demons. This must be *the* Jaitain, and the *her* they referred to must be her!

Maybe Colby was right. Maybe she should go back to the shuttle. Play it safe. Then again, maybe the straps on her gravity boots needed a little tightening, unlikely on this planet!

She could no longer hear the two males at all. She crawled to the edge of the foliage and looked out. Nothing in either direction. She came out into the light. It was dizzying for a second. She bent over, putting her head down.

"How do they live in this?" she mumbled. She knew their physiology was better equipped. The heat wasn't so oppressive for them, just normal, comfortable weather. She couldn't imagine a Caifanii on earth, in Belfast or Vancouver, but at least they could cover up. She could only try to find cover. She walked as quickly as she could back to the Hotel and went directly to her suite. She wanted to get a clear head and then call Colby.

The suite was blessedly cool, but she couldn't get the PCU online. She kept getting the same message in that ever patient, ever pleasant, simulated voice that made your skin crawl.

"You have accessed the Personal Communications System. All channels are temporarily disabled. Please try again later."

Crap. What was that about? She wondered if she should pack up her essentials and head over to the shuttle; take Colby's advice and stay there, just for the night. That might be the only way to talk to him. There was only one problem. He'd never told her where the long-term docking facility was located. It was probably somewhere near the main terminal. Then again, it could be completely off-site.

She called the hotel desk and asked for the number of the Haikon Skyport.

She dialed it in. There was one of those annoying phone trees, and she ended up on hold for what seemed like forever.

Eventually, someone came on the line, but the TLC did not work well over the local connection. She had to give up on the frustrating conversation without getting any useful information.

She strapped the PCU to her forearm, under the long sleeve of the tjong. She tossed her medication satchel into a small purse, which fit neatly onto her belt, and headed down to the hotel restaurant. She ordered a meal of fresh seafood with a white mealy grain a little like rice and a salad that looked like seaweed, and probably was. It all tasted surprisingly good, for hotel food. She ate quickly and took a digestive aide.

She left the restaurant and returned to her suite. This was proving to be one of those "Murphy's Law" days. To feel better, she reminded herself that on assignments when everything that could go wrong did go wrong, the sales contract was often a snap. While on assignments when everything went smooth as custard flan, for no apparent reason, the sales contract often fell through. She scanned somewhat aimlessly through her briefing materials, letting the day slip away into evening. She checked the PCU every twenty minutes, same lame recorded message.

After midnight, she moved a chair over to the window, and gazed up at Caifanii's two moons, both of them visible from her vantage point.

When she had first seen a night sky with more than one moon, on Gaia II, it had been mesmerizing. She stared for hours in disbelief and child-like glee. It was so eerie, so mind boggling.

That was during the first year of her position with IDS, seven years ago already. Then everything about interstellar travel had been new and exciting. Now, she was more accustomed to being in non-Terran environments. She was becoming an astro-bureaucrat, too involved in computer simulated realities and research phenomena to be intrigued by the surreal mystery of the real, the silver glow of two moons like owl eyes in the night sky?

Living on Maui would restore her sense of wonder. She tapped into that wonder now, gazing sleepily at the two luminous orbs. Both were half-full, or half-empty. Thin shards of cloud moved over and past their dual luminescence. She could not see any stars. The city center had too many of its own competing arrogantly in the soft darkness. The sky did not grow completely dark here. It was like the night sky of the arctic regions on Earth, more like shadow than darkness, softly luminous. Caifanii's Northern Continent was actually not very far north. The latitude of Haikon was comparable to that of Paris, so latitude did not completely explain the night sky.

Sola decided to let her problems rest until the morning. She got into bed and tried to fall asleep, thinking of her childhood home in Wailea, and of her current home in Evergreen, both offered galaxies of stars crowding the domed expanse of heaven on a clear night. She missed Earth.

She missed Colby. For all his cowboy boyishness, he was a surprisingly intuitive and soulful lover. She wanted him. It was a genuine longing and it made her cry. Why was she pushing away the only man who knew everything about her and still loved her, the only man other than her father, who loved her unconditionally?

Chapter 6

Day Three (morning)
Struman: Questions

The night passed slowly. Sola slept on and off between long stretches of wakefulness. She tried reaching Colby several times without success. She played lullabies on her uke.

The sun was just beginning to bring colors back into the suite. A cool breeze was flowing in through the opened windows from the gardens below. Sola slipped out of bed feeling strangely alert and tense. Turning on only the bedside lamp, she started packing a bag with a change of clothes, her prescriptions, a few sales notes, a sleep tunic and hygiene articles, in case she decided to head for the skyport to find the shuttle. She strapped her personal communications unit under her sleeve. It was still uncooperative.

Today, she would act like a tourist, but do a little investigating. The High Council's delay of her sales meeting, due to 'unexpected government business' demanding their immediate attention, now seemed much more relevant. She was quite curious what that business might be. Maybe she could get some clues today.

She stared at the overnight bag she'd just packed, and decided she was acting paranoid. She took her meds pouch and left the bag on the bed.

She slipped through the lobby quickly. There was no one at the registry desk. She would find breakfast somewhere in the city's center.

It was cool outside, and walking was pleasant in the early morning air.

The peppers had built up in her blood and she felt a marked increase in stamina despite her fitful night.

There was no motorized traffic allowed in the city center, with the exception of police and medical emergency vehicles. The streets were a series of open pavilions connected by narrow passages and decorated with an abundance of foliage and ornate fountains. She reached the restaurant section quickly, but avoided the Fuiga Nakaii. It was silly, really. Their food was undoubtedly the best. The chance of running into Jaitain there again was slim, and if he was there, maybe that could be a boon. He might have some answers to her questions. Did she trust him? She needed to shift her spinning mind into a single gear so she could move forward.

She peeked into a small cafe in an alley just off the main boulevard. It was tiny, noisy and packed with Caifanii getting ready for the business day. She found a small table in the back and felt gratefully obscured, submerged by the din of clicking voices, clanging dishes, and the high whining of a machine preparing a popular Caifanii beverage. Njin-Njin. The crowded room held its strong, bitter odor, vaguely reminiscent of coffee. She ordered some. It was thick, bitter and burned in her stomach. One sip was more than enough. She ordered grain cakes, melon and iced tea.

There was a view screen in the opposite corner to her left, high up near the ceiling, supported by a shelf jutting out of the wall. The picture was grainy and the volume was so low it was inaudible over the din of the room. No one was watching the screen, which showed a sporting event, something akin to soccer except with three balls in play at once. When she finished her meal, Sola ordered a refill of tea and sat for a while longer, her back against the cool wall watching the busy Caifanii come in and go out of the doorway. Tables were emptying. The workday was starting in earnest.

She glanced again at the viewsceen. It was now a news broadcast, a talking head shot of a reporter, then some footage of a small crowd of Caifanii yelling and running towards a large, impressive building. There seemed to be a panic. She couldn't hear what was being said, even with the cafe almost empty now, the audio was too low for her translator to pick up. On the small screen, armed officials in dark gray uniforms created a blockade in front of the stairs leading to the entrance of the building. A caption appeared on the lower edge of the screen. No use to her, she could not read Caifanii script. She wondered if the disturbance had anything to do with the conversation she overheard yesterday on the hotel grounds. It was impossible to decipher the context. Apparently, a few other patrons were also curious and the volume shot up, way up. Her TLC kicked in. The newscaster was caught in mid-sentence, "Siatja Square, Government Regulatory Buildings, Djintu City, 17 dhan, 5th Day of Kaimii. No fatalities, some minor injuries. Situation under control." That information did not clarify much. Djintu City was the capitol of the Southern Continent, so not likely to have anything to do with yesterday's overheard conversation. The Caifanii printed hard copy of their daily news, a strangely archaic practice making their non-video news sources useless to her.

She could ask around, but she preferred to keep a low profile. She was getting curious glances from a few cafe patrons, but mostly the morning crowd was too preoccupied with their own affairs to bother with a tourist, even if she was an exotic. The newscast ended, and a young Caifanii woman appeared on the screen, praising a new cooking appliance. Commercials. Was there nowhere in the known universe where you could escape them?

She paid for her meal. The rush of customers had completely ebbed. There were only six Caifanii left at the tables. She stepped outside. The street was quiet. An elderly female was selling some sort of fruit on the corner under a palm-like tree, she was yelling loudly "Fresh and tasty! Special price! Fresh and tasty!" With no prospective customers nearby, her sales pitch seemed comical. The woman yelled a barrage of product promotion at Sola as she walked past. Sola turned her head briefly to say "No thanks," amused by the scene, and stumbled directly into a short, stocky male coming from the opposite direction. He mumbled something under his breath and passed her. After a few more paces, she stopped abruptly. Standing in the entrance to a shop across the pavilion was Jaitain.

He didn't see her, yet. She darted off to her right and ducked behind a large advertisement sign with bold blue letters. She hunched low then ran into the nearest shop. It was a clothier and garments hung all along the window facing the pavilion. She peered out between two tjongs and could clearly see Jaitain. He was talking with someone inside the shop, obscured from her view. He looked serious and was nodding frequently. The conversation appeared lively. It was hot and stuffy in the clothier shop.

"May I be of service," a voice inquired, from behind her.

Sola turned around, startled.

"Uh. No thank you," she said, not wanting to take her eyes from the window. She touched one of the tjongs in the window with her gloved fingers, as if she had been admiring it. "This is a lovely color," she said. "Perhaps I will stop by again later." She glanced out of the window and saw that Jaitain was leaving. He was walking in the direction from which she had come. She left the shop and decided to follow him, on her side of the pavilion. He turned the corner, heading away from the Center. She waited for a few seconds, and then crossed to tail him. At the end of the pavilion, he turned right and she lost sight of him for a moment. She hurried and turned the corner in pursuit. They were on a narrow pathway now. She was only about 50 meters behind him. There were a few people between them. Buildings flanked the path on both sides. If he turned around, he would see her. After a few minutes, he went left. She could feel her pulse in her throat. He was heading directly towards her hotel.

She came up to the corner and peeked around. She could see him approaching the hotel entrance. She hurried around the corner so as not to lose sight of him. A small group of people had come between them from the other direction. She just caught sight of him as he entered the lobby. He was looking for her! He *had* to be. She was not there, so, most likely he would come out again soon.

Why was she so reluctant to meet up with him? Why not walk into the lobby and find out what he wanted? After the overheard conversation in the gardens, Sola was suspicious of his motives, and after tailing him, she felt awkward about casually talking to him, as if she had not followed him here. She decided to get out of sight, and wait until he left the hotel. She slipped into the secluded courtyard of the hotel restaurant. She could see the entrance to the lobby from there. She waited. Five minutes passed, ten, fifteen. The desk clerk had probably paged her room and, finding no answer, had told him she was out. Maybe he was waiting for her to return. She was getting impatient and hot. It was already 40 degrees Celsius, even in the shade.

She went into the restaurant. It was busy. She walked quickly towards the lobby entrance, hoping to be able to see into the lobby through the doors. No luck. The doors were made of an opaque, frosted glass. If she opened them to look out, there was a chance Jaitain would see her. Damn! It suddenly occurred to her that he might be in the restaurant, waiting for her to return. She glanced around, but didn't see him. She hurried back out to the courtyard.

She sat down on a bench, under a large tree offering ample shade. The sound of a small fountain was making her thirsty. She wondered if she should continue to wait. Maybe Jaitain had left while she was inside. "Damn!" she swore aloud under her breath. She should have stayed out here and kept her eyes on the main lobby entrance.

A loud shrieking interrupted her self-chastisement. A siren. She stood and moved closer to the edge of the courtyard. A hover vehicle glided into the pathway in front of the hotel, lights flashing. It parked and turned off its siren. The vehicle was small, steel gray, and identical to the one that tailed her from the skyport. Two males in uniforms like the ones she'd seen on the guards at the skyport, and interestingly also on the officials in the news program at the cafe, jumped out of the first craft and ran into the hotel, hand weapons at the ready. She watched in disbelief. A small crowd gathered to watch the excitement. After a few minutes, the two uniformed males returned from inside with a third, taller male, held between them. It was Jaitain! They were arresting Jaitain at her hotel!

They pushed him into the back of the vehicle, got into the front, turned on the siren and sped, wailing like a wild coyote, down the pathway, around the corner and out of sight.

Sola sank back down on the bench and felt the rough, solid texture of its wood against her back. They had come for Jaitain at *her* hotel. Why? How had they known he would be there? People didn't get arrested for having a bad pick-up technique. Jaitain was definitely involved in something of questionable legality, and had come here for what? To pull her into it as well? Or maybe he'd only come to invite her out to lunch and the officials had tailed him just as she had?

The air in the courtyard had grown extremely humid. She needed to go inside. This was ridiculous. She had actually enjoyed following Jaitain. It had felt exciting. It was a lark, a game, but now a dark reality had entered the scene. It was one thing to enjoy a little intrigue, quite another to be pulled into a potentially dangerous situation. She wanted no part in that sort of drama.

Sola rose with an involuntary moan, her body felt like wax in the heat, melting slowly into a shapeless puddle of questions. Her wakeful night was catching up with her.

She didn't want to show up in the lobby so shortly after the arrest. It was likely that Jaitain had asked for her at the front desk, possibly even left a message.

She left the courtyard and found a path leading around and behind the hotel.

Through the blur of burning heat, she walked into the wall of green, seeking yesterday's hiding place, the small alcove under the trees where the shade was thick. She pushed through the foliage and stumbled onto the mossy ground. She needed a quick nap to regain clarity and focus. Sleep offered a sweet, momentary escape.

When she awoke, there was a slight breeze playing over her body through the underbrush. It carried the moist, musk-like scent of tree mold, ferns, earth and coming rain.

It chilled her a little where its fingers touched her damp skin. She yawned and stretched, reluctant to get up, hovering in a surreal impression that the past 24 hours had been a dream, but here she was in this hidden little glade. Jaitain arrested at her hotel! How bizarre was that?

Eventually her curiosity got the better of her lethargy and she scrambled to her feet and out onto the path.

She entered the hotel lobby and put on her best cheerful, innocent face. The clerk was busy with another guest of a race she did not recognize. He was asking a cargo load of questions in a harsh, guttural language. At least they seemed like questions, maybe he was complaining about the huge bath sheets. The clerk seemed to have no answers, or only half understood him. It was taking a long time.

Finally, with a gruff grumble, the burly guest left, swinging his four upper appendages in a gesture of frustration as he trekked heavily across the spacious lobby.

"I regret the delay," the desk clerk said. She looked very young and seemed a bit embarrassed.

"Hello," Sola said. "I am in room 417. Has anything arrived for me?" She was hoping there was a message from Jaitain. At least that might answer some questions.

"Your name please?" the clerk asked.

"Alturas. Sola Alturas."

"There is a message, yes."

Sola felt her heart beat faster, even faster than it was already working to move her heavy blood through her system. Poor heart!

The clerk continued. "It is from the Transport Terminal. They offer regrets for the delay. Your materials are being transferred here and should arrive before the end of the day. Shall I have them brought up to your suite?"

"What?" Sola was momentarily distracted.

She'd been expecting something from Jaitain.

Colby had gotten the data processor through customs. That was good news. He must be making progress. So why didn't she feel relieved? Her instincts were still giving her flashing red lights.

"Of course, yes," Sola said. "Thank you. Please do that."

Sola turned to leave.

"Guest Alturas?" the clerk said, in a hesitant voice. "I have something else for you."

Sola turned back around.

The clerk looked nervous. "Someone came in earlier and asked me to ring your suite," she said, so softly that the translator almost did not capture the phrase.

There were no other guests in the lobby. The two of them were alone, yet the girl looked anxious. "He did not leave a message, not even his name," she continued. Then, looking very serious and scanning the entrance, the clerk leaned in close to Sola over the counter and whispered, "I do not know if I am supposed to tell you. I mean it is none of my business, but he was taken away by Central Security about, I would say, two hours ago."

Two hours! Had she been asleep in the glade that long? Sola was cautious. "I was not expecting anyone," she said quietly. "I don't know anyone here who would come looking for me," she lied.

So, he had come to see her, but he hadn't left a message. Maybe that was for the best, the message might have connected her to him, and that seemed like a bad complication considering his arrest. She didn't want to be associated in any way with Jaitain.

"Thank you for telling me," Sola said in a sweet tone of voice, wanting to alleviate the clerk's concern. "I'm sure it is nothing, really. He was probably just a business solicitor. Perhaps his previous business ventures were a little on the shady side?" She was trying to reassure the young Caifanii, and maybe herself as well.

The girl seemed appeased. "Perhaps so," she said. "It was very strange. He asked me to ring your room. When I told him there was no answer, he thanked me and went over there," she pointed to the corner of the lobby. "He stood there, for a while. Then he went into the restaurant, but not for very long. Then he came back and asked me to ring your room again. Of course, you had not yet returned, so there was still no answer. Then he went back over there and waited some more. When the officers arrived to take him away, he did not resist or protest even a little. He did not say anything at all." The clerk seemed to be talking to herself now. "He was very calm." She had a far-away look in her eyes. She probably thought Jaitain was handsome. Sola imaged that by Caifanii standards he was a hunk. The clerk snapped out of her reverie and blushed in embarrassment. "I regret, I mean," she paused. "I hope I have not upset you with this news."

"I am glad you told me, and I think neither of us need worry about it," Sola said. She smiled and pretended to make light of the situation.

"Right," the girl said, smiling as well. "Thank you. I will see that your belongings are sent to your suite when they arrive."

"Thank you," Sola said. She felt intrigued by the clerk's depiction of Jaitain's demeanor during his arrest. She had noticed it too, his lack of resistance. He had looked almost elegant out there in front of the lobby entrance, more like a dignitary escorted than a criminal arraigned.

Sola went up to her suite. When she opened the door, a draft of cool air greeted her. She eyed the shower, that landmark of civility. She undressed hurriedly and stepped into the cold relief of running water.

She felt a bit embarrassed spending so much time in a tin can rainstorm, but it helped her think, and she needed to think.

When she'd dried off and gotten dressed in some fresh clothes, she felt a whole lot smarter.

Her room monitor began to beep.

Colby! She raced over to the table and turned her module online, visual and audio this time.

"Woman! Where da hell ya been?" Colby looked sexy with a couple of days of stubble and a mass of uncombed blonde hair. A wave of reassurance rushed through her to see another human face, especially his.

"Nice to hear from you too," she said with mock indignation. "Am I ever glad to see you!" She added.

"No kidding!" He smiled and rubbed the palm of his hand over his furry jaws.

"So, what's the scoop?" she said, enthusiastically.

"Moses came through! Alan was willing to skip a few of the formalities. He was able to reset the security code and get the new one to Moses. We owe both of them, big time!"

"Fantastic! So Minerva is back to normal?"

"Seems to be."

"You know, I tried to reach you all night, Colby, but my PCU was down, completely down."

"That's strange. It took me several hours to go through each system and get everything back online, but I started with the main com system, got it functional right off. Tried reaching you on the PCU. It just rang and rang. Didn't even pop over to voicemail."

"Well, that's a mystery. It's working fine now," she said. "The last two days have been sort of psycho. I'm not sure what to make of anything. Colby, how secure is this transmission?"

"Should be solid, Pumpkin. Minerva's on her game again."

"Good." She filled him in on all the details.

Colby listened very attentively, putting in an occasional, "No kidding?" or a "No Shit?" When she finished her story, he sighed. "Well," he said, "It's not my commission on the line, so who am I to say, but I'm still for getting you out of there. I say jettison the deal. I think this place is on a questionable trajectory, and I don't like the idea of you getting swept up in what could be a big, fat mess."

"Yeah. I'm a bit nervous too," she admitted, "but also curious. Maybe more curious than nervous, you know? It's certainly making this trip a lot more interesting. Intercontinental intrigue, a possible spy ring. We could be correspondents to history!" Where was her sudden bravado coming from, she wondered.

"Listen," he continued, shifting his tone. "How would you feel about contacting IDS now that we can?"

"A few months ago, before the regime shift, I'd say let's do it. Stan was so solid, brilliant really. I completely trusted that man's judgment. I have no idea how the new corporate will react. I do know I wouldn't trust Hal Menos to walk my dog."

"Well, yeah, I'd have to agree with you, except you don't have a dog."

"I will have one, when I move to Maui! This commission means so much to me, Colby. You know I'm not a capitalist at heart, but this sale's paying my way out. If it falls through, I'll need to stick with IDS longer. That's a depressing thought."

Colby was going to make a good amount of money on this job as well, but his income wouldn't change if she bailed. Hers would take a nosedive without the added commission.

Her plan was to use that commission to pay down the premium on the condo, lowering the monthly mortgage enough to allow her to quit working for IDS and move to Maui.

Without this commission, she was stuck with the higher mortgage, and would have to keep working. IDS required her to live near their Denver headquarters, so that meant continuing to rent out the condo, a most unhappy scenario. Finding a job in Maui was not an option, unless she wanted to give surfing lessons, not such a bad idea in theory, but talk about competition. Everyone and their grandmother taught surfing on Maui.

"Okay. What if we hold off on IDS but contact the United Planets instead?" Colby asked.

"We don't have anything solid to report. There was some civil disobedience in the capital of the Southern Continent. It was on the news. The authorities roughed up some students during a protest march. You can image how I feel about that! According to the news here, no one was seriously hurt. I doubt that's enough for an investigation. Plus, Caifanii is not a UP member."

"What about the guy they arrested at your hotel? We could alert Amnesty Interstellar."

"Not enough to go on there either. He might be a political prisoner. Then again, he might be a member of an organized crime syndicate or a terrorist."

Jaitain must be some sort of troublemaker, she thought. Whether he was the sort of troublemaker who also made history, she could only speculate. Mahatma Gandhi; Martin Luther King, Jr.; Terra Kofal; Shosan Igamtulaz. History had its share of those kinds of troublemakers, people ahead of their milieu, not blinded by conventional thinking. Often, they became martyrs. She had no proof Jaitain was *that* kind of figure. He was from Djintu, and could well be involved with the civil unrest in the Southern Continent.

"Houston," Colby prompted, "this is Apollo 11. Do you copy?" He was waving his hands in the air.

"Yeah." She pulled herself out of her musings. "Sorry. I don't know, Colby. I think I should stay here. See what happens. Meet with the High Council as planned. You got my stuff through customs, that's a plus. Did you have any trouble with that?"

"Nope."

"You felt comfortable enough to have Port Authority send the data processor to the hotel. That shows a rise in your confidence."

"True, but you needed it and I needed to stick with Minerva, so I didn't have a lot of choice there."

"Still, the overall forecast looks like it's clearing up. That reminds me. Did you find any residual energy signatures in the system?"

"No. Nothing, but they could have been degraded too much to detect, so no real verdict there."

"Well, that's at least not bad news. I'm sticking with 'business as usual' for the time being."

"You're the boss, I'll follow whatever directive you decide makes sense, but I'd sure be more at ease if you were back here."

"Why don't you come here instead? Things seem copacetic on Minerva now. Your hotel suite is still here, waiting for you."

"I haven't taken any those peppers yet. Figured why get hopped up on drugs if I don't need them, but I guess I can handle taking them for a day or two."

"It takes that long for them to kick in, so you might be able to handle being on this planet without them. You're pretty tough, but I strongly advise taking them. The climate and the g force here are brutal on us mere humans."

"I'm from Houston, Hon, used to sticky heat."

"I'm from Maui, Dude! This heat is monumentally worse! Minerva's keeping you comfy with her perfect humidity and gravity!"

"Are you saying I prefer comfy to adventure? You know I love a good explore."

"Then get your butt out of the saddle, and head on over!"

"Okay, Alice! I'll just pop those pills and jump down the rabbit hole. It'll take me a while to secure Minerva. Wanna make sure she's tucked in tight. See you for dinner."

"Just come up to my room when you get here. I'm in 417."

"Any good BBQ on this planet?"

"Not with meat, but something akin to chili, pretty hot. I know a place!"

"Great! Do they serve cerveza?"

"Nope. But I'm sure we can find you something worth drinking."

"Bueno. Hasta!"

She switched her monitor off, took in a deep breath and let it out quickly through her lips. All that talk about dinner made her hungry. Breakfast sailed long ago, but lunch was in order. The hotel restaurant would have to do.

The waiter served her meal complete with a small envelope folded into the white, cloth napkin.

It was from Jaitain.

One of the restaurant employees must be a friend, or maybe Jaitain slipped someone the right amount of cash.

She placed the envelope into her satchel and ate hurriedly. She wanted to get back to her suite and solve a few mysteries.

Chapter 7

Day Three (afternoon)
Dornjan: Answers

Sola sat on the edge of the bed in her suite and opened the envelope. Inside was a small computer disk. Her computer had no drive for discs. They were old technology. Darn. The IDS data processor unit was still not in her suite. It had several disc drives. She needed it in order to access the data.

She called the desk. The clerk said she was busy helping a guest. Sola ended up on hold for a long time listening to the Caifanii version of elevator music, something super sappy with high-pitched, stringed instruments. Eventually, someone came back on the line and promised that her delivery would be there right away.

A silent, thin male was at her door with the processor within ten minutes. After he left, she locked the door.

She suddenly felt as if she had left the shuttle months ago rather than the day before yesterday.

She thought about waiting for Colby, so they could check out the disk together, but she was far too curious. She could play it again for him later.

She set up the translator unit, connected it to her computer, and placed Jaitain's disk in the foreign format conversion drive.

It was in Expert 3.2, an outdated software sold by theTaszu, who were notorious in interstellar trade. They were dealers of outdated, second-hand technologies, but they got around.

The disk was a visual message from Jaitain. He looked tense, no smile.

The lighting was dim and from below, giving him a sinister look and blurring the background into a dull brownish haze. Jaitain's voice was full of urgency and authority.

"Representative Alturas. I do not have much time to relay this information to you, and have been less than wise in my attempts to contact you. I am a leader with The Mhalanai Trust. We are a peaceful peoples' revolution. We have some visual information filmed in Djintu City, the capital of the Southern Continent, some as recent as yesterday, some going back several months. We feel this information must reach the United Planets and Amnesty Interstellar as evidence of gross maltreatment and violence on the part of Central Security as the military arm of the Caifanii global government. Because of the nature of your work here, your business reputation for integrity, and your personal history in working with Amnesty Interstellar in the past, I have reason to believe that we can trust you. You present us with a unique opportunity to bring the offenses documented on this disk to light in the interstellar arena."

He paused then continued. "Our work is dangerous. The outbreak of what the government has termed 'rioting' has given Central Security the excuse to arraign several of our prominent leaders in both the Southern and Northern Continents. I have reason to suspect that they will apprehend me at any time. We are not certain to what degree Central Security is aware of our work here in the northern capital, but we suspect we are being monitored. For these reasons, it is necessary that I reach you now. My regrets for any difficulty this may bring upon you. My earlier attempt to arrange a meeting with you informally was unsuccessful and perhaps I made you in some way uncomfortable. Please accept my regrets. It appears my social etiquette, despite my research on that subject, was not well honed to your culture."

He smiled, looked a bit embarrassed. He grew serious again. "The future of our society is poised on this fulcrum. We ask you to view these materials. Their message is clear. I hope that it will motivate you to deliver this information to the interstellar authorities. I offer you my respect and deepest gratitude. I regret to place you in such a position as this, but I see no other choice but to place this disc into your hands."

He paused again for a moment, a faint smile gracing his darkened face. She couldn't help but guess the nature of his thoughts. After all, he'd seen her hands without gloves.

He finished with what sounded like a traditional blessing of some sort. "Go with honor and strength." He bowed his head slightly and then the screen went black.

Sola hit the pause button. Jaitain was a troublemaker of *that* kind after all. Her body felt tight. The message was so personal, so confident, as if he had no doubts about her deciding to help, about her loyalties. It unnerved her, made her a little angry and a little afraid. She was unused to people trusting her on faith. In her field, she learned to be wary, to not trust anyone she didn't know very, very well.

She wasn't sure she wanted to see the footage. The word *peaceful* and the word *revolution*, were oxymoronic. Revolutions were not peaceful. She walked to the windows and looked out at the blue-green mass of the trees in the distance. It seemed certain now that the two males she overheard on the path behind The Hotel yesterday were part of this peoples' revolution. Did they know about Jaitain's arrest at her hotel? Did they know he successfully got this disc to her? Did they orchestrate that for him? She wondered if anyone else would try to make contact with her. She walked slowly across the room and sat down heavily on the edge of the high bed. Did she want to sign a contract with no idea what lay hidden in the small print?

She switched on the screen and her TLC. She sat staring out of the window for a few more minutes and then pressed the small, yellow key that would reveal everything to her.

Jaitain returned to the screen. "What you are about to see is material the Intercontinental News Syndicate edited and fed to programming yesterday regarding what they are calling an uprising in Siatja Square, Djintu City. After you have watched this segment, we will show you what actually happened in that location yesterday, the unedited reality of the events there.

The first scene was of the "riot" she had witnessed on the view screen in the cafe that morning, only this time with audio. There was a voiceover of a newscaster, a Caifanii male with an authoritative voice. Sola realized she was biting her lip and tried to relax.

"This morning," the newscaster was saying, "a small group of residents from Djintu City's eastern quarter marched along the river wall towards the Government Seat. Security says the crowd remained quiet and in restraint until it entered High Court Square just before eleven. At that point, a large group of marchers at the front of the protest began running towards the court buildings shouting, 'Free Kaleen Utjaika!' Security was able to control the riot quickly with minimal use of force. Reports say that the run on the High Court involved about 20 marchers, mostly university students. The rest of the protesters dispersed peacefully. Twelve of the youth were arrested, three suffered minor injuries due to resisting arrest. The protest seems to have been an isolated incident, spurred by the tensions of the last three days as members and supporters of the Mhalinaii Trust await news of the condition of one of their imprisoned leaders, Kaleen Utjaika. There is no report this morning as to the condition of Utjaika, who fell seriously ill and was taken to Domaliki Hospital yesterday. The High Court has made no statement regarding her scheduled trial date later next week."

Jaitain returned to the screen. "The scene you are about to witness is what actually occurred, at the same location, the same time. Only this second recording is synchronous, made by a friend of the movement who is working within the I.C.N.S. undercover."

Synchronous must mean live coverage, Sola thought. The TLC had translated the term literally. The live coverage picked up earlier in the morning, with scenes of the protest march. There were many more participants than the newscast had showed. There must have been three or four hundred in the crowd, adults and youth. They looked upset, some were crying, others shouting, others holding up their injured fellow marchers. One female's face was bleeding at the left temple.

The peaceful protesters moved into the square like flowing water, slowly filling the square with color and movement. Then they stopped and stood in silence: a stunning silence, magnificent, sad, and haunting.

At that moment, a single, female voice spoke clearly, "Utjaika will be free! You cannot impede justice!" It was as if that one voice spoke for them all, and then there was silence.

Another single voice rose out of the crowd, this time deep and masculine in tone. "Utjaika will be free! Mhalanai will be free!" The magnetic silence of the massive crowd hovered over the square with an acute outrage far more impressive and powerful than any physical force.

Suddenly, the square filled with officers in dark gray uniforms. There was an outbreak of screaming and shouting. The officials began to beat on members of the crowd with short, blunt, hand weapons. There was the hammering sound of some sort of weapon fire. Three armored vehicles had entered the square and began firing directly into the crowd. People were falling to the ground. A small group of young males broke from the mass and ran, obviously in fear, towards the Court building and up the wide stairs of its entrance with the officials in pursuit. That was the cut in the newscast. The image began to shift radically, bouncing up and down. The person recording the event must be running. In the final image he managed to record, a young woman lay on the ground, covered in blood, perhaps dead, or nearly so.

Sola shut off the monitor, not wanting to watch the additional footage now. Her hands were icy and shaking. What she had just witnessed carved out a hollow of remembered pain and indignation in her belly. She wished she had waited for Colby.

It had been five years, but she remembered the experience now as if it had happened this very morning. The swollen face of her brother Ramon, forehead and temples stained with dried blood. Ramon had been only 13 years old, a student at the University of Moez on Ortisis. Just a few months before, she had shuttled out with him. It had been the spring, just before the start of his first session. They had been so jovial together. He had been full of adventurous spirit and excitement. It was his first interspecies experience, and his first year away from home.

The University of Moez, famous for their School of Music, gave Ramon a full scholarship. He was a virtuoso percussionist, and received an offer to join the Global Orchestra of the Mediterranean to commence upon his graduation in three years. It was a tremendous honor. He would be the youngest member of the ensemble in its thirty-year history. Ramon never played with the orchestra. He never even finished his first year of study at Moez. Tensions had been building on campus for years due to long-standing racial discrimination and oppression. There had been some protests in the past, all of them peaceful and without incident, but in the fall quarter of Ramon's first year, the political climate on Ortisis shifted into the red zone. Ramon was curious and sympathetic to the cause of the protestors. He had experienced discrimination himself being Hawaiian. He and his friends joined the protestors. Without warning, police stormed the quad and began beating student protestors without provocation. They opened fire, killing several students, including Ramon. He was to perform in a university concert later that month. The whole family planned to attend, to celebrate with him. The university said Ramon died quickly and without pain. She didn't believe that.

She should never have agreed to identify his body. They knew who he was. Genetics were never ambiguous, and there were the university records.

Yet, she was required to identify him. How could she identify so much anguish in a single glance? How could they have expected her to sign that odious, white sheet of paper proclaiming him gone? "Not like this!" Her mind had rebelled. "No!"

On earth the practice was abolished centuries ago, but on Ortisis, identification by a living relative was legally required in order for her to have his body sent back to Earth for cremation and the ceremonial scattering of his ashes. Her parents had been on a scientific research mission with the

Socrates Society on a quarantined planet, unreachable for another three weeks. Her grandmother was too elderly to travel. She was the only one who could be present.

Colby and her old friend Tori Murdock had gone with her. The two of them had kept her from losing her mind over the pain, which burned like a white dwarf.

She would never be free from the memory of Ramon's face in the morgue, so pale, so boyish under the irrevocable veil of death, so strangely unidentifiable as her Ramon.

She had wanted to say, "No. That is not my brother."

There was nothing of him in his face except the physical features, the bone structure, the shape of his lips, nose. There was none of his vibrant character.

She wanted, in her heart, to deny it was him at all, so that he would not be dead. But there was, the tiny birthmark under his left eye, so small it was hardly noticeable, but she saw it, the cruel evidence. The rage had washed through her veins like a permanent dye.

They informed her that the ammunition tore through his body. She was not required to see it. At least they had spared her that. The morgue's silver sheet covered him up to the neck. He was in one of those drawers, pulled out like a document on file.

She had wanted to scream at the morgue officials and the two witnesses of the court. How can you do this? How can you treat him like this? He's a person. He's my brother. He was only thirteen years old, for God's sake, show some respect.

Instead, she had stayed silent, digging her nails into her palms. She let the rage boil inside, percolating under the mask of her composure.

At the time, she had been too scared to let her emotions show. If she had let even a trickle of that rage escape, she believed she would have gone insane.

Now, she sat on the bed for a very long time, motionless and numb.

The afternoon rain was washing against the windows and it was growing darker outside. She wished Colby would get here. She thought of calling him, but he was probably on the way.

She felt immobilized. It was difficult to grasp that the massacre in Djintu City had taken place only yesterday, and only eight-thousand kilometers away. It seemed centuries old and light years away. This kind of raw violence marred Earth's own history: bloody, mean, fear-based, those countless revolutions before the coming of The Lesser Peace.

She sighed, sent a silent greeting to her brother and asked him to help her find focus and strength.

The edited version of the newscast she had witnessed earlier in the cafe was like an acid wash on glass, meant to etch reality into an opaque blur.

Sola's mind was crammed full of questions.

Who was responsible for the distorted depiction of the event? Censorship was an understatement! The intent of the distorted newscast was obviously to shelter or pacify the Northerners. How had the crowd in the square remained so quiet, so controlled? Who were the speakers? The voices were so beautiful, so resonant, so unflinching.

There was a knock on her door.

She opened it, pulled Colby into the suite, closed the door behind him, dove into his arms and started to sob.

He dropped his duffel bag and wrapped his arms around her.

He didn't say a word, didn't ask for an explanation. They stood in that embrace for a long time, even after she'd stopped crying. He stroked her hair and kissed her head.

"When you're ready to tell me what happened, I'm ready to listen," he said.

"Wow," she said. "That was quite a storm system from the past."

They moved over to the Cafanii version of a couch and sat down, his arm around her shoulder. She told him about Jaitain's disc. She said she wasn't ready to see it again, but he could watch it later. He said he completely understood and didn't need to see it. They sat in silence while the light faded outside.

Colby reached over to the end table and turned on the lamp. It threw an amber pooling of light around them. He took her hand and kissed it. He looked into her still wet eyes and then kissed them too. "Let me hold you," he said. "Just let go of thinking, if you can. Just allow yourself to be held."

She nodded and leaned into him, her head on his chest. He put his arms around her and they sat in silence. It was what she needed. Colby always knew what she needed.

After a while, she felt calm again. "Are you hungry?" she asked.

He chuckled. "That depends on what you mean by that."

"Oh," she said. "Uhm. I meant do you want to go have something to eat."

"I know what you meant, Hon. Sorry. Are you up for going out?"

"I'm sort of a mess and believe it or not, I'm not hungry."

"You? Not hungry? That's a first!"

"I know. I'm always hungry."

She wanted to tell him she was hungry for him, that she'd been thinking of him for the past couple of days in that way. She knew it was in part a side effect of the peppers, but there was more to it. There was always a sexual tension between them, that at times was difficult to deny. She didn't want to deny it now. She didn't want to take him on an emotional rollercoaster either.

"Colby?"

"Si, siñorita."

She looked at him, at those gentle, hazel eyes. "Never mind," she said.

"You know, I think it would do you good to get out of here for a while. Plus, I'll admit sitting here in the semi-dark, with that outrageously huge bed right over there *is* making me hungry. Woman, you have no idea!"

She laughed. He laughed. Then she kissed him, and he kissed her back with such fervor that she felt it all the way to her toes. He kissed her mouth, her eyes, her neck, her shoulder, her mouth again. He picked her up off the couch and carried her to the bed. It felt like a page torn from a romance novel, but it also felt very real. Now they were on the bed together, he rolled her on top of him and looked her in the eyes with complete candor, nothing hidden.

"Is this okay? Are you going to be okay with this?"

"I think that's my line, isn't it?" she kissed his forehead. "I'm more than okay with this, Colby. I want this. I've wanted this for a while."

"For a while? Woman! Why didn't you tell me? You know I'm crazy 'bout you girl!"

He had a mischievous look in his eyes that made her feel like a teenager. She had to forgive herself for not resisting. "Stop talking, handsome cowboy, and kiss me."

He did. His tongue explored her mouth, hers explored his. He pulled her tightly against him, his hands on the small of her back. He spoke softly into her ear with his husky voice and Texan accent, "Crazy 'bout you."

She felt herself grow moist, and not from tears this time. He knew her so well. He touched her with such love and in such excellent ways that she melted completely into the moment. His tongue savored her warmth and excitement. Her mouth caressed his firmness until he was moaning in a low octave. He slid her gently down on the bed, so her head wasn't so close to the wall, and he entered her. He fit her so well that she wondered why she'd ever pushed him away. They rode together on the crest of each wave of pleasure and emotion. She held him close to her heart, her breasts pressed against his strong chest as they came together. He stayed inside her for a long time after their avalanche of bliss.

"Thank you," she whispered.

"My pleasure," he said.

They both giggled. He combed her wild hair away from her eyes with his fingers. "You are a mess, young lady. How are we going to go out for that spicy Caifanii food you promised me with you looking like you've been ravished?"

"I was ravished, and excellently so! But now I'm famished!"

"Let's clean up and go eat. I have no idea what time it is. It doesn't really get completely dark here, does it? Will the restaurants still be open?"

She checked her PCU on the nightstand. They'd been in bed for over two hours.

"It's 7:40. If we hurry we can make it. There's always the hotel restaurant or room service, but everything on their menu is seriously bland."

"Bland is unacceptable. Vamanos!"

They showered together, a humorous endeavor considering the size of the stall. They got dressed and headed for the Center to find the best Caifanii equivalent of four-alarm chili.

She took him to the Fuiga Nakaii. The candlelit atmosphere was even more delightful in the evening. They ate some generously spiced food with gusto, and then there were serious questions to answer. Would Sola meet with the High Council as planned in the morning, or would they bail on the assignment in light of the developments, in honor of Jaitain and his comrades, and in support of their own safety?

Colby's concerns were numerous. If Sola went to the meeting, would they apprehend her, the same way they apprehended Jaitain? Did they suspect Jaitain had contacted her? Who, exactly, were *they*?

"Central Security is what the young clerk downstairs called the officials who took Jaitain," Sola said. What would happen to Jaitain now? She wondered.

Sola had questions too. What was the relationship of her clients with Central Security? The High Council was an administrative body of the government, but they were responsible for commerce, not the quelling of civil disobedience. It was likely that they were not in any way associated with the events in Djintu City. It was on another continent after all. That didn't change the fact that the Caifanii government itself was the actual client, and IDS didn't make deals with overtly corrupt governments, not knowingly in any case, but that was the old IDS. The corporate behavior of the new IDS was an unknown factor. What was the most ethical course of action for her now? Was it possible to be ethical and not forfeit her commission? Those were the crucial questions for Sola.

They talked until they were the only patrons sitting in the restaurant, except for two Caifanii males at the bar who were likely to stay until they were tossed out, passed out, or both.

It was close to 11:00 by the time they got back to her hotel suite. Sola needed to get some sleep, especially if she was going to be "on" for the meeting tomorrow. She still hadn't made the final decision, but her brain was too exhausted from surveying all of the considerations and angles to make a clear-minded choice.

"Let's call it a night. I'm whooped. The meeting isn't until 10:00. Let's sleep on it."

"Am I invited to sleep here?" Colby asked, a bit sheepishly.

"If you promise to not snore," she said.

"I promise. Let's sleep. I'm zonkered."

They got undressed, crawled into the massive bed and were both asleep within minutes.

Two pillars of smoke rose from the fields behind Oilia's farm in the countryside that rolled out from the edge of the sea. Alam and Shuri, the eldest sons of her neighbors, Mita and Niuri, were killed in a protest march in Djintu City that morning. They were both students at Djintu University. Now only their remains returned to their childhood home. Their bodies, anointed with oils, and wrapped in ceremonial cloth lay on the funeral pyres. Traditional prayer songs rose from the throats and hearts of the mourners all afternoon and well into the evening. Now, near midnight, the final Sending was in progress.

Chapter 8

Day Four (morning)
Asmaliantu: Diplomacy

The morning dawned overcast with a promise of oppressive heat. Sola woke up early. She let Colby sleep. He looked so adorable with his wild hair all over the pillow. She didn't regret last night. She was grateful he was here.

She got up and readied herself for the meeting. She still wasn't 100% certain she'd go, but preparing helped her get clear. When Colby woke up, she sat on the bed and they had another potent consultation on the topic. He was still against it, but Sola made an executive decision. Despite her own and his concerns, she'd go to the sales meeting. She'd act like nothing unusual had happened. She'd play dumb, feel them out, but not raise suspicions. She had a good poker face.

Cancelling the meeting last minute could not only kill her sale, it could put the High Council on guard that something was amiss.

It seemed wiser to keep them in the dark if possible. That would better serve Jaitain and his people. Once Colby sent Jaitain's information to the UP and Amnesty Interstellar, those organizations would have time to decide what kind of intervention was needed.

They'd have time to organize that intervention with UP and Amnesty members located in regions near Caifanii without the Caifanii government having advance warning, or the opportunity to orchestrate cover-ups, or who knows what.

Sola was technically required to inform IDS of the planetary situation first, and let them decide whether to contact the UP and/or Amnesty Interstellar, but she didn't trust her new bosses to take the ethical path. Once the sale was closed, they'd want to keep things copasetic with the Caifanii government and they wouldn't want anything to interfere with that financial relationship. A signed sales contract insured Sola her commission, regardless of whether the UP shut down trade with Caifanii.

If they did enforce an embargo, her residual royalties would be on hold, but that seemed like a non-issue at this point.

She wanted to do everything in her power to assist the Mhalanai. Interfering with the political workings of other worlds was not in her job description. It was generally and legally frowned upon, but she wasn't willing to let the injustices against the Mhalanai go unchecked.

Jaitain and his people were taking a huge risk coming to her. She could have easily betrayed their trust. They didn't know her. They certainly didn't know that her personal history would make saying no to them impossible, or magnificently difficult. She was not about to stand by and do nothing. She already signed their contract. She signed it the day she signed her brother's death certificate.

She knew that much, but the small print still made her seriously queasy.

"I have to go to the meeting, otherwise, I'll be waking the sleeping pigs," she said to Colby.

"I'm pretty sure the expression is, 'let sleeping dogs lie,'" he said. "I'm all for getting both of us the hell outta here now. I see your point, but I really, really, let me emphasize this, I really don't like you putting yourself in danger."

"The High Council gains nothing from antagonizing me, Colby. They want this affiliation with IDS."

"I no longer give a shit what IDS wants. If the High Council is corrupt, then the new IDS leadership and the Council make perfect bedfellows! I say, let them screw themselves, but later. First let's give Jaitain and his crew the best possible shot at getting some interstellar help before we blow this taco stand."

"Okay," Sola said. "You sound like a man with a mission."

"That's me! I'll take the disc to the shuttle. Let Minerva recode it in a light-based format. Safer copy. Easier to transmit. I'll send it on its humanitarian mission, get Minerva ready to scram. As soon as that sales meeting is adjourned, you head straight for the shuttle and we are outta here pronto."

"That reminds me, where the heck is the shuttle parked?"

"I'll give you the address and directions," he said, "con mucho gusto!"

After Colby left, Sola showered quickly and dressed in the formal tjong supplied by Protocol Department. This one was not nearly as bad as the first, but nothing to get excited about either. It was beige, the ultimate neutral, the least likely to offend in any culture, according to interstellar research polls. It was a flattering color on her, but she felt pale and insubstantial in it today.

There was a great weight on her shoulders. She packed the briefing disks into her case to review on her way to the meeting, just to calm her nerves and get into her role. She checked to make certain she had all of the database information she would need and the demo materials for the Council. She secured her demo computer into its case.

She pulled on the light blue gloves. All systems go. Still, she felt unprepared. She knew her product well enough, but was nervous about effectively playing naive. She wondered if anyone would mention Jaitain's arrest. Probably not, and she certainly was not going to mention it. If they played dumb, she could play dumber.

According to her briefing materials, someone was meeting her in the hotel lobby to escort her to the Council Chambers in the Government Center for the three-hour meeting.

She was in the lobby only a few minutes, when a short male in a stark, gray uniform approached her. Gray, she thought, beyond neutral and into sterile. There was something passive aggressive about gray. She was feeling on edge.

"Greetings Representative Alturas," the escort said. "I am honored to provide you transport to the High Council. Are you ready to depart?"

As ready as she was going to get, she thought. "Yes. Thank you."

She followed him outside into the muggy haze. They boarded a lavish transport unit that reminded her of a limousine, long, sleek, black and ostentatious to the max. It was hovering just outside the Hotel entrance. The seats in the back were plush. It was cool inside, and there was a wet bar with a silver beaker of iced tea and a chilled glass for her. Nice touch, she thought, as she poured herself a glass. Her escort, who was also the limo driver, did not address her further. A darkened glass partition between the spacious rear compartment and the driver's seat gave her complete privacy.

As the craft took off, smooth as silk, Sola felt like a movie star in one of Colby's old films. What were their names, those glamorous beauties? Greta Garbo. Susan Hayworth. She was more the Katherine Hepburn type. She sipped the cool tea, and scanned her materials nervously. She gave up on reading. Her mind was too scattered. She gazed out of the windows as the transport made an 180° turn to ascend over the tree gardens behind the Hotel. There was no sign of other buildings in this direction. The vegetation below grew thick and wild. If they were heading for the Government Center, they were making quite a detour. They were heading in the opposite direction. After ten minutes, and no buildings in sight, she knocked on the window.

The driver rolled down the glass.

"Excuse me," she said. "How long before we reach the Council Seat?"

"The meeting has been relocated," the driver relayed. "We will be approaching our destination shortly."

After another ten minutes, Sola could see well-maintained grounds spreading out below them, surrounding a lavish, multi-storied estate. It looked like a Tuscan villa. This was definitely not the Government Center. Her briefing materials showed that center as a compound of imposing buildings with pagoda-style architecture. This estate must be the High Councilor's private residence.

The transport began a curving decent and stopped at a massive, ornate gate. There was a security hut. A guard came out and authorized their entrance. He was impressively large for a Caifanii, with a lot of upper body bulk. Not someone you'd want to run into in a dark alley, Sola thought. He looked more like a thug than a guard.

The gate opened.

They proceeded down a long drive lined with tall trees until they reached the villa. If this was the High Councilor's estate, he was what Colby called, "filthy rich."

Sola put on her best professional face and tried to relax. Her heartbeat was fluttering like a bird. The driver came around, opened her door and offered to carry her cases. She accepted.

"I will escort you to the meeting room." He sounded official, his expression polite but not friendly.

She followed him up the wide stairs to an opulent front entrance with double doors made of blue stained glass. The doors opened as they approached.

A stone-faced door attendant invited them into the foyer, which had a cathedral ceiling. A staircase swept down from above in a grand gesture.

"Please follow me," the escort said, leading her to the left down a darkened hallway, which led, after several minutes of walking, into another wing of the villa. He stopped before a massive wooden door impressively carved with a mountain scene. He knocked.

The door opened slowly, revealing a large chamber and a surprisingly overweight male Caifanii with a broad, expressive face.

"Representative Alturas. Esteemed greetings," he said, with a quick bow of the head. "I am High Councilor Htiu. Welcome to my home. We thought it would be more agreeable to have our meeting here."

Sola smiled. The High Councilor was a powerful figure. His name, however, was a powerful sneeze. She nodded her formal greeting. "Esteemed greetings High Councilor and most honored Council members."

She came into the spacious, brightly lit room. South-facing windows provided a view of lush gardens, a small waterfall, and a sizable lake. Tapestries woven in rich, autumnal colors hung on the walls, interspersed with tasteful landscape paintings. Thick red carpet covered the floor. The décor and art in this room alone were probably worth more than everything Sola owned. Htiu's estate was expansive. She imagined the plethora of rooms, all decked out to the max, just like this one. She wondered if one could get "filthy rich" on Caifanii without also getting filthy. On most planets, this kind of extreme opulence was the reserve of the elite, who inherited it; the famous, who won it by selling their privacy; and the infamous, who obtained it by illicit dealings. She was sure the High Councilor for Trade and Commerce received a generous salary, but she guessed Htui's wealth had more than one source.

There were seven Council members seated around a long, oval table, all males. They bowed their heads as a gesture of respect. She repeated the posture. There was one empty seat saved for her at the far end of the table. Introductions ensued. She wasn't going to remember all of their names.

Htiu smiled agreeably. "We are enthused to review the materials you have brought, the," he hesitated. "I regret, I have forgotten the term."

"The demo," she returned. "Yes, I have brought the data base, of course, it is not the complete volume that covers this star system. That is extensive. We offer a variety of databases, a variety of combinations: single solar systems, entire galaxies, personalized selections from several star systems. The Caifanii translations for the sample edition have received extensive review. I believe you will be pleased with the linguistic fidelity."

It felt reassuring to get into the routine she knew so well. She continued. "Our cultural exchange process is, as you know, in its early stages. The IDS encyclopedia is a stimulating addition to that process. You will be able to access information instantaneously, and begin building new trade and information networks which promise to benefit your planet." She wondered if they would benefit only the Northern half.

She glanced around the table. The Council members were openly staring at her. The unabashed, childlike faces of the Councilors made her feel somewhat reassured. They looked like they wouldn't hurt a fly. Then again, there were no flies on Caifanii. Her wavy, auburn hair was making a spectacle of itself. She wished she had thought to pin it up this morning.

Htiu spoke again. "Yes. We are most pleased with this opportunity. You must notify us of any need you have. The Hotel is comfortable?"

"Yes. Thank you," she said. She moved her hands into her lap. The gloves felt itchy, confining. "Purchasing the first data base installment, allows you to be included in the encyclopedia. IDS will send a research team to do the full development of the Caifanii entries, including your impressive cultural and natural attractions; your offerings for economic growth and development; your rich history; all the aspects that will make Caifanii a destination for trade and tourism. They will spend several weeks on the surface." This was all in their briefing materials, but verbal clarification never hurt. She continued. "There are many aspects of life here which will make excellent entry material and which will, I'm sure, lead to profitable future opportunities. The data base will also open to you many new doors for exploring other worlds and making new business, trade, and cultural connections."

She went on to explain the review process to the group. It was outlined clearly enough in the files they had received, but it was always a confusing issue. "Would you like me to go over the review process with you now? Do you have any questions which were not addressed or answered clearly in your briefing materials?"

Several heads tilted as the Caifanii all nodded in the affirmative. The gesture was more a rolling of the head than a nod. They looked as if they were practicing a yoga technique for muscular relaxation. Sola usually enjoyed sales meetings, they were a fun challenge, but this one made her feel anxious.

"All right," she said, "let's begin by looking at the potential timeline for the reviews."

Almost two hours passed while she covered the review materials, provided the demo presentation, and answered all of their questions. She was feeling more at ease, methodically moving through the well-worn terrain of her profession, but she maintained her alertness. Under the circumstances, this was not a "business as usual" situation. Another hour passed as they discussed purchasing and payment options. The Council already gave IDS strong buying signals in advance. IDS didn't send representatives to far flung parts of the galaxy unless the sale looked extremely promising. Still, no deal was "sure deal" without a signed contract.

Htiu sat at the far end of the table from her. He rose with a formal gesture. "We are impressed with your presentation, Representative Alturas. We would like to convene in private for a short while in order to make our final decision. Would you enjoy a tour of the gardens while you are waiting? We have set up a variety of local foods there for you to savor. We hear you are quite interested in cuisine."

"Yes, that sounds lovely," she said. They were ready to make a final decision today. This was excellent news. Often, clients needed to "sleep on it," and she didn't get their answer until the following day. She needed to get a signed contract today. Tomorrow, she'd be far, far away from this humid planet.

Htiu called for a servant who graciously led Sola out of room by way of a glass-paned door leading out into the gardens. She was relieved to be outside, despite the heat. The table they had set for her had an elaborate spread of local delicacies, including cheeses, which reminded her that she'd completely forgotten about the cheeses she purchased to present to the Council. They were still in the cooling unit in her suite. She'd only have a few minutes at the hotel to get her things and check out before taking a cab to the long-term parking facility, but she'd be sure to pack those cheeses. Colby would love them too.

She made a plate for herself and wandered around in the garden, trying to stay present with the tastes and textures, but too nervous to fully appreciate them. The waterfall created a cooling mist. She settled down on a small bench where she could feel the water's light spray on the breeze. After only twenty-minutes, they asked her to return to the meeting room.

There were satisfied smiles around the room, a good sign. Htiu informed her that they were all in agreement that the sales contract was acceptable and they were ready to sign. Once she had their signatures, Sola added her own, separated the contract copies and gave Htiu his in a formal folder for that purpose. She tucked her copy away in her briefcase. There was some light conversation, congratulations, the usual wrap up.

"I understand there was a bit of a disturbance at your hotel yesterday?" One of the Council members said.

The question caught her completely off guard. Was she turning red? She looked around the room.

The Caifanii were a reserved culture, not highly expressive. They were not known to possess telepathic abilities, but she sensed that there was communication going on between the Council members that her translator had no hope of accessing, much less translating for her. From the sudden increase in tension and the stern look on Htiu's face, the comment had been ill spoken. Good. Maybe she could milk them for a little information.

"A disturbance?" she said. "What do you mean?"

Htiu spoke, throwing another sharp glance at the Council member who had brought up the taboo subject. "Apparently it did not cause you any inconvenience."

He was trying to close the subject. Sola tried to keep it open. "I was out most of the afternoon, enjoying the Center," she said. "Did I miss some excitement? Was there a fire in the kitchen?" She congratulated herself on her coy demeanor.

"No, nothing of consequence." Htiu wasn't going to budge. It seemed obvious that she wasn't going to get any further details without asking for them, and that was too risky. She watched the outspoken male sink into a chair. She didn't envy his position.

"Well," she said, trying to ease the tension with her cheerful tone. "This has been a most successful meeting. On behalf of IDS I welcome you to our interstellar business family." It was a standard closing, but her heart was nowhere in it. "My esteemed appreciation for your attention and courtesy today. I especially thank you for the delightful foods you provided. That was most thoughtful."

"You are most welcome." Htiu said, assumed his dignified pose.

Then he moved closer to where she was standing, a little too close for her comfort, and just about whispered in her ear. "Miss Alturas, I am having a gala this evening, here. I am celebrating. I am the newly appointed Minister of the Drug Administration."

"Congratulations," Sola said. This was interesting news.

Htiu gloated. She could feel his breath on her cheek. It was not a pleasant sensation, but she was curious what he would say next.

"I would be greatly honored by your presence this evening as my special guest. I have sent an artisan-made formal tjong to your suite at the Hotel. I think you will find it exquisite, and the color will suit you beautifully."

Was he coming on to her? She knew he was married. She felt a combination of disgust and something akin to fear. Up close and personal, Htiu had a predatory energy. She decided to continue to play the game. It was just for another few minutes. She would let sleeping dogs lie.

"I would be honored," she said. She would relay a message to him later, from the hotel, excusing herself due to urgent family business.

"I will have one of my drivers meet you in the Hotel lobby at 6:00. Would that be agreeable?"

"Yes," she said. "I will be ready. Thank you for your many considerations and kindnesses."

He looked oily and pleased with himself.

What a slime ball, she thought. Yuk. Though, she had to admit, if the tjong was indeed exquisite, she'd keep it.

Htiu moved away and resumed his official demeanor. "Esteemed Representative," he said, smiling in a way that made her feel slightly nauseated. "We have kept you long here. You will no doubt desire some time to be at ease. One of my drivers will take you back to the Hotel."

She was happy to step out of the room and out of her role. An escort waited in the hallway, and led her back to the main entrance. Shorter and thinner than the first, this escort looked much too young to be a driver for Htiu, a position she assumed was not entry level. He seemed extremely nervous. She hoped he was better at driving than he was at walking, as he almost tripped on the way to the limo. She felt embarrassed for him. He helped her get her materials into the limo and they were on their way.

Sola was glad to see a fresh pitcher of iced tea in the limo, and eagerly poured a glass. She drank it down a bit too quickly, giving herself a brain freeze. It left a sour taste in her mouth, too much lemon or the local equivalent.

Suddenly, it started to rain heavily. The percussive drops on the limo roof reminded her of her brief stay on the small island of Puerto Rico many years ago, funny how a sound can trigger a memory. There too it rained every afternoon in torrents. The profusion of drops created an aural festival of marimba rhythms on the window louvers. That was a wonderful rain.

This rain also created a joyous ruckus. She rolled down the limo window a bit and breathed in the refreshed air. She let herself relax after the stressful meeting. It was a miraculous success. She was so relieved.

She reached down into her briefcase, pulled out her PCU, and strapped it to her wrist. She wanted to send a message to Colby, but bending down made her dizzy and disoriented, like she was about to faint.

She rested her head against the back of the bench seat.

She was suddenly not feeling at all well. Her vision was slightly blurred. She closed her eyes.

The limo came to a halt.

She opened her eyes. She had a nasty headache now.

They were at the edge of the woods. She could see the deep green of the trees, but everything was very fuzzy.

She was barely conscious, but felt someone lifting her, threads of thought stretching and tearing as her feet dragged across the carpeted floor of the limo.

Her right arm fell to her side, her hand hitting something hard. There was a brief pain, masked and distant.

Carried in a firm embrace, her cheek resting against a muscular chest, a fragment of memory escaped through the tightening net of sedation, a memory of her father carrying her to bed when she was a small child.

The memory disappeared, replaced by a shard of fear scratching at the remnants of her consciousness. She thought for an instant about screaming, but could find no sound.

She saw something just under the edge of her abductor's shirt, a small tattoo. In her haze, she swore it looked like a plumeria blossom.

She looked up, tried to discern the face of her abductor in the harsh daylight, then her mind faded to black.

Sitting behind his formidable desk, Htiu rang for his assistant.

"Prepare my private vehicle," he said into the intercom in his usual curt manner. "I need to leave for a meeting in twenty minutes.

"It will be done," the assistant assured him.

Htiu pressed the end call button.

A few minutes later, the intercom buzzed.

"What is it?" Htiu growled.

"Your private vehicle has not yet returned," the assistant's voice replied.

"Not yet returned?" Htiu shouted. "It has been hours! Do you know the reason for this delay?"

"No, Sir."

Htiu fumed. He was surrounded by morons.

"Well, call the vehicle and inform the driver to return it immediately. When he arrives, tell him he is terminated. Prepare another vehicle for me now."

He hit the end call button with enough force to flip the unit over.

This was unacceptable behavior in his driver. Htiu was not only angry, he was disappointed. He had seen potential in the youth's vigor and enthusiasm. He had promoted him to personal driver for that reason, hoping to mentor that passion, but the boy obviously had no discipline.

Htiu sighed. He turned the intercom unit back over and pressed the begin call button.

"One more thing," he hissed. "Call that hotel in Haikon where the Terran woman is staying. Make certain she was safely returned there."

Book Two

*Nidia soluantu doste
mauan din folan u pa listu*

*Life travels in cycles,
yet brings us to a new place*

The Mhalanai Book of Ways

Chapter 9

Hana, Maui. Earth

Sim amako doste fulante mani.
From darkness we are born.

The Mhalanai Book of Ways

In the deep center of the night, Sola's grandmother Mahealani awoke. Someone was knocking on her kitchen door.

Still disoriented from sleep, she pulled on her silk robe and walked barefoot to the kitchen.

It was a warm, humid night. She instantly recognized the face and the thick cloud of dark hair of the woman behind the screen door.

"Leanna. Come in. Come in. My heavens." Mahealani felt her heart palpitate nervously and her palms grow moist. Leanna was a strong seer, a Kahuna, and would not come in the middle of the night to share some ordinary gossip.

Leanna stepped into the house and the two elderly women sat down at Mahealani's wooden kitchen table, listening to the night sounds in the brush and to the soft lapping of the waves on the black beach near the house.

"I come because of Sola," the old Hawaiian said, her face expressing both concern and joy. Your grandchild is coming into a strong journey."

"Is she safe?" Mahealani whispered.

"I do not sense true danger," Leanna said, "but there is fear and great uncertainty."

"Leanna, I do not even know where in the heavens my little pearl is right now. My last communiqué came from her about three weeks ago. She was in transit from here to there, to somewhere else. You know, her life is like a plumeria petal in the breeze!"

Leanna took hold of Mahealani's frail hand and placed it with love into her own large, brown palm.

"I should not have come to take you out of your rest, my friend, but I believe that Sola could use our support on this night."

"Then I believe with you," Mahealani said. "Have I ever had reason to doubt your intuition?" She chuckled lightly. "Besides, I was dreaming about those giant flying roaches again and am much pleased to be done with it. Come, it's so hot in the house, let's go out on the lanai."

The two passed through the quiet house and out of a side door onto the uncovered porch where they reclined together, sideways, in a large hammock and stared up into the expanse of space that somewhere held their Sola.

"I too was dreaming," Leanna said. "Only in my dream there were people with luminous eyes and skin the color of early leaves. They told me that they must take our Sola on a journey, but that she would be safe with them. They were very beautiful, these silver-eyed people. They asked me to come and to tell Sola's Great Mother to send Sola peaceful feelings in order to calm her fears."

"What an unusual dream, Leanna. Was it a vision?"

"Oh, I believe all of our night journeys are visions, yes?"

"Then what are those nasty roaches trying to tell me?" Mahealani frowned and gave her head a quick shake. "They truly give me the willies!"

Leanna gave a full-bodied laugh, rocking the hammock.

"Oh, my, I don't think I can help you with that one," she said.

Leanna pointed up at the star cluster of the Pleiades.

"How bright the sisters look tonight," she whispered.

In a warm and slightly raspy voice, Leanna began to softly sing one of Mahealani's favorite songs, based on an ancient Pule Ho`ao marriage prayer.

Eia loa`a maha
O haka moe
O haka i ka lani
Pili olua e, ho`ao e
Moku ka pawa o ke ao
Ke moakaka nei ka hikina
Ua hiki ho`i la nui

Mahealani let the song soothe her heart. If Leanna believed that Sola was safe, then she was willing to believe it as well. She had known Leanna since they were both school children and she trusted her friend's mysterious wisdom. If Leanna said Sola needed their attention, let the two of them send her courage and the wisdom to allow change, and so they did.

As her grandmother and the old Kahuna of Hana were gazing up at the bright stars that, from the vantage of Earth, seemed gathered together as seven sisters; Sola was lifted in the arms of a young Mhalanai, away from all semblance of routines, and down into a labyrinth of caves where everything in her life would slowly begin to transform.

Chapter 10

Day Five (afternoon)
The Caves of Lan, Northern Continent, Caifanii

Iu ashuma ho limau pa porulo li ania pa hone.
Look into the eyes of your enemy and recognize your teacher.

The Mhalanai Book of Ways

When Sola opened her eyes, there was only darkness, deeply silent, cool and dank. She was lying on her back on something hard, with a heavy blanket wrapped around her. Its rough fabric prickled her skin. Through a haze of confused thoughts, she realized that she was not in the limo, the suite, or the shuttle. In her dream, someone had carried her away from the limo into the woods. She was aware, but unable to move, struggle, or escape. She dropped into an instant of terror. That was no dream. She tried to sit up, but found no strength in her body. Her mind was a whirlpool of disjointed, frenetic thoughts all vying for attention.

"Okay," she whispered, her voice sounding loud in the silence. "Hold it together, Kiddo," she encouraged herself, half-heartedly. She pulled her arms out from the cocoon of the blanket and combed her fingers through her tangle of curls, and massaged her temples.

She'd been drugged. The iced tea in the limo. That explained the sour taste. The sedative had left a dense haze and a mean hangover. She took a deep breath and let it out slowly.

"Let's just look at this logically," she told herself aloud, somewhat reassured by the familiar sound of her own voice in the void. "Colby will find me."

She grabbed her left wrist. The PCU was gone. She checked her belt. The TLC was there, though the earpiece had fallen out of her ear.

She unwrapped herself from the blanket. The cold was intense. This must be a refrigerated storage room. Caifanii had no natural cold like this. There was no sound. If there was a cooling unit, it was not currently running. She felt around her. She was on a hard slap with edges, a table. She sat up. Her head was pounding. She slid her legs over the edge and felt for the floor with her toes. The table was not high. She stood up, collapsed like a rag doll. She sat on the stone floor and berated herself for "drinking the Kool-Aid," as Colby would say. The iced tea was perfectly fine on the way to the meeting, no reason for her to suspect otherwise on the way back. There was no reason for Htiu to drug her. He had what he wanted. This made no sense at all.

"Shit," she whispered.

She felt around her on the floor, hoping for the PCU. She found nothing but a thick layer of fine dust. This was certainly not a restaurant freezer. She scooted around on the floor, her hands fanning out to left and right. She followed the legs of the table and went all the way around. Nothing but more dust, no PCU. She needed to know the size of the room. She stood up very slowly, using the table as a crutch. She ventured wobbly-kneed into the blackness. She took a few steps and ran into a wall almost immediately, felt along its contour until she reached another wall, felt out the space in this way. It was a small storage room with shelves along two of the walls, the long table in the center, and one locked door. No light came through the cracks along the door's edges, and the only thing she found on the shelves were cylindrical metal containers, probably canned food supplies.

Along with the damp chill, fear settled into her bones. She sat back on the table and pulled the itchy blanket around her.

After an indeterminable time in the dark, Sola heard a group of quick footsteps and one angry voice somewhere in the distance, muffled but coming closer. She felt for the thin cord of the TLC, secured the earpiece and turned on the unit. The voices were very close now. Scream for help, or stay quiet? She asked herself. She went with the second option. She ditched the blanket again, scooted quietly off the table and felt cautiously towards the shelves. She took one metal container in each hand, and positioned herself to the left of the door. She held her breath as the footsteps approached and stopped directly on the other side of the door.

There was the sound of a key in the lock. Then a loud creaking as the door opened, letting in a single beam of light. The sudden brightness burned into Sola's dilated pupils, she was blinded. She threw the two cans as hard as she could. One hit the door with a disappointing thud; the other hit its target who shouted, "Aaaaah!"

"Aaaaaaaaah!" She screamed back. She tried to scramble for two more cans. She closed her eyes for a moment and then reopened them, trying to adjust to the light.

There were three backlit figures. One approached her, limping. She was about to give him a swift knee in the groin when she recognized his face. It was Jaitain. The sheer surprise stopped her in mid-action.

"Representative Alturas! Are you all right?" He asked, with genuine concern, his face now close to hers. "I will not hurt you. I did not lock you in here. I am here to liberate you."

She stared, silent, stunned.

"Can you walk? Shall I carry you?"

This was very confusing. "I'm okay," she said, "a bit freaked out. I thought you were in prison."

"I cannot believe he locked you in here!" Jaitain's indignation was palpable. "You must be frozen." He got the blanket from the table and wrapped it around her shoulders.

"You're limping," she observed.

"Someone threw a can at my leg," he said. "I got lucky. I think she was aiming for my head!"

His humor threw her. It was not a funny situation.

He put his arm around her. "You are weak, let me help you walk."

She was too feeble to resist his assistance. They walked out of the storage room and down a narrow corridor, the two others illuminating the way with flashlights. The walls were made of raw, damp stone. The ceiling was low and uneven. After a few minutes, they passed through a low archway into a large chamber that glowed with yellow, artificial light. The air was warmer, less musty but still stagnant. Jaitain helped her sink into a beanbag-shaped chair. The others moved away, disappeared through another archway.

Sola sat staring up at him, trying to take in this experience. He looked terrible, purple bruises on his face, dried blood on his lower lip.

He seemed as hampered by disbelief as she was. Finally, he spoke.

"Please believe me. I did not approve this. I did not even know about it, until now. This is not an action of the Mhalanai Trust." He looked at her, trying to read her face. He grabbed a couple of additional blankets from a nearby pile, wrapped one around her on top of the first. He placed the other one, folded up, on the floor. He sat down at her feet. "When I was apprehended," he explained, "there was a panic. I am the principle Mhalanai leader in this sector. One of our young supporters acted completely outside of our protocol by bringing you here. Fanaticism is always a danger. We watch for it, but in this case, did not catch it in time."

"First of all," Sola said, "I am livid. I'm just not feeling well enough right now to express my anger adequately."

"Adequately enough, and justified." he replied.

"Jaitain. I did exactly what you wanted. I gave your disc to my pilot. I asked him to send it to the United Planets and Amnesty Interstellar this morning. We planned to leave directly after my sales meeting. He is waiting for me. I need to get back to the hotel, right now, or directly to the skyport. That might be better. I don't care how this happened. I just need you to fix it."

"Representative Alturas, you are not our captive. I do not wish to detain you, however, things are complicated," he said.

"It can't be that complicated to get me to the skyport."

"I want you safely on your shuttle, believe me, but it is no longer in Haikon.

"What? No. Colby would not leave without me!"

"Colby is your pilot?"

"Yes," and lover, she wanted to add, just to emphasize that he would not abandon her.

"This is unacceptable!" she rasped, then coughed. Her throat felt raw.

"I went out on a limb to help you and your revolution," she continued. "I did exactly what you needed me to do, and now your revolution has stranded me here in this," she looked around. "Where the hell are we anyway?"

"At the moment, it is better I do not tell you. If you decide to return to Haikon, anything you know will be a danger to you and to us," he replied.

She cringed.

"Well, we are obviously in some sort of cave, my favorite environment, being claustrophobic."

She regretted her sarcastic tone, getting antagonistic with Jaitain was a bad strategy. He was obviously her only way out of here.

"Jaitain, I am willing to believe this was not your plan, but I need to contact Colby right away, now. He's got to be going nuts."

Jaitain looked miserable sitting on the floor gazing up at her. He reminded her of her puppy Sam, who used to go out and eat all kinds of weird stuff and then feel ill. What was with this business of her comparing men to Sammy? She was annoyed with herself.

"Here's what I do know," she said. "I was drugged in the limo, on the way back to the hotel. That young driver, was he responsible?"

Jaitain looked at her, sighed. "You are persistent."

"Stubborn," she said.

"Before I tell you, we need to have a vital conversation. The more questions I answer now, the more risk we create. The Haikon area is crawling with Central Security and Htiu's patrols. Until we decide the safest course of action, I strongly recommend you remain here."

"Are they searching for me? Why not let them find me?"

He looked at her, a deep frown on his face. "Again, let me be perfectly clear. Representative Alturas, I have no desire to keep you captive. You are free to go. One of us will guide you back to the city center. From your perspective, I can see that going back to the Hotel, or the skyport, seems highly reasonable. Your perspective, however, does not include my experience with Central Security, and more importantly, with the personal motives of High Councilor Htiu."

"Your recent experience with Central Security certainly wasn't pleasant," Sola said. Jaitain's face looked gruesome. She suddenly felt dizzy and nauseated.

"Representative, you do not look well. You need to drink a lot of water, to flush your system, and you have not had food in many hours. I will get you some water and food, and we will resume this conversation once you are fortified. Are you willing to allow for that?"

Sola looked into Jaitain's eyes. He seemed earnest, and ridiculously formal, considering the situation. She tried to imagine him as the bad guy, but the typecasting didn't fit. The footage on his disc was enough to convince her he was the underdog and not the villain, but every fiber of her being wanted to run, run, run away. She was in some sort of a cave, without the light beam on her PCU, running away would mean becoming hopelessly lost in a dark, cold, underground maze. It was not even a remote option. She knew from experience that extreme hunger made you feel nauseated, a malevolent design for sure. Food and water sounded like a smart idea. Jaitain was unlikely to drug her again. He acted more like a Red Cross volunteer than her captor.

"On one condition," she said. "That you stop calling me Representative Alturas and call me Sola."

He smiled. "Agreed. Just rest here. I will be right back. It will only take a few minutes."

Sola wanted the situation resolved, but knew Jaitain was right. She needed to take care of her body first. What a ridiculous predicament. The signed sales contract was in her briefcase, which she hoped was somewhere in the room. Her commission was "in the bag," so to speak, but she had no way of getting the bag to the bank.

She did her humanitarian duty. The interstellar authorities were probably viewing Jaitain's videos right now. Yet, here she was, stuck under a ton of rock, having a chummy conversation with an outlaw revolutionary leader, whose fanatical young follower was the most likely suspect in her drugging and kidnapping case.

That all made for an interesting scene in a film, almost funny, but a bad real-time situation.

Jaitain was back quickly. Sola drank generously from the tall container of water he gave her, and then settled into eating something akin to warm oatmeal from a ceramic bowl.

"There's a kitchen down here?"

"A galley of sorts, yes."

"Sorry about the canned food projectile, and yes, I was aiming for your head."

"Good thing you are a lousy shot."

"I'm actually a good shot! I was a little comatose on some sort of horse pill."

"Sola, though I am reluctant to tell you anything further, you already assume the truth, so I am willing to verify it."

"That the limo driver drugged me and brought me here?"

"Yes."

"He is your fanatical revolutionary? Where is he now?"

"We have him in custody. He created a highly volatile situation. I will deal with him later."

"I lost my communicator. It was on my wrist in the limo. Did he take it?"

"He says he brought your belongings. I will find them for you, but first we need to continue this conversation."

"So you can convince me that walking away from this situation is a bad idea? Good luck!"

"I can see I will need it!"

"I'm a reasonable person, Jaitain. Give me a reasonable reason and I promise that I will accept it. Why was your young fanatical revolutionary working for Htiu anyway?"

"Cylin is a recent recruit, and a highly valued addition, until now. He was taking a huge risk working for Htiu while being an informant for the Mhalanai. He is the one who told us about you."

"The 'friend' you mentioned when we were in the restaurant?" She asked, between bites.

"Yes. The workers at Htiu's estate are prone to gossiping, and a visitor from another planet is a juicy topic. Cylin was perceptive enough to recognize the opportunity you could provide to bring interstellar attention to Mhalanai cause. As you point out, he is very young. He is inexperienced, his passion not tempered by wisdom. He was convinced you gave my disc to the High Council. He also believed you turned me into Central Security since my arrest happened at your hotel."

"You know that I didn't, right?"

"I know."

"Isn't Cylin a bit young to be Htiu's driver?"

"He is in training. According to him, after your meeting, Htiu's primary drivers were unavailable. Cylin received the order to drive you back to the hotel. Since it was an unexpected assignment, he had little time to decide how to utilize the opportunity. He thought taking you here gave us a second chance to persuade you to support our cause."

"Abduction is a sure fire way to win someone's trust," Sola said.

There was that sarcasm again. Of course, she had every right to be pissed off.

"He just happened to have a kick-ass sedative on him at the time?" She asked.

"Cylin had access to all kinds of drugs, working with Htiu's people. He claims the drug he used is not dangerous."

"Not to Caifaniis maybe. Might have killed me! Sure knocked me out, and left a bad headache."

"It was an unconscionable act," Jaitain said, "and put us all at risk. At least he covered his tracks. He took you to the house of a friend, whom he knew was out of town and left you there while he drove the limo to the Center. He parked it near the Hotel, so it would appear he had dropped you off as planned. Then he rode the bus back to his friend's home, which is quite a distance from here, and then carried you with your bags to our location."

"That's no small feat. I mean, not that I'm all that heavy."

She was feeling like a bumbling adolescent again. Jaitain had that effect on her, even now.

"Cylin succumbed to a not-uncommon hubris."

"A sort of hero syndrome?"

"Exactly. He was convinced abducting you was an act in the highest service of our cause, a stamp of honor."

Sola suddenly recalled the young man's tattoo.

"Jaitain, I'm not sure if I imagined this, but when Cylin was carrying me, I saw a small tattoo on his chest. It looked like a flower native to Earth, to my home place, Hawaii."

"Ah, it was an oplumia," Jaitain said. "It grows abundantly in the southern continent and has become an emblem of the revolution. Many young supporters get oplumia blossom tattoos. I find it admirable, but worry that it is dangerous for them to mark their allegiance so openly."

"That is pretty brave of them, and it is also a pretty odd coincidence, because we call this flower plumeria. In the Hawaiian language, it is called o'plumeria. That's a very, very similar name."

"That is indeed!"

They looked at each other for a moment, a little perplexed.

"Well," Jaitain said, "in any case, it is a beautiful and fragrant flower, and one of my favorites, for obvious reasons!"

Sola loved plumeria too. Its blossoms made a magnificent lei, though they were so fragrant that wearing the lei could make you feel woozy.

Jaitain moved back to their original conversation.

"I was a little wary about engaging Cylin from the start," he said. "He is young, easily influenced by his work cohort. In this case, that cohort is an unscrupulous band of thugs who are the cogs in the machinery of Htiu's drug cartel."

"Htiu is a Drug Lord? Wow. Why doesn't that surprise me? He can put on the charm, but he has a Mafioso vibe underneath. Did you know he just got appointed as Minister of the Drug Administration?"

"That is certainly convenient!"

"Like putting the mice in charge of safe-keeping the cheese!"

"Indeed!"

"He invited me to the gala celebration of his political triumph. A limo was going to pick me up at the hotel at 6:00. He even had an expensive tjong delivered to my suite for the occasion."

"Well, you must have made quite an impression on him!"

She blushed.

"I had no intention of going, Jaitain! I just played along to keep him appeased. When I didn't show, he must have been disgruntled."

"Well, he did have your room searched and placed two of his guards outside the door."

"Yikes. So much for the fancy tjong, and my cheeses."

"Cheeses?"

"I bought some excellent cheeses downtown, left them in the fridge in my suite. Htiu's guards probably ate them. You should see the guard he has stationed at his estate gate. The man is huge. I didn't know the Caifanii could be that tall and that massive. I am getting a clue why you are not enthusiastic about my wandering back to the hotel. Oh, crap! My uke!"

"Your what?"

"It's a musical instrument I take along when I travel."

"I do not think it made it here. That is unfortunate."

"I can replace it. Please continue. I had no idea the plot was this thick!"

"About and hour ago, Htiu gave the news syndicates a most inflammatory story of your abduction by Mhalanai terrorists, a strategic move. He was obviously indisposed at his own gala, so when did he have time to pull that together? It now makes me suspect this was a setup, that Cylin did not act on his own initiative."

"You think Htiu ordered him to abduct me? Why would he do that? He just signed a contract with my company that will bring lucrative trade to Caifanii. Why would he jeopardize that deal? I have the contract with me right here." She tapped her briefcase. "If I don't get back home, the paperwork doesn't either."

"I am only speculating. I will admit the fact that Htiu invited you to attend his soiree makes the logic of my theory questionable."

"Unless he invited me specifically to insure he would look innocent, to portray himself as the man in the white hat, and prevent me, or anyone else, from suspecting that he's really the man in the black one."

"Possibly so. I will need to talk further with Cylin."

"It's lucky for Cylin you're not likely to do to his face what Central Security did to yours."

"The Mhalanai do not believe in violence."

"Glad to hear that."

"Sola, considering the unfortunate circumstances, I am sure it is difficult for you to imagine that I am this 'man in the white hat,' as you put it, but I hope to convince you that this is indeed the case."

She chuckled.

"This is humorous?"

"No, it's just that my translator makes everything you say sound like a transcript from a court case. Super formal, you know, like you are a lawyer making a case."

"I have no desire to be seen as a lawyer! That is no compliment on this world."

"Well, lawyers do have a bad reputation, pretty much everywhere, but there are good ones. Lots of entertainment shows and books on Earth portray lawyers as the 'men in white hats.' I promise I'll keep an open mind."

"Speaking of lawyers and other crafty figures, Htiu is not the only wolf who holds a government seat in Haikon. There are numerous corrupt politicians. They subjugate the masses with fear tactics promulgated through the media, which they control tightly. If Htiu was not behind your abduction, he is certainly making good use of it by calling it a Mhalanai terrorist act. The Haikon authorities consume their own lies and genuinely believe we are the enemy. In one sense, of course, that is true. We are the enemy of their elite power structures."

"Is that why Htiu jumped to the conclusion that I was abducted by the Mhalanai? I mean, there are other possibilities. I could have gone out for the evening, fallen asleep at a concert of traditional Caifanii music with a postmodern angle!"

"I hear that concert was less than riveting," Jaitain said.

He gave her a surprisingly mischievous grin.

"It was wise of you to turn me down," he added. Then he quickly became serious again.

"In any case, Htiu is using the opportunity to paint us in blood and justify having Central Security come after us with full support. That fortifies his own campaign to use his private militia to root out our Haikon headquarters. It is also possible someone on Htiu's staff found out Cylin works for us. That is the most disturbing scenario. It compromises our safety, and puts a target on his life. Two of our supporters are sealing off the tunnel Cylin used to enter these caves, just in case. He knew only of that entrance, not the others.

"Aha! We *are* in a cave!"

"My slip. You have an odd effect on me, Representative, I mean, Sola. I will admit this. I feel strangely disconcerted in your presence."

"Really?" She was intrigued.

He seemed to be blushing, but it was hard to tell for sure because of his green skin.

"Are you at least becoming more inclined to trust my judgment on how to keep you safe?"

"I'm getting there, but telling me we are in a cave is not likely to make me want to stay put. I hate caves!"

Sola's mother was an amateur geologist, and spelunking was one of her favorite hobbies. Sola went on plenty of excursions to caves as a child. Once, she got wedged between two rock walls while crawling through a tight passage. She panicked, hyperventilated, and started to cry uncontrollably. The minutes seemed like an eternity, while her mom and the rest of the expedition worked her free. She was terrified and mortified at the same time. Ever since, being in caves made Sola squeamish.

"We will not stay here much longer, in any case."

"Well, I'm glad to hear you didn't seal up our only way out. You weren't kidding when you said things are complicated! My head is spinning."

Sola looked at the dark bruises and cuts on Jaitain's face. "They certainly gave you a mean going over," she said. "How did you escape?"

"If Htiu's thugs had taken me, I would not be here now. Central Security still has some legal safeguards, a few legitimate leaders trying to keep the organization from falling completely into corrupt hands. They had no legal grounds to hold me."

"But they decided to rough you up just for fun?"

"It is a complex story, for another time. For now, you need to decide if you are going back to the hotel or staying with us. We will do everything in our power to get you safely to your shuttle."

"I'm not keen on the idea of running into Htiu's thugs, but I'm still not clear as to why he would harm me, or keep me from getting on my shuttle and going home. It serves his interest to see me leave, contract in hand."

"He has multiple interests to consider. Trade with other worlds through connections made with your company is doubtless good for the Caifanii economy, and that served Htiu's reputation as High Council of Trade and Commerce. However, as he is now the Minister of the Drug Administration, that trade is no longer his responsibility or his boon. He will be less concerned about that contract than you imagine. Another important consideration is that Htiu has a personal vendetta on me. He has been my nemesis for many years. He is doubtless livid about my managing to once again escape Central Security's clutches without giving them any information. He now believes, or knows, that you are with me. If he takes you into custody, he will do everything he can to get information from you about our operations in Haikon. He will use you to get to me. That is my primary fear. "

"You mean torture? Like sticking needles under my fingernails, or pulling my teeth without Novocain?" Sola felt herself cringe down to her bones.

"Perhaps nothing quite so violent, but maybe things worse than that. Htiu does not treat women with respect."

"Oh, yuk! Don't even make me think of that!"

She shook her head, trying to dislodge the unpalatable image of Htiu trying to get personal with her.

"I generally prefer to stay clear of Drug Lords, not my kind of people!" She said.

She shifted the conversation. "What kinds of drugs does his cartel move?"

"He deals in a number of illicit substances. One of the most addictive and lucrative drugs is called K, short for the rainforest plant Kau'maa, from which it is made. It has psychotropic and pleasure-center activating properties. It provides a potent high. Used medicinally, it is an effective painkiller. Trafficking K is the main pipeline for Htiu's wealth and power. His only personal interest in your company would be finding an interstellar market for K."

"Shit." Sola sat for a moment, taking in this new information. It stirred up all kinds of contrary demons in her mind. "Jaitain, maybe I need to tear up that contract! You know, only six months ago, my company, IDS, had a policy of collaborating exclusively with United Planets Association members, a good policy in my opinion. Then there was a corporate takeover. The new leadership works with anyone who offers a good profit margin. I will make a considerable amount on the commission for this sale, enough to stop working for IDS and move to my childhood home, Hawaii. It pains me greatly to give up that plan, but I am not willing to achieve my dream by dealing with a drug dealer. Now that Htiu is no longer the High Councilor of Trade and Commerce, is there a chance the contract with IDS will be outside of his illicit influences?"

"Perhaps, but Htiu's cartel has clandestine operatives working in many governmental agencies, and as Minister of the Drug Administration, who knows what havoc he will wreak."

"How do you know so much about Htiu's world?"

Jaitain stared at her for a moment. "I am ashamed to say," he looked pained. "Let me begin by telling you that the ancient Mhalanai used Kau'maa for ceremonial and shamanic purposes to induce altered states of consciousness. A few elders still use it, but we generally do not condone its use. It is far too dangerous. As an adult, I completely agree, but as an adolescent, I did not yet have the wisdom to resist the allure of this drug. When I was fifteen, my father died in a terrible mining accident. The mining company disregarded safe practices because they lowered the profit margin. It is always about the profit. I was distraught, angry, I started using K to escape from the grief and anger. Within a few weeks, I was addicted. I had to have the drug. That meant I needed money to purchase it. I started selling it in order to make that money and in order to have easier access to the drug. I became a streetwise criminal. I was a K addict for over ten years. I worked my way up off the streets, became one of Htiu's most effective dealers, his personal favorite. Using K eroded my ethics and destroyed my life."

"Wow. I didn't see that coming. You are full of surprises. No wonder Htiu wants to take you down. His prodigy turns out to be the lead crusader for his demise. How long have you been clean?"

"Almost seven years." He smiled, sheepishly. "I have lost my chance to be seen as the 'man in the white hat,' yes?"

"What cowboy doesn't get a little dirt on his Stetson?"

"You have lost me. What is a cowboy? What is a Stetson?"

"A cowboy is a man on a horse who tries to make a whole lot of cattle move in the direction he needs them to go. The most famous company making hats for cowboys is Stetson."

"Hmm. Sounds like hard work, especially for the horse!" He laughed.

"Not as hard as your work! The more I know, the more I respect what you are up against."

"How are you feeling?"

"Quite a bit better, but concerned about Colby. My first priority remains contacting him, when it is prudent. I don't want to jeopardize his safety either."

"Our intelligence has not heard of any attempt to apprehend him or fire upon his shuttle, as yet."

"So, you know where he is! What happened? Why did he leave Haikon?"

"A Mhalanai Trust supporter works at the skyport in reservations. Apparently, Colby cancelled the remainder of his reservation at the long-term parking facility. Their checkout time is 5:00 in the afternoon. I am sure he expected you to rendezvous with him long before that time."

"When I didn't show, why didn't he just reinstate the reservation?"

"They already rented the space to another craft, and all the other bays were occupied."

"So, there was nowhere to park? That figures! It's like Murphy's Law decided to use us as an example of the worst case scenario."

"I do not know this Murphy's Law."

"Believe me, you don't want to know. So, where did Colby go?"

"According to our sources, he taxied to the main terminal and waited in one of the gates for as long as they allowed him to occupy it. Eventually, he was required to leave. My assumption is that he is in static orbit above Haikon."

"Crap. That is bad, bad, bad news! How am I going to rendezvous with him? It's not like we ever actually invented the transporter!"

"You have lost me again."

"I'm sorry. A transporter is something from an old entertainment show on Earth, depicting space travel before we were doing much of it. It is an imagined technology that demolecularizes you, beams your molecules through space, and then recombines them once they are in the desired location."

"I would not volunteer for such a thing. What if the molecules are not put back together in the original order?"

"I'm with you. Sounds scary to me, but it would allow me to get onto the shuttle without Colby having to find another parking space!"

"Finding parking is a big problem in Haikon."

"Finding parking is a big problem in all cities. Does Htiu have weapons capable of reaching an orbital target?"

"Not that we are aware."

"As long as Colby isn't targeted from the ground, he'll be fine. He's a fantastic pilot, and we have excellent weaponry."

"Let us hope Colby will not need to use it."

"Jaitain. It appears I have no reasonable choice but to stick with you. I don't like the odds of my going back to Haikon. I'm not fond of the idea of my face ending up looking like yours."

She bit her lower lip.

"Ooops. I didn't mean that as an insult. You have a very nice face. I just meant, you know, the bruises and all."

There was that teenaged, bumbling goofiness again.

"I mean, Central Security would probably just give me an official escort to the skyport, and invite Colby to swoop down and pick me up, but Htiu is another matter. The thought of ending up in his clutches gives me the willies. That is not a risk I'm going to take!"

He smiled. "A wise decision. So, you are with us?"

"I am. So, now that's settled, can you find my bags so I can try reaching Colby?"

Jaitain limped across the room and searched for a few minutes near the far wall, and then carried her bags over to the chair. "I assume these are yours?"

"Yes."

"It is unlikely you will be able to get a signal. There are tons of solid stone between us and the surface."

"Thanks for reminding me."

Sola rummaged through the bags and found the PCU.

"Yes!" She said, with relief.

She turned it on and the screen lit up. She punched in Colby's ID and hit transmit. The screen gave her a text message: no signal available.

"Damn. I'm getting nothing."

"We will contact him as soon as we are on the surface again."

"I can't wait!"

"We must wait, a little longer, until the risk is not as high."

"Okay. When we do leave, where will we go?"

"South."

"To Djintu?"

"Near there, yes."

"That's a long journey."

"It is a beautiful trip. Believe me, despite all this, you will enjoy it."

"Jaitain, this is a silly question, but I've been wondering, what was in that can I threw at you? It was heavy!"

"Preserved beans," he said. "Truly tasteless beans that give you terrible gas, and have left a considerable welt on my thigh," he added.

She felt herself begin to chuckle, then succumb to an involuntary, raucous laughter, a strange but effective release of pent up anxiety and fear.

It was infectious. Jaitain joined in and they both sat and laughed.

"I'm sorry," she said, finally. "I shouldn't be laughing. You're still limping."

"At least I didn't have to eat the beans!"

"Good point. Jaitain, what made you so sure you could trust me with the disc?" Sola asked, suddenly serious.

He looked at her thoughtfully. "I was convinced that you are a mijchi."

"A what?" she asked, the TLC had provided no English translation.

"A mijchi is an extremely loyal animal, often kept as a pet, but the word also means idealist, supporter of the people. It is a compliment," he said. "Please do not be offended."

"I'm not, unless you meant the first definition. I would not make a very good pet. Jaitain, you took such a major risk. You did not know me at all. You could easily have been wrong about me. Salespeople do not have a reputation for altruism, especially if it threatens their commission. How could you entrust such a vital component of your success to a total stranger?"

She looked at his strong face. It was indeed a handsome face, despite the bruises.

He moved closer to her. His eyes looked stern and sad.

"You are right," he said. "We took a risk, but we trust our intuition."

He paused, as if there was something else he wanted to add, but thought better of it.

Then he added, "You presented us with a rare opportunity. We took it."

She had connections. She was certainly more likely to get the information off planet than the Mhalanai. Still, their move was a serious long shot, from her perspective.

"I feel like Persephone in the Underworld," she said, suddenly feeling the immense weight of the stone hovering over her head.

"Nulini," he said, the word sounding gentle, like a term of endearment. "I had no right to bring you into this, by contacting you. I overstepped a boundary. You deserve your normal life."

"I'm the one who's sorry, Jaitain. Sorry for what happened to all those innocent people in Djintu City. They do not get to have their normal lives, do they? Sorry those Central Security idiots brutalized you. Sorry you lost your dad for the sake of someone else's profits on copper. Sorry that I can't do more to help."

"You have already done so much," he said.

He looked at her with a respect she felt she didn't deserve. She didn't want to be the heroine in his novel. She didn't even want to be strong or courageous. She just wanted to let the reservoir of her inner resources regain some of its lost volume.

He noticed the drop in her mood. "I think you need more food, to catch up on your energy."

He got up. "You are a mijchi, you know."

"A reluctant one, I'm afraid," she said.

He looked at her very intently. An intimacy hovered between them for an instant, and then shifted.

"You're right, by the way. I'm still way hungry!"

Food lent its own compassion. That is why it intrigued her. Not all species required consistent molecular refueling, but for those who needed it, the sharing of physical nourishment could be a ritual conjoiner.

"I can warm up some laiku," he said. "Can you eat that?"

"I don't know. Is it very fibrous?" she asked.

"I do not think so. It is puffy and soft, and made of lai, a grain. It is processed into flour and then mixed with fruit juices and steam cooked, and there is a nut paste inside."

That actually sounded good. "I'll try it. As long as it's not Rotchak worms, I'm game."

"Worms are not on the menu! I will be back shortly," he promised.

Sola pulled the blankets close around her shoulders and sank deeper down into the chair. She closed her eyes and wondered what Colby was doing, probably swearing at her for being so inaccessible. That is what she was now, warm and dry and completely, undeniably inaccessible.

Chapter 11

Day Five (evening)
The Caves of Lan, Northern Continent, Caifanii

Doste ho ulumi paania, ho huma yin straela.
In the cocoon of living, the spirit transforms.

The Mhalanai Book of Ways

Jaitain returned quickly with a plate of hot food. She took a bite of the laiku, which smelled like fresh baked bread, and forgot about everything else but her appetite. The laiku tasted terrific. It reminded her of something she had not eaten since her childhood.

"Pork bun!" she said.

"What?" He too was eating, sitting a few feet from her on some blankets on the floor.

"Jaitain, I feel bad I keep hogging the only chair you own!"

"I am more comfortable on the floor. Do not worry. What is 'pork bun'?"

"When I was eight, my family moved to an extensive orbiting lab. My father, at the time, was an organic chemist working on a project there. A family from Nanjing lived directly above us. They had three children, the oldest was a girl my age. We were in the same class at school together. The first day, she shared a snack with me. It was a pork bun, a pasty, round, white bread, steamed, like this laiku, with a small bit of pork meat on the inside."

Jaitain began to cough. "Your translator tells me that on your planet, you eat animal meats?"

"Yes, at times," Sola said. She'd obviously hit a nerve. "I didn't mean to upset you."

"I am not judging your traditions, but here we do not eat our companions," he said.

"Well that's good to hear, seeing as I am one of them now!"

"We do have domesticated animals. They provide wool and foods, like milk and cheeses."

"The cheeses I left in my suite were excellent," Sola said, "made from yamma milk."

"My aunt raises yamma and makes cheeses. I love their sharp flavor."

"Too bad we don't have some cheeses here. They would be a great match with this laiku!"

She was too curious to let the conversation linger too long on food, even though it was one of her all-time favorite subjects.

Sola wanted to know more about the Mhalanai. She knew some Caifanii history from reading her briefing materials, but the information supplied to IDS by government agencies in Haikon now seemed suspect. The historical background information portrayed the Caifanii settlers, who arrived on the planet over a thousand years ago by 'mysterious means,' as the 'founding fathers of a golden age,' an advanced race bringing peace and salvation to the savages, so to speak. A ruling paradigm always writes history to enhance its own mega-ego and political advantage.

"Tell me about your people, Jaitain. What is the story of the Mhalanai Trust, and who is Utjaika?" She remembered the silent crowd in Djintu City, the awesome coherence of spirit among the protesters, the strong cry of, "Free Utjaika."

"Utjaika is an elder of our movement," Jaitain explained. "We are trying to bring the ancient Mhalanai Ways back into practice in order to help restore the balance of our planet before our Caifanii practices and ideologies do to this world what our

Caifanii ancestors did to their own world. It became so uninhabitable that they had to leave it behind and find new territory."

"Ecocide?" Sola asked. "It almost came to that on Earth."

"We who profess to be the higher life forms are the greatest threat to the well-being and survival of all other life; such an irony, yes? Our Caifanii ancestors were technologically advanced for their era, but remarkably shortsighted. Expansionism was their model. Use, discard, and move on to new resources. They brought their service-to-self mentality with them to this new soil."

"My people were like that," Sola said. "Still are, in some places, but we are learning."

"We too are learning. It is only now that we are growing aware of the dangers inherent in upholding the present model. Please do not think I disrespect my Caifanii heritage. There are many qualities to admire in that ancestry. I am Caifanii, but I also choose to honor my first ancestry. There is still Mhalanai blood in my heart, diluted with Caifanii blood for certain," he laughed, "but enough to remember my roots."

"I carry the blood of two ancient peoples, the Mayan and the Hawaiian."

"Then you must know the challenges of mixed blood. After all these centuries, the Caifanii and the Mhalanai no longer exist as distinct races. Our struggle is no longer one of race; it is one of creed, behavior and attitude. This world is currently dominated by Caifanii perceptions and ideology, but the memories of the Mhalanai elders and the stories passed on, the Joining, some of that remains."

"The Joining? What is that?" Sola asked.

She remembered the peaceful faces of the protesters, the single voice which seemed to speak for them all. The silence filled with energy.

"The Mhalanai use the Joining under certain ritualistic conditions. It is a Sacred Way. A Way that was not completely lost. At certain times, when there is enough focused energy, and a passionate purpose, we can create the Joining of our minds.

Legend says that our Mhalanai ancestors were fully telepathic. A few of our elders still practice telepathy, but most of us have lost this skill. Those of us in the Mhalanai Trust have worked to regain at least some of our telepathic abilities with the assistance of our elders. Our modern version of the Joining ritual involves placing the same thought into all of our minds simultaneously and focusing on that one thought until we can feel a certain collective resonance. It is difficult to explain adequately."

"Have you ever been involved in a Joining?" she asked.

"Yes, several times. It is a very powerful experience, difficult to describe with words. It is an experience of temporarily having no physical form, of your perceptions stepping outside of the senses."

"That sounds intense," Sola said. "But it does make me wonder. How did the colonizing Caifanii power structure, so obviously fear-based, achieve dominance over a people of such metaphysical strength? How is it possible that Haikon can suppress this movement even now?"

"History, as recorded by the early Caifanii colonizers, describes the Mhalanai as a backward, docile people easily conquered. The ancient Mhalanai believed in non-violence, in a radiant acquiescence that made them vulnerable to the physical aggression of the Caifanii colonists who had advanced weaponry. As for today, it is difficult to say. It is not as it was over a thousand years ago. Then, there were two distinct races: the Caifanii and the Mhalanai. There is only one race now, as much Caifanii as it is Mhalanai. Our Caifanii heritage is one of dominance over others, over those who are different. Our Mhalanai heritage is one of union, of connection with others, a unity in diversity. The Mhalanai traditions of open consultation, equality, generous coexistence with those who are different, and with the sensory world, these are the virtues the Mhalanai uphold. Our revolution seeks to liberate us from ourselves, from our destructive patterns and beliefs. The Caifanii civilization was highly developed technologically, for its era, very intelligent and productive. There are many good virtues in that heritage. We do not seek to bring Mhalanai virtues in dominance over Caifanii virtues. That would, in any case, be illogical, dominance not being a Mhalanai virtue."

He smiled. "We seek to create a balance of cultural beliefs in which we can prosper by the virtues of each and heal from the deep wounds we have inflicted on ourselves and our home world."

Sola sat in silence, listening, smiling. Jaitain's words were resonating from him like the vibrant tones of a musical instrument. He was an idealist. She knew the grand terminology of social reform was only the launching pad for the implementation of actual reform, which took years of robust energy, determination, and sacrifice. She thought about the tremendous changes on Earth during the Formative Age, the turmoil of the late twentieth and early twenty-first centuries, when Earth's ecological equilibrium was so seriously upset that only a transition into a higher dimension of social consciousness could save the planet from destruction. That had been a time of leaders and idealists, but also a time for deep trench digging and raw violence in resistance to change.

"I am getting carried away with all of this," Jaitain said, perhaps noticing her attention was wandering. "I do not wish to tire you."

"No. No. It's fascinating. Please go on."

Jaitain continued. "We are working to resurrect and cultivate latent Mhalanai virtues, the Sacred Ways, like the Joining. It is a new remembering. The Government is afraid of these Ways, afraid that this revolution will usurp their control, that their power structures will be overthrown. They are trying to stop the revolution by silencing the Mhalanai Trust through violence."

"That sounds all too familiar," Sola said, "I've read enough intergalactic history to know that."

"I will do everything I can to minimize the danger to you." he said.

She suddenly felt awkward. "Jaitain, from this point on, I consider myself a free agent in this collaboration."

"You were drugged and taken here without your consent. You had no free choice. I am responsible for what happens to you now."

"Well," she said, "we just have to go forward from here."

Her full belly was making her feel encouraged. Whatever had passed had passed. Now, she needed to make the best of the current situation. She was trained to handle unpredictable situations. She just needed to normalize, to put things into perspective. Thinking of Ramon helped her do that. She was, in a way, paying homage to him by supporting this cause, these people. Wasn't that worth more than her commission, her condo, her own comfortable, narcissistic little life? She smiled at herself. If Colby already contacted IDS with the news of her abduction by terrorists, her commission might be long gone, a moot point.

"I'm curious about something," she said, shifting in her chair and giving Jaitain a searching look.

"Yes?" he said.

"We're in the middle of a revolution. Why do we have time to sit here and talk? Shouldn't we be doing something?"

He laughed, a wonderful freeing laugh. "We are!" he said. "We are getting to know each other." He looked at her with a gentle affection. "It is a reasonable question. Sometimes there is too much work and no time. Sometimes there is no work and too much time. Right now, there is too much time. We are waiting for my companions to return here with news that the situation above ground is more opportune for our departure."

"Let's hope they arrive soon! You look tired. Do you want to rest?" she asked.

"No. My mind is too agitated."

"What does Nulini mean?" she asked, "My translator has no word for it."

"It is from the Mhalanai language."

"Well that explains it. My translator doesn't speak Mhalanai!"

"It means New Rain, a gift. On the Southern Continent, there is a time of year when the rains do not come. Sometimes it is only for a month, sometimes much longer. At first, it is enjoyable to have a dry afternoon. No one misses the rain. After about a week, the temperatures begin to climb and afternoons become scorching hot. If the rain does not return by the end of a month, the weather becomes unbearable. Carrying water from storage areas into homes and to fields is hard labor. We take water very much for granted on this planet! During these dry spells, however, we pray for rain every day. People become irritable from the oppressive heat. The land is dry and thirsty. The magnificent lushness of the kali trees and the abundant varieties of plants begins to fade. Everyone is hoping for the rain to return. When the sky darkens, the clouds get heavy, and that first rainstorm hits the ground, there is a great celebration. Everyone is outside in the streets and fields dancing and getting wet from head to foot! It is something to see! That first rain is called by this special name, New Rain, Nulini."

Sola was speechless. "Wow," she managed to say. "I am honored."

It was a touching term of endearment. She expected the name to be just a diminutive like "Sweety," or "Honey," terms that made her uncomfortable. Her uncle Geoff always called her "Cutie Pie," a term she abhorred.

Sola felt her old inadequacies surface. She wanted to tell Jaitain that she was nothing like that, nothing like that incredible new rain.

She was just Sola, doing her best to get by and worrying too much about everything trivial, all the details of her own microcosm. Whatever he saw in her must be an illusion, certainly it was a standard she could not possible live up to, but she decided to let go of the old self-effacing patterns. She decided it was okay to feel honored by Jaitain's gesture of respect and affection.

He looked haggard. His bruises were swelling, and the cut on his lip looked infected. He was a willful, buoyant spirit weighed down by the ballast of too much responsibility.

"I still can't believe they beat you like this," she said. "They are the official state police! How do they get away with that kind of unwarranted brutality?" She knew well enough how such things happened, and that they happened all the time.

He laughed again, softly. "The kutnak chases the rij," he said with dramatic flair, "but will never catch her!" The expression was lost on her.

"I don't understand," she said.

"Oh," he said. "It is an old Caifanii story. They are mythological creatures, the kutnak and the rij. The rij is small and moves quickly like water over a rock. The kutnak is large, heavy and slow, yet it thinks it can catch the rij. The kutnak chases the rij and tries to catch it. It quickly becomes too exhausted to keep up the physical chase. The kutnak, however, has a fragile ego and cannot accept its own failure. So, in order to preserve its delicate pride, the kutnak does not admit to failure. Instead, it decides to pretend that it is still chasing the rij, spinning a victorious illusion in its own mind about racing after the rij with great speed and agility. Of course, it is only an illusion. The kutnak sits on a rock and watches the rij, just sits and watches and pretends to chase the rij. Then Kutnak closes its eyes and pretends to catch the rij. When it opens it eyes again, the rij is long gone."

Sola nodded her head slowly, looking down at his round, green face. The moral of his story was not completely clear to her, but obviously the rij represented Jaitain and the kutnak was Central Security, or the government itself.

"Does the kutnak ever get it?" She asked. "I mean does it ever realize that it will never catch the rij, that all of its imagined bravado is useless?"

"No. Not in the story, anyway."

He smiled. His teeth were a luminous white in the subdued light of the room. She felt a tenderness towards him.

He looked at her. Maybe he sensed her fluctuating mood. "There is no justice in them, but plenty of protocol," he said. "They did not get what they needed to hold me. They had to let me go. It has happened before. Eventually, they will have what they need. Right now, they do not need another hostage. They are busy enough with one martyr on their hands."

"Utjaika? Did she die?" Sola asked.

"No, she survived, but barely. Her illness is politically disadvantageous to them."

"So was letting you go. It seems to me," she said. "That day in the restaurant, when you left so abruptly, were they after you then?"

"Yes. Two officers, undercover, but I recognized them."

"You need to put some antibiotic on your lip, Jaitain. It looks infected, and your bruises are swelling."

"Good advice. I become so focused on the larger picture, I forget the immediate details!"

He rose with obvious effort and walked across the room. He opened a storage crate, found a small bottle and poured some of the ointment onto a cloth. He began applying it to the dark bruises on his face and to his lower lip as he walked back towards her. "They invest too much trust in fear. Bile! This stuff is fire," he said, wincing dramatically, but smiling, as he dabbed the cloth onto his wounds.

Caifanii was a stately language with an elegant formality, then again, it could be just the translation she heard. For some reason the TLC didn't translate contractions, a glitch that needed fixing. It translated everything in full. "Did not." "We will." "I am." That factor alone gave the translation an archaic taste. She didn't know if the Caifanii used contractions. Some languages didn't require them, for example, there might be a single word that meant "I am." She stretched her arms and legs like a cat and settled more deeply into the soft chair. For just a moment, she felt comfortable and safe. Then she remembered something that made her feel the exact opposite.

"Jaitain?" she said.

"Yes."

"Did Cylin bring my small green bag with the waist strap? It's not here with the others."

"I do not know. You will recognize it faster than I would. You are welcome to have a look over there. I think we need something hot to drink! I will return in a moment."

While he was gone, Sola checked through the supplies that

lined the far wall. She was relieved to see her green satchel tucked in behind one of the boxes. She needed her medications.

She tried to still her mind, to forget all of her urgent questions. She sat back down and listened to the silence that hung in the stale air, full of expectation.

Her path had taken a radical turn, the exact nature of its new direction obscured by a plethora of unknowns. She could only wait for this new countdown to reach its zero point.

Once more, she found herself on the threshold, the fulcrum.

She let her thoughts float away, watching them gain distance like party balloons drifting up into a vast, blue sky.

"E komo mai." It was the woman's voice again, the one she'd heard in her mind while she was in the airlock.

"E komo mai. Ua hiki ho`i la nui!" It said, gently, like in a lullaby.

The words felt familiar and soothing, like something long forgotten, but now remembered.

Then the voice broke into a soft, joyous peal of laughter, as light as the gurgle of a wave retreating from a pebbled shore.

The sound made her feel tranquil in the silence it left in its wake.

Chapter 12

Night Five
The Caves of Lan, Northern Continent, Caifanii

Oliai dein hua din listu maia.
Our differences bring us great joy.

The Mhalanai Book of Ways

Jaitain returned with two large, steaming mugs. "This should help warm us," he said offering her one. "Careful. It is hot tea."

She took the ceramic mug from him. It looked handmade. "This is nice work," Sola said, admiring the raku style glaze.

"Eilfina is a superb potter," he said. "You will meet her. She will accompany us."

"She is one of the companions we are waiting for, with great anticipation?"

"With great anticipation, yes."

"Jaitain. I don't know how to ask you this without sounding completely 'Looney Tunes,' as Colby would put it."

"Which means?"

"Crazy, gone around the bend, lost your marbles."

"You seem entirely sane to me, Sola. Solid as a hearthstone, as they say here."

"You may change your mind about that. A few days ago, when I arrived on Caifanii, while I was still on the Minerva, at the skyport, I heard a voice. Not out loud, not someone talking, but inside my mind, like a thought, but it was not my own thinking." She paused.

"Go on," he urged.

"Well, the weird part, well, actually the entire thing is weird, but the totally out there part is that this voice spoke in the native language of my ancestors, Hawaiian."

He looked at her with the Caifanii equivalent of raised eyebrows, minus the eyebrows.

"See what I mean? I sound insane already."

"No, you do not. I am only intrigued. Go on."

"All right, a few minutes ago, while you were getting tea, I heard this same voice again."

"What did the voice say this time?" He asked, in an earnest tone, with no trace of mockery.

"Wow, you actually don't think I'm crazy." She sighed, relieved. "It said the exact same thing, in Hawaiian, like before, but this time there was a second phrase, and then there was laughter. Not a 'laughing at you' sort of laughter, more a heavenly sort of laughter. That should have made me feel completely crazy! Strangely, it made me feel completely at peace."

"Perhaps this voice is your subconscious mind bringing you a gift?"

"My grandmother believes our inner psyche has wisdom our thinking mind needs to hear."

"Grandmothers can be our best mentors."

"Mine used to tell me, 'Listen! Honu.' She calls me Honu, which means turtle because I move so fast, no time for introspection, which is funny because turtles are terribly slow creatures. Anyway, I digress."

She felt jittery and she hadn't even taken a pepper yet.

She felt something monumental was shifting inside of her, at her core. She had no clue what it was, but she suspected the voice in her mind was a key.

"You said the Mhalanai ancestors were fully telepathic, right?"

"Yes," Jaitain confirmed.

"You also said there are elders who still have telepathic skills."

"A few."

"Is it possible?" She hesitated.

What she was suspecting was bizarre.

"Okay, here goes," she continued. "Could the voice I heard be the voice of one of these Mhalanai elders communicating with me telepathically? If it was, how does she even know about me? Jaitain, the voice spoke in Hawaiian, a language few people speak any longer, even in Hawaii."

"So what did the voice say?"

"It said, 'E komo mai. Ua hiki ho`i la nui!' That means, 'Welcome. At last the great day has come!'"

Jaitain looked startled. He stared at her intently for a moment.

"I think the second line is part of an ancient Hawaiian wedding song," Sola explained. "Well, as far as I can remember. I haven't heard the song since I was a child."

"Eh kima maia. U'hili ho listu ona," he said.

"Okay. Now *you* are making me feel crazy. What did you just say? My translator is giving me a 'foreign phrase, not in data base' message. What you said sounded a lot like Hawaiian to me, but I couldn't quite understand it."

"It was in the ancient Mhalanai language. The first phrase means, 'You are greeted with joy!' And the second means, 'At last the Great Day is here!'"

Sola's eyes began to water and her skin felt electric.

She stared at Jaitain, who stared back at her.

Neither of them spoke for several seconds.

"Sola, those are the first two lines of a prophetic section of the Mhalanai Book of Ways. The section tells of a time of a great deliverance for our people."

"That's an extremely out there coincidence." Sola said. "My grandmother claims there are no coincidences, that everything is meant to be as it is."

"Maybe she is right. Maybe your being here now, and helping us is exactly what must happen. Maybe this *is* the 'Great Day,' and you are fortunate to be part of a long-awaited moment in our spiritual history."

She was not sure if he was being completely serious. There was a hint of humor in his tone.

"You make it sound like this is just a terrific fortune I found in my cookie!"

"Your translator just told me you found a large amount of money inside a small desert snack."

"A Chinese desert snack. They fold a thin strip of paper inside a cookie with a phrase printed on it. Usually the phrase says something banal like, 'You will be successful in the coming week.' We used to joke about these fortune cookies. You're supposed to add the words, 'in bed' to whatever fortune you receive."

"You will be successful in the coming week, in bed!"

"Yes."

"Humorous," he said, with a grin that told her he understood the connotation of 'in bed.'

"Jaitain, this is quite unnerving to me. I'm only joking around because that's what I do when I'm stressed, I get funny. Well I guess it's more silly than actually funny."

"I understand. It is unnerving to me as well. I only use the Book of Ways for spiritual guidance. I do not read it as a prophetic text, but many of the elders believe it contains prophesies, including the prophecy of the Great Day. My interpretation of such things is more pragmatic than ecstatic. I believe the Great Day is every day, because we always have the choice to liberate ourselves. I believe each of us must work towards this liberation, accepting help when it is offered, but not accepting anyone else's path as our own."

"Thanks. That actually makes me feel a bit less wigged out. I like the way you put it, but sometimes, don't you feel lost? I quite often feel lost."

"That surprises me! You seem most secure."

She laughed. "I put on a good show."

"Prophecy is a heavy word. Please do not be concerned, Sola. The Mhalanai do not believe in putting anyone on a pedestal. You are in no danger of becoming our 'Holy Personage,' or some such thing."

"Well, darn. I was so looking forward to all those rose petals at my feet!"

"Flower petals can be arranged."

Jaitain smiled coquettishly. She wondered if he was flirting with her.

Their conversation was making her feel more at ease, but the coincidence remained uncanny.

"Jaitain, thanks for talking through this with me. I guess time will tell what, if anything, this experience of mine means."

"I believe you are right, but I feel for certain that it has a profound meaning. We just do not understand it yet."

"Right now, I have a profound need to contact Colby! Not only that, my translator runs on a solar cell. The artificial light in here is not charging it for some reason. I'm getting a low battery icon. If I don't get it under daylight soon, it will die and that will leave us unable to communicate. You said there are multiple tunnels down here. Do any of them reach the surface in a relatively safe location, where I can charge the cell and make the call?"

"There is one tunnel, but I must warn you it is not an easy trip. There are many turns and tight passages and it does not lead to the surface, only to a place where the light comes in."

"Why did you have to tell me that?" She could feel her stomach tighten already. "Okay, I will face my demons! Colby owes me one! When can we do this thing?"

"We can go now."

"Excellent, before I lose my nerve."

"I will bring you some warm clothes. It is cold in the tunnels." The electronic voice of the TLC was growing weaker, slower and lower in pitch.

"Jaitain, I'm losing power on the translator quickly. We may end up unable to understand each other, so stay close to me."

Why didn't that low battery icon show up sooner, giving you more time before the battery went completely dead? This always irked her, and the new unit was no better than the previous in this regard.

"Your translation is becoming garbled," Jaitain said.

"I know. No time to waste."

Jaitain reached into a bag and pulled out a thick sweater. He held it out to her and nodded, urging her to wear it. She was grateful. She strapped the CPU to her wrist. Its battery was getting low as well. Murphy's Law was still hounding her.

They left the dim room and entered the passage that led to the storage room, where they turned into another passage, and kept going. They each carried a hand-held light that created a small circle of luminescence before their feet. She stayed close behind him. They walked for ten, maybe fifteen minutes through curving tunnels with sudden switchbacks and uneven floors. The ceiling was so low in places they had to bend down to get through. The cavern tunnels were a maze. She was beginning to think they might run into the Minotaur any minute. Such an extensive set of caverns would be a protected natural monument on Earth. The Caifanii government must know about them. Were there no tours? Obviously not. It was a rebel base.

If she had been alone, she would be now be completely lost. There were too many side tunnels. Too many possible turns, and everything was space black.

A serious claustrophobia was oozing into her psyche, making her short of breath. The air in the tunnels was stagnant and oxygen poor. Their passage became narrow, frighteningly so. At points, they had to squeeze through sideways between walls.

She could feel the dampness of the stone press against her back, her clothes catching on the rough surfaces. Always, the way led upward. In the dense, black it was difficult to perceive the angle of the grade, but the growing muscle fatigue in her legs told her it was steep. Her heart was pounding. She was feeling shaky. The near panic made her want to cry, but she was too embarrassed to admit how terrified she felt.

Suddenly, the tunnel expanded into an open space that felt huge. A vacant feeling surrounded her even as the black air pressed in against her skin and lungs.

There was the sound of dripping water. The echoes of drops surrounded them.

The sound of their footsteps was hollow. Small pieces of mineral kicked by their boots rolled over an edge and fell into an unseen abyss.

She could hear the stones bounce, bounce, bounce, and keep falling.

They were walking along a narrow ledge, skirting a deadly fall into nothingness. All she could see ahead of her were Jaitain's feet and legs.

They entered a narrow tunnel again, she could no longer move her arms up or out to the side. After more turning and shuffling, it began to be a little less black, then, gradually the blackness turned to a brownish gray. The shapes of jagged walls become visible. Jaitain's body became a dark mass outlined by a faint glimmer of ambient light. The passage became impossibly narrow. She was having flashbacks.

He said something she could not understand, softly and with tenderness.

She reached for his arm. He took her by the elbow and they moved sideways, their backs against the damp, smooth wall of rock.

Slowly, they moved into a beam of pale, natural light. Her translator started beeping like a hungry baby bird for a few seconds. The canary in the coalmine had survived!

The tunnel opened into a small chamber filled with dusted sunlight. A wide beam of it came down through a jagged hole in the ceiling, a shaft of revelation, a shower of relief.

She stood under it and let the subtle warmth bathe her upturned face. She would stay here. She would not go back into that darkness.

She sighed, deeply took in the air, breath after breath, like a shipwrecked mariner waking on the warm sand of a beach, in a harbor of daylight. The translator's charge indicator was flashing.

"This is magnificent," she said. Her voice sounded loud, even though she whispered. The TLC was working again.

After about ten minutes, the red indicator light switched off. The unit recharged efficiently in direct sunlight.

She hoped the charge was the only one she would need to make from this spot.

"Sunlight is a miraculous gift," she whispered.

She wished she had climbing ropes.

The walls of this vertical chamber were slick from water runoff, no hand or foot holds. Free climbing was not an option.

"I am not looking forward to going back into the dark. Those tunnels really freaked me out!"

"You were courageous."

"I was a mess! I just didn't want you to know."

"You put on a good show."

"You learn fast."

She turned her face up into the light again, recharging her own solar cells. The PCU's indicator light blinked. It was fully charged.

"I am going to call Colby. I'll keep my voice down."

"This cavern opening is not in a populated location. I have no concern about being over heard, but we need a plan. There is minimal time to talk with him. We need to know exactly what you will say and what we need him to do."

"Good point. I guess I was just thinking about letting him know I am safe, but then what?"

"Exactly. We should have covered that ground earlier. Now we must cover it with expedience."

"Jaitain, I don't know if it's the TLC translation, but the way you speak sounds amazingly well-organized. Everything you say sounds like a well-prepared speech presented at a United Planets."

He looked dismayed. "This is a bad thing?"

"No, sorry. No idea why I even said that. I'm nervous, talking calms me." She smiled.

"I understand."

"My brain doesn't work that way," Sola said. "My thinking is disorganized. My train of thought is more like a derailment."

He stifled a laugh.

"What?"

"Your translator tells me your 'rail-based public transportation concept is off track.'"

"That's about right!" She took a deep breath. "So, we need to find out if Colby's in static orbit above Haikon, as you assume. We need to decide whether he stays put until we reach our southern destination, or if he heads in that direction as well. I have no clue. This is your planet."

"Haikon may be monitoring his position, even if they are not targeting him. If he moves, they will know *we* are moving. I recommend he stays where he is until we are safely at our destination."

"He won't like that. He probably feels like he's sitting on a duck, and just ignore whatever crazy translation you get for that expression."

"Do not tell him anything about our location or our plans. We don't know how secure the call will be. Just tell him you are safe."

"And not being held by terrorists."

"This particular terrorist would like to hold you," he admitted.

She blushed.

He blushed.

Neither of them said anything for a few moments.

"I could use a hug after all that spelunking!" she said, "God only knows how my TLC will translate spelunking." She knew she was making light of his confession, but this was not the time for whatever it was he desired, or for wherever it was he wanted to go.

"Cave exploration," he said.

They both laughed at the unintended sexual innuendo. That relieved the tension, and it needed relieving.

"I'll use audio only, no visual," she said.

"Good."

Sola punched in Colby's number, held her breath, and hit send. There was a crackling sound from the PCU.

"Sola!" Colby's voice came through thick static.

"Colby!"

"Sola! Where in the hell are you? The static is crappy. Are you okay? Are they treating you well?"

"Colby. I'm safe. There are no terrorists."

"Are they making you say that?"

"No, no one is making me say anything. Listen. I need to get back to the shuttle."

"No kidding!"

"Yeah, but, listen, I really don't know how we're going to do it. Can you tell me what you know about what's going on?"

There was a momentary pause. "I've been damn worried about you. Tried to call you for hours and hours, but your signal was harder to find than gallium. Are they treating you okay? They're not hurting you, are they?"

"I'm fine, honest. There are no terrorists."

"I know the terrorists are making you say that," he said in a low voice, "I need to know if we can talk freely, so give me a sign that you are okay, wait, let me think. Okay, I've got it. Remember that book I've been reading lately?"

It was going to be a challenge to convince him there were no terrorists.

"If you are genuinely okay," Colby said, "and we can talk freely, tell me the name of my current favorite author. If you are not okay and we can't talk freely, say you don't remember it."

"What if I genuinely don't remember it?"

"You don't remember it? Or are you saying that it's not safe to talk?"

"No. I mean. It's Louis L'Amour." she said.

"Great! So, you can talk freely?"

Sola wasn't sure how this little ploy of his proved anything, but at least Colby was convinced they could have an open conversation.

"Yes, we can talk freely," she said.

Colby launched in.

"The news agencies in Haikon are pushing a story about a Terran diplomat being abducted by terrorists, some group called the Melon Eye Trust, or some such thing. Had me crazy as a bullbat! If there aren't any terrorists, then where the heck are you and why didn't you show up as planned?"

He sounded a bit peeved, understandably.

"Colby, it's a long and complex story, and I promise I will tell you every detail, but not right now. I only have a short time to talk and then we will end up without a signal again for some time."

Technically, she *was* abducted, but not by terrorists. All of that was too confusing to explain right now.

Jaitain moved in close to her. "What is he saying?" he asked.

"What we already know, that the news says I was abducted by terrorists."

"Ask him if there are any further news updates?" Jaitain whispered.

"Sola," Colby said. "Is someone with you? I thought I heard some weird clicking or something. Are you alone?"

"No. I mean yes, someone is with me, friend not foe. Has there been any further news, anything else about what they think happened to me?"

"Not much, just that the authorities are conducting a thorough search of the area. That type of thing. I tell you, woman, I have been a fruitcake for hours wondering what to do. I have rerouted every known frequency to find you. Will you please tell me where you are? I will come get you lickety-split."

"I can't tell you right now. It might put us in jeopardy. It's heavenly to hear your feisty voice. Any chance we'll lose this connection unexpectedly?"

"Beats me, Pumpkin Pie. Cross your fingers and toes."

His goofy term of endearment felt a little awkward with Jaitain so close.

"Colby ..." she hesitated. "Hold on a second, I have to ask someone a question."

She muted the mic.

"Jaitain, I don't think they can tag this signal. Minerva has excellent communications armor. I think I can talk freely."

"It is a risk," Jaitain whispered. "Be careful. Do not give any information about where you are."

"Like I really know where I am!" she said, jovially..

"Colby, I'm back."

"What's going on? Who are you talking to?

"I'll explain in a minute."

"Right. I'm not curious. Hey, I've only been hanging on the wrong side of this atmosphere for going on eternity!" He cleared his throat. "Uh, I'm sorry. I'm a little on edge, I guess. Okay, listen, I've contacted the Pegasus. She's the closest IDS ship to our sector. She's on her way to rendezvous, but it will probably take her damned close to a week to get here. I don't want to wait that long. I want us out of here as soon as possible. I don't even want to hear a word about your commission."

"Screw the commission!" she said. "I'm in the middle of," she stopped herself and looked at Jaitain. "Colby, I need to ask someone here something again. I know this is hard on you, but please be patient. I'm so glad I finally have you on line. Hang in there just a minute, Okay?"

"I'm a regular chimpanzee in the baobab tree!" he said. "Is this a party line or what?"

She muted the mic. "Jaitain, I want to ask him if he sent your files to the UP and Amnesty Interstellar. If he didn't send them this morning, and he got the news of my abduction before he sent them, he might not have sent them at all, not knowing what to believe. I don't need to mention names. What do you think?"

"That would be excellent to know."

"I agree," she said, un-muting the mic again.

"Hey, Colby."

"Yes?"

"Did you send that information from 'you know who' to 'you know who'?"

"Yup. Might not have, if I'd seen that news report before-hand."

"I understand, but it's a relief you sent it!"

"Is 'you know who' the person you were just talking to?"

"Yup."

"That's also a relief. Seems like a good man."

"He is."

"He sent it!" she said to Jaitain, who immediately did a goofy victory dance, leaned over and kissed the top of her head, wrapped his arm around her shoulder and squeezed. He looked vibrant, jubilation shone in his face like sunlight through seawater. Sola felt a contact high from his rush of exhilaration. She was giddy.

"Colby, you are a local hero!" she said.

"Glad to hear you're happy," Colby said.

Sola felt a great weight lift from her heart, a weight she had not known she was carrying there. History's path had taken a promising turn.

"Now, my dear," Colby said. "What about getting you up here? How shall we accomplish that?"

"A good question," she said.

The realization hit her that with the file definitely sent, her role in this heroic scenario was complete. The realization left her feeling oddly lost. She didn't feel ready to walk out of the picture, and was grateful that doing so was not an immediate option.

"Any ideas, Colby?" she asked.

"I still don't even know where you are. Luuuucy, you got some splainin' to do!" he said in his best Cuban accent. She knew it was another one of his obscure 20th century television impersonations, lost on her, but apparently very humorous to him. She could hear him chuckling to himself.

"Sorry," he said. "I couldn't resist. I haven't got a clue. I was hoping you'd have all the answers. Could I talk directly with you know who?"

"Oh, of course. Do you have your TLC handy?"

"Just a minute," he said. "Yes, all right. Ready Freddy."

"Colby, here is 'you know who,'" she said, switching the unit to speaker setting, so she could listen in, and handing it over to Jaitain.

"Colby?" Jaitain said.

"Good to meet you," Colby replied. "This voice-only communication leaves a bit to the imagination, but at least we can say howdy."

"Yes. Soon, I hope we will meet in person," Jaitain said, appearing a bit uncomfortable with Colby's informal manner. "I am profoundly grateful for your help," he continued. "I find it a challenge to express the fullness of what this means to me ... and to so many others. The benefits of what the two of you have done for us are profound, truly historic. It may not be possible for you to fully comprehend the significance of your actions, but know that you are greatly respected and that we are greatly indebted to you both."

"I'm just doing my job." Colby sounded a little flustered. He wasn't one for formalities. "I'm still pretty confused about what is happening down there and how exactly you and Sola got linked up, but it sounds like she's pretty impressed with you. Are you taking good care of my gorgeous redhead?" he asked.

Colby's question made Sola feel suddenly awkward. Jaitain's arm was still around her shoulders.

She wondered if Colby felt jealous. Possessiveness was not his usual modality. Their intimate time at the hotel was connecting and soulful. It had made her think, that night, that she was finally ready to be in a committed relationship with Colby.

That was before her entire perspective on life went into the blender on whip.

"Yes," Jaitain said. His voice startled Sola back into the present moment. He took a strand of her auburn hair and caressing it between his fingers. "I am doing my best to see that she is comfortable. She is a timely and a precious gift. She is new rain," he said, glowingly.

There was a long pause. Sola could hear Colby's gears turning. "So, when does this water woman get to return to our little ship?"

His question left Sola and Jaitain both silent as if a surprise wave had caught them with their backs turned.

Sola looked at Jaitain. He looked back at her.

"Hello? Anybody home?" Colby asked.

"Uh, yes," Jaitain answered. "We, this is complex. I am most concerned for her safety. We need to be cautious. I recommend that you remain in your present position until we have more information to relay. It will take at least a few more hours, possible a day before we can reconnect."

"Well," said Colby. "I seriously don't like the sound of that plan."

"Can I talk with him?" Sola said.

Jaitain passed the unit back to her.

"Colby, it's going to take time. We need to wait until the search and rescue teams back off before we can make a move. Any indication that the search effort is losing steam?"

"If it bleeds it leads," he said, "but it seems to be bleeding less already. Haven't seen any updates in hours."

"That's actually good news."

"I get it, Pumpkin. You need to stay safe. I just hate worrying about you, and I'm real anxious to get out of this satellite corral. I don't trust these Caifanii. They make me nervous. Do they have anything that can reach me up here?"

"No, we don't believe so."

"Okay. That makes me feel a little better. I'm gonna have something to eat. I'll keep the console online. Just yell when you need me."

"Colby, you are gold itself," she said. "I am going to be out of range for a while. I know that sucks, but there's nothing we can do about it. I promise we'll talk again as soon as possible."

"Make it real soon."

Sola looked at Jaitain. "Is there anything else I need to tell him before we sign off?"

Jaitain shook his head, "No."

"I'm going to sign off now, Colby. I miss you!"

"Be careful. I'll be here. Meanwhile, I hear some pepperoni pizza calling my name. Hasta."

"Hasta," she said and closed the call.

"He's an interesting man, this Colby," Jaitain said.

"Yes," Sola said. "I'd have to agree with that."

"So," Jaitain said, a teasing look crossing his eyes. "I am not the only one who thinks you are a remarkably special."

She chuckled. "I'm a little embarrassed." She bit her lower lip gently with her teeth. She wanted to be open and truthful with Jaitain. "I've worked with Colby for five years. We're good buddies, you know, friends."

"Perhaps a bit more than friends as well?"

"There was a time, over four years ago, when we were in a romantic relationship. It was only briefly," she added. "Sometimes, though, we still spend intimate time together. Not regularly, but it happens."

"Once you have such a bond, it tends to hold its magnetism. You do not need to disclose your personal life, Sola. Colby obviously cares a great deal for you."

She could sense Jaitain wanted to know more, but he resisted the temptation to ask anything further.

"I care a great deal for Colby as well," she said. "I hate to say it, but I suppose we need to go back down. Let me soak in this light a bit longer."

"Okay."

She had no choice. She knew she could not stay here. This was not an exit, just a brief glance through a porthole at the sky. She soaked in the sunlight with her face lifted up, eyes closed, for a few more moments. Then it was time to return to the underworld. One step at a time, she encouraged herself. Don't think, just move. She held on to the back of Jaitain's sweater with one hand, her flashlight in the other with a firm grip. Don't think. Just move.

He led her back into the darkness. Each step further from daylight made her heart heavy. Keeping her inner demons at bay became more challenging with every downward twist and turn of the tunnel. Mercifully, as with most return trips, their retreat seemed shorter than their advance, but long enough to leave her rattled by the time they were back in the dimly lit living chamber down below the living world.

Chapter 13

Day Five (late afternoon)

Isamu ti u luma, ti mei u moyin.
Before I knew you, I longed for you.

The Mhalanai Book of Ways

Sola was numb from the cold. Jaitain went to make hot tea, that magic elixir.

She wrapped herself up in a blanket and sank into the beanbag chair again, her home away from home.

The trip had charged the TLC's energy cell, but drained her own. She felt crushed beneath the weight of this strange planet.

To her dismay, she started crying, perhaps from exhaustion, perhaps for reasons beyond her conscious understanding.

A female rebel, a new arrival, came over and sat on Jaitain's blankets. Gazing up at Sola with compassion, she began to sing a gentle song in a clear and childlike voice. The words were not in Caifanii. The TLC provided no translation. She assumed it was a Mhalanai song, but sounded so much like Hawaiian, it soothed her all the more.

Sola's mind drifted into a trance state from the languid tone of her minstrel's voice.

Huma kote juie. Ila Ila juie.
Ona a ili. Ona pe a ili.
Huma kote juie.

The song must be a lullaby, she thought, as she let sleep subjugate her conscious awareness.

Her dream was brief but potent.

There was a woman wearing a robe of radiant lavender. The woman stood in the center of a circle of many people. Sola also stood in the circle among them as part of a communal experience, everyone linked at the roots, like a grove of aspen. There was a feeling of swaying, not a physical movement, but an emotional wave. The entire circle was swaying like the boughs of trees in a mild wind. There was a feeling of peacefulness, of rectification. The sky was cobalt blue and filled with glistening stars, nebula clouds and swirling galaxies. The circle seemed perched in the midst of space. The silhouetted shape of a huge, hawk-like bird, wings outstretched, swooped over the gathering and circled three times before ascending away with three loud cries. As the great bird's wings plowed the cosmos, the cobalt mellowed into azure, then pale blue. The stars disappeared. It was daylight. She stood alone in a meadow of wildflowers, their aroma an overpowering musk of fertile earth and sunshine.

When Sola opened her eyes, she saw Jaitain standing across the chamber looking at her.

Caught in the act, he put on a sheepish grin, but did not break his gaze.

"I reheated your tea," he said. "You were sleeping."

"No kidding. I was zonked." She stretched. "I had a powerful dream. I think I experienced a Joining."

He looked stunned. "Really?"

She described her dream in as much detail as she could remember.

"You amaze me," he said in response. "I am beginning to believe there may be something to that old prophecy after all."

"Don't get all woo-woo on me."

"All what?"

"An old term for being overtly inclined to believe in the supernatural."

"I believe everything is supernatural!"

"Well, woo-woo to you!"

"Seriously, this dream is no trivial matter. What you described to me does indeed sound like a Joining. How could you know about this in such detail?"

"Beats me!" Sola said.

"Well, in any case, it seems like a good omen, some sort of protection."

"We could certainly use that!" Sola said.

She picked up her mug, blew across the steam and took a small sip. The taste was nothing to write home about, but it gave her body an instant rush of warmth.

"This is great!" she said, after a few more sips. "I mean, it's awful, but it's really warming me up inside. What is it?"

"A tincture of herbs," he answered, coming to sit again on the pile of blankets near her feet.

The young Mhalanai who sang to her was now nowhere in sight.

"I bought it in Nepal," Jaitain continued.

"Nepal?" She said, in disbelief. He had used the English word.

"I know, the old cliché. Everyone goes to Nepal to find a magical cure," he said, obviously finding it humorous.

She shot him a quizzical look. "Jaitain, what are you talking about? You've been to Earth?"

"Earth? No. What gives you that impression?"

"Oh. There is a Nepal here, on Caifanii?"

"Yes, of course. You mean there is also a Nepal on your home world?"

"Yes!" She said. "Your Nepal and our Nepal have the same name, at least in pronunciation. The TLC did not translate it, treated your word as if you said it in English."

"That is most woo-woo!"

She laughed. "You do learn quickly! I recently learned that Woo Woo is also the name of an alcoholic beverage made of vodka, peach schnapps, and cranberry juice! Sounds truly horrible!"

"Do they sell that Woo Woo in your Nepal?"

"I've never actually been there, so I am not authorized to say, but I doubt they have peach schnapps or cranberry juice. Vodka, you can get pretty much everywhere! Nepal is, however, exactly the kind of place to get an herbal healing, nasty tasting tea like this! It is up in the Himalayas, the highest mountains on our planet. People have been making spiritual pilgrimages there for thousands of years, looking for whatever they felt was missing."

He laughed loudly.

"Then it is nothing at all like our Nepal," he said, "which is a seedy, dirty, riotous collection of markets, illicit dealings, prostitution, and gambling. It is below sea level surrounded by levees that often flood. It is a thoroughly muddy, nasty, offensively odorous place, and, believe me, I should know. I used to live there."

"Why on earth would you want to live *there*? Let me rephrase that. Why on Caifanii would you want to live *there*?"

"Because, at that time in my life, I was a seedy, nasty, dirty, riotous young man with a few more illicit habits than I could afford."

"Your K addiction years?"

"Accurate guess. I was using, dealing, and trying to keep from getting stabbed in dark alleys. There were a few times the knife found its mark and I am lucky to be here at all. Good thing I have other obsessions these days!"

"How did you get from there to here, Jaitain?"

"That is a long story and only some of it worth the telling. My truest friends, from my old life, were willing to risk severely bruising my ego in order to save my life, one in particular. She risked her own safely to take me in when I finally had the courage to get clean and stop working for Htiu's cartel."

"Htiu strikes me as a man who doesn't allow attrition in his ranks."

"It was about like signing my own death warrant, but here I am, clean and free."

"How did you get free?"

"Miracles happen, mostly through the hearts of good people. In any case, there is nothing quite like Nepalian tea for warming the body."

"Except maybe K?"

He laughed. "Oh, that will warm you up alright, like jumping into a burning house!"

Jaitain's boyish laughter reminded her of Ramon's. He always laughed wholeheartedly at Sola's jokes, even ones she made up herself, that were not funny to anyone else. The two of them shared a quirky sense of humor, a fondness for the oddities of life. She missed the sound of his laughter. It was irreplaceable, like everything else about him.

"When they arrested you at my hotel," Sola said, "was it because of your drug history or the revolutionary activities?"

"Oh, they would *love* to get me on some drug related charge. That would hold. They would have one less stone in their shoe, but I paid that price in full, years ago."

"You did time in prison?"

"Five years, with early probation for good behavior. My white hat is getting more sullied all the time, yes?"

"I know several good people who spent years in prison. I won't judge you."

"These days, I get picked up for civil disobedience and suspicion of government subversion."

"All for a noble cause, as I see it. Jaitain. What time is it? Did I sleep long? There is no way to tell down here."

"It is always now down in the caves," he said, "but if you must know, it is well into the night." He looked tired.

"You should get some rest," she said, looking into his silver eyes. They were mysterious and beautiful. She was still wearing the blue gloves. They helped her hands stay warm. Jaitain wore no gloves. She looked at his hands. His fingers were long and delicate.

She caught his eyes again and found him looking at her in a way that made her feel warm in an all together different way.

"I would like to visit your Nepal, I think." He smiled.

He was definitely sexy, she decided.

How odd. For the past few days, she'd spent most of her time on this planet trying to get cool. Now, she was grateful for the luscious heat from the cup radiating through the cloth of her gloves, warming the palms of her hands.

"Jaitain, you don't wear gloves down here, and neither does, gosh, I don't even know your companion's name. She was here earlier and sang a sweet song for me."

"Eilfina. Her voice is like pure water." He ran his finger lightly over her gloved hand.

"The Mhalanai do not believe in this restrictive practice," he said. "It is a Caifanii structure, based on archaic codes of modesty."

Sola felt a tingling energy all the way down to her toes. "Really?" she managed to say, suddenly a little breathless. "Bare hands are not considered promiscuous in your eyes."

"Repressive social mores are just another form of oppression. Do you not agree? Your hands are most lovely."

She blushed, remembering that he had seen her bare hands at the restaurant. That was ages ago.

"I don't mind wearing the gloves down here," she said. "They keep my hands from freezing, but up there, in that heat, they are ridiculous."

"Function above social fashion!"

"Maybe they arrested you for not wearing gloves in public!"

"Could be. Sometimes I forget and walk around with naked hands, shamelessly."

What would happen if he touched her bare hands? Sola wondered.

It was taboo for IDS Reps to engage in interspecies romance during business travel. On most planets, it was not remotely a temptation. She was technically still a company rep, but in radically altered circumstances, which were far from business as usual. She would hang in with the glove protocol for now.

She could not deny that this handsome revolutionary with luminous skin intrigued her but, what about Colby?

They had their friends with benefits agreement, but she felt a new level of commitment to him after their night in the hotel.

What she felt for Jaitain was probably hero worship mixed with bad boy attraction, curiosity and hormones; a heady combination.

She sipped some more Nepalian tea. She never experienced such an unsteadying attraction for an alien before. Well, maybe once or twice, but those aliens were genetically akin to Homo sapiens, no green skin, some type of body hair, similar sexual behaviors and anatomy. Caifanii sexuality was a mystery. What about Mhalanai sexuality? That could be intense, probably involved some type of telepathic joining, like those pointy-eared, brainy aliens on Colby's favorite old TV show. Even if she wanted to fantasize about Jaitain, she had no clue as to what to fantasize!

She sank deeper into the chair, pulled her knees up close to her chest and wrapping her arms around them.

The IDS databases covered a lot of territory, but their entries on interspecies sexual interaction were marginal and mostly useless. There was plenty of data on social behaviors and norms, philosophies, aesthetics, religious and spiritual belief systems of hundreds of species, including some entries on courtship practices. Her briefing materials usually included information on the sexual norms and behaviors of the client species. It was important for her to know such things so that she would not embarrass herself or her clients, and so she would know if they were making advances. Sometimes, sexual advances were so subtle or so bizarre, you never even knew what was happening until it was too late, and then you were stuck in a sticky situation.

One time, at a social event a few years ago, the sponsoring clients asked Sola to serve the wine to the guests. They claimed this was a great honor. There was nothing in her briefing materials about serving wine. She went around the room filling glasses and feeling quite honored until the room full of guests, all of whom were male, started ogling her, making catcalls, and laughing out right. Someone finally told her the joke was on her. In their culture, only men served alcoholic beverages to others in polite company. A woman doing so advertised herself as available for the purchase of sexual pleasure. Her clients thought this was all most hilarious. Sola found it less than humorous, but laughed along with them, for the sake of the sale.

She knew some sales reps engaged in sexual activity with alien species as a sort of personal conquest, considering it a perk of their position.

That was not her style. To her sex was a meaningful bonding, a way to create sacred space with another being. Sure, it was also a lot of fun, but she never went for the fun without the foundation of love.

There was rarely anything in the ISD briefings about the specifics of alien sexual acts. The Protocol Department was a tad prudish, or maybe they operated on a "don't ask, don't tell" basis. The only thing she knew for sure about Caifanii sex was that it had the emphasis on the last syllable, "tchenjó." She found herself shaking her head slightly, marveling at the course of her thoughts.

"Great minds of the cosmos are aligned with IDS," she said to herself. "What are you waiting for?"

"What was that about the great minds of the cosmos?" Jaitain asked.

Sola felt her face flush. "Oh, nothing. Just a little slogan my company uses as an advertisement."

She took a few more sips of tea, put the mug on the floor and pulled the blanket more tightly around her.

She was suddenly feeling so cozy and amorous, she wondered if the tea was some sort of aphrodisiac.

That was a laugh! A Caifanii aphrodisiac! That would probably make her want to shake hands with everyone in sight. She smiled smugly at her own joke. She could imagine Ramon laughing at the sophomoric nonsense of it. No more boring business meetings!

She checked herself. This kind of thinking was so immature. She should feel ashamed, but she didn't. She just felt playful. For the first time on this dense planet, she felt a touch of weightlessness.

"You are beautiful," Jaitain said.

The comment was unexpected. She just sat quietly, looking at him.

"I thought so the day I met you," he continued. He paused, a grave look crossing over his eyes. "I have wondered in these past days, if these circumstances hold a deeper meaning."

"You mean like karma?" she asked, apprehensive about the direction of his ruminations. "Like as in the old expression, 'Haven't we met before, another time, another life, another planet?'"

He looked a little perplexed, the cultural nuance lost on him. "No. I do not think so. Not that exactly," he said. "More like a special coincidence, a serendipity of the soul." He smiled. "Only a few hours ago you pummeled me with canned food, and now I am telling you things I should not. I suppose I am a fool. It is just that I have thought of you often during these past days."

She wondered what kind of thoughts he entertained about her. She found him intriguing. Even at the restaurant, she felt chemistry between them. Romance could spark in a flash if the timing and chemistry were right. Whatever it was she felt for Jaitain, she was convinced it was wise to temper it, but she wasn't feeling terribly wise.

The exposed skin at his neck looked luminous in the soft light of the dim room, like the sheen on sculpted marble or ivory. She leaned forward in the chair, closer to him, her thick hair falling forward over her face. She brushed her curls away from her eyes.

He took a lock of her hair in his fingers, placed it against his mouth. Then he brushed it against his face and smiled, an almost girlish giggle escaping his lips. She could feel his breath. It was soft against her cheek, held a sweet aroma, like jasmine from a distance.

"It is very soft, yet irritates the skin. What is it made of?" he asked.

"Hair? Gee. Proteins and ... wow. Well, actually it contains everything. Everything I have consumed or been exposed to. You can tell a lot about a person's body chemistry by testing their hair."

"Interesting." He kissed the lock. "It is very strange, fascinating."

"Well, you're not having any is pretty strange too."

He was looking straight into her eyes. "Nulini, it is not wise to desire what you cannot have."

"Are you telling me this, or are you talking to yourself?"

"Perhaps revolution is a time for wisdom, not passion," he said.

"A time for passionate wisdom, certainly," she said, "and stop sounding like a gothic romance by Harnassy!"

"Harnassy is not to your liking?"

"Oh, wow! You know about him? You've read him? That explains it. When you came to my table at the restaurant, you said, 'You are looking exceptionally ravishing.' You got that line from a Harnassy novel?"

"I needed you to attend that concert with me, so that I would have ample time to talk with you in a crowded place where we would not easily be overheard or spotted. It was perhaps a foolish plan, but at the time, I thought it would work. I heard that this Harnessy's books are irresistible to women. He is an Earth-based author. You are an Earth-based woman. I figured you would find a line from Harnessy irresistible."

She felt the laughter overtake her. She laughed until her stomach muscles ached, and still could not stop. It really wasn't that funny, but all the tension in her body, some of it now sexual, needed an outlet.

He wasn't joining in, and looked up at her with a quirky frown.

"I'm sorry," she said gasping for air. "I can't help it. No wonder you sound like a gothic romance! How in the world, in your world, did you even find Harnessy?"

Marcus Harnessy was currently enjoying great popularity on Earth and outlying stations. He was a novelist and humorist.

His series of satirical romance novels emulating pulp styles were hilarious and widely translated, though she doubted into Caifanni. Jaitain was bilingual; perhaps he knew a few off-planet languages as well. Some women found Harnessy's "lace bodice ripping" style of romance enticing. Sola found it utterly ridiculous.

"There is a Caifanii translation bouncing around, unauthorized and probably not all that good. I received a copy from Eilfina. She liked it well enough. Perhaps you will laugh at me some more, but I rather enjoyed it. The book that is, not that you were laughing at me."

"Forgive me," she said, with genuine regret. "I didn't mean to embarrass you. It's not like you have a lot of choices when it comes to learning about my culture."

This was interesting. Jaitain enjoyed reading the gothic romance.

Too bad she didn't have a lace bodice on her. The thought almost made her chuckle, but she stifled the urge, not wanting to hurt his feelings again. She surprised herself by briefly imagining him ripping open her lace bodice, sending all the mother-of-pearl buttons flying.

He surprised her by placing his hand on top of hers, and tugging at the fingertips of her gloves to slide them slowly away. No lace bodice, but the effect was the same.

He was breathing quickly. Suddenly, so was she. What happened now? Did they kiss? Embrace?

He stroked her bare fingers gently with his own. She leaned down and placed her lips on his, kissing him lightly. He pulled away.

"You didn't like it?"

He smiled. "I am not sure. It startled me. Maybe if you did it again. I could be prepared."

His reaction had taken some of the edge off her emotions. "Well now, that sounds romantic. But wait, I thought you said revolution was no time for passion."

"One can be too much of an idealist. Here. Let me show you something."

"Aren't you going to tell me first so I can be prepared?" She almost succumbed to another fit of laughter.

"All right, I am going to ... "

"No, no!" she interrupted him. "Don't tell me. Just do it slowly so I can stop you if I don't like it. And, by the way, where is Eilfina?" She felt nervous enough about this turn of events without having to worry about privacy issues.

"She is asleep in another chamber."

His words resonated with warm sensuality. ·

"Let's remove your other glove," he said pulling it slowly away.

She felt like a teenager with dating jitters. She was feeling modest about her hand. Her hand! She went to nude beaches in the south of France, and here she was feeling like a school girl because he wanted to touch her naked hands. Of course, that could be it. That could be tchenjo, the whole shebang, no pun intended.

He took her hand in his own naked hands and rubbed the palm with his fingers, in small delicate motions. She felt a dense heat rise in her body. At first, his touch felt a little ticklish, then she began to feel weak and wonderful. She didn't have the right "whatever" in her palms, but his closeness; the warm, gentle touch of his hand; and his intent were enough to stir her. She let go a soft sigh and smiled down at him. He looked into her face then hesitantly put his mouth over hers. He quickly pulled away, obviously unaccustomed to the sensation.

"Nice try," she said.

She slid out of the chair and sat next to him on the blankets. She placed her arms around his slender body and pulled him close to her. A strangely soothing erotic energy flowed between them. They sat in that embrace for a long while. He played with her hair. She ran her fingers over the smooth skin at his neck, and moved her hand under the rough gray cloth of his suit down over his chest and up around his shoulder. He took her fingers and placed them one at a time into his mouth where they melted. This her body understood. After he had graced each of her ten digits with this magic, he spread out the blankets and she lay down gently on top of his lean, small frame. She touched his lips lightly with her fingertips, smiling and kissing him quickly and gently. He did not resist this time, but gave himself completely to the experience. She placed her mouth over his again without reservation and kissed him with her fullest passion. Their tongues, which did not speak the same language, found a perfect communication. They moved together in a languid dance as ancient as the Mhalanai Way of Love.

She slowly undid the fasteners on his body suit and pulled it away from his upper body revealing his slender but strongly built chest. She kissed his sea-green skin. It felt as soft as rose petals and smelled deliciously like some vague memory of autumn. Beneath his silken skin she felt strong muscle. She touched him with great tenderness and his movements and sounds were enough to encourage her explorations.

He smiled mischievously and unbuttoned her clothes pulling them away from her almond colored skin and revealing her browned, muscular shoulders and the soft skin of her breasts.

"Touch me here," she said moving his hand over her left breast.

"This is exquisite," he said, obviously intrigued by her body. I have not seen a Terran body before, without coverings that is. Do all females have these wonderful … alahini?" He was looking at her as if he might devour her.

The TLC didn't offer a translation for the word he'd used. "What's alahini?" she asked.

"A special Mhalanai treat. It is wonderful! I have to find one for you when we are in the south. It is a round, soft bread. You eat it warm, right from the oven covered with a powdered spice that tastes a little bit tangy and a little bit sweet. It is my favorite. They say alahini is an ancient Mhalanai sacred food, but that may be only legend. In any case, it is supremely delicious."

"I'll consider it a compliment then!" she said. "You can taste my alahini if you like."

He did and she began to think that maybe their two species were not so different after all.

They spent uncharted hours exploring each other's surprising anatomies, touching, caressing and tasting each other, breathing deeply into their sensations and emotions. Their desires burned slowly and with graceful power. Sola felt all the while that the core heat generated from a soulful connection that had its fire in the metaphysical as much as in the physical.

When they finally began to drift towards the edge of sleep, they were entangled together, wrapped in the glowing embers of their passion, in a gentle silence, smiling.

"It is raining," Jaitain said. "Up there. I can feel it." He placed his arm under her head, rolled onto his back and pulled another blanket over them. They both stared at the rough ceiling of the cave. Sola felt briefly claustrophobic at the thought of all that stone hanging above her, but she was so relaxed, so at ease, that it passed without taking hold.

"It is raining in Djintu City," he said, sounding distant, suddenly sad, "washing away the blood."

"There is no escaping it, is there?" Sola said, moved by the vivid image.

"No. It is a part of my being, under my skin, a dye, and a great urgency."

"Can you ever forget, even for a moment?

"I just did." He turned to face her, smiling again, then touching her forehead with his lips.

She ran her fingers over his smooth scalp, as she had felt an impulse to do that day in the restaurant. "What do I do? I finally feel at home, but it's not my own home; it's yours, and I'm constantly reminded that I can't stay?"

"You come and hold me," Jaitain said, "and try to remember exactly how 'home' feels, so you can carry it with you."

He wrapped his arms gently around her body, making a warm cocoon of himself for her.

For the moment, she felt safe in that cocoon.

Jaitain relaxed into sleep. Sola remained awake, her heart tugging at her thoughts.

How could she feel so connected with Jaitain so quickly? He was essentially a stranger, and a man caught up in a dangerous revolution.

Was she crazy? Last night, she opened her heart to the possibility of getting back together with Colby, as his partner, for the long term. Now, she was in deep with one of his little green men.

What was wrong with her? Was she so afraid of true intimacy that she was sabotaging her relationship with Colby by being with Jaitain? That possibility made her angry with herself, but it didn't feel accurate.

Something else was happening, something with a mysterious and mystical meaning. She could feel the buzz of it in her bones. She wished she could talk with her granny. Mahealani always found sage insight into any situation Sola managed to get herself into, but even her wise kupunawahine would surely call this one a doozy!

Jaitain slept silently, lying close beside her. She felt his body heat absorb into her skin. Several layers of blankets on top of a futon-like pad kept the stone floor from leeching their warmth. Sola found sleep elusive, her entire life seemed surreal to her down here in these tunnels created by molten mineral flows billions of years ago, and then carved out by water. How insignificant were human and Mhalanai concerns on the timeline of geology.

Eventually, Sola allowed sleep to lull her into a state of acquiescence.

Chapter 14

Day Six (morning)

U isamu ho luma, ho mei moyin.
To know the end, transforms the beginning.

The Mhalanai Book of Ways

Sola woke up to kitchen sounds. She was alone on the sleeping pad. Jaitain must be making breakfast in the galley. She pulled the blankets close around her. Her joints and muscles ached. She needed to take her meds. She sat up and scanned around for her clothes. Her naked skin was unhappy about the prospect of getting out from under the covers before getting into some clothes. She shot up out of the bed, gathered up her scattered clothes and pulled them on as quickly as her sluggish body and brain could muster. This involved some crazy hopping around and teetering on the brink of falling down. She was glad she had no witnesses. Once dressed, she realized her shirt was inside out, but she was not about to take it off. The cave felt arctic after a night of warm sleep.

She found her boots and pulled them on, then followed the sounds of breakfast to the galley chamber.

"Good morning," she said to Jaitain, who was busy at the makeshift counter and stove.

He turned to smile at her. "How did you sleep, Nulini?"

"Like a baby."

"That is not so good!"

"I know, right? The term means you slept well, but I agree, it's not an accurate statement."

"Babies are awake much of the night! So I hear. I don't have one myself." He smiled awkwardly, put down a bag of some sort of flour, and turned around to embrace her.

"How wonderful to be with you last night," he said tenderly into her ear, making her skin feel alive all over. He took a strand of her wild morning hair between his fingers and studied it.

"The color reminds me of a tjong my mother often wore when I was a child. It has the same evening sunlight."

She smiled at him. They wrapped each other up tightly with grateful arms.

"Did we eat up all the laiku?"

"Yes, afraid so. I am making something else."

"And here I thought all the food was take-out."

"Take-out?" he asked, puzzled.

"Getting food from a restaurant and taking it out with you to eat at home," she explained.

She could use some fresh carrot juice from The Alpha Planet Juice Bar right now, and those incredible non-dairy pastries with fruit filling and rice custard wrapped in thin layers of crispy filo dough from Arnaud's in Boulder, but Colorado was a distant speck across the cosmos. Reaching Arnaud's would be a challenge even by astral travel. Of course, if you leave your body behind, you can't eat pastries! She found herself chuckling softly at her own musings.

"What are you thinking, Nulini," he asked touching her cheek lovingly with the back of his fingers. "You look like you are in another world."

"Very observant," she said, enjoying his intuitive prowess. "I was, and a very distant world at that. A particular take-out treat had me back on Earth. You'd love this stuff." She looked at him with affection. "Maybe someday you can come to my home world and I'll take you to Arnaud's for pastry!"

He nodded his big, round head and said, "I would like that, very much. What is this pastry?"

"I guess you could call it a dessert breakfast. It has some nutritional value, but mostly, you eat it because it is delicious, a fun food. Like alahini!" she said, remembering his audacious comment about her breasts.

"Well, I am afraid filij is not anything like pastry," he said in a dramatic tone, "although, perhaps I may indulge in some alahini a little later?" He had a sly look in his eyes.

"That might be arranged," she said, grinning. "So, filij. That, I assume, is our breakfast?"

"Yes, it is almost ready."

"This kitchen is surprisingly well-equipped. How did you get all this stuff down here through those horrible tunnels?"

"Through the tunnel we sealed up."

"Well, many thanks to Cylin," she said.

"I have grown quite grateful to him lately. Without him, you would be far, far from Caifanii by now, and I would not be able to do this." He kissed her, with a natural passion, as if kissing were something he'd practiced since adolescence.

"May I reiterate for the sake of emphasis," she said, feeling warm in all the right places, "you are a fast learner!" She wondered how he managed to be so light hearted. She expected revolutionaries to be a somber lot, bitter and angry. This one was oddly content and at peace.

The galley wasn't much of a kitchen, but for a subterranean rebel base, it wasn't bad. They had a small cabinet for cups, bowls, plates, utensils, and stores of food. Of course, there was also that horrible storage room. There were two huge jugs of water, a long makeshift counter to work on, a two-burner stove, and several canisters that looked like they held fuel.

"Isn't that dangerous?" she said, pointing to the fuel canisters.

"It is all dangerous. The whole thing. Every minute of it."

There it was again, that lightness.

He spoke of the danger as if he were talking about an exciting adventure not a life-threatening revolutionary struggle. She knew there was much to learn from his attitude. She felt critical of her own heaviness in the face of her minor challenges, like coping with Caifanii's gravity and muggy weather. Those were inconveniences, not dangers. They did not threaten her survival, just her comfort. That is, as long as she was not exposed to them too long. Maybe if you looked death in the eye every day, you got used to its gaze. Maybe you just learned to wink and say, "G'day mate!"

What about looking death in the eye when it is staring at you from the lifeless face of someone you love? That was different. That had broken her completely. Jaitain must have lost friends, even members of his family. This struggle had years of history. The massacre in Djintu City only just happened. Jaitain's friends and relations were likely involved, possibly dead. How did he stay light in the face of such darkness?

The penetrating darkness of the caves was enough to rattle her composure. She wondered what the next days would bring, and hoped they would bring her out into the lighted world again. The last few days now seemed more like a few weeks. Colby, her job, her commission all seemed light years away. She had enough meds for three months, a standard precaution, but she wondered if three months would be enough. She might be back on board the Minerva in a day or two. She might never be back. The future was a big question mark.

She watched Jaitain place several ingredients into a bowl. He lit one of the burners and placed a pan of water on the open flame. She stood behind him, placing one hand over his solar plexus and moving the palm of the other hand slowly up and down over his left shoulder and upper arm, feeling the warmth of her energy reach into him with affection, feeling the strength of his body reassure her. He was short, she could easily see over his shoulder. She had shared intimacy with human males of less stature than her own. She was a tall woman. This was different. Jaitain was not only short he was slight and smaller-boned than she was, although equally muscular and perhaps stronger. Still, his body seemed feminine to her.

"How did you know I would be at the Fugia Nakaii?" she asked, resting her chin on his shoulder.

"You think I knew in advance?"

"You said you didn't, but I doubt you had that much luck."

"The luck of experience! It is a very popular place, especially for out-of-town visitors. I often see foreigners there. No houbob!" he said.

He poured the contents of the bowl: some white powder mixed with a yellow grain, into the hot water now bubbling in the pan, and stirred the mixture with a long handled spoon. She could feel the muscles in his back tighten and release as his right hand turned the spoon with a steady, gentle motion.

"Does it take long to cook?"

"No, just a few minutes. I will warn you, once it starts to congeal it begins to smell strong, and it tastes as bad as it smells, until you get used to it."

"Am I obliged to try it?" she asked, beginning to cough a little as a pungent odor reached her nostrils and throat. It reminded her of the sulfurous odor of a spoiled egg. "It smells atrocious," she said. "How can you stomach that stuff? It smells like the bowels of the earth spit it out."

"Ha!" He laughed, pushing the muscles of his abdomen out against her hand, where she embraced him. "I thought you were interested in interstellar cuisine!"

"How did you know that?" she asked, kissing the back of his bare head.

"I know all kinds of wonderful things about you," he answered, teasing her.

"Well, don't take it personally, but I don't think this stuff is going to make it into my new cookbook."

"Filij is the most nutritious thing on the planet," he said. "That's why we put up with it. It never spoils, or if it does, it does not seem to matter. It always tastes the same." He gave the mixture a few vigorous twists as it thickened against the spoon. "This gourmet delight has been called the curse of the revolution! In fact, do you know what it means, filij?"

"No," she said. "The TLC is translating it simply as filij. That means there is no English equivalent in the database."

The odor was now so obnoxious, she moved further away.

"It means stinky feet!"

"No way! Yuk! That's about perfect. I don't think I want my portion of stinky feet!"

"I will add something sweet to make it more palatable."

"Sweet stinky feet, sounds like a bad country song."

Just as Jaitain was pouring their portions into two ceramic bowls, there was the sound of laughter.

Eilfina and three other rebels burst into the galley with radiant faces and several white boxes tied up with strings.

"Tell me you brought take-out!" Sola said.

"Laiku to the rescue!" Eilfina said, pinching her nose with her finger at the stench of the filij.

"Your timing is impeccable!" Sola said.

"The cook is quite insulted," Jaitain said, holding the two steaming bowls, "but he will get over it quickly!"

They all laughed and dove into the boxes to eat the laiku while they were still warm. Sola indulged and ate two. Everyone was silent, fully engaged in the joy of eating.

Eilfina spoke first. "Sola, these are our companions. This is Mako," she said, pointing to a young male with stunning silver-blue eyes, "and Dukal," she continued, nodding to her left. Dukal was taller than the others, and athletic in build. "And, this is Jumein," she said, putting her arm around his shoulder, "our youngest freedom fighter."

He blushed. He was adolescent, maybe twelve or thirteen years old.

Sola nodded. "Well, I suppose you all know I'm Sola," she said. "Pleased to meet you."

There was a lot of nodding of heads and smiles.

"So, what is happening in the Center, and at the Hotel? Did you talk with Rain?" Jaitain asked.

"Who?" Sola asked. He had spoken the English word: rain, which the TLC translated as: rain.

"Rain," Jaitain said, "the head waiter at the Hotel restaurant, the one who gave you the envelope I left with him."

Oh," she said. "I never actually met him. He delivered the envelope with my breakfast, wrapped in the napkin."

"Clever."

"What did you say his name was? It sounded like you said rain."

"No. It is Rain."

"Right."

Right as rain, she thought. Rain appeared to be like the word Nepal, it sounded exactly like it was spoken in English, even though it was not. Perhaps the word rain meant rain in Caifanii, but not in Mhalanai. She assumed some part of the name Nulini meant rain in Mhalanai. This was confusing.

"What does his name mean, and is it a Mhalanai name?"

"It means eldest son of the wagon maker. Of course, there are no wagon makers now, have not been for centuries. It is an old name, very traditional Mhalanai."

"I see. The sound, the pronunciation of your friend's name, is exactly the same as the word for rain, as in precipitation, in English."

He laughed. The sound echoed briefly on the cave walls.

"That is wonderful!" he said. "Rain will like that! I will tell him. Appropriate too. He is as reliable. The word for precipitation is lini."

"Ah, as in Nulini! New rain." She smiled. "I guess nu means new. How curious. So, Rain is with the Mhalanai Trust?" she asked.

The others chuckled.

"He is my eldest brother," Jaitain said.

"Really?" she said. "So which son of the wagon maker are you?"

"Number three, but Jaitain does not mean third son of the wagon maker.'"

"What does it mean?"

"It means endurance. It was a long birthing for my mother. Does the sound Jaitain also mean something in English?"

"No, but it means a lot to me," she said, lightly squeezing his arm, "but I interrupted your update. Please continue. I don't want to get in the way of important revolutionary business!"

The Mhalanai lightness of being was rubbing off on her.

Eilfina spoke. "I think we have a good window tonight. Central Security is no longer on full patrol. No clear idea what Htiu's legions are doing, we lost our eyes there."

"Anything further on Cylin?" Jaitain asked.

"He is a foolish child, but he was not compromised. As far as we can gather, he acted on his own. He is with Tinir now."

"Good. He will be safe there."

"Rain says the Hotel placed Sola's belongings into storage this morning. They are preparing the suite for use by Caifanii guests."

"Not wasting any time," Sola said. "Gotta keep that income coming in!"

"A good sign, no?" Eilfina said.

"Yes, but I'm glad I am not waiting to be rescued. Sounds like Central Security gave up on finding me already!"

"They just gave up on you returning to the Hotel." Jaitain said. "They are still searching."

"Is Rain coming with us?" Sola asked, hoping that maybe he could bring her ukulele.

"He is unable to take time from work right now, and we need him in Haikon," Jaitain said.

Sola realized it was probably a pipe dream anyway, or a uke dream. Rain worked in the Hotel restaurant, how was he supposed to get to her uke locked away in some storage room. The thought made her sad. She wanted to rescue her sweet little instrument.

"You look downcast," Jaitain said, softly to her.

"I miss my ukulele, that instrument I left in the suite."

"Perhaps Rain could liberate it and send it south!"

"That's what I was hoping, but he's not coming south with us."

"It would be risky, but we can explore the possibility of finding your instrument and smuggling it here. I can see it means more than you admit."

"True enough, but not so much that it's worth taking any kind of risk. Promise me no one will take any risk. My uke can be replaced, you are all irreplaceable."

"When do we leave?" Mako asked.

"I think we have a good window tonight," Eilfina said.

"Well, I'm all for jumping through it!" Sola said.

"Then we better start packing," Jaitain said.

Chapter 15

Day Six (afternoon)

Yeaku hoim loti din mi Iaho porulaom.
We greet what awaits us as an old friend.

The Mhalanai Book of Ways

In the caverns, it was impossible to tell the time of day by instinct. Sola was usually good at gauging the hour. Even on planets with days considerably longer or shorter in length than those on Earth, she was rarely more than an hour off, but in the caves, her special talent vanished.

Time decanted itself without precision, day mixing with night into a homogeneous blend.

Hunger and the need for sleep created their own schedule, but even that was irregular. Sometimes, she was constantly hungry. Other times, she had to remind herself to eat. Sleep came when she was too tired to stay awake.

Without checking her PCU, she could not be sure if she was sleeping under two moons or a sun. She wondered if being out of daylight for a long enough period would derange her biological clock until time became irrelevant altogether.

She wanted sunlight on her skin and fresh, wind-blown air in her lungs.

Jaitain and the others were busy arranging for their journey to the southern continent.

They spent the morning talking through possible plans. He sent Mako to the surface to inform several key supporters. Mako had a gentle face. His smile was shy but generous. She liked him. Five Mhalanai rebels would join them on the journey. Three of her current cave companions: Mako, Dukal, and Eilfina, plus an older female named Olanii, who would join them later at a point some distance from the caverns. Because he was still so young, and everyone felt protective of him, Jumein would stay in Haikon at a safe house.

Their journey would be on foot for considerable distances and they would need to move quickly. Sola had few possessions left. She'd take some papers from her briefcase, but leave the case behind. She'd take her med pouch. Eilfina gave her some clothes. The rebels did not wear traditional Caifanii clothing. Even the females wore pants. None of them wore gloves. Eilfina's pants were much too short and a bit too tight on Sola, but they would have to do. She wasn't going to hike in a tjong. Sola didn't want to have to carry her portable computer, but she didn't want it left behind, so it would come along. Of course, she'd take the PCU and the translator.

There was nothing further she could do. Her offers to help the others were met with smiles but, in the end, most of the preparations required more experienced hands as she had no clue what did and did not need to come along. The rebels treated her like some great personage, the hero of their revolution. She felt at once celebrated and lonely.

After a while, she realized that following the others around like a puppy was making everyone nervous, so she sat back down in the beanbag chair and serenaded them with Hawaiian songs, sans her uke, but still soothing. *Ahi Wela*, followed by *Hi'ilawe*. Her companions were noticeably uplifted by the singing, and it calmed her own nerves. She thought about her mother. Envisioned her cutting samples from the plants in her air gardens at the lab, as she used to do, smiling in that deeply conscious way of hers, smiling at the plants, at the Universe, at her daughter off on another space adventure. Mom, I sure miss you, she thought.

Jaitain returned carrying several large, overstuffed bags. He set them down carefully and began extracting various instruments and supplies. She didn't want to interrupt his focus. Within a few minutes, he came over to her with a dark blue backpack.

"It is lightweight, and holds a good amount." He plopped the bag down at her feet and sat down next to her.

"So, how's it going?" she asked. "Are we on schedule?"

"Yes, I think so. I would prefer to be at our rendezvous point before sunrise and that means we need to start as soon as it is fully dark. Shall I help you pack these things?" he asked, scrutinizing her pile of belongings.

"Jaitain, it doesn't get dark on this planet."

"What?"

"You think it gets dark?"

"Yes."

"I guess you have never seen a truly dark sky, so you don't know that you don't have one here!"

"Dark enough to provide some cover for our departure." He smiled. "Why have I not heard you sing before now? Your voice is sunlight."

"It's the sound of my homeland, Hawaii. I wish I had my ukulele, the songs are sweeter accompanied by it. I have played the ukulele since I was a child."

"We have an instrument here, well, in the South, called a himalina small in size, light tone, made of wood. It has strings and a high, lovely sound. Perhaps it will be something like your ukulele. We will find you a himalina! The songs you sing sound so like our language, Mhalanai!"

"Kindred spirits, the Hawaiians and the Mhalanai. You know there is a similar history of oppression too. I'll have to tell you that story some time." She touched his cheek for a moment. "I'm glad you like the songs."

Sola hadn't backpacked in years. The last time she camped out was over six years ago in the Sierra Nevada range in northern California. She hiked a magnificent section of the Pacific Crest Trail out of Ebbets Pass towards Lake Tahoe.

These days she was accustomed to five-star travel and accommodations. In getting from point A to point B, she was definitely used to going First Class.

This was going to be an adventure. The circumstances were dangerous, no doubt. Nonetheless, she felt excited!

Jaitain sat down with her in the beanbag chair. It was comforting to be so close. He enclosed her with his long, slender arms. They were taking a break from plans and packing.

"I want to stay with you as long as possible," she whispered.

"Yes, but the longer you stay, the wider the river becomes, between here and your home."

She leaned her head back onto his shoulder and could feel the soft heat of his breath against her neck.

"I'm not sure what to think, really," she said, beginning to feel overwhelmed.

Her initial role had been clear, to get that file to the UP and Amnesty. With that accomplished, did she have any further business being involved with this revolution, with this revolutionary?

Maybe she needed to consider, one more time, any options to get back to Colby now, not take this journey and prolong her stay and increase their risk as well.

"I am tremendously grateful that you and Colby were able to get the files to their destinations. Yet, I feel a germinating sadness because of the uncertain future of what we have created between us. The revolutionary in me is ecstatic! That we achieved success so quickly is truly miraculous, but the thought of losing you from my life creates a turbulent eddy in the flow of my emotions."

"Jaitain," she said. "Do you always think in poetic metaphors?" She shook her head lightly. Jaitain and Colby, they were worlds apart. Jaitain was like a Phillipe Rosario to Colby's Mitz Krueger, a Henry Thoreau to Colby's Ernest Hemingway.

"Well," she said, "I've never set much stock in miracles, but we could use one or two more. Do you think Central Security or Htiu will go after the shuttle?"

"I do not believe so. As long as Colby stays in orbit, he poses no threat and he gives Central Security an excuse to leave him alone. I doubt they are anxious to be in contact with him."

"They are acting like the kutnak, you mean?"

"Yes, and at the same time they want to make sure that the public does not hold them responsible for your disappearance. They jumped at the opportunity to make us look aggressive and dangerous. I doubt they have a clue as to how to handle things from here."

"How much does the public really know about me, or care to know? It's not like I'm a foreign dignitary, or a pop celebrity."

"Oh, you would be surprised how much of a celebrity you are. The public may not know who you are, or why your disappearance matters, but the news programs are constantly showing a photo of you, so they believe you must be important and that your disappearance must matter a great deal. Nulini, it is easier than you suspect to become a celebrity. The media can make a simpleton into a sensation."

"Are you calling me a simpleton?"

"No. It's only an expression."

"So, I'm about as invisible as King Kong on the Empire State." Her analogy was a classic Colbyism, not translatable. "Doesn't that make our getting away from Haikon even more dangerous? I don't exactly look like a native. You'd be safer traveling without me."

"We are not going without you, Nulini."

"I know we talked through this before, but maybe things are different now. Maybe we need to reconsider. Maybe our plan is too risky. What if I went straight to Central Security? You said there are still trustworthy people in leadership there. Wouldn't that protect me from Htiu? I am technically a foreign diplomat. I doubt they would risk harming me. Sounds like they would be relieved to get me off their hands, deliver me safely to Colby."

He frowned. "I wish it could be that simple."

"It might be. Maybe it's easier than we think. What if I tell them, when I return to the Hotel, that I went on a sightseeing tour out of town, or some such thing, became ill and needed to recover. If they do not allow Colby to land and pick me up, I could threaten that they are creating an interstellar incident and that they need to comply."

She was beginning to convince herself. Jaitain was remaining strangely silent. She continued, fueled by a nervous hope that she might be able to go home now.

"I could tell them that the IDS Pegasus is on its way here. It's not true, but it could be a successful bluff. Who knows, the UP may in fact be sending a ship already, maybe it's not such a bluff."

"It is possible that they would let you leave," Jaitain said, brushing his fingers across her brow lightly. "It is more likely that they would take you into custody and try to get information from you regarding our operations first. I doubt they will believe any story you tell them. They might even bring Htiu in to assist with the interrogations."

"Why does that evil man get to have his finger in all the pies? Sorry, I keep using these idioms that must translate poorly."

"Htiu does have his tongue in all of the puddings. He is in the picture no matter where we focus the frame. Htiu may convince Central Security that you sought us out, intended to support the revolution all along. That would shift things in a highly dangerous direction. Corrupt officials permeate all levels of the government. It is even possible they will assassinate you in order to make certain you are silenced."

"Jesus!" A deep, cold, shiver shot along Sola's back. "Are you serious?"

"They could do it efficiently using top secret personnel," Jaitain continued, his voice sounding tense, dark.

"Everything is already in place for them to make it appear that you were killed by us. The population in the North is still asleep. They believe what they see in the media without thinking to question the voice of authority, and they consume on high drama like a drug."

"Why would they do that? Why would they risk an interstellar investigation? Do they think my company is just going to write me off? Could they be that stupid?"

"You are judging them by your own standards. These people are not used to operating in an interstellar arena. They are not even concerned with the repercussions of their policies and actions on a global level. I know it is difficult to believe, but the threat to your life is very real. I am not willing to take that risk. Are you?"

"Of course not, I just thought the only real threat was Htiu, now I see it is more complex."

Maybe Jaitain was right. Her logic was the product of understanding values, regulations and legal repercussions present in her own society. She had no proof these were even present in theirs. Maybe IDS's opening of this new territory was premature. Without prevalent extraplanatary social awareness, a culture's behavior in the interstellar marketplace was unpredictable at best. She felt the eye of the hurricane collapse as the far edge of the storm moved in on her emotions.

She curled up close to Jaitain's warm body. He held her. "It's not that I don't want to go with you," she whispered. "I want to be with you as long as possible. It's just that it makes everything so much more complicated. I guess I was hoping there was still a simpler way out. My Granny always says, 'The only way out is through.'"

"Then we will go through. Nulini, you are under the protection of our elders, I trust this much. We will be cautious. We will be together."

When everything was ready, all the packs lined up against the wall, Jaitain suggested that they gather for a moment of quiet focus. They stood together in a circle, facing each other. The others closed their eyes. Sola watched the tension drop easily from their faces as they began breathing deeply. She wondered if they were attempting a Joining, but assumed that they were just getting into a centered state of mind. After a few minutes, she too closed her eyes. She had trouble meditating these days. After Ramon's death, she was too angry inside. She didn't want to face her demons. Now, she decided to give herself to the process. She breathed deeply and let the crowded thoughts in her mind drift into the background. She felt a tingle of energy rising slowly up along her spine, moving over the back of her head, and pouring like a warm waterfall over the front of her face and body, then up again along her spine, this time more quickly. Soon, the energy was circulating and she began to feel a permeating heat. Why had she not done this earlier to get warm?

"Silly goose," she thought. "Shhh, noisy monkey mind," she told herself, silently.

The gentle harmonic resonance she associated with reaching an alpha state began to wash over her consciousness. For years, she practiced an ancient Chinese form of energy work called Chi Gong. She was happy to find she could still circulate her chi.

After an indeterminable time, she heard Eilfina's soft, lilting voice calling everyone back. Sola felt refreshed. The faces around the circle were radiant. Sola looked into the eyes of her companions. They, at least, had some idea of what lay ahead. She was about to embark on uncharted course. Well, she thought, it beats boredom!

With their gear hoisted on their backs and small packets and canisters hanging from hip belts, the small party twisted through a series of tunnels. Sola was relieved that these were wider than the ones she had traveled to recharge her solar pack, and frequently opened into cavernous rooms where the air felt less dank and oppressive. The depth of the darkness that engulfed them astounded her. She felt as if they were thousands of miles beneath the surface, "Journey to the Center of the Earth" she thought, one of Colby's favorite movies. Except, of course, that this was not the Earth. They moved slowly, the soft auras of their five light beams bobbing before them. No one spoke. There was only the hollow sound of footsteps, the soft passage of air in and out of lungs, the swish and rustle of cloth rubbing against cloth and occasionally the rasp of a sleeve or pant leg against the stone walls in the more narrow passages. If time had seemed undefined in the chambers, it now became non-existent, as if everything had stopped, all rotations had ceased and the world was only this black, cool void of space without stars.

They continued walking, always gradually upwards, in silence. The muscles in her legs grew sore from the tension of walking so carefully in the darkness. This route to the surface was much longer than the one they used to recharge her solar cells, already twice as long, she guessed.

At least her mind felt relatively calm, the panic of claustrophobia abated perhaps by the steadying energy of her earlier meditation.

After what seemed like a small eternity, Sola felt a movement of air, fresher and wilder than the stagnant rations she'd been breathing. Slowly, the darkness began to erode. She could see a mass of stone looming ahead on her left, then the ragged edge of the cavern ceiling just ahead where the tunnel began to descend. Temporarily they moved down, before the tunnel opened up into a large chamber filled with cool, bluish light.

Moonlight! They came into the fresh air of an evening sky, an inverted bowl of stars! The others began to crawl, hand over hand, out of the cave up a steep incline of rock, dirt and small shrubs.

Sola just stood still, her face turned upwards. Stars jumped out of the sky at her senses. The air was moist and warm on her face. She filled her thirsty lungs with the fresh oxygen in deep, satisfying gulps.

She felt suddenly lightheaded and lost her balance. Her pack pulled her backwards and broke her fall so that she was half sitting, half lying on the ground, like an overturned turtle. Giggles erupted from her throat. Jaitain sat down beside her.

"The oxygen is making you dizzy," he said, helping her sit upright slowly. "Just rest a moment."

"No kidding," she said, trying to breathe less deeply to prevent hyperventilating. Her lips were tingling, and the stars overhead were starting to spin like a lighted carrousel.

When she felt back in balance, they climbed out of the rocky entrance of the cave and stepped onto the soft, mossy soil of a moonlit forest glen.

Sola began to cry quietly with relief and sheer delight. Perhaps the others were too accustomed to their routine of living above and below ground to experience this exquisite liberation.

Sola wanted to drop her pack and dance, to take off her boots and feel the damp soil on her bare soles, to kneel with a knightly reverence and kiss the sweet essence of the living world! Emergence from the caves elated her, enchanted her like a magical elixir. The others moved away into the shadow of the trees. Sola stood locked in the moment, freed by its ecstasy, her heart reborn in this night air, her spirit drenched in this pale, cool nectar of moonlight. Her soul felt rooted, at home, truly at home in this moment.

The thought jolted her out of her reverie. Would she ever be 'home' again, on Earth? She looked at the strange, soft-leaved trees around her. She missed the spruce, juniper and aspen of Colorado, and the Norfolk pine of Hawaii.

Jaitain walked back to where she was standing. He placed his hand against her cheek a look of tenderness and concern in his shadowed eyes.

"I'm all right," she said. Her whisper sounded formidable in the dense silence.

"I understand," he said. "The underworld eats slowly at your heart. When you emerge into the air again, you can feel the wound begin to heal, feel the empty places fill themselves like ravenous animals with life."

She stared at him, shaking her head. "Do you ever write these things down?" she asked.

"What things?"

"Like what you just said. You have a phenomenal mind, Jaitain."

He smiled broadly, his white teeth looking garish in the shadowy light. "When I am old and settled down, I will write my memoirs and send you a copy."

She felt herself wishing that she could simply stick around until he was old and settled down, wishing she could grow old and settle down right along with him. These thoughts were a peculiar tangent to her independent, "Rambling Rose" credo. She shook her thoughts out into the breeze, like crumbs from a tablecloth, and prepared for the next course of action.

"I'm ready," she said. "Sorry to hold us up."

"We are not likely to be detected here," Jaitain said, "but we are having a race with the dawn, a race we cannot afford to lose."

They walked under a spell of urgency for what seemed like hours, winding through the trees. There was no discernible path. They followed Mako's lead through the lessening darkness, and the odd quiet of a forest without frogs or nocturnal insects, without the crisp crunch of dry leaves underfoot like the crackle of fire, just soft padded mulch and an occasional, lonely call from a distant unknown creature.

They came into a large clearing. The trees gave way to low grass. The others moved purposefully towards the opposite side of the meadow where Olanii awaited them. Without exchange of words, the entire group began to remove the foliage that provided camouflage for a hidden transport vehicle. There was a buzz of excitement. No one spoke, but it was obvious all were relieved to have come this far undetected.

The transport was a hovercraft with a large view-window at the helm, and a small side hatch. They boarded. Inside, there were two seats before a main control panel and four seats further back. It was more spacious inside than she expected. There was a small galley in the stern, and four fold-down bunks, two each on the starboard and port sides of the inner hull. They stowed their gear into large containers located beneath the folded bunks, then settled into their seats and strapped in. Everything handled with precision and fluid grace. This scenario was no premier performance. Well-rehearsed, it found its agile routine by repeat experience.

Nonetheless, Sola held her breath as they prepared for takeoff. She wondered how long the craft had been lying dormant in the forest, and hoped it would function properly. The engine started without a sputter and purred smoothly. It sounded reassuringly well maintained, and utilized a rotational field propulsion system, a typical hovercraft design.

Pale grey light began to permeate the dark grey sky, slowly extinguishing the stars. Both of Caifanii's moons were waning gibbous in the pre-dawn glimmer. The craft rose stealthily into the embrace of day, the rosy pink of sunrise, lifting its steely hull through a thin mist of dew evaporating from the meadow grass at the touch of first sunlight.

Once they were at a cruising altitude, the compartment burst full of excited chatter. They maneuvered very close to the ground, dangerously so. Olanii piloted with expertise, she was obviously used to this kind of flying. After two hours of nerve-jarring maneuvering through an increasingly mountainous terrain, the craft ascended to higher altitude and an expanse of blue spread out before them on the view screen, the ocean!

Olanii gave over the controls to Dukal. Mako moved into the copilot position. The rest of the small crew shuffled off to the rear of the craft, pulled down the folding bunks, and hoisted their tired bodies onto the mattresses and off to sleep. Sola followed suit, but despite the comfort of lying nestled in a bunk, sleep was evasive. After two hours, she found herself still awake despite her exhaustion.

She noticed a marked change in the pitch of the engines. The transport was descending. Sola got out of the bunk and came to the front of the ship. She sat down in a chair behind Dukal. There was nothing but ocean in the view screen. There was a loud rumble and a brief, muffled explosive sound.

"Are we in trouble?" Sola asked, her heart skipping a beat.

"No. No trouble," Mako said.

"What was that loud noise?"

"That was the two pontoons being deployed from inside the lower hull, and self-inflating. We are turning this ship of the sky into a ship of the sea!" Mako explained, with pride.

They set down with remarkable ease on the placid surface of the water. Mako pulled over a ladder and climbed up through a hatch on the top hull. He disappeared.

"He is going to erect the masts, and set the sails," Dukal explained.

"Can I help?"

"Absolutely."

She climbed up the small ladder and stepped onto the flat roof of the craft. It was now the deck of their ship. It was bright outside. Sola squinted into the hot, white sunlight. Mako quickly assembled the main mast, constructed of segments of a synthetic material that fit together as components and locked into the top of the outer hull. Sola helped him with the rigging of the main sail, which was bright blue and had rigid battens, like Chinese junk rigging. They assembled a smaller mast near the bow for a jib sail, which also had rigid battens.

They hoisted the main sail, which fanned out and quickly caught the wind, sending the craft across the water at a sudden and impressive speed. Sola and Mako both shouted for joy as the craft, now essentially a trimaran, tilted to starboard. They found their sea legs and set the smaller jib sail.

The sails were a close match to the color of the cloudless sky stretching in all directions, and a few shades lighter than the expanse of blue-green water, a clever bit of camouflage. Sola sat down near the bow, and gazed out at the horizon where the blue-green water kissed the blue-green sky. Her father would enjoy this scene. He came from a long line of Scottish men of the sea, a sailor down to his DNA. The two of them used to spend Saturdays sailing his 26 foot Jeanneau out from Lahaina when she was in her teens, to swim with pods of dolphins off the coast of Lanai, or snorkel with sea turtles at Molikini. Once, while anchored off Lanai, another boat came into the bay. It was a homemade catamaran with Chinese junk rigging. Her dad talked with the owner for hours about his unique design. He just completed a solo journey from Panama to Maui and found the junk rigging much simpler to handle alone. Now, she was sitting on a similar ship. It was magnificent. The blue sails were oriental fans carrying them swiftly across the gentle swells. She missed her dad. She could use a bit of his dry wit and a good squeeze on the shoulder from one of his strong, stubborn hands. When this adventure was over, Sola promised herself, she'd spend some quality time with him, maybe even go sailing.

The rolling pitch of the ship and the warm sun made Sola feel luxuriously sleepy. She slipped below deck, crawled into the bunk and drifted immediately into dreamless oblivion.

Chapter 16

Day Six (early evening)

Tonia yin pa iumo au iumate.
Depth is a reflection of insight.

The Mhalanai Book of Ways

The beeping of her CPU dredged Sola up from a deep sleep. She'd left the unit on her wrist. She hit the answer button, still groggy.

"Earth to Mars! Earth to Mars!" Colby said. "What's going on comrades? Hello! Hello!"

"Hey, Space Cowboy! What's up?"

"I'm gettin' mighty weary of this particular view. Too cloudy."

"It's been clear here."

"Where exactly is here?"

"We made it out, Colby! We're on the ocean now."

"Don't you mean *over* the ocean?"

"No, at the moment, we are sailing, can you believe that?"

"Sounds like a slow boat to China!"

"We really are! You should see this thing, it has junk rigging!"

"What? The sails are made of junk?"

"Colby, you crack me up. No, the sails are like those fan-shaped ones on Chinese Junks. We're in a hovercraft that's amphibious. Turns into sort of a trimaran. Pretty wild."

"Sounds like you're alright, mate! Heck, sounds like you are having *way* more fun than this cosmic sailor!"

"I wouldn't go that far!" she said.

"Hey, speaking of sailors, I'm afraid we won't be getting any assistance from the Pegasus. They won't be sailing any time soon. Major failure in their hyperdrive, blew a serious gasket. They're stuck at some spaceport a good two light years from here. So, can I skedaddle and pick you up any time soon?"

"Let me see if the man with the answers is available. We're all super tired so there's a lot of napping going on around here."

"Did I wake you up?"

"Yes, but I am so glad to hear your voice, I don't mind." She was awake now, and feeling the benefits of her nap. "Hold on a minute, while I round up Jaitain. Not sure where he is."

"Wow, must be some yacht you're on."

"No, it's quite small, just don't know if he's sleeping or up on deck."

Sola got out of the bunk and snooped around as quietly as possible. Two of the others were asleep in bunks. She couldn't tell which two, they had their backs to her, though she was pretty sure neither was Jaitain. The Caifanii still looked alike to her. Familiarity breeds recognition, and she had very little familiarity, except with Jaitain. How was she going to approach that topic with Colby? In person, and when this was all behind them.

Mako was sitting before the console, reading a book.

"Where's Jaitain?" Sola whispered to him.

"He is up top," Mako whispered back.

She climbed up the stairs and through the open hatch. Jaitain was sitting at the bow, wearing a wide brimmed sun hat with a tightly cinched chinstrap. The sails were still full and the wind was providing a good clip.

She walked gingerly towards him and settled down. "I've got Colby on the line," she said. The ocean air felt refreshingly cool after her sleep in the stuffy cabin.

"Colby, I found Jaitain. I'll be right here, so we can both hear you."

"Colby," Jaitain said. "How are you faring?"

"I'm okay. One heck of a cloudy planet you've got. The whole Haikon area is socked in."

"Yes, that is true, though we have sun at the moment."

"Then you are a long way from Haikon."

"Are you certain this transmission is secure?"

"100% secure. You have my word on that."

"Excellent. Has there been any attempt by the Haikon authorities to contact you?"

"Not a peep."

"No signs of aggression?"

"Not a one. They're not even being El Paso Aggressive!" He chuckled.

Sola got the joke. Jaitain, of course, did not.

"Well, I am certain they are monitoring your position, Jaitain said. "If you move, they will assume Sola has left the Haikon area."

"Sola told me you are on a sailing expedition. Where are you headed?"

"We are heading south. In the near future, you will need to shift your static orbit to a more southern position, to the latitude of Djintu City, so we can arrange a rendezvous."

"Can't wait."

"For the time being, I am afraid waiting is what you will need to do. Stay alert. The government may come to consider you a threat. From my experience, their tactics are not rational. They can be unpredictable, but they are not our only concern. I do not know how much Sola told you regarding High Councilor Htiu."

"The Big Sneeze, yes."

Jaitain gave Sola a quizzical look.

"I'll explain later," she said, softly.

"He is a highly dangerous man," Jaitain said.

"I thought the old fellow was the head of trade and commerce."

"He was just appointed Minister of the Drug Administration, but he is also the head of a powerful drug cartel that moves illegal substances on both continents." Jaitain said.

"Sounds like a bull I don't wanna ride!"

"Colby, the translator tells me you have no interest in sitting on a male yamma. I do not know what this means, but it sounds quite ridiculous."

"A bull is nothing like a yamma," Sola said. "Think three times the size and ten times the power."

Colby laughed. "It's a traditional sport where I come from. You ride on the back of a massive critter with two sharp horns that doesn't appreciate your presence and tries quite violently to get rid of you."

"A good way to break your back." Jaitain said.

"And both legs to boot. Speaking of bulls, I'm not interested in wearing a bull's eye on my ass, pardon my French, so let's hope neither party gets trigger happy. My guess is this little filly has more shielding than anything they can throw my way."

"Htui can afford newer craft and better weapons than the government, so he is a greater threat." Jaitain said.

"A no-account fellow that Big Sneeze! Can I talk to Sola again?"

"Of course." Jaitain handed her the PCU.

"Colby," Sola said.

"Hey, looks like I'm stuck on the ranch for now and we'll have to figure out how to link up later."

"That sounds about right," she said. "I will stay in touch on a regular basis. It will take several days for us to get to our destination. I'm not sure where that is exactly, or why we are sailing rather than flying, but there must be a good reason. I'm glad no one has decided to use you as target practice. That's good news, at least. Hang in there. I'm not taking any of this for granted you know. I mean, you're the best!"

"Geeze woman! We're a team. When this is all over, let's go play in your new backyard, chase some of those wacky humahumanukanukaapuaa! Deal?"

She laughed. "Deal!"

Just like Colby to cheer her up with the crazy name of Hawaii's national fish!

"Just keep yourself safe until I can pick you up, okay?"

"You betcha," she said and switched off the unit.

"Jaitain," she said. "Why are we sailing instead of soaring above the water? It would be so much faster."

"That particular question has a very ornery answer," he said, reaching for her and pulling her close to him, "but I need to hold you before I explain," he said. "That shipmate of yours is a character. I had trouble following him."

"He comes from a unique part of my country called Texas. The Texans are a breed extraordinaire!"

They sat together on the bow. The ship moved up and down over the swells, as the wind carried them forward into the apparent endless sea and sky, the two meeting at the far horizon where magenta and orange streaks foretold the coming sunset.

"Do the others know about us?" she whispered into his large alien ear.

"Yes, of course," he said, taking her face in his hands and holding her forehead so that it touched his forehead lightly for a moment. It was a Caifanii gesture of affection, but seemed humorous to her. She let herself relax against his body, leaning her head against his chest.

"So, what's the answer to that ornery question of mine?" she said.

"The question is not ornery, Nulini," he said, "just the answer." He laughed lightly. "It is not a short answer, are you certain you want to hear it?"

"Yes, you bet."

"There are two reasons. The first has to do with fuel, the second with security. This craft is not a long-distance vehicle. It is a city transporter converted to sleep five and turn amphibious at our command. The internal fuel tanks do not hold enough to fly coast to coast. We could store extra fuel in portable canisters, land in the water long enough to refuel the tanks, then take off again. However, storing the fuel canisters in the cabin is dangerous. It is highly combustible. I do not want it close to the galley. The fumes of the unburned gas are toxic. We do not want the canisters close to our lungs. Storing the fuel canisters on deck works when we are sailing, but not when we are flying."

"That's quite a conundrum."

"Add to the fuel issue the fact that there is a radar detection system monitoring cross-oceanic flights. If we fly, we are visible to that system. If we sail, we pass beneath the detection grid. There is little commercial boat traffic on this particular route due to frequent and sometimes violent storm systems moving through. All things considered, sailing remains our best option.

"Let's hope there are no violent storm systems heading our way!"

"Indeed," he said.

"Any reason why you opt for sailing first and flying later?"

"Storms are less likely to brew in this section of the ocean than the area closer to the Southern continent. I also want to maintain flight capacity at all times once we approach the continent. There are drug runners, and pirating vessels in the straights of the archipelago. We want to be able to give them a wide berth."

"Believe it or not, I had no idea this trip was going to be so dangerous. You do this on a regular basis?"

"Three or four times in a year."

"Well so far, it's pleasant. I'm enjoying myself."

"I am enjoying you as well." He kissed her teasingly. "The light is almost gone, Nulini, time to head back down."

"Let's see what's cooking! It smells darned good," Sola said, following the aroma coming from the open hatch.

The sea air gave everyone a strong appetite, and Olanii's cooking left them all satisfied and feeling lazy. There was jovial conversation into the night, peppered with laughter, and occasional seriousness.

Around ten, the small crew climbed into the bunks to sleep. Eilfina would captain the boat for the first watch, followed by Jaitain, then Dukal. Sola was grateful to have the entire night to rest. As usual, being on this planet left her exhausted at the end of the day.

Chapter 17

Day Seven (late morning)

Soma yin kote di taah.
Truth is an invitation for trust.

The Mhalanai Book of Ways

The growing warmth of the morning coaxed Sola awake. She was lying in one of the bunks. Jaitain was sleeping next to her, his arm over her waist. Sola was curious about the day, the weather, their location. She moved Jaitain's arm gently away, and slipped out of the bunk, careful not to wake him.

She grabbed her eyeshades and her translator and climbed up top.

Eilfina was sitting at the bow. Sola didn't want to startle her, so she cleared her throat lightly.

Eilfina turned to face her. "Greetings! Did you have a good rest, Sola?"

"Yes. I was out for the count!" Sola said.

She realized this would probably not translate, and that she herself didn't have a clue to what that expression referred. She'd picked it up from her father, along with a plethora of other figures of speech, mannerisms, odd habits and core beliefs. She'd have to ask him some time.

"You look refreshed," Eilfina said.

"I feel energized!" Sola said. "Must be the sea air."

"Are you hungry?" Eilfina asked. "You must be. I myself ate enough for two this morning."

Eilfina laughed and rubbed her belly. She wore a shirt with

a low neckline that exposed a small plumeria tattoo just over her heart.

I see you wear the oplumia," Sola said.

"You know about it?" Eilfina asked, in surprise.

"Yes, Jaitain told me about it. It's beautiful. I admire your devotion."

Eilfina smiled.

"The revolution is my life," Eilfina said. "Devotion is simple. So, there is plenty of good food," she continued, "I would be honored to bring you a bowl of something nice and hot."

"Thanks!" Sola said. "That sounds excellent."

Eilfina came towards her and gave her an unexpected embrace.

The top of her spry companion's head barely reached up to her shoulder and Eilfina probably weighed 40 kilos, if that much. Sola felt like a mighty giant, with a mighty giant's hunger.

The food was delicious, filling and slightly sweet. It was some sort of grain with small pieces of dried fruit mixed in. It reminded Sola of oatmeal with raisins. After her meal, she sat on the flat of the deck in the shade of the main sail for some time gazing out to sea and letting random thoughts dive into her mind like fishing pelicans. She missed birds. This ocean seemed strangely sterile without the cry of albatross and the white glint of flapping wings.

She felt pleasantly homesick, another anomaly to her personal credo. What was going on with her? Since leaving the caverns, she had a subtle but persistent feeling that this was no ordinary journey. Of course, it was no ordinary journey for many reasons, but she sensed there was something going on deeper than even the unusual circumstances and experiences themselves. She first felt it during the bold rush of emotion that hit her at the sight of the night sky spinning with stars, as she came out from the dark tunnels. It was a vibration in her core, fortified by the almost visible energy field radiating from the trees in the forest. Now it was mellowing, settling into her consciousness like a gestating seed. Something magical was happening around her, *to* her.

She was nervous and excited. It felt good to be alive. The warmth of the morning sun radiated through her body. She felt content in the moment, which was not her typical style.

Eilfina sat at the stern eating a piece of fruit. She waved and motioned for Sola to join her.

The ship's rudder was controlled from down below, an awkward arrangement. Always better to have sails and rudder under the same gaze.

Sola moved cautiously to the back of the craft, the wind was picking up and they were listing to starboard.

"We're going to knock the rest of the crew out of their bunks if this wind keeps up!" Sola said, jokingly.

Mako tends to hug the tiller a bit too eagerly," Eilfina said. "At least both pontoons are still in the water."

"I certainly hope so!" Sola said.

Years ago, while racing through choppy seas off Lahaina, Sola was nearly thrown from a catamaran listing so far to port that only one outrigger hull maintained contact with the water. It was not unlike riding a bucking bull, she thought.

"I don't have my sea legs back yet," Sola said, laughing at her prudent movements.

"You will get them soon enough," said her bright companion.

Gazing in all directions, there was no land in sight. "This is a serious stretch of water," Sola said.

"Not the shortest route between the continents, but the safest one for us. We call this area of the Great Sea the Minor Sea because there are atolls and it is not as rough as the open ocean to the east," Eilfina explained. "We would not attempt to sail that expanse in such a small craft. There are massive currents and frequent storms. Once we reach Sum, we will trade this lovely beast for something with a little more vigor," she said, patting the deck affectionately.

"I thought we were refueling near Amarillo?"

"In Amilio, yes. Then we will use this craft to cross to Sum where we have close friends who harbor our other vessel. Most of the peninsula's population is Mhalanai Trust supporters, although not openly so, but there are plenty of loyalist and government agents in the mix. That area is a targeted outpost. The authorities monitor movement in and out of the location closely. There are only a few channels and bays that are worth risking."

"How often have you made this trip?" Sola asked, sitting sideways and keeping a firm hold on a guide rope. It was a balmy late afternoon. Sola entertained the notion of going for a swim, but the boat was moving too quickly now.

"This will be my fourth time, not including my trip north when I first became active in the movement," Eilfina said. "Jaitain has taken this journey many, many times. He is quite the expert in these waters."

"Do you think we could take a swim sometime?" Sola asked, excitedly.

Eilfina looked suddenly coquettish, her face lighting up like a child at an ice cream parlor. Sola liked Eilfina's large, open eyes and the way she tossed her head a little whenever she laughed, which she did often.

Eilfina smiled broadly and without a word dove gracefully into the water. She came up with a sputter.

"Yaaouw! It's cold!"

She was quickly a long distance behind the boat.

Sola panicked for a moment, but Eilfina was calm, as if this was something she did all the time. She waved to Sola to join her. Sola never said no to water. She slipped off her shoes and placed her translator and PCU inside of them. She pulled off her pants and dove in wearing just her shirt and underwear.

Her body tingled all over as she rose from her dive. This was heaven! There were fish! This planet's oceans had plenty of active life forms! Less than twenty feet away hung a massive school of large, yellow fish with red stripes. The boat was soaring away from them so fast it made her panic for a moment, but Eilfina, swimming nearby was so unconcerned, Sola trusted that all was well. She felt a strong sense of impending magic.

She took a deep breath, held it and dove. She could see Eilfina gliding towards the school of fish, sending it off in a new direction like a cloud of balloons in a sudden blast of wind. Her companion moved her body like a dolphin through the clear water. Sola sank just under the surface, so she could watch Eilfina. She felt her hair float out around her like the tendrils of a jellyfish. She rose for a new breath and went down again, a little deeper.

Four yellow fish were heading her way. One came over to nibble on her hair, which probably resembled some sort of seaweed. She tugged on the strand of hair and the fish stared at her with its big, black eye on the side of its narrow face. Its body flared out wide and was whimsical in color. The red stripes were closer to a deep purple up close. The water was much less saline than the oceans on Earth and, although it stung her eyes somewhat, Sola could keep them open underwater.

The raucous color of the fish, now hovering just in front and above her made her gleeful.

She held her breath as long as she could and then rose above the surface gasping.

Sola checked back over her shoulder to see that the ship was leaving them far behind.

Eilfina surfaced about twenty feet from her and swam towards her. They both started heading in the direction of the ship but even their quickest strokes brought them no closer. The wind was picking up and the distance between them and the ship was growing wider every second.

"Juitiana partjo fin," Eilfina said.

Sola heard only the Caifanii. Her translator was safely aboard the ship. She sensed by her tone of voice that Eilfina was trying to calm her. Her companion seemed genuinely unworried.

"How will they know we are here?" Sola asked, realizing her words had no meaning for Elfina. "We didn't tell anyone. We just jumped ship!" She felt a jolt of panic.

Eilfina swam in close to her and took her hand, urged her to roll onto her back and float leisurely.

The two of them floated, their bodies lifting to the surface where the water was warmer. The sky was growing cloudy, the wind bringing in a storm system from the east.

Suddenly, Eilfina let go of Sola's hand, and dove under the water. She emerged again, and laughed. "Naia!" She shouted. "Naia!"

Naia was the Hawaiian word for dolphin. Sola wondered if, like the word "rain," this word too had a completely different meaning and only sounded like a word she understood.

Eilfina was so excited and joyous that Sola felt uplifted even though she didn't see any reason for her friend's exuberance. The sky was turning dark, and they were alone in the midst of an ocean with no apparent means of rescue.

"Iu! Iu! Sola!" Eilfina shouted, then rolled over and swam away with vigor.

Sola looked around, treading water. She saw only the ship in the distance. Suddenly, she felt a rush of water on her left. She rolled over in the water almost taking in a mouthful. Then she saw them.

About five feet from her, two sleek, brownish bodies moved with effortless grace in the now cobalt water. They resembled seals but were twice as large, had a dorsal fin, spotted skin, and spouted water from a small blowhole in the top of their heads.

One of them moved in closer and made eye contact with her, and then swam gently very close to her.

She reached out cautiously and ran her palm over its skin, which felt rubbery but surprisingly smooth, just like a dolphin. It nudged her gently at the elbow with its nose as if to say, "Come on! Grab on! We need to get going."

She took hold of the dorsal fin with both hands, letting her body align with the sea creature's form just beneath her. Instantly, they were moving through the water, gaining speed quickly. She heard light peels of Eilfina's laughter behind her, and then Eilfina sped by, carried by another spotted sea surfer.

Water raced by, making a roar in her ears. The creature's body beneath her was a powerful engine. Sola felt her arms strain to keep hold. She worried that she might lose her grip, her undies, or both.

As if sensing her concern, the creature slowed its pace a bit. They moved easily through the water in the purple reflection of the coming storm.

A dark shape approached them in the distance. The ship had come about and was heading back for them. Eilfina must have known these creatures would come to their aid, or she would never have been so calm all along.

Sola was in a state of bliss as she and her carefree taxi approached the ship. Just before they reached the side of the craft, the creature slowed and came to a gentle stop.

It made a series of short, high-pitched noises, then came close and poked Sola gently on her belly with the front of its head. Sola felt a jolt of heat and energy shoot through her and, for a second, she sensed a presence in her mind, a glimmer of a thought not her own. It was a peculiar sensation, very physical and very pleasurable. It made her feel simultaneously lightheaded and very clear mentally. Then the creature gently touched her forehead with its nose. She felt a rush of energy, almost electrical in nature, just for an instant, and then the creature sped away.

It leaped out of the water three times about ten meters from her, and then dove and was gone.

Jaitain and Dukal lifted Sola out of the water and Olanii wrapped a large towel around her. The craft tacked into the wind and began its journey into the deepening dark.

The entire crew sat on the deck and watched as a pod of six naia rode the soft luminescent wake of the boat, leaping out in pairs and threes again and again, bringing elation and gratitude.

"They are blessing us, those naia," Jaitain said.

"Jaitain," Sola said. "Eilfina knew they would come to help us, didn't she?"

"They are never far away in these waters."

"On Earth, there are similar creatures and they are called dolphins, but in the Hawaiian language they are called, naia!"

"Somehow that surprises me less than it should!' Jaitain said, enthusiastically.

"It was the strangest feeling," Sola whispered, "like the naia could read my mind."

"They are very intuitive. Ten years ago, one saved my life after the craft I was piloting crashed. It carried me for over eight hours. I also felt as if it knew my thoughts. Some of the Old Ones believe that the naia have telepathic abilities. It may be only a legend, still I have wondered if, perhaps, it is true. Telepathic or not, they have an uncanny ability to be there just when you need them."

Eilfina came and sat close to Sola.

"They saved our lives!" Sola exclaimed. She gave Eilfina an affectionate squeeze, and felt pure joy.

When Sola was in her middle-school years, she spent her summers with her maternal grandparents, whose home was in Hana, on the island of Maui. While swimming and diving every day, Sola developed a special relationship with two dolphins, which came to play in the secluded, black sand cove near her grandparent's beach house. The dolphins always kept their distance, never coming closer than about 15 meters. She would tell her grandparents that she wished the dolphins would come closer and take her for a ride, but secretly she was a little afraid of their strength and power in the water. Perhaps the dolphins knew this secret fear and respected it with their distance.

As an adult, Sola had returned to that cove many times to look for her childhood dolphin companions, but they never came to her again.

She had not been to Maui since her mother's funeral service two years ago. She had spent a week on the island then, mostly in tears and mourning.

One day, during that stay, she took a long walk on Makenna Beach, where the ocean is fierce and the waves bone-crushingly strong. She needed the raging water to speak the immediate language of her heart.

By chance, she met the famous marine biologist, Alger Kölorn, who was also taking a long walk. She was familiar with his work and listened to him talk of his most recent experiments. Kölorn developed a tonal language for communicating with dolphins. The language was very successful with bottlenose and spotted dolphins, although spinners seemed less inclined to respond to it. The language was still limited to a few key words but was a breakthrough program. As far as she knew, telepathic communication with dolphins was still in the realm of myth rather than science, although her grandmother claimed that certain Kahuna in the islands practiced it.

Sola was surprised that her longtime dream of swimming with a dolphin was still so vital. Now, that dream had manifested here on a planet light years away from her home with a creature every bit as delightful!

"I felt like it allowed me to read its thoughts too, for an instant," Sola said.

"Yes!" Eilfina said. "How magnificent! I am so glad for you! I've enjoyed this experience many times. They offer to share their perceptions for a brief moment, and I offer to share mine. It is like welcoming someone into your home."

"It felt like that," Sola agreed.

"Eilfina has a special affinity with the naia," Jaitain said. "Sometimes, she pushes it a bit, if you ask my opinion," he said raising the ridges above his eyes. No more spontaneous dives, please. I know how tempting it is, but we are on a tight schedule, Fina."

Eilfina bit her lip and looked sheepish. "My regrets, Tain. I wanted so much to share this gift with Sola. I suppose it was not the most intelligent choice. I won't jeopardize our journey again." She sounded serious, but her characteristic lightheartedness was just beneath the surface. "I am hungry as a masop!" she added.

"A what?" Sola asked.

"A masop! You know, oh, I guess not!" That light bubble of laughter again. "A small farm animal with a remarkably large hunger. It can munch an entire field of grass in a single day."

"Jaitain!" Sola suddenly froze in shock.

"What?" He looked at her with concern.

"My translator! I'm not wearing my translator but I can understand everything you're saying!"

Jaitain looked like his eyes were going to pop out of his head. "What!"

"No," she said. "This is not possible. This is too weird! I am speaking English. You are speaking Caifanii, but I understand you, and you apparently have no trouble understanding me."

"Sola! You're right. I understand you perfectly. I had not even noticed that you were speaking English until now. Amazing!"

"It is a gift. It's a gift from the naia!" Eilfina piped. "Legend has it that they have special powers."

"Are you serious? Eilfina, what are you saying, that the naia just made it possible for me to understand Caifanii? Boom, just like that? No offense, but that can't be possible. How?"

"I've heard about such a thing as well," Olanii said. "Oh, I thought it was another myth perpetuated by the Elders, but it must be true. Ailva told me once of a child who was healed of a fatal disease after being in contact with the naia. I admit I was skeptical when she told me the story, but Ailva does not speak of such things lightly."

"Who is Ailva?" Sola asked.

"Ailva is a great Tumasei, an Elder. You will meet her when we arrive at Sum."

"Does Ailva live in a small cottage in the forest at the edge of a clearing?" Sola asked.

Olanii chuckled. "We all live in a small cottage at the edge of a clearing in the south. The rainforest is our world."

Sola wondered if it was Ailva who had welcomed her in the airlock and appeared to her in her dreams. She would find out soon enough.

"Nulini," Jaitain said, coming to sit close to her, "I once heard a legend that the naia can breach barriers in the brain. Perhaps there is some truth to that legend. Perhaps this naia broke away a barrier to verbal understanding. Perhaps it established a quasi-telepathic matrix for you. If so, you are even more blessed than we thought!"

"This is wonderful and everything, but it's also creeping me out, big time," she whispered. "A quasi-telepathic matrix? That sounds seriously woo-woo!"

How could a sea mammal, however intelligent, cause her brain to change so radically that she was suddenly able to understand Caifanii, a complex language with such nuance of inflection that it would take her years of training to learn it? And yet, that was exactly what they were experiencing.

"Jaitain. Do all of you usually speak Mhalanai when you are together?"

"Yes, we were using Caifanii because of your translator. We doubted Mhalanai was in your database!"

"No, it certainly was not. Say something to me in Mhalanai, anything. I want to see if I will also understand that."

"I love you," he said.

"You do?" She smiled a little bashfully, self-conscious in the presence of the others. She wasn't used to their level of public intimacy. "Say something again," she prompted.

"But, I don't know what to say," he said.

She heard his Mhalanai words. Mhalanai sounded sweeter and rounder than Caifanii. There were no clicking sounds, just a melodic flow of mostly vowels, amazingly similar to Hawaiian. She did not understand the language itself exactly, but immediately understood the meaning.

"This is fantastic!" she exclaimed. "I can't believe it, but it's happening. It's happening right now. Wait 'till I tell Colby about this. He's going to think I've gone completely bonkers! What about the other direction?" she asked. "If the naia gave *me* this ability, how come you understand what *I'm* saying when I am speaking in English?"

"I don't know," Jaitain said. "I can hear you speak in English, and I do not understand the sounds as words, but I understand you anyway. It is like telepathy, but different."

"Maybe," she paused, pondering her logic. "Perhaps I gained the ability to psychically read thoughts you project to me through verbal language, and the ability to project my thoughts to your mind through the same mechanism."

"That sounds plausible," he said, "and makes me wonder if you haven't explored this territory before."

"What do you mean?"

"You sound more ready to believe in telepathy than I suspected."

"Well, I will admit the possibility of being telepathic has always fascinated me. My grandmother's people are very spiritually inclined. Intuition played a big role in my childhood. My grandmother always knew exactly what I was doing. She could just about read my mind. It was very frustrating as a child, and even more so as an adolescent! I could never get away with anything. She was always on to me, just like that."

"I've heard heightened intuition can be passed on, and perhaps the naia brought that latent trait to the surface."

"Then again, I might just be dreaming and I will wake up in a bunk down there any minute with a headache from having bumped my head in my sleep!"

Sola put the palms of her hands over her face and yelped in mock indignation.

"What is it with this planet?" She said.

She removed her hands and shook her head. "I don't know what to think anymore, but, I'll tell you one thing, that naia certainly did something to me. A blast of heat and energy passed through me when it touched me. There was an electric sensation in my head, an opening up that made me feel superbly clear and unified with everything."

Her mind tried to wrap itself around this miraculous development. Maybe she just needed to accept the gift without a clear explanation of its mechanics. It worked and it was a tremendous blessing.

She felt instantly more connected and at ease on this alien world, now that she didn't need to wear a computer chip in her ear in order to understand her companions.

"You love me?" she said to Jaitain. "Really?"

"Undoubtedly!"

"Wow!" she said. "I love you too! I'm so awestruck you could tell me I've turned green and lost all my body hair and I'd be inclined to believe it!"

"Oh, don't do that! I absolutely love your color and your hair!"

"My grandmother used to tell me that life was much more about magic than about science. I always thought she was just a wonderful, silly old lady, but maybe she was right. Or, maybe science is more magical than we think."

As if to emphasize the point, a group of four naia came leaping out of the water at once in perfect symmetry. At the top of their arch, they received a loud "Aaahh!" from everyone on board, and then it started to pour curtains of rain.

Chapter 18

Day Ten (late morning)

Ho tianmi lomasu cai ho bosa u fiono.
The liberator will emerge from the mouth of a dragon.

From The Prophecy of the Great Day
The Mhalanai Book of Ways

The next two days passed without incidence. If anyone was looking for them, they were looking in the wrong places. Sola spent considerable time on deck sitting in the shade of the main sail. In the sea wind, her hair was an undulating auburn veil. She kept an eye out for naia. They passed by the ship every day, in the early morning and early evening. She had missed their morning visit by sleeping late, but was hoping to catch sight of a few stragglers.

Her new abilities remained intact. The brain is highly adaptive. She was already beginning to find it less bizarre to receive the thoughts of the others when they spoke to her in Mhalanai. The communication was in one aspect similar to using the TLC. She still heard and did not understand the actual words, but in every other aspect, it was significantly different.

When her companions spoke, their meanings, even with subtle nuances and colloquial expressions mixed in, were instantly clear to her. If this talent remained with her, it could boost her career to unprecedented heights. She could be fluent in any language.

Maybe leaving her sales position was premature. She could still ditch IDS. Plenty of other companies would hire her in a snap with this new skill. There was the distinct possibility, however, that the gift functioned solely to assist her here, on this planet. Perhaps it worked only with members of the Archaldian species, who had some telepathic capacity. Perhaps her new abilities would function only in communication with telepathic or empathic races.

Sola felt more than a twinge of discomfort at the hubris of her thoughts. This was a special gift and here she was thinking about financial gain and career advancement. This assignment had already taken her into territory beyond any call of duty to which she was obliged, so perhaps the Universe would not begrudge her a little financial benefit for her trouble, but it felt less than honorable to follow her current train of thought. In any case, her career with IDS was finished, a distant reality, one she was happy to leave behind.

She had not heard from Colby since yesterday. He was not answering her calls this morning, which concerned her a little. Most likely nothing had changed on his end, he'd gone to Cancun, had a few too many shots of tequilla, and was sleeping off the hangover. It was his own fault for not switching to synthehol, but he claimed it tasted 'like a bad idea gone sour,' and didn't have the buzz of the real thing. She was not fond of the taste of alcohol in any of its varieties, including the synthesized version, and got a better buzz from a good gourmet meal.

Beer was Colby's gourmet passion. How could she blame him for honoring his taste buds, when she was always honoring her own? She missed him and hoped there was nothing wrong.

It was approaching midday and the sea stretched in all directions without sight of land.

Sola turned to face away from the bright glare of sunlight on the water's surface.

Jaitain and Olanii were sitting close together near the bow, talking in low voices and trying to adjust a malfunctioning communications unit. So far, they were having little luck. The unit sent out periodic squeals and the static of band fluctuation, and then fell completely silent again.

There had been a discussion earlier about the potential hazards of using communications equipment at all, even her PCU. Olanii and Dukal were concerned loyalists or Caifanii military personnel might detect the transmissions. Jaitain hoped to make audio connections with Amilio and Sum to inform rebel supporters of their imminent arrival. In the end, their equipment itself won the argument in favor of radio silence, and Sola agreed to hold off on using her PCU. Eilfina and Mako were below making noise in the galley, and Dukal was at the helm.

Sola sank down onto the deck, her head under a fickle sliver of shade from the main sail.

The air was cooler than usual, and there were banks of clouds forming along the starboard horizon. She wondered if the weather was going to turn on them. The rainstorm at the close of her encounter with the naia, was the last one they'd encountered.

That seemed odd to her, given this planet's regular propensity for afternoon cloudbursts. She'd asked Dukal about it. He said that the dry weather was unusual for this stretch of sea at this particular time of the year and that they could simply count themselves lucky. The steady winds and lack of rain might cut as much as a day from their travel time.

Sola settled into the luxury of laziness. She was beginning to think she was a cat, sleeping every other minute! The ship rose over each wave as if taking in a deep breath, and relaxed down again between swells. She closed her eyes and let her mind drift along the borders of sleep, her thoughts crossing over into last night's unfinished dreams, in and out of consciousness with the rise and fall of the ship.

Thunder roared like a disgruntled lion close enough to take warning. A spray of seawater washed over the railing and onto the back of Sola's head, instantly waking her.

Water was collecting on deck and she was awash in it. The clouds congregated overhead in a hurry. It began to rain, hard.

Sola grabbed hold of the mast and stood up. Jaitain and Olanii were taking down the jib sail and securing it to the deck. The ship lunged, throwing Sola off balance and thrusting her forward. She held tightly to the mast, the moisture making her grip difficult to maintain. She started working to take down the mainsail. The ship rolled substantially in the heightened swells. Jaitain and Olanii came to help her. Together they folded the sail and secured it to the deck, then they scampered, squirrel-like, towards the hatchway in the heavy downpour, soaked to the skin. The ship was heeling considerably. Sola struggled to get below.

"Sola," Eilfina said. "You're wet as a fish! Let's get you into something dry. This storm really came on hard, and quickly!"

Sola followed Eilfina into the rear of the compartment. Jaitain and Olanii were also there looking for dry clothes.

"I am out of clean clothes at the moment," Eilfina said, "but we can find something for you Sola."

Once Sola was dry and dressed, she dropped into a rear seat. Mako and Dukal swiveled their seats around to face her.

Mako looked at Sola's outfit. "I think those look quite a bit better on you, Sola!" he said, poking Dukal and breaking into a chuckle.

"These are yours, Dukal?" Sola asked, tapping her pants and shirt, and feeling a little awkward.

"Yes," he said, looking embarrassed. "I'm honored," he said, sheepishly. "You are welcome to take my clothing anytime."

She doubted he was being flirtatious, he seemed innocent, reserved, but the unintended joke was a good one.

"Very funny, Dukal!" Mako said, reaching over and rubbing the top of Dukal's head.

"Are we running on instruments?" Sola asked.

"Yes, but it means very little," Dukal said, glad to be out of the previous conversation. "We are using a small motor to maintain our position as best as possible. There isn't much we can do in this weather." He pointed to the view screen in front of them, which looked like a murky aquarium. "We can't see anything."

"Is it dangerous, being out in a storm like this?" she asked.

"Not terribly," Mako said. "In some ways, it might be less dangerous. We're not likely to be spied from the air in this kind of weather, plus the winds are out of the north, so even without the sails we will gain some distance."

"So, you think we're still undetected out here, Mako?" she asked, rubbing her hair with a towel to soak up the moisture.

"It's difficult to say," he responded. "We've been lucky so far."

Dukal frowned. "I worry they know exactly where we are and plan to meet up with us once we reach the waters off Amilio."

"Why do you think that?" Sola asked.

"Because he is paranoid." Mako said, trying to keep the mood light.

"I am not paranoid, Mako. I just find it difficult to believe that we have sailed for over three days under a completely clear sky without somebody, somewhere spotting us!"

"So what if they did?" Mako said. "They probably assumed we were a pleasure cruiser."

"Right!" Dukal said, his voice coming to an edge. "A pleasure cruiser made out of a city transport vehicle! Not likely!"

"You have a point, my friend," Mako said. The tone of his voice was soft, calming. "Maybe we are just blessed with luck. Maybe Sola brings us good fortune."

Sola felt her cheeks flush. She hoped Mako was right. Their luck certainly had been good so far. She didn't want any credit for it, but she was ready to be grateful.

"Well, no one is likely to find us in this storm!" she said, trying to sound cheerful.

The craft was listing severely from side to side. Sola felt seasick. Without sails, they would make slower progress. An outboard motor was not going to give them much propulsion in a sea this rough.

"Will the storm last long?" she asked.

"As long as it pleases," Eilfina said, coming to sit in the seat next to Sola and placing her hand affectionately on Sola's knee. "We'll be fine. I have seen weather ten times worse than this out here!"

Sola wondered about the personal protocols between these rebel comrades. No one wore gloves, no one seemed to notice each other's naked hands and everyone showed a level of affection not customary to Caifanii behavior, as she understood it.

She wondered about the potential intimate relationships between the others. She and Jaitain were the only ones sharing a bunk. At least one of the crew was on duty at all times, so four bunks were sufficient for the six of them.

Eilfina was very physically affectionate with everyone, offering a quick embrace or a light touch. It was difficult for Sola to gauge Caifanii attractiveness with complete accuracy, but there was no doubt Eilfina was stunning and a real fire ball.

Mako had tremendous charm and was flirtatious. Dukal was so self-absorbed that it was difficult to read him. His always seemed somber and carried his introspection like a protective cloak held tightly around him. He was obviously the youngest, by several years.

Olanii was certainly the eldest, probably a good decade older than Jaitain. She had a stately posture and self-assured manner. Her eyes were such a light shade of blue-gray they looked almost translucent, giving her face a mystical quality. She had the gaze of some ancient mage. Sola imagined Olanii with hair. It would be silver, long and thick and it would make a curling, wild spectacle of itself all around her earnest, intelligent face.

Sola realized, in the process of her musings, that she had grown very fond of her companions, especially Eilfina who treated her as a sister. She never before found this level of companionship on an alien world. Her assignments did not allow her the time or occasion for developing friendships. That continued to be the main pitfall of her career choice. She missed her friends and she often lamented the lack of genuine socializing associated with her adventurous, "here today, gone tomorrow" lifestyle, or her, "here today, gone to Maui!" lifestyle, as the old expression goes. She soaked in the affection she felt now, letting its vital energy seep deeply into her dry roots.

The storm lasted the better part of the night. The others traded shifts at the helm to keep an eye on instruments and see that the craft stayed on course, as much as possible.

Sola knew how to sail, but this craft was no yacht. To console her sense of uselessness, she filled the water kettle, heated it on the stove, which rocked from side to side, and kept her companions supplied with cups of tea. Staying down below was the only dry option, but turned her stomach. Sleeping in this much of a roll was impossible. She got miserably seasick trying. Instead, she kept each of the helmsmen, and women, company through the night.

By the time Jaitain was at the helm, in the darkest center of the night, the swells calmed, and the rain came from behind them, lightly, and still on a steady wind from the north. Jaitain decided it was time to hoist the sails. He woke up Mako and the two of them went out into the remnant of the storm. Jaitain was luffing the craft to get as much forward motion as possible, and to keep it from sideswiping in the swells. They needed to increase their speed to make up for lost time. Sola was in desperate need of some fresh air, and stuck her head out of the hatch to fill her lungs with it and quiet her turbulent stomach. The rain was gentle and warm. The storm was passing.

They ran for several hours with the north wind filling the sails. Near dawn, the storm had blown itself out completely. The wind died down to almost nothing. The ship was close to lying in irons. It was a good time to catch up on rest.

Sola's sleep was deep and left behind a nasty headache. She heard someone moving about in the cabin, as she now affectionately referred to the compartment of the vessel. She got up, had a drink of water and went on deck hoping to take a brief dunk in the sea to wake up and clear her head. Dukal was sitting with his back against the mast. Both sails were slack. There was not a breath of wind. The ship rolled softly in the gentle swell. The sea was a calm lake. It was an eerie contrast to last night's chaos.

"Greetings, captain," she said to Dukal, raising her hand in mock salute.

"Did you have a good rest, Sola?" he asked.

"Yes, I guess so. I could use a quick swim though. Do you think it would be all right?"

"I don't see any reason not to. I doubt we are moving a millimeter at the moment," he said. "Our outboard motor ran out of fuel in the night from running it nonstop through the storm." He looked worried, then again he always looked worried. Perhaps today he had good reason. They were losing valuable time, but Sola wasn't ready to worry. The storm was history and that was enough to make her grateful, especially for the sake of her stomach!

Sola didn't want to embarrass Dukal by shedding her clothing in front of him, especially since it was his clothing. She decided to take her dive from the rear of the ship, in her underwear, behind Dukal and out of his view. The water was a shock. It felt cold, although it was probably no less than 20° C. She floated on her back and let her hair drift out around her head. After a few minutes, she turned and took a shallow dive to see what might be frolicking beneath the surface. She didn't see any action, no schools of bright fish, not even the many smaller inhabitants of the blue. The sea looked empty. It was an odd feeling and made her slightly nervous. Where was everyone today? She surfaced and swam out a little from the boat. It felt wonderful to move, to stretch her muscles. The water felt almost warm now that she had become accustomed to it. She rolled over and looked at the cloudless, slightly hazy sky. The moment was delicious.

She kept an eye on the boat to make sure she wasn't drifting too far out.

After taking in a good dose of warm sunlight on her face, she dove again hoping to see some colorful wildlife this time.

The sea was eerie and silent. Maybe the storm chased the fish elsewhere. Something moved, about 50 meters away. Even from that distance, it looked large. It was definitely not a fish. It moved like a snake through the water but had legs, some sort of sea lizard. It looked prehistoric. Its long, reddish shape snaked stealthily in her direction. Her body shot full of adrenaline. The creature bore a striking resemblance to the mythical sea monsters painted on the edges of 12th century world maps, sea monsters with dragon tails, fiery eyes, and scaly heads.

She swam towards the ship. It had drifted a considerable distance, or maybe it had begun to move forward. Between breaths on the surface, she swam underwater, sideways so that she could watch the creature's movements. It did not seem interested in her. That was good, but it was definitely getting closer. That was not good. Whatever this thing was, it looked nasty and might be the reason that all of the other fish were nowhere in sight.

She tried to calm her mind, and keep her movements smooth, knowing that predators read frenetic movement as an invitation to dine. She surfaced next to the ship. The ropes on the pontoon were well out of her reach. The rubbery material of the pontoon was too slick to gain a handhold. She could attempt to force herself up out of the water high enough to maybe reach the rope on the top of the pontoon, but if she failed, her attempt would create just the kind of turbulent water ballet that identified her as prey.

She swam along the side of the craft towards the rear, looking for another rope or ladder. After her previous swim, the crew had hoisted her aboard. Maybe there was no rope or ladder.

She called to Dukal. She couldn't see him from sea level. Maybe he was no longer on deck. She sunk back underwater to check on the position of the creature. It was only about twenty-five meters from her, the length of a lap pool, and gliding back and forth. She felt stalked. It was close to two meters long, and looked like a giant red iguana. She guessed it could move fast, if it wanted.

She tried to calm her mind. This was no shark, but she sensed its shark-like aggressiveness. She tried to recall the protocol for a shark encounter. She remembered a story about a man whose craft crashed into the Pacific. He survived for two days before his rescue. He spent those two days floating around in an inflated body suit, punching sharks in the nose with his fist to ward them off. Why was she thinking about this? She surfaced again and called Dukal at the top of her lungs. This time his head appeared.

"Help!" she shouted. He came running and leaned over the pontoon. She reached her arm as high up as she could manage. He caught her hand and hauled her out of the water just as she felt something grab her left leg. A sharp pain shot up her calf. The creature had her leg. Dukal was screaming and pulling her up while beating on the creature's head. Mako arrived, and began to beat on the creature as well. There was a loud explosion. She felt the creature release its hold, as the pontoon began to deflate beneath her. Dukal and Mako pulled her up and she collapsed on deck. Blood covered her foot.

"Get the medical supplies, quick!" Mako shouted.

"It's swimming over here now!" Eilfina shouted from the starboard side.

Sola saw Dukal run over to her and heard the two of them shouting and then throwing something heavy into the water to ward off the creature.

The ship was listing seriously to port. Water was starting to flood the deck. Sola lay back against Mako, who sat behind her holding onto the main mast so as not to slide off the raked deck. She felt dazed. Her body was flooding with endorphins. Something was very wrong with her leg. The pain was almost overwhelming her capacity to stay conscious. She also felt extreme panic, the kind caused by chemicals like epinephrine. Her heart raced. It was difficult to breathe.

Sola heard Jaitain shout. "We need to go airborne, now! This pontoon is half empty."

Mako crawled to the hatch, pulling Sola behind him, and carried her down into the cabin. Her leg was on fire with pain.

She screamed, not able to contain the sound. Mako's face looked blurry. There were odd clouds of color washing over her vision, pink, green, yellow. She closed her eyes. The wash of color remained, became more pronounced. She was floating in clouds of almost fluorescent color, in and out of consciousness.

There was a lot of noise, shouting, banging, more shouting, more banging, and then another loud explosion as the creature apparently ripped into the starboard pontoon. Everyone scrambled down below deck. She heard the roar of engines and felt the craft lift. They were airborne, hopefully without their vicious hitchhiker!

She opened her eyes again. Jaitain was holding her hand and stroked her forehead. Mako produced a nasty looking needle and said he wanted to give her a shot for the pain and to antidote the poison.

"Poison?" she said, her mouth felt dry. She nodded and closed her eyes, keeping them open made her dizzy.

"Don't worry," Jaitain said against her ear. "He is a trained doctor. He knows what he's doing."

She felt the sting of the needle going in but it was brief, already subdued by the veil of stupor that clouded her awareness.

Whatever the stuff was, it worked fast. Within a few minutes, the pain became less intense and more distant. She looked up at Jaitain's worried face almost obscured by a swirling cloud of chartreuse light, and then she felt herself fade away into a drugged sleep. A violent dream erupted in her mind.

She was in a burning building. There were hundreds of people and animals, some Terran, some from other worlds. Everyone ran, screamed, trying to find a way out. There were mothers with small children, and frail elderly people stumbling around. She was shouting to everyone to get down on the floor to escape the accumulating smoke and fumes. No one listened to her. Three zebras passed in a small stampede, knocking her to the ground. She felt the heat of the smoke-filled air burn her throat and lungs.

She began crawling down a long, dark corridor. There was a narrow band of light shooting out from under a doorway. She tried to reach the light, but the closer she came to the door, the smaller the band of light became until it disappeared. The fire rapidly approached from behind her. She felt the furnace of its draft shoot out ahead of its path. Her left foot began to singe from the blast of burning air.

She gasped, cried out in pain. Suddenly the doorway before her exploded with a back draft of fire and smoke that hit her body like a wall of molten heat. She felt her body burn like a dry tree. She felt her spirit funnel up out of her physical form like a whirling tornado sucking life force from her body and expelling it with explosive power from an opening at the top of her head.

Her consciousness raced violently up through the center of this funnel of energy until it flew out of the cone at its apex into a swirling cloud of charged particles and glittering light. Her consciousness entered a violet and rose nebula cloud. There was no physical sensation, no emotions or thought. She was no longer aware of any separateness. She was in the nebula cloud. She *was* the cloud. She *was* light. She was outside of time, outside of physical dimension. She floated as essence in a non-material expanse.

Sola woke from the dream, disoriented in her physical body, and in dimensional space.

She heard the drone of the engines. The luminescent colors were gone. She opened her eyes. There was only a deep blackness, so complete and vast that she was not certain if she was, indeed, awake. She felt her head resting on a pillow and her body on the mattress of the bunk beneath her. She was awake, but all she could see was darkness.

"I'm here, Nulini," Jaitain whispered, grasping her hand firmly, calling her out of her dream state and into a different nightmare. Her left leg from her toes to her hip was on fire with pain. She was lying on a bunk in the cabin. It was so dark, much darker than the partial dark of the Caifanii night. She could not see anything.

She drew in her breath and winced. "Jaitain, what's happening? Why is it so dark?"

She could hear his voice, but it was a struggle to understanding what he was saying. Swirling clouds still confused her thinking.

"Nulini, you need to rest. Let me explain when you are lucid."

"Please explain now," she whispered, "Please."

"Okay," he said, gently. "As Dukal lifted you out of the water that creature, its called a kygne, bit into your leg."

"I saw it in the water. It looked like an ancient dragon."

"Encounters with the kygne are rare, and almost always lethal. It does not live in these waters. It is amphibious and lives on an island hundreds of kilometers north-west of here."

"A good island to avoid," she whispered.

"My guess is, it was swept south by the storm currents. It was desperate to climb aboard our floating island. It's not a long-distance swimmer."

"Desperate to take a bite out of me!" she said, hoping humor would save her from the fear growing inside of her mind.

You were fortunate. It had a loose fang, likely abscessed inside the gum. Biting down must have caused it considerable pain. Having Dukal and Mako beat on its head at the same time, and then the explosion as the pontoon ruptured was enough to make it abort its mission to consume you! The loose fang came out, along with a considerable amount of the creature's blood. The fang remained imbedded in your calf muscle."

"So all that blood on my leg was not my blood?"

"Not only your own, also the creatures."

"Gross!"

Jaitain hugged her.

"If that fang had been healthy and strong," he said, "the kygne might have held on, possibly breaking your bones with the pressure of its jaws, and tearing off your lower leg completely."

Sola winched involuntarily.

"I will stop," Jaitain said, "this is causing you additional trauma."

"No. I need to know. How bad is it?"

"There is penetration damage from the fangs to your muscle tissue, but luckily no torn tendons. Mako repaired the damage as best as possible, but you need additional medical attention."

Minerva had surgical energy fusers onboard that could restore damaged tissue instantaneously, but Colby was miles above them, staring down at this planet floating like a huge blue marble in a sea of star spangled black.

"The kygne injects poison to subdue its prey," Jaitain continued. "It managed to deposit its venom into your blood stream before it broke free. That's why you are in such pain."

She was silent, and searched for his hand. He grasped it immediately. She held on tight, beginning to realize, with a rush of panic, that the darkness around her was not a lack of light in the cabin.

"Jaitain," she said, "I'm blind! I can't see!" Her mind flooded with fear and anxiety.

"Yes. I understand, Nulini," he said. "It should be temporary. We have to hope it is temporary. It's a reaction to the poison. The kygne blinds its prey. The individuals who survive kygne attacks lose their vision for a matter of some hours, it returns if they are treated properly."

"Hours? Have I been treated properly?" she asked. "Will I be able to see again?" Her heart felt like a pile driver in her chest.

"Mako was able to inject a general antidote into your bloodstream only minutes after the attack. I think you will fully recover."

"A general antidote?"

"A plethora of poisonous creatures live on the southern continent. Our medical kit always includes a general antidote. Kygne bites are rare. We don't carry anything to counter its specific poison."

"That's not reassuring," Sola said.

She was starting to feel exhausted just from talking.

"Your general antidote is designed for Caifanii body chemistry. Will it even work for me?"

"We can only hope, Nulini. The fact that you are conscious is a very strong indication that the antidote is working."

All of this information was coming to Sola through a veil of mental fog, from far away, as if it were unrelated to her life. She tried to talk again. She didn't have the physical energy. Instead, she focused her thoughts, directed them at his mind without verbal words.

"Yes," he said, sounding excited. "Yes. I can get the green bag for you. Is there something in it that might help?"

She told him, with her mind, to give her two of the pills in the small red vial in the white pouch marked with a red cross, and to place these under her tongue. She waited to see if he had heard her thoughts.

She felt his hand release hers. She heard him move away. After a few minutes, he was back. She heard the zip of her bag opening. He had understood! The red vial, she thought again trying to direct him.

"Yes. The red vial," he said. "Under the tongue. Yes. Open your mouth, Nulini, I have two pills here."

She opened her mouth, her tongue felt heavy as she lifted it. She felt him slip the pills into her mouth. They tasted sour. Indrohl was a strong herbal concoction of ancient Chinese origins that muted pain without numbing the mind. In a while, maybe, she would feel a little better.

"I keep telling myself that I cannot blame Dukal for letting you swim," Jaitain said, perhaps more to himself than to her. "These waters are widely known to be safe."

"Why didn't the naia come rescue me again?" she said, mostly to herself.

He stroked the back of her hand. It was a gentle gesture and so common among humans that she almost forgot the sexual overtones it might imply for him.

"The kygne is an apex predator. It eats anything that gets close enough. The naia are smart to stay far away, and they tend to seek calmer waters during a storm.

"We have creatures called sharks," she said, "in our oceans on Earth. They are not rare, but not poisonous either, although they can be deadly if they are provoked or hungry. Sharks rarely attack humans. I have seen them often viewed from the safety of a ship, and twice while in the water, surfing. They were not hungry. I was lucky."

"Nulini," he said, his voice sounding warm. "We saved the fang in a jar for you. We will have it thoroughly cleaned. It can be a talisman of your good fortune."

She hardly considered this experience good fortune, but, then again, she *was* alive and still had her left leg. She had been extremely lucky to survive.

She smiled feebly, "I seem to attract large sea-dwelling creatures?"

"And a few not so large land dwelling ones," he said caressing her hand affectionately. "You were doubly fortunate. It grabbed onto the pontoon with its claws and not onto you. Its claws do much more damage than its fangs. It punctured the pontoon in six places when it tried to crawl aboard."

"That explosion probably scared it off too."

"Yes. It swam to the other side, and tried to climb aboard there, shredding the starboard pontoon so badly we almost sank. It took some serious teamwork to get the masts down and get us airborne before the engines swamped."

"I almost feel sorry for it. I would grab onto whatever I could find out in the open ocean too!"

"I had a brief inclination to toss something out there it could float on, but saving its life puts a lot of other lives at risk, and I was too busy trying to save our lives!"

"I guess my recreational swim messed things up pretty badly!"

"I am angry at Dukal for encouraging you, but I can't really blame him. These waters are considered safe. We need to get you to Sum as soon as possible. I know someone there who can help you heal."

"A doctor?"

"A Tumasei," he said. "In the Mhalanai tradition, the Tumasei is the keeper of the spirit medicine."

"Kahuna," she whispered, it was the Hawaiian word for a shaman.

Sola always chose modern science over ancient ceremony when it came to medicine, but she knew an old Kahuna in Hana whom she would trust with her life.

"A Kahuna is someone who practices ancient healing ceremonies, an expert with herbal cures and energy medicine?" Jaitain asked.

"Yes," she said, taking in a deep breath, and letting out a deep groan. "I need some spirit medicine!"

"Then it is our luck there is spirit medicine in Sum!" he said.

"High ho, Silver!" she said, almost inaudibly, trying to feel optimistic.

It was one of Colby's expressions. Poor Colby. He was up there somewhere, clueless about what was transpiring here on the surface, but probably worrying himself silly about her. Bless his soul.

"Can I try to reach Colby?" she asked. Every other second the darkness all around her and the thought of its potential permanence made her cold with fear.

"We are approaching the archipelago. I do not want to risk off-planet transmissions, too many potential ears nearby. Let's wait until we are safely in Sum."

"I can't talk anymore anyway."

"Close your eyes, Nulini. Rest so you can heal."

He was probably right. She squeezed his hand and closed her eyes. It didn't make any difference. It was dark either way. At least, with her eyes closed, the darkness felt more normal.

"Jaitain," she whispered, "the poison, hallucinogenic? Psychotropic? Psychedelic dream. Bad dream."

"I don't know," he said, "but the antidote is mixed with pain medication, an intravenous form of K, and that, my dear, can take you on quite the trip!"

"Trippy dippy." She was barely conscious.

She felt his lips touch hers lightly. She burst into tears from exhaustion, pain, and fear.

"I'm scared."

"I know, Nulini. I'm here. I'll stay with you."

He stroked her hair. "There is a line from the Prophecy of the Great day, in the Book of Ways," he continued, softly, 'The liberator will emerge from the mouth of a dragon.' I previously interpreted this as a purely metaphorical creation myth, but perhaps it is literally true."

"That thing sure looked like a dragon!" She said, feeling herself drifting into the relief of sleep.

Chapter 19

Day Eleven (morning)

Caio ye ruo umasi, caio ye ruo u nidia.
When we come close to death, we come closer to life.

The Mhalanai Book of Ways

Sola slept on and off through the night. The pain in her leg kept waking her and her fear of permanent blindness kept making it hard to fall back asleep. While awake, she said silent prayers to angels who might hear them. The thought of being in darkness indefinitely made her sanity feel insubstantial, like it might slip away at any moment.

Now, she lay very still in the bunk listened to the soft, regular breathing of the others sleeping. She did not hear anyone stirring in the cabin, but knew someone must be at the controls.

Last night, after she kept waking up, Jaitain offered to sleep apart from her so as not to disturb her or accidentally bump her in his sleep and cause her more pain but, she insisted he stay with her in the bunk. She needed him close. She could not bear being alone with her fear.

She heard the others begin to stir.

Jaitain woke up and gave her a gentle embrace.

"How are you feeling? Did you sleep?" he whispered."The pain is less severe," she said. "I drifted off."

She gazed into the grey place she knew contained his face.

"I can see the outline of your head. Oh, wait! I just saw your eyes, for a brief moment!"

"That's excellent progress!" he said, and kissed her on the forehead.

"Land!" she heard Olanii shout. She must be at the controls.

That got everyone out of bed in a hurry. Sola heard them scurrying to dress.

"I'd better go to the helm," Jaitain said. "We are coming to the most dangerous passage of our journey, well, not including our encounter with the dragon! Do you want to sit with us? Do you feel ready? I could carry you to a chair."

Sola decided it was worth a try. "Sure."

Jaitain got up, carried her to the front of the cabin, and deposited her into a chair.

Everyone was happy she was out of bed and there were loving words all around her.

How is your vision this morning?" Mako asked.

"I am seeing some shapes and the darkness is definitely not as dense. I even got a glimpse of Jaitain's eyes a while ago!" Sola said.

"That's a treat!" Eilfina said. "He has such gorgeous eyes, yes?"

"Stop," Olnaii said, "you'll make him blush."

"You'll make him vain!" said Mako. "Sola, you are showing wonderful improvement. This likely means the blindness will not be permanent."

"I think I will keep *my* eyes closed," Sola said. "What I can see is pretty disorienting."

"Whatever's best," Mako said.

"I can describe what we see in the view screen for you," Olanii offered. "We are about 100 kilometers from the coast. When I first spied it, it was like a mirage of a dark, green ribbon floating on the horizon. Now, we can discern the coastal range with its jagged ridges and we can just barely make out a few slivers of beach." She chuckled lightly. "Eilfina is doing a little dance. Oh, wait, now Mako has joined her and they are dancing together to celebrate coming home."

Sola felt their excitement even without seeing them.

"Sola," it was Dukal's voice. "I know that you will recover," he said earnestly.

"Thank you, Dukal," she said.

"I do not understand how this happened to you," he continued, "after the naia gave you such a rare gift. I can't understand it."

"That makes two of us. I guess we have to ride the swells and hope for the best." Sola's optimistic tone belied her inner turmoil.

"Is it still very painful?" Dukal asked.

"My leg still hurts, but nothing like before," she said. "My eyes do not hurt. I am keeping them closed because what I see is a dark fog and it makes me dizzy."

"Perhaps you would prefer to not talk about it," he said.

She could hear him scuffling around.

"No," she said, trying to reassure him. "I appreciate your concern, Dukal. I think it's probably good for me to talk about it. It makes me feel less afraid."

"I am happy to help you if you need anything."

Dukal's concern touched her because it was so out of character for him to share his feelings.

"Thanks, Dukal. That means a lot to me."

"I need to run some scans," he said, "stay vigilant."

She heard him turn his chair back around to face the control panel. His worry was well justified. If they could see land, it could probably see them.

"Do you think they know we are up here?" she asked Jaitain, who was standing next to her chair, holding her hand.

"I guess we will find out soon enough," he said. "We're running a cloaking transmission to shield us from electronic detection, but it is difficult to know if the device is effective, it's experimental."

Sola sensed a cautious anticipation and guardedness among the crew. Their earlier exuberance evaporated.

"Everyone seems pretty worried," she said.

"We know this is the risky part," he said. "In fact, I need to get actively involved at this point. Would you like to stay up here, or would you prefer to be back in the bunk? How do you feel?" he asked.

She thought about that for a moment. "I don't know. I think I want to stay here, to be close to all of you."

"Good. It will take us a while to reach Amilio, where we will land. We will keep a good distance from shore until we are closer to that destination. We have some cloud cover moving in, so that's helpful." He smoothed her hair with his hand, kissed her head, and then moved away.

Nothing much happened for some time. Sola sat listening to the others talk and move around in the cabin.

Eilfina came and sat next to her and talked for a while. Later Mako came to check on her wounds and look into her eyes. She could see shapes more regularly, and the fog was no longer as dense. She felt reassured and dosed off to sleep in the chair.

"On the left!" Mako shouted.

Sola woke with a start from the sound of weapons fire.

Something hit the ship. It was knocked off course, but the hull was intact.

"I need twice as much power to the rear thrusters!" Jaitain said.

"This is all they have!" Dukal shouted.

"I am trying to redirect power to the weapons array, but the commands are not responding," Mako shouted.

"Keep trying," Jaitain said. "I will continue to use evasive maneuvers."

There was more weapons fire off to their right. This time not directed at their ship.

"I think that second ship is on our side," Dukal said.

Sola felt her body thrust from side to side in the chair. She closed her eyes tightly. Even a glimpse of her foggy vision at this particular moment made her terribly dizzy.

She had a million questions, but everyone was obviously too engaged in trying to save their lives to provide any answers.

She heard a shockingly loud explosion and the sound of an engine sputtering to a halt.

"We lost the starboard engine. Direct hit. We are losing fuel, a lot of it!" Dukal shouted.

"The ship could blow at any time!" Mako shouted.

"Bile!" Jaitain shouted. "Keep me level as best as you can. We need to get as close to the water as possible without hitting the surface."

The ship was careening out of the sky at an alarming angle.

"Abandon ship!" Jaitain shouted. "Now!"

The ship was shaking violently.

Someone unfastened Sola's safety belts, pulled her forcefully out of the seat and carried her just a few steps before a harrowing moment of freefall. She hit water, feet first. An explosion of pain shot up her left leg. She blanked out. She was pulled to the surface of the water.

She opened her eyes for a second and was shocked to see Olanii's face clear as a bell and very close, before the fog returned and she closed her eyes again.

There was another explosion, outside of her body this time. Olanii yelled, "Breathe deep and hold it." Sola did. They dove deep together and stayed down for as long as they could. She felt the impact of something heavy on water above them. When they surfaced, Sola sucked in a desperate gulp of air. Debris was floating all around them. The more buoyant remnants of their vessel bobbed in sullen silence. She could see them! She reached out for something to help her stay afloat. Olanii followed suit, then grabbed hold of Sola's hand and pulled her along. Sola tried to kick, but the pain was too intense.

She heard the sound of more weapons fire above them. Anticipating the worst, she dove again, Olanii followed. They went down even deeper this time, and stayed down in the cool darkness until Sola felt her lungs might burst. She could hear her heart beating. It sounded like a shaman's drum rising to the climax of a ritual dance.

She lost Olanii's hand, became disoriented, not sure which direction was up. Panic rushed into her veins as oxygen rushed out of her mouth. She could hear the bubbles rise up past her nose and forehead, becoming a compass.

She propelled herself upward, like a dolphin, using her whole body, not kicking her legs. She broke the surface and took in air with the dire hope that she would not pass out.

Something floated into her from behind, scaring the living daylights out of her, except she had no daylights. It was soft and buoyant. She turned and reached out. It was a seat cushion. She pulled it eagerly close to her chest and rested her head, breathing hard.

She thought of the kygne, wondered if it was still alive, desperately seeking land. There were periodic flashes of light in her eyes, but she could no longer see anything.

"Sola!"

The caller was not far away. She heard splashing and then the voice was very close.

"It's Dukal," the voice said, reaching her.

"I'm okay," she answered. "What's happening?"

"We are being rescued!" he said. "We need to move in this direction." He wrapped his arm around her waist and gently pulled her to the left. The seawater lapped at her face like the cold tongue of a dog.

Soon there were other voices around her.

"I can't believe it!" Olanii's shouted.

"How's Mako?" Dukal asked.

"Bleeding heavily," Jaitain said from somewhere behind her. "We have to get him out of the water! I can't slow the bleeding while he's in the water."

"Whose ship is that?" Olanii asked. Sola could hear the roar of engines high above them.

"I don't recognize it," Jaitain said. "Whoever they are, I'm glad to see them!"

"They certainly took care of that Loyalist vessel!" Dukal said.

Sola obviously missed a lot of the action, and was glad it missed her.

"How are you doing, Nulini?" Jaitain asked.

"I don't know," she said. "I feel like I am half dead."

The roaring of the engines above them grew even louder.

"The ship has a rope ladder descending towards us at this very moment!" Jaitain said.

"Mhalanai?" Sola asked.

"We assume so, they just vanquished our attackers."

"I need to get Mako up first. Dukal will help you up right after me."

Sola floated upright, the cushion clutched tightly against her chest. She felt very numb and wondered if she was going into mild shock.

She could hear a lot of splashing and then none. Jaitain must be on the ladder with Mako. After quite a few minutes, Dukal and Eilfina were beside her in the water. They helped her locate the rungs of the ladder. "They are only about this far apart," Eilfina said, directing Sola's hands.

"Yes, I think I can manage just using my right leg," Sola said. She tried to focus her attention. Something was nagging at her thoughts. "Eilfina! My green bag! I need my medications! Can you get it from the cabin? It is under the bunk on the right side."

"Sola?" Eilfina said, gently. "There is no cabin. The ship was completely destroyed." Her voice sounded calming but worried.

Yes, of course. She knew that, but for a brief instant, she forgot what happened. "I'm sorry Eilfina. I'm okay. I do remember. I was just confused."

"You may be going into shock," Eilfina said. Dukal and I will hold the ladder as steady as possible for you."

Sola began to climb.

It was much harder than she thought using only one leg. Without her companions to keep the ladder from spinning, she'd be a lost cause.

Her mind was on fire. No medications! No PCU! Why hadn't she kept it strapped to her wrist! She would have to deal with the implications of all of that later. She needed to focus. She was holding up traffic.

Sola opened her eyes. She saw the ladder clearly for a moment. She closed them again as the dark fog returned.

Her hands were shaking. When she reached the top, someone grabbed her securely beneath the arms and hoisted her up into the vessel. They led her further into the ship and asked her to wait on a bench seat.

She heard Eilfina and then Olanii come up the ladder. Dukal was last. There was the metal against metal sound of the hatch closing and locking into place and then immediately they were moving upward and forward. She reached out to grab hold of something to steady herself. She found an arm covered with a material unfamiliar to her touch.

"This is our esteemed guest, Sola Alturas," Olanii said. "She has done incredible work for the liberation, and has temporarily lost her vision," she explained.

"How is Mako?" Sola asked.

"We have him on monitors," an unfamiliar voice said, the voice that went with the unfamiliar material on the arm she was still holding tightly. She released her grasp now that the ship was steady.

"Do you think it was a single patrol unit, Olan?" Dukal asked. "Did they have time to radio for support?"

"Who can say," said Olan. His name sounded like a masculine version of Olanii. Olan continued, "It wasn't an official military vessel. It was older, but renovated in some unusual ways. It was not easy to overpower their weapons system, fairly advanced. No identification on the hull. Certainly loyalist, but not a vessel we've encountered before. Whoever they were, let's hope that they didn't relay their location before they went down."

"I think we need to assume they did," Olanii said. "Did any of their crew survive?"

"We searched the debris," Olan said. "Found no survivors. The impact was severe."

"That is unfortunate," Olanii said.

"Yes," Eilfina said, "but fortunate that our lives have been spared! Let us rejoice in that!"

"Without your assistance we had no chance," Olanii said. "Our vessel had such limited fire power. How did they appear so quickly? I have never experienced an ambush of this sort. Luckily, you showed up quickly as well."

"We spotted your vessel prior to spotting theirs. It did seem to appear out of thin air. We could not get a signal lock on their craft until after it began to fire on your vessel," Olan said. "Let's move up to the bridge. I'm not being a very good host."

Jaitain was already on the bridge and came to embrace her.

She'd mustered all of her energy to stay standing on her right leg, and appreciated his support. He led her gently by the arm, and they sat down in chairs.

After only a few minutes, Sola heard Jaitain rise from his chair. "Meil!" he said. "How tremendous to see you! How long has it been? A year?"

"Try two! The last time I saw you, we were at my sister's wedding!" Meil said. His voice sounded rich and commanding. It was the voice of an older man, Sola decided, and a very charismatic one.

"I've been keeping up on my underground networking," Meil said. "I knew you would be in the area soon and thought you might need some assistance. I didn't expect it to be of *this* kind."

Sola could feel the genuine love these two had for each other. Her empathic powers seemed to be progressing. She could feel the joy and warm affection these two males had for each other as if it were a tangible force.

"I want you to meet someone very special, Meil," Jaitain said, touching her arm lightly. "Sola, this is one of my best and longest standing friends, Meil," the words were spoken with tender respect.

"By 'long standing' I suppose you mean that I am still standing despite all of the dangerous assignments I seem to attract!" Meil said. "Sola Alturas, I am honored to meet you."

Sola wanted to show her respect for this person so obviously dear to Jaitain. She pushed herself up out of the chair to stand and promptly passed out cold.

She regained consciousness on the floor. She opened her eyes and saw a gathering of anxious faces peering down at her. Jaitain was holding a glass of something green. Olanii and Eilfina were rubbing her arms and Meil looked particularly distraught. It wasn't until a good two seconds had passed that Sola realized the significance of what she was seeing: the fact that she *was* seeing!

"Hey, I can see all of you!" she said.

Everyone relaxed to have her back among the living. Sola felt a little giddy, this time with relief. She smiled up at Meil's handsome, fatherly face.

"I am very glad to meet you Meil," she said. "I guess I wasn't a very long standing friend." She thought the pun was grand.

Meil laughed. "Well," he said. "It is good to see that you have a valiant sense of humor, a valuable trait for any Mhalanai supporter. We will get you some ice for your leg, and we are making arrangements for you to see Ailva as soon as you arrive in Sum."

"Ice sounds excellent," she said. "Thank you. Jaitain, can you help me up onto a chair. I think I'll be all right."

"Now, do not rush anything, Nulini. You blew out like a candle. Here, drink this. It will help restore your electrolytes."

"Oh, damn!" Sola said, as her vision disappeared again.

"What is wrong?" Jaitain asked.

"My eyes have gone cloudy again," she said, closing them once more. "But, heck, that was a good several seconds longer than the last clearing."

Olanii propped Sola up a little to help her drink. "I'm feeling quite pampered, I want you all to know," Sola said.

"And well you should be!" Olanii said. "Eilfina, can you go get some ice packs from Olan?"

"Sure. I'll be right back."

"Talk about a rebel indoctrination!" Olanii added. "You've had quite a day!"

"Meil," Sola said. "Let's have another formal introduction when I am back on my feet okay?"

"That sounds like a good plan, Sola. Please rest."

Jaitain lifted Sola carefully up onto a cushioned bench where she could lie down for a while. He was very strong for his size. Sola was amazed at how well she sensed people's presence without seeing them, another aspect of the gift she received from the naia.

Eilfina arrived with some ice packs, which she placed carefully around Sola's swollen leg.

"That feels good," Sola said. "I appreciate it. How is Mako?"

"He is stabilizing, but still unconscious. His injuries are severe. Olan is taking care of him, but I need to return to him too. Just let Jaitain know if there is anything further you need."

She smiled, but her eyes looked frightened.

"Thank you. I will."

Sola said a little prayer to her angels for Mako, and then dropped off to sleep.

When she awoke, she felt considerably better. Her electrolytes must be back in balance. She took a deep breath, hoped for the best, and opened her eyes. Her vision was clear! She sat up slowly. Other than a mild headache, she felt decent. She scanned the room to get a sense of the space. There were several instrument stations and a large view screen currently filled with a stretch of clear blue sky. She didn't see any of her crew mates, but Meil was standing at a workstation a few meters away.

"Meil?" she said softly. He turned and headed over to her.

"Sola! You are feeling better?" There was such affection in his voice, that she felt physically warmed by it.

"Yes, much. Thank you."

"I'm calling everyone together for consultation in a few minutes. We are well underway to Sum, and we need to discuss plans. Are up for joining us?" he asked.

"Yes," she said.

Meil went to gather the tribe.

Chapter 20

Day Eleven (afternoon)

I'll see you on the dark side of the moon.

Brain Damage
Pink Floyd

When they arrived, Sola greeted them with open eyes. "I'm a veritable falcon!" she said. "I can see normally again! My leg feels a bit better too, from the ice treatment."

"That's fantastic!" Jaitain said.

"Let's use my conference room," Meil said.

Jaitain placed his arm around Sola's waist, gave her a squeeze and carried her into the room.

There was a small oval table made of some kind of metal in the center of the room and nine chairs encircling it. Everyone sat down. Jaitain, Sola and Olanii sat along one curve facing Meil, Dukal and Eilfina on the other. Eilfina looked pale and withdrawn.

"Sola," Meil said. "You're not standing at the moment, but let's have our formal introduction, as you requested. I wish to say a few things that I wanted to say earlier."

He paused for a moment, then went on.

"My new friend," he began in an elegant tone of voice, "you have quickly become a hero in our revolution. News travels fast through our underground networks, and faster still if it's good news. I am honored to meet you."

"Thank you Meil," Sola said, trying to sound as elegant and serious as he had. "I too am honored. Anyone who is so deeply respected by my friends receives my respect without question."

She and Meil looked at each other with respect. "There," said Sola. "I'd call that a very good formal introduction."

"I agree," Meil said. "Now, on to the business at hand."

"Yes," Jaitain said. "We planned to refuel near Amilio, then go on to Sum, obtain a faster ship from Atrina's eldest son, Finu, and head to Mhalnor, on the outskirts of Djintu City. Now, of course, we have no vessel to refuel."

"You *do* have a vessel, my friend. You have mine! I would not dream of anything less."

"Meil, you are a true brother. You'll bring us to Sum then?"

"Damn, Jaitain. You underestimate my offer. I'll take you to wherever you need to go!"

"So, you will take us to Mhalnor?" His voice filled with a mixture of incredulity and gratitude.

"I would take you to the moons, and it sounds like that is precisely where you ought to go, my friend!" Meil said.

"What do you mean?" Jaitain said.

"I will explain in a moment." Meil said. "First, shall we offer a moment of silence," his voice took on a somber tone, "for the crew members of the loyalist vessel?"

"Their loss is our loss," Jaitain said, with genuine sadness.

Everyone sat in silence, mourning the deaths of the loyalists who had tried so damned hard to kill all of them. Sola was surprised and touched by what was obviously more than just a token gesture to love ones enemies.

After a considerable time, Meil spoke again. "Friends, I suggest we leave this tragic event behind us, and return our focus to what lies ahead."

Jaitain reached for Sola's hand and held it firmly.

Meil continued, addressing Sola now.

"I want to talk about how we may reunite you with your shuttle and her pilot."

Jaitain must have updated Meil about her situation. The entire purpose of this journey was to reunite her with Colby and send her on her way to her own world.

Somehow, she had misplaced that purpose in the midst of the intensity of the past days. It felt surreal to her now to think that soon she could be leaving Caifanii, perhaps never to return.

Since leaving the caves, she had not thought at all about her inevitable separation from Jaitain. It had been easy to imagine that she would stay here and celebrate his ultimate victory, but that was a romantic fantasy. She would go home, and Jaitain would return to Haikon, to the caves, to the unpredictable life of a revolutionary.

Instead of feeling elated at the thought of going home, she was almost dreading it. If it weren't for Colby, who would be ecstatic to see her, and whom she truly missed, she'd actually feel depressed.

Sometimes, when she was all over the map on some issue, Colby called her a complex carbohydrate. Her feelings were certainly complicated right now.

"May I suggest a plan?" Meil asked.

"By all means," Sola said. She stuffed her personal chaos under the rug, for later perusal.

"Forget meeting the shuttle in orbit. I do not think any Mhalanai vessels have the technology to create a docking bridge, or the agility and defensive shielding to withstand potential military attack. I hate to be blunt, but we can't rule out the probability that the agenda in Haikon is to find Sola and make sure she does not leave the planet."

"I still don't see the logic in that," Sola said, "but I recognize the leadership in Haikon does not follow my kind of logic."

"Meil," Jaitain said. "That's the absolute worst case scenario. Surely, there are other possibilities."

"Jaitain, I'm sorry. You know how I am."

"Do you think Colby is in danger?" Sola asked.

"Your pilot?"

"Yes."

"Our intelligence informs us that your shuttle is no longer in orbit above Haikon. If your pilot was concerned for his own safety, he might have gone for backup, or possibly moved his shuttle to the dark side of Lipo, our nearest moon."

"He is not just my pilot," Sola said. "He's my friend. He certainly would not leave me behind!" She felt a sickening twinge of concern that maybe for some reason that made total sense to him, Colby had done exactly that!

"He would not leave you behind!" Jaitain said, reassuringly.

"What if he was convinced I was dead?" she asked. "Haikon might be broadcasting that fiction."

"He saw the disc I gave you, right?"

"Yes."

"Then he knows not to trust Haikon. He must be using the moon as shielding."

"And that," Meil said, "is a perfect introduction to my alternative plan."

"You are a strategic wizard," Jaitain said. "There is no doubt about that, but before we engage in future plans, how are things looking right now? How safe is this air space?"

"We are monitoring all channels including secret military ones."

"Then you are even more of a wizard!" Jaitain said.

"You have to be clever, brother, just to survive, as you well know!"

"I lost my personal communications unit in the battle," Sola said. "Can we attempt to contact Colby?"

"Soon, but let's not draw any attention to ourselves with an off-planet transmission right now."

"I understand," Sola said. She'd just have to trust Colby was okay.

"Shall I tell you my plan?" Meil said eagerly.

"I'm all ears!" Jaitain said.

Sola was amazed at the translation of colloquialisms made possible by her semi-telepathic capacity. She was certain that Jaitain's original words did not translate directly as "I'm all ears." The TLC would probably have translated them as "I am listening."

She enjoyed the highly descriptive informality of this new form of translation, and the more informal feel of conjunctions.

"I'm all ears too!" she said. "And my eyes aren't doing as badly either!"

"Sola, I offer my regrets to you in advance for any details which may appear distasteful," Meil said. "I think this plan has a very good chance of working."

"Go ahead," Sola said, putting on her best grin. "Now you have intrigued me."

"The plan has two vital components and several crucial stages. The first component involves transporting you, Sola, to a waste containment facility on Lipo, and then arranging for Colby to rendezvous with you there."

He paused, looking nervous.

"The second component," he continued, "involves creating a staged death for you, Sola, making it appear to the authorities that you are no longer alive. That will buy us time, and get them off our tail. Both components will be more difficult to execute than they may at first appear." Meil gave each of them a searching look.

Sola smiled at Meil's use of the word execute and wondered if the double entendre was intentional.

The plan sounded sketchy, but she wouldn't judge it until she understood it better.

"That sounds like a dangerous plan, Meil," Jaitain said. "Is there life support on Lipo Base T-5? I am assuming that is where you intend we transport Sola? It's no longer a manned operation, if I remember correctly."

"Yes," Meil responded. "It was converted to computerized maintenance about three years ago, but the base headquarters was not dismantled."

"Well, a building is one thing, but what about atmospheric controls? They will not be operational. I doubt any power conduits remain intact."

Sola didn't like the sound of that.

"I'm badgering you with questions," Jaitain continued, "which I am certain you have already considered in detail. Please continue."

"We have connections inside the Municipal Waste Transport Department, which operates a facility about 26 kilometers from Djintu City," Meil said. "We could get Sola aboard a carrier."

"Are these reliable connections?" Jaitain asked.

"Very solid." Meil assured.

"Like the waste they are transporting," Sola added. It was a funny scenario, except for the unfortunate factor of her potential participation in it.

"Sorry, you sort of handed that to me," Sola apologized.

"I would never hand solid waste to you, my dear!" Meil said.

Everyone laughed.

"How is Mako doing?" Sola asked, suddenly reminded of his absence. He always appreciated a good joke.

Olanii answered. "I think he will make a full recovery. For now, he is resting in stasis. Thanks to his sister's donation of blood, his vital signs are back to a safe level."

"You are Mako's sister?" Sola whispered to her. Eilfina nodded.

Meil continued. "I realize that all of this sounds like a stretch, but let me provide some more details. Information we received just a few hours ago may provide a better alternative than using the Base T-5 headquarter facility."

"Okay, please continue," said Jaitain.

"The carrier Dahlnar is scheduled to transport a large quantity of waste materials to the lunar base in three days."

"Three days! That doesn't give us much time." Olanii said.

"The Dahlnar is essential to the plan. There are regular transports to T-5 every week, but only the Dahlnar has what we desperately need in order for our strategy to work, an on-board emergency shuttle craft."

"Aha!" Jaitain said.

Meil smiled broadly and paused for dramatic affect.

"Plus, the captain of the Dahlnar is a Mhalanai supporter!" Meil added. "She has been for years. I have many friends who are willing to vouch for her loyalty. My connections in the department have informed me that, as captain, Tjarlii will have the access codes for the carrier's shuttle bay and the craft."

Sola shook her head. Her deliverance might come from a female garbage truck driver named Charlie! That was a hoot!

"You think Tjarlii could allow Sola to use the craft to rendezvous with Colby? As captain, wouldn't she need some sort of authorization to use the craft, some sort of actual emergency?"

"That could always be doctored, but I have a different scenario in mind. I doubt the emergency shuttle has the capacity to dock with another craft in space. I am suggesting that Colby use the Dahlnar's shuttle bay. We don't know yet if the bay is large enough for two craft, but if not, Tjarlii could take the emergency shuttle out of the bay, letting Colby enter, pick up Sola, then depart. How large is your shuttle?" Meil asked Sola.

"It's fairly large, not as large as this ship, but close."

"That might be problematic. The bay is probably just large enough for the emergency shuttle, which is likely to be a small craft."

Everyone was quiet for a moment.

"There is another option," Meil said, "but it's pretty risky. Tjarlii could use the emergency shuttle to take Sola to the dark side of the moon. We get Sola set up with a spacesuit and oxygen.

Colby lands at their coordinates and Sola takes a moonwalk, hopefully not a very long one!"

"That is seriously risky!" Sola said.

"Yes, but it actually sounds workable," Jaitain said, "except for the spacesuit. Where do we get one of those?"

"Well, before we even go that far, let me admit that we have not yet contacted Tjarlii. We need to make sure we have thought of all contingencies and that everything is planned out carefully before we make any actual arrangements."

"So we don't know if she will do it," Olanii said.

"In theory, she should be able to help us," Meil said.

"It will be a risk to her career," Jaitain said. "She is enough of a supporter to take that kind of risk for us?"

"Everything has to be done very carefully," Meil said.

"What about her crew? How many on the vessel?" Jaitain asked.

"Now that's the real beauty of it!" Meil said. "There is only one other crew member because the vessel makes a quick journey, about 20 dhan round trip, *and* the other crew member on this particular trip..."

Eilfina interrupted, "Is a Mhalanai supporter?"

"No," Meil said, "is on vacation, and there will be no replacement for that particular run."

Jaitain waved his hand in the air, a Caifanii version of two thumbs up. "Yes. So we get Sola on board. Tjarlii uses the shuttle to take her to the moon. How does Colby arrive there at the same time without Haikon following him there with a fleet of military assistance?"

"That is where the fake death comes in!" Meil said, with perhaps a bit too much glee.

"Oh goody!" Sola said, putting on a mock frown.

"Again, let me offer my regrets, Sola," Meil said, "but I think this will be the most secure measure for your safety. Unfortunately, the details for this part of the plan are not yet well defined. Let me sketch them out as best as possible. Wait." Meil hesitated. "I think I have an even better idea." He paused, obviously pondering something intently.

Everyone watched him with anticipation.

"Why not?" he burst out. "The raid off the coast of Amilio."

"I begin to see your mind working!" Jaitain said.

"Is it not possible that Sola was killed during that raid?"

"Yes! Of course!" Jaitain said. "So our ship was not lost without a cause."

He ran his hand over his head, as if smoothing invisible hair. "We spread the word among the supporters that the Terran woman, Sola Alturas, was killed during a raid on our vessel by loyalists. We let the news saturate the underground in the Haikon area. Central Security and Hti's patrols will pick it up quickly."

"Wait a minute," Sola said. "Colby will pick up on it too. I don't want that!"

"We would contact him first, of course, let him know our plans."

"We'd better have a solid RJS," Sola continued, speaking mostly to herself.

"A what?" Eilfina asked.

"Oh," Sola said. "It's, well, it has to do with an old piece of literature about two young lovers from feuding families." She looked around the table. Everyone was staring at her.

"Do continue," Eilfina said.

"But we have more important things to discuss," Sola said.

"A good story is always useful," Olanii said.

"And this sounds like a good story," Jaitain added.

"Okay. Here's what happens. In order to escape her father's decree that she marry another man, the young woman, named Juliet, is secretly married to her lover, named Romeo. Juliet fears that if her father finds out what she has done, he will kill Romeo, or someone in her family will do so! Juliet's family priest, who married the couple, helps design a plan that will allow them to escape from the city and live in peace, without their families knowing what has happened. The plan reminds me of another plan I just heard about. Juliet fakes her own death by taking a temporary poison. She first sends a letter to her lover telling him to meet her outside the city limits, after the poison has worn off. Tragically, her lover, Romeo, never receives the letter. Instead, he hears the news that Juliet is dead without knowing that it is a ruse. Overcome with grief, he goes to Juliet's sarcophagus, sees her body, cold and silent. Not wanting to continue his life without her, he takes his own life by his own blade. When Juliet awakens from her state of temporary paralysis, she finds Romeo dead at the foot of her sarcophagus. She's overcome with grief and takes her own life, not wanting to continue without him. I think the story is supposed to illustrate the evils of feuding, but it makes a dramatic case for avoiding poor communications planning! Somewhere down the line, someone came up with the term, 'Romeo and Juliet Safety' to refer to security measures on critical communications. Now such measures are termed, 'RJS' for short. Sorry. I guess that was more than you really needed to know."

Everyone looked pained.

"Such a sad story!" Eilfina said.

"We will make sure Colby gets the message!" Dukal said. It was the first time he spoke during the meeting.

"We will make certain to have this RJS!" Meil said.

Sola felt only marginally reassured. "So what's next?" she asked, trying to sound chipper. She was beginning to get a very nasty headache. She needed a pepper and they were at the bottom of the sea, or in the belly of some colorful, and now hyped up fish.

"We are nearing Sum," Meil said. "Mako and Sola can receive excellent care from Ailva."

"Yes," Sola said. "Jaitain told me about her." she hesitated, collecting her thoughts. "Jaitain, I haven't had a chance to address this, but I lost everything on the ship, including my medications. I'm getting a nasty headache. My environmental stabilizers are beginning to wear off. I don't know how I'll feel without them, but I predict it won't be good. Eventually, it will be dangerous. Do you think there is anything Ailva can do for me?"

"I don't know, but she is a tremendous healer. She will be excited to meet you." Jaitain said.

"We can spend the night in Sum, but it would be prudent to continue on as soon as possible. Jaitain, I recommend we leave Mako in Sum. He will need additional medical care and time to recover."

"Yes, I assumed that as well." Jaitain said.

"It seems that main issue now is whether we contact Tjarlii," Olanii said.

"Yes," Meil said. "Let's decide if we want to pursue this."

There was about an hour of discussion.

Ultimately, Eilfina was the only one who remained skeptical of the plan, expressing her concern that it placed the fate of Sola into the hands of someone none of them knew personally.

Sola got the feeling that Eilfina's concerns were more an expression of her desire to keep Sola close to her.

Tjarlii seemed to have very stalwart credentials as a supporter and Meil, Jaitain and Olanii had all heard of her.

Olanii said she had even met Tjarlii a couple of times, a few years ago, and that she had been very impressed with her intellect, character and spirit.

If the plan had a flaw, it was not likely to be the dependability of the transport captain. Sola was more concerned about how Colby could rendezvous with them on the moon's surface. He was a dynamite pilot, but the shuttle was built to dock in the more hospitable terrain of a spaceport.

"It seems to me," Sola said, "that we need to talk with Colby before we make our next move. We need to know where he is, for starters. When will I be able to reach him?" Sola asked. "When we arrive at Sum?"

"Yes," Meil said.

"We cannot release word of Sola's death until we have spoken with Colby, but our plans demand immediate action. If we are going to use Tjarlii's craft, we need to contact her soon."

"That part of the plan does not require our reaching Colby first, does it?" Eilfina asked. "I mean, we can at least find out how feasible Tjarlii thinks the plan is, and if she is willing to help."

"Right." Jaitain said. "Everything can be arranged on a tentative basis dependent on the results of our communication with Colby."

"Tjarlii is doing the run in three days regardless of whether Sola is on board," Olanii said. "Eilfina's point is well taken. We can at least begin to move on that aspect of the plan. If the scenario changes we can adjust as we go."

"We can contact Tjarlii from Sum," Meil said.

"When will be arrive there?" Sola asked.

"We are approaching the outskirts now," Meil replied. "We can have a good, warm meal with our friends Kail and Raftja."

"I will make arrangements for you to see Ailva as soon as she's had a chance to work with Mako," Jaitain said.

The dense energy of discussion broke open into a flurry of excited movement and anticipation. They would be landing in Sum in a matter of minutes.

Sola was looking forward to meeting Ailva, hopeful that she would be able to get some relief for the headache that was now pounding in her temples. She was almost taking her sight for granted again, when only hours ago, she was living in dread of never regaining her sight at all. Now, seeing the world was just another expected sense. She tried to hold on to the wonder of it. Her blindness had made sight miraculous when it returned. She wanted to hold on to that miracle, to remember that it was all a miracle, the whole of life. Yet, even now, so far outside of her normal routines, it was easy to take things for granted. She didn't want to miss the myriad miracles imbued in the everyday.

The environmental stabilizers were definitely wearing off. She was beginning to feel heightened adrenal function, the first sign of increasing physiological stress.

Everyone strapped in. The landing was smooth and quick. Sola heard the engines slow, and then shut off completely.

Dukal left the bridge and returned in a few minutes with Olan. They carried Mako on a stretcher. He was conscious and lay smiling up at Sola.

"How are you feeling, comrade?" Sola asked.

"Like large parts of me are missing," Mako said, in a small voice.

"You look pretty good," Sola said in earnest.

He had good color in his face, although that might have been from the light reflecting off the silvery blanket wrapped around him.

"They have you rolled up like a burrito!" Sola said, knowing her metaphor was lost on him, but enjoying the apt description herself. "Looks like you're getting first class service."

They carried Mako carefully into the lift that would take them to the docking hold. Eilfina slipped her arm around Sola's waist and helped her hop on her right leg slowly after the medical team. Meil and Jaitain were up ahead and Dukal and Olanii were directly behind.

They waited in the hold and then the outer hatch opened to reveal three beaming-faced Mhalanai with arms outstretched in welcome.

Sola stepped across yet another threshold and into the warm embrace of a stranger.

Book Three

Ti comone u maya

I hold your name

The Mhalanai Book of Ways

Chapter 21

Day Eleven (late afternoon)

Miasi po uma li seim po iuwe.
Close your eyes and open your vision.

The Mhalanai Book of Ways

Jaitain helped Sola walk from Kail and Raftja's farmhouse across a flowering meadow to the small cottage where Ailva lived.

Sola stopped for a moment to stare at the scene before her. The cottage resembled the one at the edge of the forest clearing in her dream. She felt like pinching herself to make sure she wasn't dreaming now.

"Is it like your dream?" Jaitain asked.

"Yes," Sola said. "Almost exactly, and look there are so many plumeria trees here!"

"Yes. The o'plumia are abundant here, near the coast. They thrive on the moisture from the sea."

"I feel like I have just arrived home on Maui!" Sola said.

They entered the cottage and sat in the silence of a small anti-chamber, waiting for Ailva, who had been working with Mako for some hours, and likely needed to have a few moments of down time before seeing her next patient.

"Ailva will be here for you soon," Jaitain said. "I want to give you some privacy. Do you mind if I head back to the house?"

"I'm okay here alone. I'll see you in a while."

"I am certain you will feel much better then!" he said.

He kissed the top of her head and quietly left the room.

The afternoon heat teased beads of moisture from Sola's skin. She thought about Colby. He always raised his eyebrows when she did anything he considered off the wall.Something like this. Meeting with a shaman. Sola was looking forward to the healing. Her head had a pile driver inside of it, and her leg felt like someone was branding her.

She had tried to reach Colby earlier on Meil's communications system without success. If Colby had moved behind the moon, to shield Minerva from detection, they would need some of Meil's technological wizardry to reach him. Meil was working on it. Her PCU would have done the trick, but it was on its way to becoming part of a coral reef.

Sola heard the soft creak of a door opening. A provocative voice gently called her name, the voice of someone who knew things, secret things, an old voice but not a frail one, a familiar voice. It was the voice she'd heard in the airlock, and in her dreams.

"I am here," Sola answered.

Ailva came into the waiting room. She stopped and looked at Sola for a long while, smiling. Then she placed her finger tips against her lips.

"Oh, I apologize," Ailva said. "It's just that, well." She hesitated, and let the rest of her thought remain unexpressed.

"I am most honored to meet you, Sola," she finally said.

"And I am most honored and grateful to meet you, Ailva," Sola said.

"Please, come this way," Ailva continued, helping Sola up and keeping her arm under Sola's to steady her as they entered the adjoining chamber. The soft light of candles and the scent of sweet herbs welcomed her.

Ailva's moon drenched eyes reached out to her with a wave of energy that felt like a physical embrace. Sola was soothed and completely at ease.

"We will heal those bite wounds," Ailva said. "I am so sorry you had to suffer such pain and fear. It is a miracle you survived! A kygne does not usually leave without its meal."

The room's décor was aquatic, deep greens and blues. There were draperies and rugs covering the walls and floor, creating in the space an audio flatness that made sound hover close.

Sola looked at Ailva in the subdued light, recognizing her luminous face and gentle eyes. She was definitely the woman who had appeared in her dreams.

"Ailva," Sola said. "I don't know how to ask this, and I feel quite awkward about it but," she stopped mid-sentence, not sure how to proceed.

"Don't be nervous," Ailva said. "Please, tell me your thoughts."

"Was it you who greeted me when I first arrived? And was it you who appeared in my dreams?" Sola asked, already knowing the answer.

Ailva looked startled. "You heard my greeting? That is quite amazing. It was not directed at you personally. At that time, I had no idea who you were, or even that you were here on Caifanii. I was welcoming an energy I felt, a promise of something new and wonderful coming into being. But as soon as I saw you, just now, I realized our connection. You must be very telepathically sensitive to have heard me back then, before we had even met!"

Sola was perplexed. "I not only heard you," she said. "I understood you."

She felt awkward about launching into this paranormal territory with a woman she had just barely met, a woman who had so graciously offered to heal her. She didn't want to come off as pushy, or to invade this lovely woman's privacy, but her curiosity was too strong to ignore.

"When you spoke to me telepathically, or not to me specifically I guess, but that first time," Sola said, "you spoke in an ancient language of my home world, Hawaiian."

Ailva looked intrigued. "That is most fascinating. My greeting was in an ancient language, yes, but it was in ancient Mhalanai."

"Can you say it again?" Sola asked. "What you said then?"

"Eh kima maia. U'hili ho listu ona," Ailva said.

"That's exactly what Jaitain said," Sola exclaimed. "He said the first part was a welcome, the second was a line from your sacred text."

"The Book of Ways, yes." Ailva said, looking even more intrigued.

"What I heard," Sola said, "was, 'E komo mai. Ua hiki ho`i la nui!' which is Hawaiian."

"That is remarkably similar indeed! Perhaps your mind found a way for you to understand me by using this other language that was familiar to you."

"I guess that sort of makes sense," Sola said, mulling it over, but not convinced. "But you also appeared in my dreams. Did you know about me then, about my presence on this planet?"

"Yes, and no. In my own dream world, a woman appeared to me here in the forest at my cottage, and later in a Joining Ceremony. That woman looked exactly like you. That is why I was so amazed upon first seeing you. I didn't quite know what to say. I didn't feel it was appropriate to start our first conversation with, 'Oh, my! You appeared in my dreams!'"

They both laughed, releasing some tension.

"I had the same feeling," Sola said. "I recognized you instantly, but what could I say?"

"Perhaps," Ailva conjectured, "we shared these dream experiences and became connected without our being consciously aware of it at the time. It certainly bodes of some profound significance, yes?"

"Jaitain said something exactly like that when I told him of the greetings I'd heard."

"Great minds think alike!"

"Ha! We have the same saying on Earth!"

"See, exactly!" Ailva said. "Now, let's get you healed!" Ailva said. "Please, let's sit."

She gestured to some green cushions in the center of the room.

She helped Sola sink down onto one.

"That looks like it bothers your leg," Ailva said, noticing that Sola winched.

"Let's just have you lie on your back. Let me help you."

After settling Sola, Ailva sat on a pillow beside her.

"I'm going to gently roll your pant leg up to expose the wounds. I have an herbal salve I need to place on them."

Sola looked at an ornate sculpture resting on a low table next to them. The base resembled a large seashell. Its color was iridescent, reminiscent of mother-of-pearl. A slender stem rose from the base and terminated in a cluster of three flower-like shapes made of a delicate metal the greenish color of oxidized bronze. There was a mesmerizing blue light emanating from the center of each of the sculptured flowers.

Sola wanted to ask about it, but felt shy.

"It is an Olvino Saad," Ailva said, noticing Sola's gaze. She dabbed something cool onto the wounds.

"It is an ancient instrument of communication. This is not an original of course, but made in accordance with descriptions from the ancient texts. It is believed that the ancients used this type of instrument to amplify telepathic communication beyond this planet and dimension."

"Did you use it when you sent the greeting I heard in the airlock?" Sola asked.

"No, I only need it for communicating to those not on this home world."

"Right, a long-distance service," Sola said.

"I could call you when you are back on your home world," Ailva said with a coy smile.

"I will need to find my way back first," Sola said.

"You will. I am certain."

Ailva's hands hovered slightly above Sola's wounded leg. She felt heat moving into the wounds.

"This will be quite intense for a moment. It won't last long. Keep breathing."

Sola gasped as a sudden jab of hot pain entered both bite wounds simultaneously. Then it was over. She relaxed.

"That was intense for sure," she said. "Wow!"

"Just rest a moment. Try to relax."

"I think it helped. I can't feel the wounds as much now."

"Excellent."

"Are the wounds anesthetized?"

"No. They just received a deep healing. You will still feel soreness, but the wounds should no longer be quite so painful, and the infections will heal."

"Thank you!"

They were both silent for a while.

"Ailva?"

"Yes?"

"Jaitain told me that in the Prophecy of the Great Day, there is a teaching that says the liberator will emerge from the mouth of a dragon, or something like that. I think he believes I might be that liberator, since my leg emerged from the mouth of a dragon. The kygne certainly looks like a dragon, but isn't that a bit of a stretch?"

"Jaitain has never been a believer, but it sounds like his view may be changing. Some of the elder Mhalanai, including myself, have been expecting the arrival of a liberating energy, a liberating combination of events in this special time based on centuries old teachings including the Prophecy of the Great Day. Who is to say? Perhaps you are playing a part in that scenario. I sent my greeting because I felt a distinct shift, a powerful energy. That greeting was somehow focused towards you, though I did not know you at the time. There may be some deep significance in that. Don't you think?"

"I do not mean to be rude," Sola said softly, carefully, "but I am not a prophetic incarnation. I'm just me, ordinary me. Please, do not mistake me for anything more profound."

Ailva laughed a kind laugh.

"We have outgrown the need to manifest our saviors long ago! I only mean that your presence here at this time may have an influence far beyond what either of us currently understand. Time is a blanket many times folded. I am only saying that some of us have seen that blanket spread and have witnessed the ecstatic intricacies of the patterns woven into its immaterial foundation. Those patterns are connections which are only partially visible while the blanket lies compressed, but once the blanket is spread, they are easily discerned and quite astounding!"

"You are saying that you saw me in the blanket?" Sola asked, smiling.

"You might say that, yes. We saw the arrival of a point of connection and its crucial effect on the patterns of our current reality. That point of connection may very well be routed through you at this time, and the effect could be quite astounding."

At least these people were not expecting her to be some sort of Messiah. That was a relief. Sola tried to follow Ailva's analogy with her mind, but Ailva's voice was so luxurious Sola's mind gave up on analysis and instead basked in the aural and energetic resonance, no longer aware of whether the voice was reaching her as sound waves on her ear drums, or as thoughts set deeply within her mind. Her normal process of thinking morphed into a more receptive mode of communication. She was listening with her heart.

Where do we go from here?" she asked.

"I will help your body adjust to our home." Ailva said. "Does that sound all right?"

"That sounds great!" Sola said.

Whatever this Kahuna could do to help her body deal with Caifanii's gravity and extreme heat was welcome, even if Sola didn't understand how it worked.

"I lost all of my environmental stabilizer medications in the wreck," Sola explained.

"You will no longer need them," Ailva said. "Please, relax and calm your mind. I will lead us through the process."

Sola relaxed. She felt the soft carpet under her fingers, and marveled at how her leg was only slightly sore, no longer painful. She knew she could trust Ailva, and that was a huge relief.

"Sola," Ailva said. "This process will be much enhanced if I can work with you telepathically. If you give your permission, we will establish a contract that will allow us to share our thoughts, but only when we both give consent. Our thoughts will remain private unless we choose to share them. Are you willing to do this with me? You can always stop the sharing at any time for any reason."

"I'm not sure I am capable of that," Sola said. "I'm not telepathic."

Ailva chuckled. "Yet you heard a telepathic greeting I sent into the cosmos from another continent!"

"You have a point," Sola admitted. "It actually sounds pretty exciting. I'd like to give it a try. Yes."

"Wonderful! Just close your eyes. Your receptivity to my thoughts will bring them into focus in your mind."

Sola closed her eyes and waited. Within just a few moments, she could hear Ailva's voice speaking to her in her mind.

"Intention is the inception of all manifestation," Ailva said. "First, you need to set a clear intention to bring your body into perfect resonance with this physical environment. Imagine yourself able to breathe easily, your heart pumping blood without strain, your muscles able to handle the gravitational force without any effort, your mind quiet and alert. Good. I can feel the strength of your intention. Just continue to hold it gently in the back of your thoughts. You no longer need to focus on it exclusively. Now, I will guide your body through a series of subtle energy shifts, these will increase your molecular vibratory frequencies, stepping them up to higher levels gradually. When we are finished, your vibratory rate, at an alpha state, will align with that of this planet, in accordance with your intention."

"What will happen when I leave this planet?" Sola asked.

"This process is completely reversible and you will not need me to guide your body back to the correct megahertz frequency for space travel and life on your home planet. Your body will learn this process on a cellular level and your intention will activate it, though it may take a day or two."

"Could you explain further?" Sola asked.

"I know you are familiar with the concept of physio-planetary resonance."

"Yes," Sola responded, trying to remember the details of the theory. Human brain waves in an alpha state closely resemble one of the Earth's own resonant frequencies. It was a concept that had been around for several centuries linked to the work of Tesla, a radical scientist and inventor.

"That is the general concept," Ailva assured her.

"How will this realignment help my body adjust to the atmosphere and gravity?" Sola asked. "I mean, I am not from this planet and I am not genetically adapted to its environment. Even if I am more resonant with the planet's frequencies, the gravitational stress and atmospheric differences will still affect me, right?"

"True," Ailva said, "but there is a relationship between frequency and density. This planet's gravitation field will create less stress on your physical structure if that structure is less dense. This can be accomplished by raising your resonant frequency."

"I've always wanted to be less dense!" Sola said. "I can be a real heavy sometimes."

"I can relate. I was overly serious as a young person."

Ailva smiled. "Lightness of being, at any level, is a blessing."

"Very well," Sola said. "Let's get started."

"Wonderful," Ailva said. "Reconnect with your intention."

Sola breathed deeply and slowly. She felt her chi move through her like a subtle electrical charge. She focused her mind on the intention of raising her frequency.

"Good. You are creating a very strong circuit. I will be guiding a gentle but potent energy through your body, just to assist you," Ailva said. "You will experience this energy as light moving through you from the top of your head to the soles of your feet. You will be able to direct this light."

Sola felt a blue light enter her body through her crown chakra. It flowed like a river through her meridians. With her eyes closed, but she sensed Ailva's hands hovering over her, working with the energy. She aligned her mind with Ailva's, allowing her to guide the process. Sola felt something shift, something change on a molecular level. It was an odd feeling, a tangible realignment. She saw herself, in her mind's eye, at the cellular level, as if through an electron microscope. Her cells pulsed with the radiant, blue light. She found that her intention made their structure stronger, more vibrant. She observed with her inner senses, and began to experience a profound joy evolving within the very core of her molecular reality.

The cellular vision she experienced expanded until she floated freely in a cosmos of amorphous clouds of pure color, no longer sensing herself as a separate being, but completely integrated into a universal wholeness. The experience was not unlike the psychedelic dream induced by K, but the feeling nature of it was entirely opposite, ecstatic rather than fearful. Her expanded awareness was blissful.

Eventually, she opened her eyes. She found it difficult to believe that she was back in the small, darkened room. She felt amazed to be contained again in her body, but it did not feel like the same body! It felt lighter. The exhaustion and lethargy were gone. Her heart no longer worked overtime to pump her heavy blood. Her mind no longer felt sluggish or clouded. She was healed and full of energy!

"Good morning," Ailva said from across the room.

"Morning? I was out that long?" Sola felt just like herself, on Earth, actually, even better!

Ailva's eyes were jovial. "There are no words are there?" she said.

"Words are too limiting!" Sola said. She placed her hands on her belly. "Wow, I'm so hungry!"

"You used a tremendous amount of energy during the transformation."

"I feel totally energized, and totally ravenous!"

"Let's go eat! By the way, you will be able to eat anything you wish. Your body will be able to assimilate this planet's harvests, without exception."

Sola smiled slyly. "Even a kygne burger?" she asked.

Ailva laughed. "That would be karmic justice."

"Ailva, thank you so much! You're amazing!"

Sola sat upright too quickly and felt lightheaded. "Oops!" She plopped back onto the rug.

"Move gently. Your body needs to adjust. I will bring you something to rehydrate your system."

Ailva returned with something very green that tasted like ocean water.

Sola drank it down slowly, making a face at the taste. Ailva laughed.

"What exactly happened to me?" Sola asked. "I mean it felt more spiritual in nature than physical?"

"I helped your energy body create a mapping of a more appropriate physical alignment for this planet."

"A blueprint?" Sola asked.

"Yes, an energy blueprint to which your physical form, while you are here on Caifanii, can be tuned."

Sola leaned forward and placed her forehead against Ailva's high, majestic forehead, as a gesture of deep respect and gratitude.

"I don't understand exactly what you are saying on a mental level," she said, "although I do feel that I comprehend it on a level that sinks much deeper than my rational mind. It's not that I am unaware of these concepts, but I am not used to feeling them in my body. I'm used to tossing them around in my head, as interesting ideas. This is so different. It's like," she hesitated, looking for an apt description but not finding one.

Ailva placed her hands on Sola's temples. "I do understand," she said, silently. "You can talk about a fruit you have never tasted, and profess to know its sweetness, but once you actually taste its exquisite nectar, it is enough. Speaking of fruit, let's go eat with our companions. I will help you walk."

"Thanks, I'm wobbly as a Raggedy Ann!"

A growing shaft of sunlight played on the wall near the doorway, beckoning the two women to leave the darkened space and rejoin the outer world.

Chapter 22

Day Twelve (morning)

Ti u comone dosteu aesti cael.
I welcome you into my mind.

The Mhalanai Book of Ways

At the farmhouse, Raftja had laid out an elaborate, morning meal of fresh breads, legumes, tubers and a local delicacy: altona, a type of seaweed rich in nutrients and protein.

She'd never cared much for sea vegetables but the altona smelled enticing and her guests were so anxious to please her that she decided to give it a try. Kail said proudly that Raftja's recipe for sautéed altona was a regional legacy. Sola could see why. The dish had a wonderful, smoky flavor. It was crisp and buttery. If Raftja agreed, Sola would include it in the new "Cuisines of the Cosmos."

Everyone sat gathered at a long, rugged, wooden table and, after warm greetings, settled into the feast. For several minutes, there was no talk, only the sounds of everyone filling their plates, passing dishes from hand to hand around the table.

Meil was sitting directly to Sola's right. He took a long drink from his earthenware cup, and then sighed.

"This is a taste of heaven," he said. "I hate to bring up serious business in the midst of this enjoyment, but our sources report that two government ships are at the crash site investigating the wreckage."

"We expected that would happen soon," Jaitain said.

"Central Security officials are currently searching the Amilio area, asking questions, telling shop and restaurant owners to keep their eyes open for a tall, alien female with strange, red growths on her head," Meil said.

"That makes me sound quite grotesque," Sola said.

"If we are going to utilize our plan, we need to disseminate news of your death right away."

"It's a good thing we did not stop in Amilio. No one there saw anything unusual." Eilfina said.

"We need to leave this location as soon as possible. Central Security is far too close now." Jaitain added.

"Have you found a way to reach Colby?" Sola asked.

"That is proving to be more of a challenge than anticipated," Meil said.

"We can't move forward until we reach him," Sola said.

"The Romeo and Juliet Safety, yes I realize that." Meil said, looking pleased with himself for remembering the term.

"I can't put Colby through the trauma of thinking I am actually dead. Minerva will be able to pick up broadcasts from Haikon, even from his position. Frankly, I'm not certain what he might do if he hears about it before we tell him our game plan. He can get a bit crazy when he's angry, and believe me, he'll be plenty angry."

"Any ideas anyone?" Jaitain asked.

"Actually, I do have an idea," Sola said. "I don't know if it's feasible, but it might be worth a try."

"Let's hear it," Jaitain said.

"What about contacting him telepathically?"

Everyone was looking at her, with surprised faces.

Ailva leaned in, "You mean using the Olvino Saad?"

"Yes. Are you willing to try?" Sola asked. "I don't mean to put you on the spot, but we are out of technical options. The moon is blocking our communications signals from here."

"I think it is a most marvelous idea! You are a quick convert to the usefulness of telepathy!" Ailva said.

"But Colby isn't telepathic, so even if it works he may not

understand what's happening. He may think he's having an aural hallucination. That is what I thought the first time when I heard your greeting."

"He will likely experience it as a premonition, an intuitive feeling," Ailva said. "We need to make the message very clear and send it to him several times. He may not understand where the thoughts are coming from, but he will receive the information in the thoughts."

Sola laughed softly to herself.

"It's really very humorous," she explained. "Colby is such a tech-head. He never gives his intuition much credence. He will find the experience disturbing, but I think he'll pay attention to it. How will we know that he got the message?"

"We won't. We will just have to have faith," Ailva said. "I suggest you create the content of the telepathic message, Sola. It might help if you incorporated something personal, something Colby would instantly attribute to you."

"I think I know just the thing," Sola said.

"The message needs to be brief, clear and personal," Ailva said. "It will need to be presented as specific concepts, rather than in the linear format of speech. I can work with you to prepare it."

"Let's ask him to move the Minerva deeper into space away from Lipo, so we can communicate the more complex information of our plans." Sola said.

"Exactly, as long as he stays in the penumbra shadow to avoid being detected from Haikon," Meil said.

Sola turned to Ailva. "How long do you think it will take for us to be ready to send the telepathic message?"

"No more than an hour," she said.

"Then let's make it high noon," Sola said, thinking it was a perfect time for a cowboy who loves Western films and books.

"Oh, but I will need to specify which high noon. I assume we are not in the same time zone as Haikon. Colby has the Minerva's local time counter set to Haikon time."

"Haikon is two hours behind us." Meil said.

"Oh, well so much for high noon! We need to make it high

ten o'clock. Does that sound workable?"

"Yes," Jaitain said. "Meil and I will be ready. You have our absolute support and gratitude, Ailva," Jaitain said, smiling with deference. "Best of luck!"

It was clear to Sola that everyone held Ailva in great esteem.

Ailva was not at all aloof or haughty. She simply carried herself with the grace of a respected elder.

After completing their meal, Sola and Ailva excused themselves from the gathering, returned to Ailva's cottage and went back into the quiet, darkened room.

Ailva was already on task. "It will be best if you compose a brief message to Colby, as if you were writing a letter." She walked across the room and brought back a pad of paper and a pen.

Sola took the pen. It was elegant, carved of wood.

In a few minutes, she had a message on the paper. She read it aloud to Ailva.

"Space Cowboy, it's Pumpkin. Some Caifanii are telepathic. This is not an hallucination. I'm alive, in perfect health. News of my death is false. Part of a plan to get me back to you. My CPU is gone. Move deeper into space behind moon, hidden from Haikon, open to Djuntu City, so we can reach you at ten o'clock." Sola scrunched up her face. "That's way too long!"

"It's a good start," Ailva said, "Let's see what we can do to streamline it." She rose and sat next to Sola. "What about this," she said, motioning for Sola to write. "Space Cowboy. Me Pumpkin. Telepathic Message. I'm safe. Not dead! No PCU. Move deeper into space. Hide from Haikon. Expose to Djintu. Will call you at ten." Ailva stopped. "That communicates the essential information."

"Okay, sounds good," Sola said.

"Sola, it will be necessary for *you* to send this message."

"I thought you would send it. I'm just barely getting the hang of telepathy, of controlling it, in any case."

"I will help you use the Saad. I will not be able to send the message, as I do not have a personal contract to communicate with Colby telepathically."

"But just because I know Colby, doesn't mean we have a contract, does it?"

Ailva smiled. "You have known Colby for a long time, yes?"

"Pretty long, yes."

"Excuse my blunt question, Sola, but in that time, have you ever had an intimate relationship with him?"

Sola blushed. "Do you mean, like" she hesitated, "having sex?"

"Yes. Sex creates a psychic contract."

"Oh, wow. Okay. Now I feel embarrassed."

"No need for that."

"Gee. That's kind of important to know isn't it? I mean, that having sex with someone creates a telepathic contract with them."

Sola suspected Ailva knew that she now also had a contract with Jaitain. That made her blush again.

"Ailva," she whispered. "This is all quite overwhelming. Until a few days ago, I was just here to make a bunch of money. A really big bunch! That seems so shallow to me now."

"It's what the majority of us do. We freely give up our most exquisite treasure, which is our conscious connection to the divine, for the illusion of security. In seeking to control our physical reality, we sacrifice our innate capacity to exist in a realm vastly more creative and malleable than the limited material world we perceive as real, and we are proud of that choice!"

Ailva shook her head and sighed. "Are we not a lovable collection of fools?"

"Dragon's mouth or no dragon's mouth, I don't think I am the liberator. I think *you* are liberating *me*!"

"It is an exchange. We give to each other. Speaking of giving, I need to share with you some basic principles of the Mhalanai teachings on telepathy before we can begin our work with the Olvino Saad."

"Okay."

"The telepathic bond is created through trust. Trust is the foundation of the contract. When we choose to share a portion of our mental-emotional-spiritual reality, our thoughts with another, we enter into a contract of trust in which we provide information which will, in some manner, affect the reality base of the recipient. Both sender and receiver remain centered in trust in order for the information to remain neutral in the balance of power. Information transferred outside of a contract of trust becomes manipulation and upsets the balance of power."

"That sounds like it applies to non-telepathic exchanges as well."

"Definitely. An imbalance of power in any reality construct results in dissonance, and dissonance is the root of disintegration in the overall energy pattern, or grid, which functions as the collective creative mind. Such irresponsibility can have serious effects on the meta-reality."

"That makes a lot of sense, especially the balance of power issue. I do feel a little tarnished. I mean, I buy and sell information for profit, or I did."

Sola wondered if that part of her life would be over now.

"I know that information transference can have spectacular effects on reality," Sola continued. "I've seen more than a few planets evolve dramatically from the receipt of information. That's what we call progress, in our society. We are, self-termed, an information-based economy, but as far as responsibility, I think our understanding of the nature of change is still so rudimentary that we believe any transference of what we consider advanced information is a good thing. Our history doesn't even support that belief. We've caused all kinds of havoc by transferring 'advanced' information to supposedly 'under-developed' civilizations with results ranging anywhere from mild disruption to downright social upheaval."

"Remember," Ailva said. "The responsibility is mutual. Those who receive information are not victims. We believe that there is always a contract. At times, the nature of that contract may not be in the highest order. There are those who seek to make an exchange based on personal or societal gains without respect for the ultimate repercussions. The concept of oppressed and oppressor is a naïve concept."

"You sound like Paulo Freire."

"Who?"

"An historic social revolutionary on Earth. I enjoy his writings. So, the Mhalanai do not consider themselves oppressed?"

"The circumstances here do involve oppression, but both sides of the conflict are oppressed together. We seek not only to liberate those of us who follow the Mhalanai Ways, we also seek to liberate those Caifanii who do not, who are actively opposed to the Ways. I don't want to belabor this conversation, my dear. We have important work to do! I am, however, under the obligation to give you these insights. I know you are open to understanding."

"Yes. I am," Sola said, "although I do feel a bit overwhelmed by it all. I hope that's not a problem."

"Considering everything you have experienced in the past few days, overwhelm seems appropriate! Let us then make this exchange with the highest responsibility. Agreed?"

"Agreed," Sola said. "How do we begin?"

"With intention!" Ailva smiled. "Let's sit on opposite sides of the Olvino Saad."

They adjusted their positions, and sat in silence. The morning light barely penetrated into the heavily curtained room, sifting in at the edges of windows and sending soft shafts filled with the glitter of dust across the muffled, quiet space.

"The unit is a transistor, a mental transistor, if you will."

"Does it require an energy source?" Sola asked.

"You are the energy source," Ailva said. "It is powered by your thoughts, your energy field."

Ailva handed Sola a thin, transparent tube. It resembled optical fiber and came out of the base of the Olvino Saad.

"This will connect you to the circuit," Ailva said. "Hold it like this, lightly between thumb and forefinger."

Sola did as Ailva instructed.

She expected to feel something, but there was no sensation, just the thin, round tube between her fingers.

Ailva spoke directly to Sola's mind.

"The message comes from the mind but is sent through the heart," she explained. "The heart amplifies the communication. The mind is rarely in a state of purity as refined as that of the heart. Place your focus on your heart."

Sola let her attention rest on her heart chakra. After a few deep breaths, she felt a slight vibration in her fingers where she held the tube.

"Telepathy utilizes emotion as a carrier," Ailva said. "In order for you to communicate with Colby, you need to establish a heart connection with him first. Let your heart open completely. Visualize a cord connecting your heart center to his. Imagine his heart opening to yours. As you breathe in, take away all pain and suffering from his heart, move them through your heart, cleanse them with love. Then, as you breathe out, send only joy and peace to his heart."

Sola smiled. That was exactly like the ancient Tibetan healing art of Tonglen. She had experience with Tonglen. It felt reassuring that spiritual practices aligned even across light years and time.

She breathed in slowly, imagining any fear, pain or suffering in Colby's heart being gently pulled into her own, she warmed these emotions, let love purify them and transform them into joy and peace.

She breathed out, sending that joy and peace to Colby's heart. After several minutes of doing this, she felt a sudden heat in her heart chakra. Her fingers too felt very warm where she held the tubing.

"Excellent, Sola. Your heart connection is strong. Now, you can send the information. Create an emotional image for each part of the message. Don't move on to the next part until you can feel Colby's energetic response."

"Space Cowboy," Sola thought, visualizing Colby riding the cosmos on their silver steed, Minerva. The image made her feel deep affection for him. She sent that affection through the connecting cord to Colby's heart.

She kept sending the affection until she felt an energetic response returning to her heart. It was working!

"Pumpkin Pie," she thought, feeling the joy of eating her favorite desert, smiling at the thought of Colby's term of endearment, sending all of that joy to him. She suddenly felt the color orange return to her heart. She wasn't sure how you could feel a color, but she did. Colby was getting her message loud and clear.

"I am safe," was the next part of the message. She felt the inner calm of safety and sent it to Colby until she sensed his heart receiving the calmness and understanding its meaning, then returning the same energy to her.

She went through all of the other parts of the message. Each concept brought up a clear emotional state. It felt effortless, it just flowed, until she got to the last message, the time. It was challenging to create an emotional state around the number ten. Colby's emotions radiated back to her, and seemed confused. Then suddenly, she got an image from him, a blue ribbon. She remembered that he once showed her a photo of himself on the day he received that ribbon at a horse show, when he was ten years old! He understood. He had all the information now. She felt something return to her, not a response to her previous message, simply a whole lot of Texan love. She returned a big aloha to him, and then she let the connection release.

"That was fantastic!" Sola said. "I can't believe how easy it was."

"I congratulate you! Well done." Ailva said. "Your friend must have a good heart, and a natural affinity for this gentle form of communication."

"Now we just have to wait for our Space Cowboy to ride his silver steed into the path of our radio waves!"

Chapter 23

Day Twelve (late morning)

Masi yin pa don prina.
Death is a silent music.

It was mid-morning and raining hard when Sola and Ailva stepped out of the cottage and ran across the meadow to the main house. The tropical rain came down with such force and volume that they were both soaked to the skin within moments.

They entered the house full of mirth and beaming with their success.

Meil greeted them at the door.

"Ah! Congratulations!" he said, seeing instantly that their venture had come to triumph.

"Yes," Sola said. "I think Romeo will not be deceived."

"Good," Meil said. "Then we will plan our little ruse."

"This rain is a little early, isn't it?" Sola asked. "It never rained in the morning in Haikon."

"It rains here any time of the day or night, especially in the rainy season." Jaitain said.

"I take it we are in the rainy season?"

"The start of it, not the monsoon heart of it, then it rains nonstop for about two months."

"No one is praying for nulini at that time of year!"

"Nulini is always a blessed concept," Ailva said.

"What can I do to help?" Dukal asked.

"I'm certain we will find a task for you, Dukal. There will be many!" Meil said.

Jaitain placed his hand on Sola's shoulder. His gesture made her ache in a sweet way.

"We will find you some dry clothing," he said, leaving the room and returning shortly with towels and fresh clothes.

The two women entered an anti-chamber, changed and returned quickly. Plans were under way and there was a tangible excitement in the air.

"I will remind us to move back to the Naia well before mid-day to make our call with your friend," Meil said.

"Your vessel is named the Naia?" Sola asked. "That's wonderful! Did Eilfina tell you of our rescue by the naia, the ones who live in the ocean?"

"She did not, but the naia are well known and beloved for their helpful and cheerful nature."

The others were already moving on to the subject of how to best disseminate the news of her faux demise.

"I don't think we will need to spread much in the way of details," Meil said. "We can keep it simple, let the details formulate from speculation, and from whatever official news sources care to divulge. We can disseminate certain key points. Dukal, can you get us an update on what local news channels are currently broadcasting regarding the incident?"

Dukal nodded and left the room, obviously pleased to be of service.

"They will find the bodies of the deceased Loyalists, but they won't find bodies of any of the occupants of the Mhalanai ship," Sola said. "Doesn't that ruin our plan?"

"The Loyalists' bodies were retrieved and claimed by their families prior to any official investigation." Meil replied.

"So, Central Security may assume the same is true for the Mhalanai bodies?" Sola asked.

Meil furrowed his brow. "It's more likely that they assume all occupants survived, since they are searching Amilio. Their only known targets are you and Jaitain. The rest of you maintain a cloak of anonymity. It may be fortuitous for us to add Jaitain as a casualty in the crash, along with the tall, alien female with red waves on her head." he said, jovially.

Jaitain was not the only one with a remarkably light sense of humor in the midst of tense, dangerous times.

Jaitain smiled. "My being dead could be very convenient for me! At least, until someone catches on, I will be able to have greater freedom of movement. I will be a ghost revolutionary!"

There was laughter around the room.

"Excellent!" Meil said, "We will make certain to have our Romeo and Juliet Security in place with your friends and family, Jaitain." He winked at Sola.

"What about evidence?" Sola asked. "Once they hear of our demise, won't the officials want to see bodies?"

"Our custom is to cremate our departed and place their ashes in sacred urns blessed by a Tumasei." Meil said. "All we have to do to provide evidence is have a good old fashioned Mhalanai cremation ceremony for the two of you!" he said, with a wicked grin. "Please pardon my impudence, but I think we need to burn your supposed remains in a public display."

"Come on baby, light my fire!" Sola sang, leaving everyone looking confused. She didn't bother to explain.

"Good idea, Meil!" Eilfina said. "We can stage an elaborate passage ceremony for you. It is an ancient Mhalanai ritual. A Tumasai blesses the body with sacred oils. Then we wrap the body in cloth, and place it on a high platform made of wood. We burn the body using the dried leaves of the Emar tree as fuel. We scatter some of the ashes onto the land, and some onto the sea, the rest are contained in a ceramic urn, also blessed by a Tumasai."

"The ceremony takes place within the first three days after the passing of the soul, so our timing will be appropriate," Meil added.

"Raftja and Keil can hold the ceremony and Ailva can be the presiding Tumasai," Jaitain said. "She can document the passing and cremation. That is all that is needed to make our deaths official."

"I have two urns for the ashes as well," Ailva added.

"Won't they test the ashes to make certain they are Caifanii and human remains?" Sola asked. Always the pragmatist, she thought, but an important detail for sure.

"Opening the urns is unsanctified," Ailva said.

"I have not found Central Security to be overly concerned with sacred protocol," Jaitain said, "but I doubt they will open the urns."

"They may scan the urns to check for pulverized bone fragments," Meil said.

"Now you are being macabre!" Olanii said.

"He has a point," Sola said. "We need bone fragments in whatever you burn as effigy. Do you happen to have the remains of an old yamma that just passed on?"

"No old yammas have passed recently," Keil said, "so no luck there."

"What about Alam and Shuri Mhipali?" Eilfina said.

"You mean Mita and Niuri's boys who passed in that horrible massacre in Djintu?" Olanii asked. "Why are you thinking about them?"

Eilfina hesitated, looked around at everyone for a moment then continued.

"Excuse my suggestion, I mean no dishonor, but there is a way to allow those boys' deaths to have some meaning, some purpose in service to the Trust. There are two sacred urns of their ashes less than 70 kilometers away."

"You are suggesting we borrow the urns, and claim the ashes are those of Sola and Jaitain?" Olanii said.

"I know. It's too much to ask." Eilfina said, looking embarrassed.

"No, my dear," Ailva said. "I think it is a powerful way to give Mita and Niuri some small solace. Their boys were doing so well at Djintu University. Losing them to such brutal injustice must be unbearable."

Sola understood all too well.

Ailva continued, "Aiding the Trust in this manner will be a way to honor their sons."

"But how do we make such a delicate request?" Jaitain asked.

"I can contact my friend Oilia. Her farm is adjacent to the Mhipali's," Ailva said "She will be able to make the request for us with kindness and wisdom."

"Oilia is also a Tumasei," Jaitain explained, for Sola's benefit.

"You are lucky to have so many Kahunas!" Sola said.

"If we are all in agreement," Meil said, "then I suggest Ailva make that connection right away."

Everyone nodded.

Ailva bowed and excused herself. "I will return shortly, my friends," she said.

Ailva left the room just as Dukal returned.

"Dukal," Jaitain said, "your timing is excellent! What did you find out?"

"The news reports say that two vessels were destroyed in a skirmish between Loyalists and Mhalanai Trust supporters off the coast of Amilio. They say evidence found at the crash site strongly suggests that the alien female abducted by Mhalanai terrorists last week was on the destroyed Mhalanai vessel."

"They probably found your belongings," Meil said. "Any chance your PCU or computer could survive extended contact with sea water?"

"Those systems aren't built to be waterproof," Sola said. "Salt water is corrosive, the computer data and the communicator will be useless to them."

"But useful to us, as they prove you were on the vessel," Meil said.

Sola visualized her sales contract decomposing on the bottom of the sea, bloated with salt water, the ink of the signatures she had valued so highly, blurring and lifting from the page. Oddly, the loss of her commission meant nothing now. Her past as sales representative with IDS now seemed quite surreal.

Sola let that image fade from her mind. The present needed all of her attention.

"Jaitain may be able to disappear, become a ghost revolutionary, as he put it," Sola said. "But what do we do about this tall alien female with red waves on her head? I am pretty darned easy to spot."

"We will need to think creatively about that. I am sure we will find an adequate solution." Meil said.

"Wait a minute," Sola said. "I have an idea that will help, at least a little." She sat in silence for a moment, thinking it through.

"Go on," Jaitain urged.

"I will be less of a target without a red flag on my head! How about I shave off my hair and look more like a true Mhalanai!"

"Your hair?" Jaitain said, looking distraught. "You'd shave off your beautiful hair?"

"It'll grow back, Jaitain," she reassured him.

"I think she's a real mijchi!" Eilfina said.

"No doubt about that," Jaitain agreed, "but you'll still have brown-skin, Nulini. Not exactly the norm around here."

"Maybe Ailva has some magic potion to turn my skin temporarily green!" Sola offered, smiling at the thought.

"It's not impossible," Eilfina said. "She has a deep knowledge of herbs. Let's ask her when she returns!"

"Eilfina, I love your enthusiasm!" Sola said. "How is your brother doing?"

"Mako is making a rapid recovery, thanks to some of those miraculous herbs from Ailva!"

"That's great!" Sola said. "I'm so happy to hear that!"

"He's not coming with us, however," Eilfina said. "He needs a lot of rest."

"Of course. Can I see him before we leave?"

"He would love that."

"I can't leave without wishing him well and saying goodbye!" Sola said.

"Ailva!" Eilfina said, as their Tumasai walked into the room. "Was your mission successful?"

"Yes, very much so!" Ailva said.

"What happened?" Eilfina asked.

"I contacted Oilia, and told her about our need. She talked with the Mhipalis. Both Mita and Niuri are grateful to be of service. They are, of course, still in deep mourning, but expressed to Oilia that this opportunity brings them some sense of usefulness, which is a healing balm. One of Oilia's apprentices is on his way here already to deliver the urns to us. He will be most discreet and stealthy!"

"Brilliant news!" Jaitain said.

"Yes indeed!" Meil said. "We'd better head for the Naia now. It's approaching noon. Let's see if Colby has come out of hiding!"

Jaitain and Sola followed Meil out to the field where the Naia was itself hiding from view beneath branches and green netting camouflage.

"A little tricky to get inside with all this cover, but it seemed wise not to advertise her presence here."

"No problem, Meil," Jaitain said, lifting aside the netting so Sola could enter the ship.

"We have been so busy planning your funeral; we neglected to plan our conversation with your friend!" Meil said.

"Oops!" Sola said. "I'm sure we can talk through the details as we know them and Colby will have his own questions, I'm sure."

They reached the bridge and all sat before the main console. Sola was again impressed by the ship's technology and comfort.

"Nice job outfitting your rig, Meil," she said.

"Thanks," he said. "What's a rig?"

"Your ship!"

"Ah, well, she's a bucket of bolts, but she's got a good brain!"

Meil turned on the system and set the communicator to the frequency Sola provided.

There was some static, a few beeps and then a loud, ecstatic yelp from a lone space cowboy.

"Colby!" Sola exclaimed. "You got my message?"

"Yup! I've got to tell ya it was a wacky sensation!"

"I know. Been there, felt that."

"Good Lord, woman! Am I ever happy to hear your voice! How the hell are ya?"

"I'm pretty darned good, considering. We don't want to take too much time on this call because we don't want Haikon to figure out where we are."

"Oh, just let me worry about them. I have masked this frequency pretty effectively. They won't be able to tag it. So what, exactly, is the plan?"

"Well, we have some of the details, but not the whole enchilada."

"Give me what you have."

Sola explained the situation. No small feat. It was even more complicated and complex when she tried to lay it out as simply as possible.

"Dang, girl! That's some scenario. Glad it ended as well as it did," Colby interjected after she told him about the Loyalist attack and their rescue by Meil.

She let Jaitain explain their rendezvous plan.

He and Meil had talked with Tjarlii while Sola was getting her healing with Ailva.

Colby listened attentively, asked a few questions, said "Okey-dokey" a few times.

Sola had to admit the plan sounded far-fetched, but Colby was willing to go with it.

They planned to contact him again once they reached their destination near Djintu City.

When Jaitain was finished talking, Sola wanted to say goodbye.

"Colby, I miss you dude! Hang in there! You must be utterly bored up there by your lonesome."

"I've mostly spent my time going out of my mind worrying about you, Pumpkin! At least now, I can divert my attention to something less onerous. I've got to admit I'm getting tired of looking at the back side of this moon."

"I recommend a classic. Got any Pink Floyd handy?"

"Great idea!" Colby said. "Nice soundtrack for the visual experience up here."

"Well, I never thought I'd have the opportunity to say this, but 'I'll see you on the dark side of the moon!'"

"The lunatic is on the grass!" Colby said, then laughed, a sound she'd missed hearing.

"The lunatic is in my head!" she replied.

"You ain't lived 'til ya heard the Austin Lounge Lizard's version of 'Brain Damage!' Remind me to play it for you. Tickled pink to know you're alive and kickin'!"

She debated whether to tell him she would be bald and possibly green, but decided he'd find out soon enough. She was sort of looking forward to seeing his reaction in person.

"Beats the alternative!" Sola said.

"See ya on the flip side!"

"Hasta!" They signed off.

During the next hour, Jaitain, Meil, Dukal, and Eilfina prepared for their departure from Sum.

They would be her continued companions for the next stage in the adventure. Olanii's family lived in Sum, so she was staying behind. Olan would also remain to support Mako's recovery. Eilfina wanted to stay behind with her brother, but Mako insisted that she would just get on his nerves by being overly concerned and attentive. Eilfina decided he was probably right, and she really didn't want to miss traveling further with Sola and the crew.

Sola spent some quality time with Mako. His rapid recovery was astounding. Ailva was working her magic on him. For a few minutes, he was adamant that he could join them. He tried to sit up in bed. The effort made him groan involuntarily from the pain. He reluctantly accepted that coming along was not an option. They shared a bittersweet farewell.

It was now time to transform herself into a true Mhalania. Sola wondered how she would look without her hair. She knew it would grow back, but she had not worn it shorter than shoulder-length since she was five. It would be a shock to have it all gone.

Ailva was very gentle and considerate.

"I will give you a hat to wear when we are finished, my dear. Your scalp is not used to the sun."

"My ego isn't used to being bald!"

Ailva cut Sola's hair with shears first, close to the scalp. She gathered all the fallen locks and gave Sola the hair and a white ribbon. Sola braided the ribbon in with her hair and tied the ribbon in a small bow around the end of the braid.

"This is for you," Sola said, giving Ailva the braid. "An odd gift perhaps, but something of mine for you to have."

Ailva smiled. "I know how much you treasured your hair, so I will treasure your gift," she said, holding the braid to her heart for a moment, and then placing it on the table near the Olvino Saad.

"Now for the finale," Ailva said.

She picked up an electric razor that looked like it could shear a small sheep. Sola was concerned about what it might do to a tender human scalp.

"That looks a bit aggressive," Sola said.

Ailva frowned.

"I'll admit, it's not optimal, but as we have no hair ourselves, we have no razors designed for us! We use this one to shear pikoli. Don't worry. I have thoroughly cleaned and sterilized it. Pikoli are much smaller than yamma, less than half the size. I wouldn't dream of using a yamma shear on your delicate skin. Pikoli have extremely soft fur. We use it for light blankets and bedding. It is cool to the touch and breathes well. I have the shear on its slowest setting. The pikoli are quite sensitive animals. I think it will be kind to your skin.

Sola took a deep breath, and closed her eyes. "Go ahead," she said.

The sound of the razor gave her goose flesh. She bit her lip.

The actual sensation of the shearing was surprisingly pleasant, like a tingly massage on her scalp.

"We'll need to remove the hair on your eye ridges as well," Ailva said. "It will be even more noticeable when the rest of your hair is gone. I will be very, very careful. Keep your eyes closed."

Sola sat very still, with her eyes closed. She had not thought about her eyebrows. Losing them felt somehow more disturbing than losing the hair on her head.

When Ailva was done, Sola ran her hand over her naked scalp.

"Would you like to see the results?"

"No," Sola said. "I think I will wait. Let me process this before I give myself the visual! Now that I've come this far, you wouldn't happen to have a way to turn me temporarily green?"

Ailva laughed. "Eilfina already asked me that very same question! As it turns out, I did find something."

"As long as it's not permanent."

"It will work as long as you continue to take the herbs. It will fade from your skin within 24 to 48 hours as soon as you stop taking them. I will go mix them for you now. I'll only be a minute."

Colby would flip when he saw her looking like one of those little green men from Mars. Well, a little green woman from Caifanii, to be exact. It was hard to imagine she might be seeing him within days.

Ailva returned with a small glass jar filled with a dark green powder and a cup of water.

"Mix a small spoonful of this in water and drink it before you go to bed each night. Here is your first dose. I have strengthened it with some additional herbs that will help your body absorb it more easily, so that the tint will show more quickly."

"How long before I'm green all over?"

"About an hour. I suggest you rest here while your body assimilates the first dose."

"Any side effects I need to know about?"

"None, except perhaps a mild state of shock at your own appearance!"

"I think I can handle that."

"I will come get you when it's time to rejoin the others."

"Thank you, Ailva. I didn't sleep much last night. This rest will do me good. I am deeply grateful to you, for everything."

"My pleasure. Rest well."

Sola had no trouble falling asleep. She slept restoratively for an hour.

Then Ailva came to awaken her, so they could join the others in the commons room of Raftja and Keil's farmhouse.

When she and Ailva walked through the door, Eilfina squealed, ran over to Sola, took her by both hands and did a little dance with her.

"You are truly one of us!" she said, bubbling over with joy.

Jaitain, who had been facing away from the door, just about fell off his chair when he turned and saw Sola.

He sat and stared unabashedly at her for several moments. Then he got up, walked over to her, and kissed her passionately in front of everyone.

"I had no idea the transformation would be so complete," he said, "or that you would still look so exactly like you, only also like us!" he exclaimed. "Have you seen yourself yet?"

"Nope. That might be a good idea, huh? Do you think I will recognize myself?"

"I think you look even *more* like yourself!" Eilfina said. "I know that sounds crazy, and I do miss your beautiful hair, but you are positively glowing!"

"Green is definitely your color!" Meil said, giving her a flirtatious wink.

"Okay, so where can I find a mirror?" Sola asked.

Raftja, who spoke very little and kept herself out of the way and busy in the kitchen for much of the time, walked up to Sola and took her by the arm.

"We have one in our bed chamber," she said "Please, come with me."

"I want to go along!" Eilfina said. "Don't want to miss the moment!"

Upstairs, Sola stepped in front of the mirror and was indeed in a mild state of shock.

She'd expected to look like someone dressed in an elaborate Halloween costume, involving green body paint and a skullcap. What she saw instead was a very tall Caifanii female.

"Wow! I look like one of you!" She placed her fingers over her mouth in a moment of reverence and amazement.

"Your eyes look even more spectacular than they did before," Eilfina said.

The three women stood and stared into the mirror at Sola's image for a short while, mesmerized.

Returning downstairs, they found the room a buzz with excited talk. The urns had arrived. The pieces of their puzzle were coming together.

Keil was out in the field preparing two funeral pyres for the ceremony that evening.

The local community was invited. Those who knew Jaitain personally also knew it was a ruse, but the others would believe it was genuine.

"I feel like part of me *has* died," Sola confided to Ailva. "I mean, so much has happened. I know that I am not the same person I was a few weeks ago. I can feel it here," she rubbed her solar plexus. "I've changed."

"I agree. You've evolved into greater fullness." Ailva hugged her.

"Sola," she whispered, "I have decided to accompany you on the journey. Your psychic powers are activated, but still quite untried. I think it's wise for you to have my support."

"I couldn't ask for better news!" Sola said, beaming. "Do the others know?"

"Not yet. Our plan had required that I remain here to confirm your death when the officials arrive, but I have spoken with Oilia, as you know, she also is a Tumasei. She has offered to come and replace me. We often cover each other's responsibilities. A death certification with her signature will be equally acceptable to the authorities. Oilia will be here in a matter of hours. I planned a go to Djintu City to visit with my sisters weeks ago. If anyone were to ask about my absence, the neighbors have all heard me speak of that planned trip."

"Ailva, I am so happy you want to come with us. Let's go tell Meil and Jaitain."

Meil and Jaitain at first expressed concern about Ailva's safety, but then acquiesced.

It was obvious that Ailva made the final decision about what Ailva did.

"We are honored to have you join us," Jaitain said.

"We will do our best to make the trip comfortable for you." Meil added.

"Comfortable!" Ailva exclaimed. "If I wanted to be comfortable, I would stay at home! I am looking forward to a little excitement!" she said. "I can be ready in less than a thought."

"Well," Meil said, "then we'd better move quickly to catch up with you!"

Everyone burst into activity.

Ailva went to her quarters to pack.

Meil and Jaitain went out to the field to clear off Meil's vessel, and to contact Atrina regarding Jaitain's change of plans. He no longer needed to use her son's vessel. The Naia was far superior in speed, technology and weapons power.

It also had an experimental deflection device that created a barrier to scanning frequencies. That could make their passage far less dangerous.

Raftja was readying a few food supplies for their journey to the outskirts of Djintu City. It would only take them about a day to get there, but everyone was enthusiastic about having a few of Raftja's excellent dishes along, especially Sola.

The clock was ticking and there was no time to lose. According to Mhalanai Trust sources, Central Security and Htui's patrols were fanning out their investigations from Amilio. They were certain to head in the direction of Sum any time now.

Within the hour, they all crowded into the foyer of the house to give thanks and say farewell to their gracious hosts.

Ailva recited a traditional blessing of protection for their expedition, and then the party filed outside.

They headed for the Naia. When they arrived in the clearing, the camouflage had been removed and the ship was fully exposed. Sola found it difficult not to laugh. This was the first time she'd taken a good look at the vessel from the outside.

The hull was made of unmatched pieces and spare parts from various other vessels. Meil incorporated state of the art technology on his bridge, but the outside of his ship looked like a science project put together in a junkyard. If this ship truly had masking capacity, Sola thought, it was a good thing. The Naia was an eyesore! Good thing the ship was not a book to be judged by its cover.

Everyone placed supplies in holding bins and compartments and then found a seat or a bench against the side hull and strapped in.

Dukal took the co-pilot position next to Meil. Within a few minutes, they were settled in and running systems checks. Sola was grateful to have Ailva sitting in the seat directly beside her.

"Welcome to the Naia, my friends," Meil said with an edge of pride in his voice. "Her complexion may be scarred, but her heart is full of power. She's got enough 824 Nilan parts to qualify as fighter class, and she was built with 100% Mhalanai love and labor."

824 Nilan meant nothing to Sola, but it was apparently a feather in the Naia's cap. This vessel had saved her life. That was more than enough to qualify the Naia as a top-notch ship in Sola's opinion.

The liftoff was smooth, completely vertical, and fast. In fact, so fast, that Sola was glad to be securely strapped into her seat. The ship definitely had advanced technology by Caifanii standards.

Sum quickly took on the dimensions of a toy village below them, and within minutes, they were out over the blue expanse of the sea. Aside from occasional islands, the ocean's blue would be the dominant view on their flight.

Light conversations picked up now that they were on their way in earnest. Djintu City was on the opposite side of the Southern Continent. They needed to stay off the coastline by a good 50 kilometers, flying over the open ocean rather than directly across the continent over land. It was the safest route, but longer. They would not arrive until deep into the night.

The atmosphere aboard was relaxed, almost jovial. There was plenty of time to listen to Ailva's steady voice delivering folktales and mythology from her vast knowledge of the Mhalanai oral tradition.

Just after sunset, in the field far behind Keil and Raftja's farmhouse, mourners sang blessing songs for the departed souls of Jaitain I'lliana and the alien female, Sola Alturas. Two body-shaped bundles of wool and wood wrapped in ceremonial cloth lay atop the wooden platforms. The smoke from the funeral pyres rose into the deep azure sky, telling of the ascent of the dead. Those who were trustworthy enough knew it was an elaborate ruse. Those who were inclined to gossip made certain the news of these two deaths spread as quickly as the flames on the wool and wood bodies they assumed were flesh and bone.

Chapter 24

Day Twelve (evening)

Tokai seah ruom uho tii.
Always move closer to the heart.

The Mhalanai Book of Ways

The afternoon passed without incident, but Meil and Jaitain remained vigilant on the command console. The Naia was not a commercial vessel, and had no authorized flight plan as a private craft. Their passage through the coastal airspace was illegal. Meil claimed government surveillance was rare over these waters. There were few coastal settlements between Sum and Djintu City, and no major population centers. The vessel's anti-detection shielding should allow them to fly through the more regularly scanned areas closer to Djintu City without registering on radar. The masking technology required considerable energy. They could only utilize it for short, infrequent bursts.

It was now well after sunset and the funeral ceremony would be complete.

The news of Jaitain and Sola's deaths would spread quickly in Sum by word of mouth. It would not be long before Central Security got wind of the news.

Meil and Jaitain requested that Keil not contact them. Any communication from Sum to the Naia could jeopardize their safety. That meant curiosity was scratching at the door for every occupant aboard the ship. They could only wait and hope their ruse was a success.

Meanwhile, there were other things to worry about. There was a major storm system in the forecast. It was due to make landfall quite a distance north on the Djanai Archipelago, but the rain had been relentless all afternoon and continued to be heavy, making visibility marginal. Pockets of turbulence created by shifting layers of hot and cooler air made the ride rough. Sola stayed in her seat. Her weariness managed to get the better of her queasy stomach, and she drifted off to sleep in her chair.

In her dream, she was swimming with the naia. This time there was no ship anywhere in sight. Calm, azure water stretched in all directions. Waves undulated gently over her shoulders as she floated, only her head above water, her legs moving in slow rotation in the warm sea. Three naia circled her playfully, occasionally leaping out over the surface and sending white sprays of water over her head.

She felt supported, loved, accepted by these robust, oceanic mammals. She lay back into the swell of a wave and floated, gazing up into the hazy blue sky. Suddenly, she felt her body elevate above the surface of the water, the bulk of a slick-skinned naia pushing up beneath her, lifting her out of the water. The exhilaration of contact and the swiftness and power of the naia's body took her breath away.

She expected to fall back into the sea. Instead, she found herself afloat in a vacuous space full of distant starlight and empty of sound. She could see her hands and feet floating in the void, but could not control their movement. She could breathe normally.

She felt no fear or anxiety, just curiosity. In the distance, off to her right, a point of light was growing larger, heading in her direction. She found that she could alter her position by focusing her mind. She rotated herself to face the approaching light. It took form. It was a ship. It was the Minerva. It was Colby.

Below her, she saw a large celestial body, dark and void of life, a moon. Colby changed course and headed for the moon. Sola rotated to observe his trajectory. Below her, she could make out the shapes of several industrial structures on the moon's surface.

There was something else there too, hovering just above the buildings. It was another ship.

She saw the glint of its silver hull. It was not the garbage barge. It was much smaller. She felt a sinister energy radiate from the silver ship. The Minerva was now between her and the moon.

Suddenly, there was a bright flash of vermilion light. Her body felt the impact of a shock wave as she witnessed the Minerva beneath her explode into a shattered crystal of debris.

Sola awoke with a start, her body moist with sweat, her mind racing with fear. She was breathing quickly and her heart was beating violently from excess adrenaline.

"Colby!" she shouted, her voice raspy and breaking with tears.

Ailva took Sola's hand. "It's all right. You were dreaming."

"It was horrible."

"You are safe, Nulini," Jaitain said. "We are all here with you."

"I felt the impact of the dream," Ailva said. "Will it help to share the dream with us?"

"It might."

Sola told them the details.

"Is it a warning," she asked, "a prediction of what will happen if I try to rendezvous with Colby on the moon's surface?"

"It is possible," Ailva said. "It is certainly a potent sign, and should not be ignored, but dreams rarely show the exact nature of future events. They come from a subconscious construct in the mind, which doesn't employ logic, as we think of it."

"I know, they are usually symbolic, but this was so real, so graphic."

Sola looked at the time and realized she had only slept for about ten minutes.

"Do you think Htiu or Central Security could actually destroy the Minerva if Colby takes her to the moon's surface?"

"I don't know," Meil said. "It's possible."

"I can't let that happen. I can't lose Colby!"

"Whatever the wisdom in your dream, we will find it," Ailva said.

"I hope so," Sola said, trying to shake off her fear. "I hope so."

Chapter 25

Day Twelve (late night)

Ye idia min hokai efena.
We are never the same twice.

The Mhalanai Book of Ways

It was approaching midnight. The view screen was still full of rain. Meil was listening to a weather report, coming in through heavy static. The storm system was moving faster than predicted and turning south. This was bad news. They were now directly in its path. The wind strength was already in the low end of hurricane force.

Sola leaned forward in her seat and tapped Meil on the shoulder. "Why are we not heading for shore and putting down until this passes? The waves look like they are peaking close to three meters down there."

"I wish that were an option. See those high, jagged peaks?" He pointed to the right of the view screen.

"It's too rainy. I can't make anything out."

"Trust me, they are there. It's the Mhika Range. They dominate the entire coastline from here to near Djintu. There is no safe place for us to put down. The wind could push us into a mountain. We have to ride this out."

It was oppressively hot. All available power was diverted to the engines and guidance controls. The cooling system was working on reserve power only. Everyone was tense, except Ailva, who sat in the chair to Sola's right in a state of deep meditation, probably calling on higher powers.

Sola played aimlessly with the end of the safety strap that lay across her lap. She couldn't stop thinking about her violent dream, and its possible implications. Jaitain was sitting on her left. He reached over to take her hand.

"We haven't had any private time in too long," he whispered. "I miss holding you."

"I could use some holding at the moment," she replied. "I'm still rattled by that dream."

"If it is an omen, we will be led to another solution," he said. "I refuse to believe we have come this far only to find tragedy."

"I hope you're right. Kind of wish I could talk to Colby. Can't shake this feeling that he's not okay. I wouldn't tell him about the dream. Don't want to freak him out."

"I doubt we could reach him though this electrical storm."

"My PCU would have no trouble. It's designed to operate under fiercely challenging conditions. Magnetic fields in deep space have a meaner bite than anything an atmosphere can throw at you."

"No use kicking the dead rat."

"Good one! Beats 'crying over spilled milk.'"

"I like that too!" he said. "I rather like this as well." He kissed her.

She kissed him back. It was good to forget about everything for an instant. The wind and air currents tossed the ship around like a carnival ride.

"If I'm stuck on this rollercoaster," she whispered, "I might as well enjoy it!"

"I hate to disturb you lovebirds," Meil said, "but I have something on the radio you may want to hear. I have no idea what it is, a pattern of some sort, not one I recognize. Jaitain, can you and Sola switch places with Dukal and Eilfina and come sit up here?"

"It will be a crazy game of musical chairs," Sola said.

It was more like bumper cars at the County Fair, but they all managed to make the switch with minimal bruising.

Meil had the com system on reception only.

The storm system was wreaking havoc on radio signals. The nearest weather station came and went, mostly there was static with an occasional burst of content. There was something else going on in the background, a faint percussive pattern.

"I hear it," Sola said. Then it disappeared beneath heavy static. "Crap."

They all watched the rain slam violently into the view screen. There was a bright flash of lightning, a loud thunderclap followed close on its heels.

"Shit! That was close!" Sola said.

"We must be right under the storm cell," Jaitain said.

"That's not going to help us retrieve that phantom radio signal," Meil said. "We'd better sit tight and wait for this to pass south."

There were more lightning strikes. Sola counted to see if the electric storm was moving away. It was. The thunderclaps were no longer right on top of them.

After what seemed like forever, but was only a few minutes, Meil spoke.

"Let's see if that odd pattern is still there." He turned the radio up.

Sola not only heard the pattern, she recognized it this time. "That's an S.O.S."

"What does it mean?" Meil asked.

"It's a distress call in Morse code, something I learned as a child. Colby must be sending it. Oh, shit! He must be in distress!"

"Not necessarily," Jaitain said. "Maybe he's just trying to get your attention."

"Well, he certainly succeeded."

"Can you send a reply using the same code?" Meil asked.

"I could repeat the same pattern back, so he knows I received it."

"Sounds smart."

"Is there some way I can generate a variable pulse signal? I need to send the message using pulses of sound, some short, others longer in duration."

"I have just the thing," Meil said, with a gleam in his eye. "Invented it myself. See this switch controller?" He tapped a small toggle on the board. "Push it to the right to send a signal. The longer you keep it to the right, the longer the pulse."

"That's perfect!"

Meil found an obscure frequency, low on the band, and Sola fired away.

"Dot-dot-dot, dash-dash-dash, dot-dot-dot," she said aloud. She hadn't been a Girl Scout for nothing!

Within a few moments, a distinct pattern was coming in on the same bandwidth.

"It has to be Colby!" Sola said. "Who else would be answering in Morse code?"

"What is he saying?" Jaitain asked.

"Heck if I know!" Sola said. "S.O.S. is all I learned. Guess I wasn't thinking ahead."

"We can switch to voice transmission for the rest of the communication," Meil said. "Since he now knows that we are listening."

"Won't that be like sending up a flare to mark our location?" Sola asked.

"This storm will cover our tracks. It will also give us a ton of static, but it's worth a try. I'll dial the com onto this same low-frequency."

"He must have something urgent to tell us," Sola said. "Otherwise why send the S.O.S."

Meil pushed a short series of buttons on the main console. He moved through several tunings until he got to the lowest part of the band, and there were only abstract beeps and shrill tones. Sola's father owned an antique shortwave radio. These strident sounds were familiar to her ears, mysterious and in some way disturbing, like the whining of lost souls.

Suddenly there was Colby. "Sola, if you're hearing this I'll be the happiest ham operator in the star system!"

Sola leaned over the small microphone in the console. "I just love to make you a happy ham!"

"Damn girl, are you okay? You had me scared to death!"

"What do you mean? You had *me* scared to death with that S.O.S. message!"

"I couldn't get through to you on the audio channels, so I thought using Morse might get your attention."

"It got Meil's attention. Colby, any chance this conversation could be overheard?"

"Doubt it, but if your buddies would feel more comfy, how about going back to Morse? I can't believe you remembered that, by the way. I'm impressed."

"Don't be too impressed, S.O.S. is the sum total of my vocabulary."

"Good enough for government work."

"Yeah, but it's the government I'm concerned about."

"I highly doubt anybody's going to pick up on this frequency," Colby said, "nothing but cosmic garbage this low on the band. If you're not precisely tuned in, it sounds like Cyborg Acid."

"What the hell is that?"

"My new least favorite band."

"So, if everything is copasetic, why the distress call?"

"I thought you were in distress. I had this weird experience. You know how you sent me that telepathic message before?"

"Yeah."

"It felt like that, except it wasn't a message, it was an image, a freaky image of an exploding ship, and then a lot of fear. I thought you were trying to tell me your ship was under attack. I wanted to race to the rescue, but I don't know where the hell you are. So, you're okay, no explosion, no attack?"

"No, we're fine, just flying through a bad storm."

"That explains why I couldn't reach you on the com."

"I did have a vivid dream earlier that involved an explosion."

"You mean I saw part of your dream telepathically?"

"I don't know. Maybe you just felt the intensity of the emotions I experienced from the dream and that transferred the visuals somehow."

"That's possible," Ailva said, from behind her, "since you were recently connected."

"So, you gonna fill me in on the details of that dream?" Colby asked.

Sola frowned. There was no point in making him feel paranoid as well. "It was just a nightmare, you know, probably caused by stress or something I ate."

"Right. Hey, by the way," Colby continued, "I checked the local news earlier. Your death is making headlines. Thanks for giving me a heads up on that. I would have had a coronary for sure."

"You're welcome. Least I could do."

"I wish you could do something more, like get back on Minerva with me! I've become a permanent landmark up here. Satellite Colby! Can I just swing on down and pick you up, now that you are far, far away from Haikon?"

"Not unless you are willing to risk making my dream come true."

"Hold it. You mean the ship that gets blown up is Minerva?"

"Shit. I didn't mean to tell you that, but yes."

"No wonder you were so upset. I really felt that, you know, it was like bam! Straight shot to the heart. I thought you'd died, and I mean for real this time. Super glad that's not true."

"Me too! Hey," she said, "any news from Amnesty or the UP?"

"Nope. Too soon, I think. I did get a nice message from some French intellectuals who are in the neighborhood. They say they can join up with me in my cozy moon shadow resort within 24 hours. It's a research vessel, the Cousteau, so not much tactical assistance, but nice of them to offer. Maybe they're getting sick of their own company. It gets lonely out here. Hint, hint."

"I know. I'm sorry. I miss you too! You should take them up on that offer. A little moral support never hurts, and who knows, maybe they can be of assistance to us somehow."

"Maybe so, and they might have some descent rations."

"Mais oui! Baguette au brie!"

"Maybe a little sauvignon blanc! So, when can you get me the exact details on this crazy lunar plan of yours?"

"Hold on," she said, turning to Meil. "He wants to know when we'll have exact details on our plan?"

"Within the day," Meil said. "We'll contact Tjarlii as soon as we make landfall."

"Okay," Sola said. "Colby, we're going to have to call you again tomorrow on that."

"Just whisper sweet nothings in my ear, and I'll come a runnin' Darlin'," he said.

"Keep your psychic antenna tuned. I'll be calling you, but probably just from Meil's com system."

"Okay. I'll just be moon gazing as usual."

"I'll try not to have any more bad dreams."

"Well, I do appreciate that. I'll see if I can make an appointment with some French cuisine!"

"Ooh la la!"

"Over and out."

Chapter 26

Day Thirteen (pre-dawn)

Kalanias alimo do meyat au nidia.
Plans are a comfort within the chaos of life.

The Mhalanai Book of Ways

The storm shifted to the west, moving out into the open ocean. It left behind an eerie silence as the Naia flew over calmed waves in the semi-darkness of the Caifanii night.

It was time to catch up on sleep. Jaitain and Dukal took the first shift at the helm, while the rest of them went below to sleep.

The night passed quietly until just after Meil and Eilfina took over the controls.

"We are being scanned!" Eilfina announced, over the intercom. "Shall I put us under cloak?"

"Hold off," Meil said, with a groggy voice. "Let us see what we are dealing with first. If we cloak now, we will give away our secret. I'll be up there in a moment."

Everyone was awake now, so they all went back up to the bridge.

"Their scan is picking up six Caifanii," Eilfina said. "That's odd. They are not reading Sola's pattern as Terran."

"Another advantage of our work," Ailva said, with a wink to Sola. "Her frequency is as high as ours now."

"Ah," Eilfina said. "So, according to their scanners, Sola is showing up as Caifanii!"

"Well, that's great news!" Sola said. "But who exactly are *they*?"

"It's likely a routine robotics check point," Meil said.

"Let's hope that is the case," Jaitain said. "We don't need some official border patrol asking us a lot of questions."

"We have drifted a bit too near to the shoreline," Meil explained, "There are routine surveillance buoys out here which check traffic. Mostly they record activity in the trade routes. We are passing through a surveillance area now. We should have gone under cloak earlier, but with the storm system we were pressed slightly off course."

"Will they demand more information?" Sola asked.

"Possibly," Meil said.

"I'm getting an incoming transmission," Eilfina said. "They want to know our business license code and the nature of our transport activity."

"So," Meil said. "We will give them what they want."

"We have a license?" Jaitain asked.

"We may not have a flight plan, but we do have a license! You travel these waters without one, my friend? You are braver than I am." Meil said.

"Not braver." Jaitain said. "Perhaps more foolish."

"Or, not as well connected," Eilfina suggested.

"Here," Meil said, pulling up a series of numbers on the small computer screen at the top of the console. "Transfer these to the buoy."

Eilfina shook her head in apparent amazement. "How did you get these?" She asked, as she sent the numbers. "And what exactly *is* our business?"

"We are transporting executives." Meil said with irony.

"Business personnel?" Ailva asked.

"Yes," Meil said. "I have an uncle who retired a couple of years ago from that business. He is with the Mhalanai Trust and decided to continue his license so that I could use it to move between continents. The likelihood of our being harassed is slim. The government does not like to ruffle the feathers of the elite class. It's really a clever license to have, wouldn't you agree?"

"A taxi service," Sola said, wondering if there was a similar colloquial term in Caifanii or Mhalanai.

"Well, in any case," she said, "I'm glad that buoy didn't discover my true identity. I'm pretty sure I am the only human on this planet at the moment."

"Well," Eilfina said, "we just got clearance. No problem."

"Good," Meil said, "but we should travel the remainder of the journey under mask. This license holds up fine for these routine autoscans, but a visual lock would be a different matter."

"Oh, I don't know," Sola said. "I've seen some beat up looking taxis in my day!"

Everyone laughed.

"True enough," Meil said, "but this vessel does not exactly look like it belongs to Aklin's Executive Transport and Touring."

"No. I suppose not," Sola conceded. "Why didn't your uncle give you his ship as well as his license?" she asked.

"I think he could not part with the pretty sum of money it was worth on the black market."

"And you couldn't afford that sum?" Sola asked.

"I can't afford the clothing on my back!" Meil said.

He laughed. "But no matter, this vessel is twice the ship! Just not half as pretty! Eilfina, let me exchange places with you. I think we need to slip into something a little less conspicuous."

Meil and Eilfina switched places and Meil activated the anti-detection device. "We will feel this. It will draw quite a bit of power. According to anything they could scan us with, we have just become an air current," he said, smiling.

"Meil," Jaitain said, a worried expression clouding his face. "Turn up that radio broadcast. I think I just caught something we'd better listen to."

Meil turned up the volume. It was a local news program, and in the middle of a story. Everyone listened.

"…vow to stop work at 6 dahn tomorrow. Again, a late breaking story from Djintu City. The Municipal Waste Removal and Processing Department has declared a workers' strike in protest of what they are calling the massacre at High Court Square last week. City officials are not releasing additional details, but the Mhalanai Trust has assumed responsibility for the walkout. It is not known at this time how the strike will affect the city's waste removal and processing operations. The Municipal District may try to provide replacement workers. However, the Mhalanai Trust has declared it will do all it can to prevent such replacements within the means of their policy of non-violent resistance."

Everyone sat in stunned silence, and then broke into simultaneous discussion.

"Of all times to go on strike!" Meil said.

"If this was planned in advance, why did Tjarlii not mention it?" Eilfina said.

"It must have been in the works for at least several days," Jaitain said.

"If she knew, Tjarlii would have told us," Meil said.

"I guess this means no trash deliveries to the moon in the near future." Sola said.

"Looks like it." Jaitain said. "If the workers walk tomorrow, our plan is defunct."

"I think they call this being 'hoisted by your own petard!'"

"What does that mean?" Dukal asked.

"Blown up by a bomb of your own making, technically, but in the modern sense, being screwed by your own plans."

"The Mhalanai Trust just blew up our plans!" Dukal said.

"Rather ironic," Ailva added.

"Can we contact Tjarlii?" Sola asked. "Maybe she can tell us more."

"I'd prefer to wait until we are safely out of this transit zone. I will head us back out to sea," Meil said. "I agree we need to know what's really going on."

No one spoke as the Naia turned her nose south, away from the coast.

After about twenty minutes, Meil proclaimed them safely out of reach of the checkpoint buoys, and called Tjarlii.

She was on the line right away. Meil put her on speaker.

"Nice timing!" she said, in a loud voice. "Who's running this revolution?" she added, with a sarcasm lacking bitterness. "Meil, except my regrets. I had nothing to do with the decision process on this. Our original plan may be in the trash," she chuckled.

"Or rather, not in the trash!" Jaitain said.

Tjarlii continued. "I'm grounded until my comrades decide we can go back to work. Municipal Waste strikes are highly effective, usually they don't run long. The City gets mighty stinky without our services. The strike is primarily a protest measure, but I'm sure the Trust will make demands, most likely the release of Kaleen Utjaika.

If I were planning such a thing, I would milk it for all I could get."

"Those demands could delay things considerably," Meil said. "I'm a bit bruised that I was not consulted about this. Then again, I've been under cover for some time, and our good friend Jaitain here, well he's technically dead. So, we are both out of the loop."

"If we're lucky," Tjarlii continued, "it might be just a one-day strike."

"Even so, won't that change all the schedules?" Meil asked.

"Possibly, more likely, there will be overtime shifts to catch up. If the strike goes past 24 hours, we could push back our plan to my next trip. Let me check my schedule. Hold on." They heard Tjarlii shuffle some papers, then curse under her breath. "Not good news," she continued. "I am not doing that run again for another ten days. If that timing works for you, I am happy to oblige, but I assume you don't want to wait that long."

Meil looked at Sola, half in apology, half in question. "Another ten days?" he asked.

"Colby will have a fit," Sola said, "but okay, if needed."

"We have nothing else lined up, Tjarlii," Meil said. "For now, let's keep to the original plan and hope the strike ends within 24 hours. If not, then we will resume our plan in ten days. The strike will surely be negotiated by then."

"If not, Djintu will be engulfed by a massive methane cloud!" Tjarlii said. "One toxic kaboom!" She laughed.

It was a big scratchy-throated laugh. Tjarlii sounded like a rough and ready character, Sola thought, a woman who lived up to her masculine name.

"Keep in touch," Tjarlii said. "If I hear anything interesting, I will contact you."

"Our thanks to you, regardless of what happens," Meil said.

"Glad to help."

The radio went silent.

"This may sound nuts," Sola said, "but I don't feel terribly bummed, I feel sort of relieved. I mean this moon thing, ever since that awful dream, I've had my doubts about it. Maybe this will force us to find a better plan. Maybe this garbage strike is a type of protection. You've been calling for protection this entire time, haven't you, Ailva?"

"I certainly have!"

"Shall we contact Colby? Let him know what's happening." Sola asked.

"Colby does not expect to hear from us until tomorrow," Jaitain said. "We've taxed Meil's stress hormones enough making the call to Tjarlii, best to leave the com quiet."

"You have me pegged!" Meil said. "Let's get out of this hot zone as quickly as possible! We have some people who are expecting us for breakfast!"

"Now that sounds excellent!" Sola said.

Chapter 27

Day Thirteen (near dawn)

Ho pikom idia olanaom.
The mountains are elders.

The Mhalanai Book of Ways

In the grey light just before sunrise, Sola gazed out of the view screen in mild confusion. What she was seeing was so contrary to expectation that she felt she must be imagining it.

"Snow!" she said.

"The highest passes hold snow even this far into the year. High altitude creates its own climate."

"They look like the Rockies," Sola said, "a mountain range that stretches through the western center of North America, where I currently live."

It was odd to see snow in a tropical climate. Then again, she used to ski on Mauna Kea!

"I didn't expect we'd be in the mountains!" she said.

"Not completely in the mountains," Jaitain said. "Tikoi is an agricultural plateau at 1530 meters, right against the front range."

"Can we go into that front range, hike around, breathe the fine mountain air?"

Jaitain smiled, pushing back into his seat and giving her a devoted look.

"Are you a mountain woman, Nulini?"

"I do love the mountains. I have a house in the Rockies now, a massive mountain range on Earth. I also love the oceans.

So, I've always been torn. Mountains or oceans? I love them both. Are you a mountain man, Jaitain?"

"He was born in the shadow of Kailtu, the highest of the range," Eilfina said. "You can see it from here." She pointed to a distant peak at the far end of their view.

"Does your family still live there, Jaitain?" Sola asked.

"My father, yes," he answered. "My mother died eight seasons ago, serving the revolution."

"I had no idea," Sola said. "I'm so sorry." She was surprised he never mentioned this to her. Then again, had she ever mentioned to him that her mother had passed? Her pain was still so fresh, she tended to bury it.

"She was a very courageous woman," Ailva said, "a doctor. She saved many lives, including our own hero, Meil!"

"No hero, my dear, just a humble servant at your command," Meil said. "Jaitain's mother was on shift at a hospital known to serve the revolution, when the entire building was destroyed by a suicide bombing. Two young Loyalists drove a transport loaded with explosives directly into the hospital structure. Sixty-seven people died. There were no survivors."

Sola was stunned. "Terrorism," Sola said. "Our history on Earth is also marred by that type of collective insanity, it's a wonder our species survived at all."

Dukal burst into sudden tears. Ailva came over and held him.

"Dukal's mother died that day," Jaitain explained in a hushed voice. "She was a nurse, and my mom's closest friend. Dukal, my friend, our regrets that this conversation is bringing up your pain."

"This kind of fanaticism runs deep with the loyalists. They are often the neighbors of Mhalanai supporters, sometimes even childhood friends. It drives a knife through our communities." Meil said.

"Do Loyalists ever change sides?" Sola asked.

"Yes," Ailva said, "and, lately more so. The violence is wearing so heavily on all of us, that it's actually bringing some of us from both sides together in an effort to stop it. There are now many youth in our movement who come from loyalist homes, even some whose families are government officials." Ailva smiled knowingly and gestured to Eilfina.

"My parents are Loyalists," Eilfina volunteered. "Mako and I were raised to mistrust Mhalanai supporters. We were taught that the revolution is wrong, subversive, and to be stopped at all costs."

"Do your parents know that you and Mako are revolutionaries?" Sola asked.

"We no longer speak with them," she said. "Mako and I tried over the last six seasons, since we joined the movement, to help our parents understand our position, but there is too much anger in them. They disowned us. They say we disgraced the family. They have become even more involved in Loyalist activities in order to prove to their Loyalist friends that they do not share our values."

"How awful!" Sola said.

"Eilfina and Mako lost their own family, but gained a new family," Ailva said, giving Eilfina a hug. "We are all family now," she said, embracing both Dukal and Eilfina.

Eilfina added, "That includes you too, Sola!"

"We are in our approach for landing," Meil said. "So I recommend we all strap in. There will be air turbulence coming off the mountains. As we lose altitude and speed, it could give us a few surprises."

"It's beautiful," Sola said. "Right out of a storybook."

"There are ruins of sacred Mhalanai temples from a time before our written history hidden in the front range," Eilfina said.

"These mountains have a deeply calming effect on the mind and heart," Ailva said. "Some people experience spontaneous healing here. It is a very sacred location for us."

"And an oddly protected one," Meil said. "We have used this area as a base camp many times without incident. There seems to be something here that keeps danger at bay. It is a sanctuary."

"I can always feel it," Eilfina said, "whenever I come here. I feel the energy."

"My Danu claims this place is home to Beyond Beings." Jaitain said.

"You mean, like angels?" Sola asked.

"Yes," he answered, "those who have passed from the physical realm but remain available to us as guides. There are stories of unexplained mountain rescues, serendipitous meetings, people miraculously saved from avalanches, all kinds of unusual circumstances. My Danu says this place holds magic."

"What is a Danu?" Sola asked.

"A guardian," Ailva said, "someone chosen by a Tumasai shortly after the birth of a child to act as spiritual teacher for that child, aside from his or her parents and family."

"I'd like you to be my Danu, Ailva," Sola said, spontaneously.

"I am honored!" Ailva responded. "To be a Danu is a great blessing, and I am happy to be yours!"

"To be Sola's Danu," Jaitain said, "of that I am envious!"

"And many would be envious of you!" Ailva said.

Sola flushed at Ailva's obvious allusion to her romantic relationship with Jaitain.

"No need for embarrassment, my dear," Ailva said. "This bridge of love between you is well regarded. I am only teasing him. He is too serious, don't you agree?"

Jaitain laughed, the others followed suit.

Sola was still not used to being among such candid, openhearted people. There was no need for her usual guardedness, yet it surfaced out of habit. She admired this generous culture and wondered why her own was plagued with such insecurity.

Meil began a graceful descent into a pastoral valley. Tikoi looked like a Swiss village nestled in the lush green. As they glided closer and closer to the gathering of small houses and barn-like structures, Sola could see the hilly terrain was dotted with sheep-like creatures, probably yamma, grazing the pasture without regard for the drone and bulk of the metal object dropping out of the sky above them. Meil set down the Naia at the edge of a wooded area, in the elbow of an open field. His piloting skill impressed Sola. His landing was precise and smooth. She could have sipped tea from a brimming cup without spilling a drop!

"Nice work, Meil," she said.

"He's the best!" Jaitain said, giving Meil an affectionate pat on the shoulder.

The small company emerged from their scrap-metal cocoon in single file, carrying their personal supplies and chatting amiably as they strolled across the fresh grass. The scent of moist soil reached Sola's nostrils. She took it in deeply. There was a crisp breeze and the cool, astringent mountain air bit at her skin, waking her senses.

"Aaahh!" she exclaimed. "I'm in heaven!"

Eilfina set down her bags and began to run across the field, her laughter trailing behind her like the tail of a kite.

Sola took her lead, set down her bags, and sprinted.

She stretched out her arms and made loud squawking noises. She wanted to soar like a hawk, her cawing sounded more like a crow, but she was a happy crow. She felt lighter than she had in weeks.

She caught up with Eilfina and the two of them tumbled down into the soft, almost fluorescent green blades of grass and rolled onto their backs. The sky was pure blue, untouched even by a single cloud. It was a perfect sky. Perfect except for one thing, Sola thought. No wings cut across the azure expanse. The only cry of flight had been hers.

After their moment of indulgence, the two of them rose, went to retrieve their bags and hurried to join the others who were almost to the village.

Jaitain explained that Pjetri and Lena's farmhouse was the first structure at the edge of the village, directly in front of them. As he pointed, two figures appeared in the doorway.

Pjetri and Lena made a handsome couple. Both were short and muscular. Pjetri had eyes almost as enchanting as Jaitain's, but with a touch more mirth. Lena had the face of an angel, a Beyond Being. Lena was ethereal despite her athletic physique. Her face was soft, round and childlike. Her eyes were silvery lagoons into which you could plunge and expect to find nothing earthly.

Certainly nothing quite so earthly as her voice! Lena had the voice of a jazz diva, deep, resonant, sensual. Sola marveled that such a rich, dense sound could escape from between such delicate lips and such a sprite-like face. Lena was a marvelous contradiction.

Pjetri, on the other hand, had little else but earth in his features, deep gray eyes, strong nose and full lips, and a voice robust and confident. Sola felt an instant comfort, a mellow ease around him. He reminded her, she realized with a start, of her maternal grandfather, Juan.

"Are you hungry?" Pjetri asked, as he invited them into the farmhouse.

"As hungry as the sky is blue!" Meil said.

They piled into the house. Sola was surprised to find it more spacious and sunny than it appeared from the outside.

Pjetri told them to deposit their bags in the hallway, and go sit at a long wooden table near the kitchen.

"We have prepared a morning meal for you," Lena said. "Come sit and let's enjoy some food together!"

During their meal of fresh bread, cheese and garden vegetables, excited talk abounded. After they finished eating their fill, Pjetri served tea in delicate cups.

Sola sipped her hot tea. It tasted like mint, strong and refreshing.

"Let's move into the living room," Lena said. "We will be more comfortable there."

They all moved into the open living space at the front of the house, where they lingered on soft chairs and cushions by the light of a small fire. Everyone looked worn-out from being awake almost the entire night.

Sola felt oddly awake and energized, as if the mountain air were an elixir that clarified her thinking and made her more alert. She shared a small sofa with Ailva. They sat near the fire, watching the colors of the flames, enjoying the heat.

"Ailva," Sola whispered.

"Yes, dear."

"Can I talk to you about something? Something sort of difficult to talk about?"

"Of course."

"I was wondering about the massacre, why no one mentions it. I mean, you must all have lost friends, even family members."

"Yes. One of Meil's close friends from childhood was there. One of my sisters teaches at the university. Two of her students died. And as you know, Oilia's neighbors lost both of their sons."

"How can you all be so resolute about it? All this time, you seem to be at peace, almost joyful. I lost my brother in a similar event, five years ago. I'm still not over it. It haunts me. All kinds of things remind me of him and I just ache so badly. I have a huge hole in the middle of my heart," Sola said, rubbing her palm just left of her sternum.

She looked at Ailva, wanting to share all of the loss burning inside that huge hole.

"I also lost my mother two years ago," Sola said. "She died of a completely curable disease due to negligence on the part of the medical staff at a research outpost. I have tried to forgive those doctors, but I can't do it. It's almost easier to forgive the police officers who killed Ramon than to forgive the doctors who didn't keep a crucial antibody in stock. The officers were probably very young and indoctrinated to follow orders and act blindly. The doctors were educated adults with professional responsibilities and a code of medical ethics they ignored."

Ailva looked into Sola's eyes for a moment. It was a penetrating look, filled with empathy but also inquiry.

"Does your culture have a cleansing ritual, a Grieving Ceremony?"

"You mean like a funeral?" Sola asked.

"Describe a funeral," Ailva said.

"Well, we hold a special service. Family and friends come. It's a time to grieve and express our emotions, but mostly it's a time to remember the person who passed away and honor them. Is that what you mean by a Grieving Ceremony?"

"Similar, but your funeral does not appear to offer a deeper level of healing. The guidelines for the Grieving Ceremony are included in the Book of Ways, the ancient teachings of the Mhalanai."

"I am very curious about those teachings. Jaitain talks about them frequently. I do want to hear more about the Grieving Ceremony, but can you tell me more about the Mhalanai Book of Ways first? Is it a written text?"

"It was preserved as an oral tradition for centuries. The ancient Mhalanai did not have a written language. They did use sacred symbols in their rituals. Some believe that there is a written text of the Book of Ways containing all the teachings using only these sacred symbols. In ancient Mhalanai society, Guiding Tumasai learned to recite the Way from memory. They were responsible for keeping the purity of the Way, and bringing its wisdom to the community. According to legend, they also held the key to finding the secret location of the written text."

"Do you believe the legend?"

Ailva smiled. "I remain undecided. Sometimes it's nice to have a little mystery. Don't you think?"

"Do you know the Way by heart? Is that part of your responsibility as a Tumasai, to speak the Way?"

"I am able to speak the Way, and part of my responsibility is to help others learn and internalize that sacred journey. However, we also have printed copies of the Way now, so that everyone can have their own."

"How long does it take to recite the entire book?"

"I don't generally recite its entire length, only sections specific to a ritual or a need. To speak the entire book, I'd say under an hour, it's not a long text, it is a deep text."

"Can you tell me more about the Grieving Ceremony now?

Is it like a Joining?"

"It takes place within a Joining, to release and cleanse grief. It can assist a single individual or a large group in releasing their grief. We held a Grieving Ceremony in Sum shortly after the massacre in Djintu City. It allowed us, as a community, to cleanse our anger and loss so that our minds and hearts could be clear and we could move on with our work. We believe that grief and anger are dangerous when held in the physical body. They can become the cause of illness and fatigue and can leave the mind and heart clouded, and confused."

"How does it work?"

"When we come to understand that emotions are forms of energy, we can redirect that energy and transfer its impact from negative to positive outcomes. Grief and anger are two of our most powerful emotions. They are fountains of great energy. If that energy is blocked, if we hold on it, don't allow it to flow, then grief and anger become detrimental. The Joining helps release blocked energy. It's helpful to do this with the support of others. We are sometimes reluctant to give up our grief and our anger because the mind harbors the erroneous belief that the power of the emotion will dissipate if the immediate experience of the emotion is released."

"I've often wondered about that. Maybe I don't want to let go of my grief because I am convinced it means letting go of my mom and Ramon completely. I will always have the good memories, but the grief creates such a strong connection to both of them in my mind."

"Exactly. When the mind holds on to grief and anger, it forces the body to accommodate the energy of those strong emotions. This creates tremendous strain. Holding energy is not the purpose of our molecular structure; moving energy is! We take in and release all forms of the life force: air, water, physical nourishment, emotions, thought constructs, actions. To hold any of these creates stagnation, blockage. We take in air, water, food. We process these and retain what is needed and useful, releasing the rest back into the environment. We do not reprocess these things. We drink our water only once, and let it move through us, incorporating only what we need to sustain our physical form. We digest our food only once, and release the waste. We do not continue to process it. It is wise to do the same with our emotions. We can learn to efficiently process and digest emotions, retaining what we need, and letting the residual energies pass. If we try to hold on to these energies, if we persist in feeling and analyzing them over and over again, these energies begin to stagnate and create blockages in our physical and spiritual being. It is not difficult to see how this causes great harm."

"That sounds reasonable enough, but how do you put theory into practice? I've been baffled by something ever since I was in the caves. I don't feel the tension between individuals that I am used to feeling when I am with other people. Well, I did feel it, in Haikon, especially during my meeting with the High Council! I don't feel it with you, with the Mhalanai. Even in the most stressful times, you are not tense. I am skeptical when people claim to have rid themselves of all stress or all negative emotions. I used to work for a small medical office. The doctors who ran the clinic claimed they rooted out all negative thinking and thus overcame all stress. What they actually did was transfer all their negative energy and stress onto their staff!"

Ailva chuckled. "How very clever and how very unfair!"

"I agree! That was the most stressful job I've ever had, but that's not what you do. You don't transfer your stress to others, you genuinely don't appear to have any! I am impressed at how well you all treat each other with concern, patience, and humor. I just love the humor that permeates everything here."

Ailva took Sola's hand in hers and smiled.

"I believe this is because we are a happy people. Despite our struggle, we have a love of life that gives us great joy. We would not be able to access this joy if we were constantly preoccupied with old emotions. The act of relinquishing emotions after their initial impact is the key. It is not an easy art to achieve, but it is an art we value and practice regularly."

"I'm learning a lot from being here," Sola said.

Sola squeezed Ailva's hand gently. "I'll admit I can be a real pain sometimes because I assume that I know it all, that I come from a more advanced society. I'll tell you, my experiences here are beautifully humbling, and freeing. I can finally just be myself. Let down my perpetual guard. What a relief!"

Sola sighed deeply, letting her tight shoulders relax. "Do you think a Grieving Ceremony could help *me* let go of *my* stuck emotions?"

"Absolutely!" Ailva said, giving Sola's hand an affectionate squeeze. "I think we need to hold one for you. While we are here! Let's make that dream of yours come true, shall we?"

"I would love that! I would be so honored!"

"Good, then I will see to the planning, but not quite yet. I didn't sleep a wink last night. I am going up to my chamber to rest!"

"Marvelous idea! I think I'll do the same. Seems all I do on this planet is sleep."

"Oh, you've done a few other things. You got Htiu, one of the most notoriously dangerous men on the planet, to sign your sales contract. You so impressed him, he even invited you to his private soiree. A fanatical young revolutionary drugged you and abducted you. You spent all too many hours underground in a base camp. You could not pay me enough to spend even ten minutes in those horrible caves! You swam with the naia, and they blessed you with their linguistic magic. A kygne almost took off your leg, and its poison left you temporarily blind. You learned to use telepathy more quickly and more effectively than any apprentice that I've ever worked with. You voluntarily shaved off your lovely hair, changed your skin color, and increased your molecular vibration. You traveled safely from Haikon to the Southern Continent illegally, and a leader of the revolution is quite madly in love with you. I'd say you've been remarkably busy!"

"No wonder I'm worn out!" Sola said. "That is quite a saga! I think I deserve a nap."

"Indeed!"

Ailva suggested it was time for everyone to rest, and like obedient kindergarteners, the crew filed dutifully up the stairs and into their bedrooms.

Chapter 28

Day Thirteen (afternoon)

M'ti ili, ti atai oiu weloas kala.
If I listen, I hear angels call my name.

The Mhalanai Book of Ways

Sola went upstairs with the others. Her room was spacious and faced the mountains. Her body longed for rest, but her heart longed to spend some time with Jaitain.

Leaving her door ajar, she wandered to the large bay window, soothed by the view of white-capped mountains against a blue sky, she thought about dancing, slowly to the elegant sounds of bass, piano, muted horn and the slightest touch of a high-hat cymbal.

She closed her eyes and imagined floating over a dance floor with Jaitain, his heartbeat louder and more distinct than the walking bass line.

She smiled and rested her head lightly against the wooden frame of the window that held the mountain scene.

As if in answer to her unspoken wish, Jaitain opened the door of her room, knocked softly against the wood.

"May I join you?" he asked, in a hushed voice.

The words sparked her memory. They were the first words he had spoken to her, in Haikon, at the restaurant, in another lifetime, it seemed.

"Just so long as you let me finish my bean pie!" she said, teasing him.

He laughed, lightly, also remembering. He walked over to stand beside her. The mountains held both of their attention.

"Magic," Jaitain said.

"They look like they will watch over us as we sleep," Sola said.

"The mountains never sleep," he said, "but I suppose we ought to."

"Will you stay," she said, placing her hand gently against his cheek.

"Let me close the door," he said, moving away from her.

Sola felt the sweet warmth of arousal. When he returned, she relaxed into his embrace and began to place soft kisses against the smooth, jade skin of his neck.

He smiled. She kissed the edges of his smile. He placed his fingertips against her lips, then replaced them with his own lips.

"Now, we are both Mhalanai," he said. "No hair, green skin, bright eyes."

His touch lifted her into the breathless altitude of desire.

He pulled the semi-translucent curtains over the windows for privacy. The mountains were still visible as scroll paintings on silk as he led her, step by backwards step, to the bed.

At its edge, he sat. He placed his hands behind the small of her back and drew her body down onto his as he lay back into the soft expanse of a feathered mattress.

The passionate intent of his touch electrified her skin, making her feel completely alive and aware of every sensation. Less reserved and unsure than before, he urged her body to accept new erotic territory, a sexuality not human but nonetheless divine. They once again discovered each other's ecstasy and rose together in its ascent, riding into the arch of its cresting wave.

Being green-skinned, like him, made Sola feel even more intimate with Jaitain.

"We are having our own joining," she whispered against his earlobe. "I hope that's not an inappropriate thing to say."

"This is a most sacred joining," he said, turning her head and kissing the nape of her neck until she wanted to devour him and have him devour her, which is exactly what they did.

After a mutual rapture in joyous turmoil, they lay wrapped around each other in the silent, luxurious space, a beam of sunlight coming through the crack between the curtains and falling across their naked skin.

Sola felt his breath against the curve of her jaw, a delicate, warmth traveling just to the lobe of her ear. His hand rested just above her navel. She could feel his skin meld with hers from his shoulder all the way down, along both their forms, to their feet.

"How will we give this up?" she asked, not wanting to even think about it. "I want to be in the moment with you, right here, right now, but we have so few of them left. Don't we need to talk about what's ahead?"

"We can only speculate."

"This location seems safe enough. Why haven't we discussed Colby swooping down here to pick me up?"

"Does the Minerva have cloaking capacity?"

"For signal detection, but not for visual detection."

"So, as long as no one physically sees him, he's safe. Due to the protests in Djintu City, there's extra security in the area, and not just on the ground. Dukal is checking the news regularly. Central Security appears to have accepted that we are genuinely dead. After a few sensational headlines, and a brief flare of interest, you and I have lost our celebrity as quickly as we gained it. I'm not so sure Htiu has taken the bait. That's harder to verify. After your dream, I am disinclined to expose Colby and you to potential danger, if it's not essential to do so."

"Your concern for his welfare is admirable."

"It's completely selfish. He may fly down here solo, but he'll be leaving with my Sola!"

"Good point. Damn! I don't like the sound of that. I don't like the thought of my leaving you at all!"

"That makes two of us, Nulini."

They curled up together and tried to regain the peace of their previous moments without success.

Sola's mind was too active.

Suddenly, she heard Jaitain's voice, inside her mind.

He looked at her with a loving gaze deep into her eyes.

"I hear you," she said, into his mind.

"I wasn't sure if you could do this without Ailva's help."

"Apparently, I can!"

"This is wonderful. I have wanted to share with you in this way."

She pulled in close to him, holding him with an almost desperate affection.

"Are you really leaving us?" he asked.

"I'm not sure," she said, feeling her thoughts ebb from her mind and flow into his, the light cycle resonating between them, an umbilical of love.

"All this time, we've been working to reunite you with Colby," he continued. "All this time, I've asked myself if perhaps you could remain here with us, with me. Is it selfish to want you to stay? It might not, after all, be the best thing for you."

"I know. I feel the same way. I'm on the cusp of reaching my goal of going home, but now I'm uncertain as to where *home* is?"

"If you did stay, you would be welcomed, tremendously loved. Not just by me, by all of us."

"I do know that. I can feel it. I wish there was more time. Maybe I could wait until the UP and Amnesty Interstellar arrive?"

"How long that will take?"

"Hard to say. Could be weeks, could be months. They will try to respond with as little physical presence as possible, mostly negotiation."

"I will be grateful for any additional time we can spend together, regardless of your final choice."

"This is so wonderful. I could get used to this telepathy thing."

"We do not use telepathy frequently. It's a sacred practice."

"Kind of like wearing your Sunday clothes?"

"I'm not sure what that is, Sunday," he said.

"A special day of the week," she said.

"Yes, It's not appropriate for every occasion, for every ordinary conversation."

"This is no ordinary conversation! It's more like having psychic sex!"

"We should try both together some time."

"Now that is a platinum idea!"

"I agree!"

"I always thought telepathy was just mind reading," Sola said. "Now, I understand it differently."

"It doesn't work without deep respect," he said, looking at her with deep affection.

"I've heard of people trying to use this form of mental joining for personal gain or to achieve power," he continued. "It doesn't work. The one who instigates such an attempt ends up with a deep energy burn, a sort of echo effect."

"A boomerang!" Sola thought. "We call that karma."

"The energy of the light cycle will not flow if the intention lacks respect. The energy then builds up in the solar plexus of the initiator. It literally burns. It is both physically and emotionally painful and takes a long time to heal. It's enough to dissuade most of people from improper use of telepathy."

"I guess so. Ailva explained to me about the need for mutual respect and the establishment of a contract in order to use telepathy. She said we already have a contract because of our sexual intimacy."

"She said that?" He seemed surprised.

"I imagine it's pretty obvious how we feel about each other."

"Ailva is not timid about speaking the truth."

"Well, she didn't tell me about that burnt solar plexus risk."

"Maybe she didn't want to worry you."

"Is it possible to use telepathy improperly without meaning to?"

"If your intention is pure, you cannot be endangered."

"Well, I'll try to have pure intentions then!"

"I cannot imagine my life without you, Nulini."

"Jaitain, if I stay, what will I do here? Will I travel with you? Will I have to live in those depressing tunnels for months at a time? Will I live with Ailva and see you only occasionally when you were passing through? Will you stay longer in the south to spend time with me? Will I be able to assist the revolution in some way? What will be my place?"

"That's a lot to think about. Much of that is up to you, but you know that my work will consume much of my time. Are you willing to live an uncertain and dangerous life with me?"

"I want to say yes, I really do, but I worry that it will be too difficult. I wasn't born here, and I wasn't raised to be a Mhalanai. I'm the spoiled child of a couple of wealthy research scientists. I got to do just about whatever I wanted for most of my life. I've created a pretty cushy existence. I'm fascinated by idealism, but I'm a realist and I can't ignore more practical considerations."

"What about Colby?" Jaitain asked. "Do you love him?"

"Wow. That was an abrupt shift in the conversation."

"I hope I am not upsetting you with the question, but it's an important one to ask, don't you think?"

"Yes. I do love Colby, as a friend, definitely! I've struggled for years with whether I can love him as a romantic partner, in the long run. I'm not sure we are a good match. He is such a rogue, such a prankster. I find it difficult to take him seriously half the time."

"What about the other half of the time?"

"It's ironic actually, right before I was abducted, I was seriously thinking of taking Colby seriously!"

"But not now?"

"I don't know. Sometimes, I can't even think of him, of my former life, as real. It all seems surreal, like a dream. I don't know if I can even step back into that reality now."

"Does he know about us?"

"No."

It bothered Sola that she had not told Colby. All along, she'd thought the time wasn't right and that a better opportunity would come along soon.

She wanted to tell him in person, but the longer she remained physically separated from him, and therefore unable to have that conversation, the more she dreaded having it at all.

Jaitain kissed her forehead. "I understand. I didn't mean to cause you any anguish."

Sola realized her private musings had not been private, as their thoughts were connected.

"I want to give you more mental privacy around this. I think I've overstepped a boundary, please accept my regrets for that. Shall we shift back to talking?"

Sola looked at him. "You just read my mind."

"Yes, I did."

They went back to speaking aloud.

"That was a wonderful experience, Jaitain. Thank you for doing that with me."

"Of course, but now you are going to have to tell me what you're thinking, if you want me know what you're thinking."

"Right. I want you to know that it pains me about Colby, about not having told him. There's so much water under the bridge now, it's a challenge to know how to even begin that conversation. He's stuck up there behind the moon with only worry and boredom for companions. It seems cruel to tell him while he's making such a sacrifice for me."

"A reasonable argument."

"A truckload of monkey mind, if you ask me! I'm just being a wimp, and I feel terrible about it."

"Be kind to yourself, Nulini. You haven't had any time for a private talk with him."

"That's true, plus he's always joking around. It's hard to get him into a serious zone. Jaitain, I've kind of avoided thinking about this, but I also worry that if I tell Colby I'm in love with you, he'll flip out. He'll be so hurt and pissed off. No telling what he might do. He might leave without me."

"You really think he would do that?"

"No, but still, it's not outside of probability. He's been in love with me for years, and I have not made that easy for him.

I've been clear with him about my feeling, but my feelings have been seriously wishy-washy. I was shocked at how easily he was able to communicate with me telepathically. I misjudged him. I thought he was too much of a tech head to be open to that kind of thing. He's obviously much more emotionally connected with me than I thought."

"And you are more connected with him than you thought."

"We've worked together for seven years."

"Which means you've essentially lived together for seven years."

"During assignments, yes."

"That's created a lot of experiential overlap, a strong foundation for any relationship."

"I know. You're right. You and I don't have *that* kind of history, but we've shared some powerful experiences together in a very brief time. That creates a strong foundation too. I just wonder if I could ever truly belong here. I want to belong here. I've never felt at home anywhere. I move around so much. I wonder if I could handle living in one place, even on Maui, let alone on a planet light-years from Earth. I want to call one place home, settle down into a nest like a content little sparrow. There aren't even any sparrows on this planet. No birds at all, and I love birds. Maybe I *am* a bird, a fast one like a hawk or a falcon. I wish you could see a hawk or a falcon, such regal creatures. I don't think I could live without seeing a bird fly ever again." She realized she was just meandering around. "I don't mean to confuse you, Jaitain, I'm just trying to understand myself."

"Everything you're saying makes sense to me, Nulini.
You need to be sure, and yet there is no way to be sure. You don't need to make the decision in this moment."

"I do want to stay with you, Jaitain. I'm just not sure if I can."

"Nulini," he said, placing the palm of his hand over her heart. "I will be with you, right here, no matter what planet you're on."

"You are the quintessential romantic," she teased.

They held each other tightly.

"I will be with you too," Sola said, "but it's not the same as being able to do this."

She kissed him.

"I love you, Nulini."

"I love you, Jaitain."

He kissed the top of her head. It was an odd sensation to feel the kiss directly on her scalp.

They lay together in the soft light. Sola drifted over the precipice of consciousness into sleep.

Chapter 29

Day Thirteen (late afternoon)

Selanio koko mu ye datu.
Opportunity knocks until we answer.

The Mhalanai Book of Ways

Sola woke from her nap. Jaitain was still asleep. She was certain he had not slept at all last night, so she didn't wake him. She slipped out of bed, washed, dressed quietly, then went downstairs.

She needed to contact Colby.

She found Meil in the living area, by the fireplace.

"Sola," he said. "You look rested."

"I feel great. Did you get some rest?"

"I slept like a mountain."

"Are the others still resting?"

"Eilfina went out for a walk with Dukal. Ailva is with Lena somewhere in the village, and I have no idea what Pjetri is up to."

"Any news from Tjarlii?"

"She called to say the strike continues. Negotiations so far don't look promising."

"That's bad news, though not surprising."

"Tjarlii has no work due to the strike, so she's flying in tonight. She'd like to meet you."

"Really? Now that *is* surprising. That's great!"

"Ailva is planning a Joining," he added.

"I know. Has she already begun to make arrangements?"

"She's a whirlwind once she has a plan. Tjarlii wants to be here for the ceremony."

"Nice! When will it be held?"

"Tonight."

"That soon?"

"If the strike ends, you'll be flying to Djintu with Tjarlii in the morning."

"Wow!" Sola felt a sharp pain in her heart. She wasn't ready to fly away in the morning.

"I'd like to contact Colby," she said. "Can we do that now?"

"Of course, let's head out to the Naia."

They walked across the field in late afternoon sunlight. There was a chill in the air.

"Altitude makes quite a difference!" Sola said. "I never expected to feel cold on Caifanii!"

"Except in the Caves of Lan!" Meil said.

"You've been down there?"

"It's a Mhalanai rebel's initiation! Right?"

"No kidding. On Earth we have an expression, 'initiation by fire!'"

Meil laughed. "Here it's more like initiation by freezing your ass off!"

"Good one, Meil. I hope to never be down there again."

"I spend most of my time on the ship. Guess that has its benefits."

"What time will the Joining begin?"

"Once it is fully dark."

"It never gets fully dark here, Meil."

"What do you mean?"

Sola smiled. "On my planet, at night, it's actually black dark. Here you always have some half-light."

"Black darkness sounds disturbing, though it must be amazing to be able to see more deeply into the cosmos. Our moons are too bright."

"You must come to Earth," Sola said. "The night sky, especially out in the high desert, away from cities, is spectacular. It will leave you dizzy!"

"That is an invitation I accept gladly!"

They reached the ship. Meil placed his hand on the ship's hull. "I love this old beauty, but I doubt she'd make it all the way to Earth!"

They boarded the Naia and Meil started up the communications system, which was still tuned to the frequency they'd used before to reach Colby.

"Colby," Sola said into the microphone. "Hey, Space Cowboy, are you there?"

She could hear the sound of movement, then the clearing of Colby's deep, rusty voice.

"Howdy," he said, yawning. "I was taking a cat nap. Any news?"

"Bad news," she said, "or maybe it's good news, depends on if you have anything else to offer. Our moon plan is questionable due to a garbage strike."

"Yeah, I heard about that, been listening to the news from Djintu City. I don't get it. Aren't the folks you're with part of that Melon Eye Trust thing? Didn't they know you needed to hitch a ride on the garbage truck?"

"It's Mhalanai not Melon Eye, and it's ironic for sure. Unless it turns out to be a one-day strike, we're out of luck."

"A one-day garbage strike? Not much chance of that," Colby said. "Things don't start smelling bad that quickly."

"They do in the tropics!"

"Hey, does this mean I don't have to get blown up?"

"Yeah, guess that's one good thing, huh?"

"Can't complain about that! Pumpkin, any chance we can have a private conversation for a few minutes. I feel like we've been doing nothing but talking shop since you've been down there."

"Of course, hold on, let me explain to Meil." Sola felt a sudden knot in her stomach.

Was she about to have *the* conversation with Colby?

She really felt it would be wiser to wait until they were together.

"Meil," she said. "Colby is asking for a little private time to talk with me, would that be okay?"

"No problem. I will go down below, just hit this button when you want me to return, It's the intercom."

"Great. Thanks."

Meil left, and Sola took a deep breath.

"Colby, I'm all alone now."

"I don't have anything super confidential to say," he said. "I just really miss you and wanted to be able to express that, you know, without your compadres around. Are they still treating you good?"

"Very good, Colby. Aside from the hazardous circumstances, I'm being pampered like a princess around here."

"Well, I hope you're not so pampered that you don't want to come home!"

It was a perfect lead in, and Sola was about to take the plunge when Colby continued.

"I'm so chomping at the bit to come down there and pick you up, and you don't even need to remind me that it's a bad idea. I can see the potential for unfriendly fire written on the wall. The airspace around Djintu City looks like a beehive. I can't get anywhere near there undetected. There's constant news about protests and increased security, bla, bla, bla. This planet is a mess. I'll feel a hell of a lot better when you're off of it!"

"We're not exactly in Djintu, but still too close for comfort."

"Where exactly are you anyway?"

"Probably not wise to say, just in case, you know. Then again, I don't really know exactly where we are, to be honest, but it's a Shangri-La magical kind of place. Wish you could see it!"

"I can be there before you can say, Camelot!"

"Let's keep that plan in our back pocket, Lancelot."

"A little too risky, I presume," he said.

"Yup. I'd be royally bummed if someone decided to take a pot shot at you on the way down."

"Well, I don't mind jousting with another knight," Colby said, "but a squadron of trigger-happy Caifanii security teams all aiming for my ass is more than I'm equipped to fend off."

"Any news from that French science vessel?"

"Nope, I haven't heard back from them. I hope they are not ignoring me. I will contact them again. They might have some clever ideas. They told me they do all sorts of cutting-edge scientific experiments. Who knows what they might have up their sleeves. They sounded like a bunch of eccentrics to boot, might get a kick out of helping us."

"Why don't you call them and get back to me. I'll be busy until late tonight though."

"You got a hot date or something?"

Damn, Sola thought, another perfect lead in. She lost her nerve. She couldn't step up to the plate and hit the pitch.

"Uh, no, I'm taking part in a ritual healing ceremony."

"No kidding! You *have* gone native, Pumpkin."

"You have no idea!"

"Okay. I'll get back to you as soon as I know something."

"I'll check in with you after the ceremony."

"Will you be clean and sober?"

"I don't think it involves mind-altering substances, though I'm sure it will be a mind-blowing experience!"

"Wish I were there!"

"Me too!" she said, and meant it.

"I miss you like crazy, woman" he said, suddenly tender.

They both fell silent for a moment.

Then Colby continued.

"I want you to know that I understand that what you are going through down there is no easy deal, and that it is having a big impact on you. I'm not so naïve as to think your connection with these people is so shallow that you can just walk away without looking back, or feeling a loss. I've been thinking about that, a lot. I really wanted to talk with you in private, so I could tell you. These folks are sort of like your war pals now. I've never been a soldier, and I'm grateful for that, but I've read a lot of wartime novels and seen plenty of old wartime flicks. Don't feel awkward about having mixed feelings about leaving these people behind."

Sola was stunned. She couldn't even think of what to say. Colby had just blown her out of the water.

"Sola? Are you still there?"

"Yeah. I'm here, I'm so touched by what you're saying. This whole experience here is unlike anything I've ever been through, Colby. I want to talk with you about all of it, when I'm back on Minerva. I promise, I'll tell you everything then. Right now, I just need to deal with those mixed emotions. You're so right, it's not easy."

"Just know that I totally respect what you're doing."

"Thanks, Colby."

"Not everyone has the courage to stand with an honorable cause, no matter what. I'm proud of you!"

"Colby. I'm so grateful to you for being supportive and hanging in with me. Your situation isn't easy either."

"Oh, it's not so bad. I'm getting all caught up on my back burner projects. Getting a tan in the Cancun program.
I'm fine, just looking forward to some quality time with my best bud."

"Me too!"

"Okay, until later then."

"You bet."

They signed off.

Sola sat in the chair staring out of the view screen. The green camouflage netting that hung over the entire ship was all she could see.

She'd call Meil on the intercom in a moment, but first she needed time alone to think about what just happened.

Colby was her best friend, he'd proved that many times over, and he'd just proven it again. She wasn't sure if he suspected that she'd become romantically involved with one of the Mhalanai, but she was sure that he would be a lot more understanding when she told him about Jaitain. Kudos to Colby. He was a trooper.

Sola called Meil and they walked back across the field towards the farmhouse.

"Colby was contacted by a Terran research vessel in this sector yesterday," Sola said. "He's going to ask for their assistance. Their vessel probably has all kinds of new technologies that could prove useful for us, and they could be here within a day."

"That sounds promising!" Meil said.

"I need to contact him again later tonight, to see if he was successful. Will that be possible?"

"You mean after the Joining?"

"Yes. I doubt he'll know anything before then."

"It's not a problem, though you will be in an altered state!" Meil said, with a knowing grin.

When they reached the gardens behind the house, they found Ailva sitting in a chair enjoying the fresh air and the view.

"Sola," Ailva said, "do come sit with me a while."

Meil bid his adieu and went into the house.

Sola settled down on a small bench under a blooming tree. Red flowers trailed down from willow-like branches all around her.

"I'm nervous," Sola said.

"You look delightful with all that red around you," Ailva said, beaming with a maternal affection. "Maybe we will weave a garland of those flowers to place on your head. I do miss that amazing hair of yours."

"Is there anything I need to do to prepare for tonight?" Sola asked.

"No," Ailva said. "It will help if you are rested. Did you get some sleep this afternoon?"

"Yes, I did, but I'm confused. I don't know what to do."

Sola leaned in against Ailva resting her head against Ailva's shoulder.

"I'm thinking about staying here," she said.

Ailva wrapped her arm around Sola's shoulder.

"You would certainly be welcomed," she said.

"All this time, we've focused all our energy on getting me home. Now, I wonder if my *real* home is here with all of you! I'm all tied up in knots about it, and I have precious little time to make a decision."

"I feel for you, my dear," Ailva said. "I suspect there is no wrong decision," she added. "You can create happiness on either path."

"That doesn't help much," Sola complained. "I feel that one or the other must be the better choice. I've changed so much here that I no longer know my own needs well enough to judge how to fulfill them!"

"An interesting dilemma!" Ailva said, shivering a little.

"Would you be more comfortable inside?" Sola asked. "It is getting a bit chilly out here."

"No." Ailva said. "This is too wonderful, those mountains are too extravagant to miss. Besides, there is so much clatter and chatter in there. It's peaceful out here in Lena's lovely garden."

The garden had a scattering of wild flowers bordering a cultivated plot with rows of remarkably large vegetables.

"I love the garden too. It's soothing to be out here," Sola said. "I hope the Joining will help me figure things out."

"That is one of the benefits," Ailva assured her. "The experience will deeply connect you with your heart. The Grieving Ceremony will also free any pent up emotions. With all that compressed energy released, things will be simpler. Our guests will begin to arrive soon," Ailva said. "I'm going to take a walk out into the meadows to find a suitable location for our gathering. Would you like to join me?"

"You bet," Sola said, "a walk would be just the ticket."

"Good," Ailva said. "Are you ready to go now?"

"First, let me get us both something warmer to wear," Sola suggested.

"That's very thoughtful, my dear. I will wait for you here."

"All right," Sola said. "I'll be back in a jiffy."

Sola returned with two shawls woven from yamma wool. They strolled out into the open fields. The sun was on its descent in the sky, but the breeze had settled down, so it was pleasant, especially wrapped up in Lena's warming handiwork. Yellow, purple, and blue wildflowers spiced up the field grasses.

"Do you have a place in mind?" Sola asked.

"Yes," Ailva said, "a place where we held a Joining, let me think, well, I can't remember exactly how long ago, a good while. I am hopeful I still remember how to find it."

The fields stretched out towards the foothills. There was plenty of space all around them. Sola wondered why one area would be any better than another.

"Will we meet out here in the fields?" She asked after they had walked for about ten minutes.

"There is a meadow up ahead," Ailva said.

The two of them walked in silence.

"The meadow is a completely clear place," Ailva continued. "There are no black streams."

"Black streams?" Sola asked.

"Some landscapes carry high densities of natural electromagnetic radiation from the planet," Ailva explained. "Fissures, fault lines, veins of certain mineral deposits, these all increase such radiation. We call these areas black streams. It is unwise to build a dwelling over such a place. It can cause everything from poor sleep and irritability to physical illness. In certain places, this radiation is multiple. That is, one black stream may cross over another. I am always careful in choosing the location for a Joining. Participants will experience heightened awareness and receptivity. I wish to protect them from any negative influences. The Joining is assisted by choosing a proper location where the planet's natural energies are in harmony."

The high grass ended abruptly, and they moved into a meadow of softer, lower vegetation, a type of dense moss.

Sola looked back.

The farmhouse was a long way behind them.

The meadow remained level for several hundred meters and then began to slope gradually up into the low hills.

Ailva stopped. She turned slowly, stretched her arms out a little from her body. With the palms of her hands facing down, she closed her eyes and turned very slowly in a complete circle.

"This is the place," she said.

They both perused the land. From here, the mountains dominated the view with even greater impact than from the village.

The deep green of the moss provided a dramatic contrast to the foothills and peaks beyond. Whereas the field grasses had softened the lens, the open meadow focused the image so that the mountains looked more sharply defined and formidable.

"This is impressive," Sola said, looking up at the majestic mountains and finding herself dizzy from the thin air and the view.

"You look a bit lightheaded," Ailva said.

"I could fly away right now, or at least be blown away!" Sola laughed.

"I am going to walk the perimeter of the area, to feel the energy of the land at the circumference of our gathering. I will not be long," Ailva said, "but I will need to be alone, silent, and focused for a little while."

"I won't get in your way," Sola assured her. "I think I'll walk up into the hills a bit further. Just call me when you're ready to leave."

Just over the first rise, Sola came down into a second, smaller meadow full of wildflowers. Gleefully, she picked a bouquet of pale-blue, butter-yellow, white, orange and magenta flowers. She would give them to Lena.

After too short a time, she heard Ailva's voice calling softly in her mind.

She picked a few sprigs of green to augment her arrangement and wandered back to meet her Danu.

Chapter 30

Day Thirteen (sunset)

Ho Lea shau ho tii.
The Joining heals the heart.

The Mhalanai Book of Ways

The last frail rays of sun reflected off the icy summits of Mount Mudriat.

Sola went upstairs to wake Jaitain. She opened the bedroom door. Pale alpine glow illuminated the space through the thin curtains. Jaitain lay on his side, facing the windows, his breath slow and deep with sleep.

She crawled into the bed and spooned him, kissing his shoulder.

"Wake up, Sweet," she said.

He stirred and slowly turned to face her. His eyes clouded with remnants of dreams.

"Nulini," he said, a satisfied smile growing across his sleep-creased face.

"You were out like a light," she said.

"I slept like a mountain."

"That's what Meil said too. On Earth we sleep like a rock."

"A mountain is a giant rock."

"True enough," Sola said.

"How long was I asleep?" Jaitain asked.

"Hours, but you needed it. Guess what?"

"You missed me?"

"Yes, I did, but I have two pieces of news. Ailva has planned a Joining, for tonight!"

"That's excellent! Perfect! What's the other piece of news?"

"Colby may have some allies who can assist us."

"Really? How so?"

"Some researchers from Earth, of all things, are in the neighborhood."

"From Earth? That's amazing!"

"I know, miraculous, actually. Colby thinks they may have some new technology that will come in handy, though he doesn't have a clue exactly what that might be. He's going to ask them if they would be willing to help us."

"I have a good feeling about this," Jaitain said.

"I know. Me too!"

"It's getting dark. I'd better get up and dress. Did you eat?"

She kissed his cheek.

"No. Lena and Eilfina are cooking up a feast, and guess who's coming for dinner? I almost forgot that news. Tjarlii!"

"I must have been asleep for a week. I've missed all the excitement."

They held each other watching the pink light on the mountains through the scrim of the curtains.

"I love alpine glow," Sola said. "It turns the rugged harshness of rock and ice into a fairyland as fine as gossamer."

It was quiet upstairs, but kitchen noises drifted up from below.

Sola rested her head against Jaitain's chest. This might be their last intimate time.

Soon, she might be back in the green-less, sun-less void of space, back in the clinical world of techno talk and artificial light.

So many important changes in life came in bits and pieces, strung together over time. A new fabric of reality spinning and setting its patterns before you even realized you were making monumental change.

After all the events and transformations of the past days, Sola wasn't sure she could step back over the threshold and return to her old life.

Habit was a strong force. She knew that. It might take time to adjust, but eventually she would probably realign. She could let her well-worn routines urge her back into the day-to-day details of her previous life, and she'd be fine, but was that what she wanted?

There was something fresh on this planet, with these openhearted people. She felt emotions so vividly here with her sensuous and genuine lover.

Once she returned to Earth, would she long for the life she'd experienced here? Would she feel homesick for Caifanii? If she stayed here, she would miss Colby, her father, her grandmother, Maui, and all the wonders of Earth. She would miss them in a deep, aching way.

She was torn and unable to make a decision. She hoped the Joining would bring clarity.

"You are in another universe," Jaitain whispered.

"I was thinking of Earth, of all the wonderful things I will miss, would miss."

"I'm glad to hear you haven't made a final choice to leave."

"I can't imagine leaving you."

"Then don't imagine it. Let's go down and see what wonderful things Lena has placed on the table for us!"

Chapter 31

Day Fifteen (evening)

Ho tiloa cama au yin ionane.
The final face of grief is gratitude.

The Mhalanai Book of Ways

Sola was delighted when, during their evening meal, Tjarlii made a boisterous entrance.

The garbage barge captain strode into the house with an air of bravado. She was wearing a large coat that reminded Sola of a cowboy's duster. It hung unfastened and flowed amply from her strong shoulders like a great cape.

Tjarlii smiled as she entered the dining area, her heavy boots making a clatter on the wooden flooring. She was slender, sharp-eyed, and her curt laugh hinted at a few good stories.

"Greetings!" Tjarlii said, in a sonorous, raspy voice that sounded like it was no stranger to whiskey, or the Caifanii equivalent.

"Tjarlii!" Meil said. "Welcome! Please come and eat with us, you must be hungry from your journey."

"My regrets for such a tardy arrival," Tjarlii said.

She took off her coat and hung it on a rack on the wall near the entry, as if she'd done so a hundred times before, totally at home in the room.

"The strike has everyone out of sorts and I had some business to attend to in Djintu," she said.

"No problem, my friend. We are all so happy that you are able to be here with us for this Joining," Meil said.

He led Tjarlii, who was tall for a Caifanii, to the empty seat next to Sola.

"Let me introduce you to Sola Alturas," Meil said.

Sola turned in her seat to face Tjarlii.

"I am honored to meet you, Tjarlii," she said.

Their new guest settled into her seat.

"And I am honored to meet the the famous Terran revolutionary!" Tjarlii said.

"Is that the story you've heard?"

"Oh, there are many stories," She gave Sola a wily look, and a wide grin.

"Well, I hope they are all good ones," Sola said, blushing.

"Mostly tales of courage and beauty, and I can see that these are less exaggerated than I'd guessed. Do not judge me by my frankness. I can be a tad assertive, but be assured I hold you in highest esteem."

Tjarlii made a slight bow of her head.

"Thank you," Sola said, feeling an instant connection with this rough edged, candid woman. "I regret we may not have the opportunity to ride together on that fine garbage barge of yours."

Tjarlii laughed. "That ship is nothing to regret missing, I assure you! As for our adventure, we will see what transpires in the next hours of the strike. We may still have a chance, but I am keeping all of you from your meal; and knowing Lena, it is a glorious feast!"

"Please," Sola said, "have some bread. It's still warm from the oven, and here," she passed Tjarlii a bowl of fresh garden vegetables in a delicate herbal sauce, "These are terrific!"

Dinner continued amid the cacophony of excited conversation in anticipation of what lay ahead.

After the meal, everyone moved into the living area to drink tea, just as guests began to arrive for the Joining.

The earlier din and buzz settled down into a preparatory quietude as the room began to fill to overflowing.

Ailva walked to the room's center.

"Thank you, everyone for coming on such short notice. We are pleased to have you here with us for this momentous occasion. Please follow me outside. The villagers have donated lanterns, blankets, and cushions for us to use. Please help carry these and let's begin our journey to the chosen site for the Joining."

The evening was calm, the sky cloudless, and both moons close to full. A caravan of nineteen participants walked out into the fields, some carried small lanterns. Everyone had received a warm blanket and a small cushion to bring. There was some light talk, but the overall mood was one of reverence.

Sola walked silently next to Jaitain. They were near the head of the party, which followed Ailva across the field.

Sola felt as though she walked through a dream world. She wondered if angels would be in their company tonight. She was floating in the procession of small lights, which moved into the semi-darkness under the steady gaze of Mudriat Peak, and of the two moons, looking like giant owl eyes peering down at them.

She expected to feel excitement. Instead, she felt trepidation, not about the Joining, but about the decision that lay ahead of her.

No matter which choice she made, to stay or to leave, she was going to suffer a loss. She tried to let it go, just walk, let the night take her into its cool embrace and empty her mind of thought.

When they reached the meadow, everyone began to move in single file to form a large circle with Ailva standing, like a Druid priestess, in its center.

Sola recognized the vision she had dreamed long before she had even met Ailva. Tonight, Ailva's robe was a very light blue, not lavender as in the dream, but that was the only difference.

Everyone stood fairly close together in the circle. They placed their cushions on the moss, but remained standing. Sola followed suit.

Jaitain stood beside Sola on her left, Eilfina on her right. Between these loving souls, Sola felt comforted.

She expected someone to build a fire in the center of the circle.

That seemed a requirement of outdoor rituals in the nighttime, but apparently not a requirement for a Joining.

In fact, everyone turned off their lanterns, and stood silent in the moonlight.

Ailva was a silvery blue figure at the circle's center. She addressed the entire gathering in a resonant, regal voice.

"Let us begin our Joining by offering our contract to become connected through our hearts, and minds."

Within a few breaths their hearts and minds began to join together.

Sola gasped, it was such a powerful experience. She breathed into the feeling, allowing herself to become part of the loving embrace. She wanted to hold hands with Jaitain and Eilfina, but everyone was standing with their arms at their sides.

Ailva continued speaking. This time telepathically.

"Let us now address the directions in thanksgiving."

Ailva raised her arms, facing away from Sola. The entire circle faced East as Ailva's voice continued in all of their minds.

"We praise and thank the East, direction of new light, of new hope. We praise and thank the color red, color of birth and rebirth, color of our ancient memory. We praise and thank the mineral realm, foundation of time and place. We praise and thank the Home World, Mother of all life, provider of all nourishment and progress." Ailva paused.

Sola breathed deeply, let her shoulders relax. She instinctively took a Chi Gong position, knees slightly bent, energy centered at her solar plexus.

Ailva made a quarter turn to the right. They all followed suit.

"We praise and thank the South, direction of summer, direction of fruitfulness, of faith and healing. We praise and thank the color yellow, color of joy, color of cleansing light and wellness. Color of our optimism. We praise and thank the plant realm, foundation of sustenance, replenishment and beauty. We thank water, vehicle of our cleansing, bringer of clarity and peace of heart."

Sola shifted into an altered state. It was a physical sensation, as if her feet no longer touched the ground. All of them in the circle connected with Ailva as the hub of a wheel of energy with spokes of light connecting each individual to that hub and to each other.

Ailva's voice flowed into her mind like white light. All of them turned again to the right, without thought, as one being.

"We praise and thank the West, direction of our release, direction of our intuitive power, direction of our intention. We praise and thank the color black, the color of the void, of the creative force. We praise and thank all two and four-legged creatures who share our world, may they guide and teach us as they have done since the days of our ancestors. We praise and thank fire, the instigator of illumination, purification, and transformation."

Ailva's words welled up in her mind like water from a spring, as pure concepts.

Sola began to feel a soft tingling throughout her body, throughout her molecular being. She felt a vibration of energy at the cellular level. She felt the vibration of all the others move through her. Her perception of her individual self, her definitive identity, transmuted to a perception of greater wholeness. She felt at one with all in the circle.

She began to notice other thought forms entering her mind, moving into her awareness like tributaries of energy.

The thoughts and feelings of love and joy, which filled her mind and being, were no longer exclusively hers.

They were a collection of the thoughts and feelings of all of those present.

For an instant, it occurred to her that this ought to be alarming, that her mind might not be able to contain so much energy, so many collected thoughts and feelings.

She breathed deeply. The worry was fleeting and instantly replaced with peacefulness. Everything was flowing together into a river of light and reverence. She let it flow through her. It was rapturous.

Ailva's thoughts now came without voice, without literal form, as pure ideas, as all of them turned in unison to the right.

"We praise and thank the North, direction of the mind, direction of the spirit's knowing, direction of return. We praise and thank the color white, color of tranquility, humility, acceptance and understanding. We praise and thank the Beyond Beings, servants of the Light, and ensigns of love. We praise and thank air, vehicle of ecstasy, of crystalline perception, mindfulness, inclusion, life."

Sola felt a great urge to sit down and as she sat, she felt that they were all sitting now, eyes closed, minds connected through Ailva to each other.

She felt warm and content, aware of her physical body as an anchor, the rooting of her being, but no longer a separate, distinct entity.

She felt that her physical form expanded to include the entire circle of beings and the powerful form of Ailva at its center.

She felt no concern, hesitancy, or fear. She felt only the basic, grounding current of love passing through her, connecting her heart with the hearts of her companions, and with the Universe beyond and within them.

Ailva's words now felt like they originated within her own mind. "We praise and thank you, Great Spirit, provider of all life, fountain of all thought, source of all energy. We ask that the power of love transform us from that which desires a singular reality to that which desires a unified plurality. We ask that the infusion of light bring us together as one mind, one insight, one understanding, as it is in the Spirit World. We praise and thank you Mother Mhalanai, harbor in space, planet of our material resource and spiritual manifestation. Bring us together in harmony with your vibration, in harmony with your intention. Let us be guided to our ancient wisdom with honor, simplicity and reverence for all life, all thought, all vibrations of Being."

These thoughts coursed through each mind in the circle as a continuous circuit, and then expanded beyond each personal identity, as a unified field of the Life Force itself, expressing its nature through all beings.

The collection of thoughts and emotions contained within the individuals gathered in the circle transformed into a pure emotional state; unspoken, unvoiced, unanimously experienced in a timeless framework of Being.

Thought transformed into instantaneous conception. Conception into Light. Light into Energy. Energy into All that Is. Time ceased. The pre-organic connections of the Universal Structure of Love transcended all organic definition.

Out of this timeless state, energy began again to form into light, into conception, into thought. Wholeness remained, but individuality emerged into distinct qualities and vibratory patterns. What had melded into oneness began to separate again into diversity, yet each part remained complete, a holograph of the whole.

After an indeterminable time, Sola recognized distinct thoughts in her mind. Some were her own some were clearly the thoughts of others. She heard Ailva's voice in her mind.

"The Joining is accomplished. Sola, it is time for you to voice your question."

Sola formed her question as a concept in her mind. "Shall I remain here to live on Caifanii?"

The sensations that followed were odd beyond description.

Sola felt her question lifted out of her mind, like a child from a crib, and passed to Jaitain, who held it for a while, gave it love, and then passed it on to the person on his left. In this way, her question moved around the entire circle. She could follow its progress.

Eventually, the question came to Eilfina, who held it lovingly and then passed it back to her. All of the thoughts and emotions of each member of the Joining provided a new energy, a new illumination to the question. Through this spiritual sharing, the essence of the question grew and developed into its own answer.

Sola listened to her question, returning to her like her child, having been tenderly held and nourished by each heart that carried it through the circle.

The answer was succinct and poetic. "Carry our heritage to your home and you will carry us with you. Return here when we are whole, and you will find your home with us."

Sola held the concept in her mind, letting it settle. While her mind remained uncertain as to the exact meaning, her heart felt a great sense of ease. She knew the answer was sufficient even though her mind was not yet able to grasp its full meaning.

She wanted to express thanks to her companions for formulating this answer with her.

She held the thought in her mind, "Thank you. I am deeply grateful." Again, the thought lifted gently from her mind and passed along the circle. It returned to her as, "All hearts feel your thanks. All receive it with love and return it with love."

Sola rested in a radiant contentment. There was a sense of well-being present in the entire circle.

She again heard Ailva's voice in her mind. "Sola, do you wish to experience the Grieving Ceremony within this Joining?"

"Yes," her mind answered, without hesitation.

"Then we will accomplish this together," Ailva responded. She addressed the circle as a whole. "Our companion has suffered two great losses. She still carries grief and anger. Are we willing to assist her in the release of these heavy emotions?"

The circle collectively answered, "Yes."

"Then," Ailva's voice guided, "we ask that Sola's blocked emotions surface, are experienced in pure form, and then released from her heart, mind and body."

Sola listened, in repose, staying open.

"Sola," Ailva's voice said. "We collectively call forth the residual emotions connected to the loss of your brother, and the loss of your mother. We collectively hold assistance for you in surfacing, experiencing and releasing these heavy energies. We call on our Protectors in all realms to act as sacred witness to this cleansing and to allow its process to take place without harm or distress to any participant. Are you ready to begin?"

"I am ready," Sola said, in her mind, feeling an intuitive preparedness and sensing the steady support of her companions and of other, non-embodied energies surrounding their circle.

It came. Straight out of her heart like a rush of wind. Anger. A hot red feeling shot into her consciousness, making her throat constrict and making her body burn with its raging heat. She experienced acute but mercifully brief pain in her kidneys, then in her groin, her colon, her stomach, her joints, her throat, her eyes, her jaws, her forehead.

She felt the anger lift out of her physical body.

Its energy moved rapidly around the circle, not staying with any one person long enough to cause distress, and dissipating in potency with each passage from body to body.

Each member of the Joining retained a small portion of her anger, and then passed the rest on to the next participant, who did the same.

In this way, her anger divided among the participants. Each person transmuted their small portion of the emotion into pure thought energy by honoring its power and then releasing it out of the circle.

By the time her anger came full circle back to her, it was so manageable that she was able to transmute it herself into pure thought energy and let it go completely.

A cooling energy passed through Sola's body like anointed water.

After the clearing of her anger, a new, more profound emotion surfaced.

Grief.

Again, it originated in her heart like a burst of wind and moved into her physical body causing her lungs to ache profoundly for a moment, then her throat, her ears, her reproductive organs, her temples, her lower back and the back of her neck.

Again, as soon as she felt the pain, the emotional energy passed from her, to her left to move through the circle.

Again, each member of the Joining retained a small part of the grief, transmuted it to pure energy and released it, passing the rest along until the residual grief came back to her so diminished as to be almost nullified.

Sola released the remaining fragment and felt it go, felt it replaced again by the cooling sensation of holy water.

Sola felt light, as if she might float up off the ground. Her heart filled with an uncontainable mirth.

Soon, she was laughing, and the entire circle was laughing along with her, sharing her delight.

They laughed, and laughed, and laughed.

Sola's muscles ached from the powerful belly laughs. There was such release in this simple joy. It was a new freedom.

She felt an immense wave of love pass through and over her from all those present.

In the lingering warmth of this love, she realized that her thoughts were her own again, single, not multiple.

The Joining had closed with divine humor.

Chapter 32

Day Fifteen (deep night)

Imalatu yin muti aru
Intuition is our second sight

The Mhalanai Book of Ways

Everyone wandered back to the village, arm in arm with companions. Some sang softly, others were still chuckling. It was approaching midnight. The guests were staying with various villagers. Everyone acted giddy.

Meil came up beside Sola as she walked arm in arm with Jaitain.

"Do you still want to call Colby?" he asked.

"Oh, I completely forgot! Thanks for reminding me. I'm high as a kite, but I promised I'd call him tonight."

"As of a few moments ago, it's morning" Meil said.

"Well, then good morning my dear friend!" Sola said.

She felt drunk with happiness, and gave the night sky a big, "Whoopeee!"

"You are in grand spirits!" Ailva said, catching up to them.

"I am!" Sola kissed Jaitain on the cheek, and then turned to kiss Ailva as well.

When Meil pointed to his own cheek, Sola gave him a kiss too.

"Wait for me!" Eilfina said, running up from behind them.

They all joined Sola in heading for the Naia.

They climbed aboard.

Meil switched on the com and called Colby.

"Colby!" Sola said.

"Hey there, Cinderella!" he said. "I was beginning to worry your carriage had turned into a pumpkin, Pumpkin!"

"I know. The ceremony was pretty long, and beyond amazing! I'm super high!"

"You sound like you've had a few too many margaritas, señorita."

"Not a one, my friend. Not a one! Just high on love."

"Gee, wish I could get some of that!"

"Plenty to go around, around here." She *was* feeling delightfully tipsy.

"Sorry, it's not nice to flaunt my joy to a guy who's been stuck on the dark side of the moon for days!"

"I've named all the craters. There's a spectacular one called Solace."

"How very kind of you," she said. "So, any good news?"

"How's your French?"

"About as good as my Swahili!"

"Quel dommage," he replied, with a generous Texan accent. "No worries. I think these chaps will speak English if you ask real nice."

"You mean the Cousteau is going to help us out?"

"Bien sur! How would you like to be a soil sample?"

"Not very much, thank you, but do explain."

"They have something called Molecular Energizing and Reconfiguration Technology, or MERT. Their parent company initially developed it to extract soil samples from planets with inhospitable environments, but now they're using it to transport all kind of things, including themselves, between their ship and the surface of hospitable planets. They'd be happy to snatch you up from Caifanii, and could do it without even infiltrating the official orbital boundary."

"Shit! That's really out there." Sola felt suddenly quite sober. "Wow! I've heard of MERT, but had no idea anyone was actually using it. That's pretty wild, but aren't they going to break interstellar law by taking something, or someone, off this planet without prior clearance?"

"As far as we know, Haikon thinks you're dead, so they won't exactly miss you, and you are not Caifanii property, so they aren't technically stealing anything, plus the head honcho on the Cousteau insists this situation is an exception. According to him, Amnesty Interstellar has classified you as a 'prisoner of war,' and that authorizes Amnesty to utilize United Planets Association member vessels to liberate you if possible, as long as there is no use of force and no prospect of immediate retribution. Get this! Their captain, believe it or not, is named Jean Luc!"

"No way!"

"Way! He got pretty excited about the whole thing, went on and on about how this brought back old memories of his missions with Greenpeace."

"I'm beginning to think I'm hallucinating. Are we really having this conversation?"

"I assure you we are. I am very real, and so is the pain in my ass from sitting up here all this time."

"Sorry, cowboy. We'll get you out of the saddle soon."

"I'd much appreciate it!"

"I'm not exactly a 'prisoner of war,' but close enough for government work, I guess. Legalities aside, how safe is this MERT? Is it certified? I don't want my molecules whisked through space and gathered back together with a few important parts missing, or in the wrong place!"

"Are you worried your nose may end up on your forehead?"

"Yeah, maybe, or something less obvious but more lethal, like losing cell regeneration capacity."

"Ouch! That would be bad," Colby said. "They did send me a link to the official brochure."

He put on his best commercial voice. "MERT has now been perfected to transport equipment and life forms, including research teams, to and from planet surfaces. Scientific trials have proven the method to be safe and reliable."

"Really? I can't believe we haven't heard about this before."

"I know! I've been waiting for someone other than Picard to say, 'Energize!' for decades."

"Picard is definitely my favorite Star Trek captain! Wow! I can't believe I'm going to be able to say, 'Beam me up, Scottie!'"

"It's even better than that! You're going to be able to say, 'Beam me up, Jean Luc!' and Jean Luc will actually beam you up!"

"Outrageous!"

"So, does this mean you're in? They will be here in about eight hours."

"Wow! That's soon!"

"Shall I inform Jean Luc that we accept their generous offer?"

"Wow! Let me think about this for a few more moments."

"That's a lot of wows."

"I know. It's a seriously wow situation."

"Take your time. I'll wait. I'm getting seriously good at that!"

"You're the best!"

Sola took a deep breath and let it escape with a sigh.

She turned to her companions.

"Well, it looks like my rescue is imminent. That Terran research vessel I mentioned earlier is offering to pick me up. Their technology is very cutting-edge. They have the capacity to transport me directly from the planet surface, at fixed coordinates, to their vessel without their even entering Caifanii regulatory space."

"How would they do this?" Meil asked, incredulous.

"Something called Molecular Energizing and Reconfiguration Technology, MERT. My molecular body would be highly energized for a fraction of a second, transferred to their vessel as light, and then de-energized back to its normal molecular state and frequency."

"Oh!" Eilfina said. "That sounds kind of like death and resurrection."

Sola hadn't considered it quite that way.

Certainly, for a moment, she would technically be dead, and then revived, or rather recombined.

"I guess it is pretty cosmic," she said, "but it does make me worry about my nose."

"What?" Eilfina asked.

Sola pulled at the end of her nose, twisted it around a bit, and then pretended to stick it to her forehead.

"Oh, I see!" Eilfina said.

"How soon could this take place?" Jaitain asked.

"Their research vessel will arrive in about eight hours, so some time after that," Sola answered.

It hit home to her that she was going *home*.

The Joining had been a catalyst for her final decision. She was leaving, and as soon as later this morning, hopefully to return, but the future never offered guarantees. Her stomach filled with fluttering butterflies.

Everyone stood in silence, experiencing the gravity of the moment.

"You are leaving us then?" Jaitain asked. His eyes filling with tears.

"Oh, shit!" Sola said. "Now I've made a revolutionary leader cry."

"That doesn't happen too often!" Meil said, giving Jaitain a gentle slap on the back.

"In the Joining it was clear that you will return again," Ailva said.

"Then we will focus on that reunion!" Jaitain said, smiling through his tears.

Sola's eyes filled with tears too, and then they were all laughing and crying, and making a general emotional fuss over each other.

"Houston, do we have a problem?" Sola heard Colby say over the com.

She turned around to face the console. "No, just a lot of blubbering going on over here."

"I can hear that. You must've made quite an impression on those folks! So, I take it you are on board with the plan?"

"I am!"

"I'll get the fine print from Jean Luc. They will need a specific time, and the coordinates of your chosen location, outside is best. So, think about that and let's talk again after we've both had some sleep. Call me at high noon, your time."

"Sounds good, Colby. Sorry to keep you up so late."

"I'm on satellite time up here. No problem."

"Hasta mi amigo, y gracias!"

"De nada!"

Chapter 33

Day Sixteen (morning)

Taah yin kote di taah.
Trust is an invitation for truth.

The Mhalanai Book of Ways

Jaitain spent the night with Sola. They wished their intimate time together could stretch out to forever, but knew they had only a few hours of bliss.

They left the curtains open to savor the view of moonlight on the mountains while holding each other in the bed. Both still delightfully high from the energy of the Joining, their silent embrace flowed easily into making love while telepathically connected. Sola's consciousness expanded so profoundly at her heart chakra, that afterwards, she was sure MERT could offer nothing as cosmic or potent. All tension released from her mind, body and heart, she fell into a deeply relaxed sleep.

Sola woke up feeling at peace. It was a surprisingly normal feeling that had not been the norm in far too long. Sunlight streamed into the room. She thought about Ramon and about her mom, and was grateful to find no anger or grief in her heart, only love. It was a miracle.

Jaitain was already up and gone.

Sola stretched luxuriously, longing for a morning kiss.

She would go find him and get one.

Instead, she found Ailva in the garden with Pjetri. She joined them, settling onto the bench under the flowering tree.

Pjetri explained that the tree was called a kadit tree, and it offered long pods in the spring which, when dried, were used to make a rich dessert called kaditan. He went into the house and returned with a sample for her from last spring's harvest.

To Sola's amazement, it tasted just like bittersweet chocolate.

"Be careful you do not eat too much," Pjetri warned. "It will make your heart race, and," he added with a sly grin, "it will make you feel amorous! Well, so they say." He laughed. "I have not myself experienced this second effect."

Sola smiled, pleased with Pjetri's easy manner and delighted to taste chocolate, or a close cousin, after so long. Non-simulated, genuine chocolate was hard to find these days, even on Earth.

"I will wrap some up for you to take along," Pjetri said.

"That's wonderful. Thank you so much, Pjetri, for that and for all of your hospitality!" Sola said.

"You are welcome. I am going to go do that right now, before I forget and you end up with no katidan and a big frown for Pjetri!"

"Ailva," Sola said. "Can we talk about the message I received during the Joining? I'd value your opinion, your interpretation."

"It is the meaning you extract that matters," Ailva said.

"Perhaps, but your thoughts are still very welcomed."

"I do strongly believe that you will share our teachings and your experiences here with others when you return to your world. Even prior to the Joining, I was convinced that such work would be natural for you as a writer."

"Well," Sola said, "writing cookbooks is more a culinary art than a literary one."

"That may well be, but I believe the Joining urges you to share our stories and our teachings with your people, and perhaps with others as well, in whatever way is best suited."

"That makes sense," Sola said. "I don't want to misrepresent your culture or your wisdom. I may have some experience with your teachings but my knowledge is a drop in the proverbial bucket, and my memories of the experience will lose clarity over time."

Sola felt a sudden head rush from the kaditan.

"Wow! This is excellent!"

Ailva smiled with affection and came to sit next to Sola on the bench. "You are under no obligation to do anything in particular with your experiences here. If you do decide to share them, I can assist you. We can work together, telepathically."

"Ailva, you must be joking. I will be light years away!"

"True," Ailva said, looking like a poker player with an ace up her sleeve. I will be back momentarily." She rose from the seat and walked back into the house.

In a few minutes, she returned with a large, ornate box cradled in her arms. Thick burgundy wrapping paper decorated with an ornate golden flower pattern covered the box.

"What is it?" Sola asked, as Ailva placed the box on Sola's lap.

"My gift to you, Nulini," Ailva said, "regardless of what you choose to do with your future."

Sola sat with the large box on her lap. It was not heavy. She gave Ailva a searching look and felt like a child at a surprise birthday party.

"Shall I open it now?" she asked, timidly.

"Absolutely!" Ailva said.

Sola carefully undid the wrapping paper, wanting to save it. She exposed a highly polished wooden box with three ornate clasps, one at the front, one at each end. She undid the clasps and lifted the surprisingly lightweight lid. Tucked meticulously inside, surrounded by a thick velvety material was the Olvino Saad.

"Ailva!" Sola said, her hand coming up to cover her mouth.

"You don't need this to communicate with us here, but it will enhance your skills when we try to connect over a great distance,"Ailva said.

"Are you sure? Are you *sure* you want me to have this? Is it the only one?"

"I do not personally own another, but there are others here in the South. This gift is from all of us. Will you accept it?"

"I will accept it. I am so moved, really, I am speechless. I will protect it, keep it safe always."

"May it protect *you!*" Ailva said.

"I hope I remember how to use it!" Sola said. "I've only used it once."

"If it will make you feel more confident, we can use it one more time before you leave, as a refresher."

"I'd appreciate that. Any chance we could do that now?"

"No time like the present!" Ailva said. "Let's use my bed chamber. There is a small table there and two chairs."

The women went into the house, which was curiously empty and silent.

"Where is everyone?" Sola asked.

"Maybe Lena took them out for a demonstration of sustainable farming!" She said, chuckling to herself.

They entered Ailva's chamber. Ailva closed the drapes against the bright sunlight.

"To help the concentration," she said.

She quickly cleared some personal items from the table and Sola placed the box in its center. They sat, across from each other in the two wooden chairs.

Ailva lifted the unit out of the box by the base, supporting the stem with her other hand. She set in on the table and placed the box gently on the floor by her feet.

Sola recalled the details of her first session with Olvino Saad. She took the tubing in her fingers, calmed her mind, and centered her energy.

"Excellent," Ailva said, "Now, find and focus upon a well-defined thought."

"A well-defined thought," Sola whispered. "I don't have any of those today."

She searched through the myriad wandering thoughts in her mind until something jumped out at her. She giggled.

"If you're happy and you know it, clap your hands," she sang.

It was a childhood song. Why it popped into her head now, she had no idea, but it was a well-defined thought.

"Now, choose someone with whom you have a telepathic contract. I suppose Jaitain would be a good choice."

Sola filled her heart with love for Jaitain. She sent that love out to his heart, and immediately felt warmth in her heart and a tingling in her fingers. She sang the song to Jaitain in her mind. The more loving emotion she placed into the song, moving it from her heart to his heart; the more she felt the warmth and vibration. She stayed with the love and warmth for some time, and then let the connection release.

"It's quite easy, really. I felt Jaitain connected with me, but shall we find him and see if it worked?"

"Oh, it worked," Ailva said. "He will be clapping his hands and wondering why!"

"Maybe not," Sola said. "I mean, maybe he isn't so happy right now."

"Why should he not be happy?" Ailva asked.

Sola gave Ailva a quizzical look. "Because, I am leaving."

"He will miss you dearly, Nulini. We all will. However, I think he will not allow his emotions around your departure to cause him unhappiness. Joy is the root of life. We do not relinquish it easily and we do not allow ourselves to let it ebb out by painful emotion. I am lecturing, a bad habit. Are you unhappy, dear?" she asked.

"Yes," Sola admitted. "I think I've let my joy leak out."

"Hmm," Ailva said, with a deep sigh. "It will take time for you to learn how to experience your emotions and then release them, not allowing them to color your overall state of being. We live each day, we learn, we change, we always have opportunities, is that not true?"

"Yes, I suppose so," Sola said. "When I want to talk with you, when I'm rushing through space like a monkey in a supersonic cage and I'm crazy for some sane advice, do I just do what I did now? That's it? That's all?"

"Yes," she responded. "As you continue to use the Saad, your skills will improve. Your ability to send and receive messages will improve. You will be amazed at the sophistication of the telepathic art."

"So, if I send you a message using this, and I can feel the tingling vibration in my fingers, I can be sure that you heard me?"

"Yes," Ailva said. "I will doubtless respond to your message in an instant, unless I am asleep, though possibly even then! That will be proof enough, I should think. Even by your scientific standards, yes?"

"There is no lag time? I mean, this is instantaneous, even across light years?"

"Yes," Ailva said, "Space and time are merely constructs."

"Does telepathy operate outside of space and time?"

"Now you are thinking!"

"Is it inter-dimensional?"

"Now you are thinking even more clearly!"

"Speaking of thinking," Sola said. "I've been thinking about the second aspect of the message from the Joining.

"I believe I will return here, to live with you, when things are more peaceful. I think that's what the message is saying, the part about my returning when you have become whole."

"It certainly seems so," Ailva said. "Let us hope that the time of peace is close at hand. Then we will not have to be apart for very long!"

"Last night was a miracle. I actually tried to connect with my pain and grief about Ramon after I woke up this morning, just for a moment, just to see what I'd feel. All I felt was love and a sense of joy! I have done so much therapy over losing him, and it never worked. Not like this. I finally feel healed! I don't know how I can repay you, all of you, for that gift!"

"You have no debt to us, Nulini. We share in your recovery."

"Thank you. Thank you for making it happen for me!"

Sola wanted to rush outside, to smell the fresh mountain air.

She wondered if Jaitain was clapping yet.

Chapter 34

Day Sixteen (late morning)

Ti comone u maya.
I hold your name.

The Mhalanai Book of Ways

Jaitain came walking across the field, looking like a farm boy wearing Pjetri's big woven hat against the strong sun.

Sola stood on the garden patio watching him move through the ripening crop of nicha, a tall grass, which she learned from Lena was a highly nutritious grain.

When he saw her, Jaitain raised his arms above his head and moved his hands together making wide, slow arches. The sound of his clapping reached her as a muted staccato carried by a mild breeze.

She bit her lower lip gently, staring at his youthful figure backlit by the sun and made diminutive by the stark rise of the etched mountain peaks behind him.

She wanted to remember him in this moment, so full of life, so innocent.

In this moment, he appeared not as a revolutionary hero weighed down by responsibility and ideology, but as a free man, running across the field, a dream image, only half-real, only half hers.

"Ailva's gift!" Jaitain said, slightly out of breath as he approached her. "We will be able to talk, over all those vacuous leagues of space!"

That was true! She hadn't thought of the wider implications of having the Olvino Saad. She needed to establish some other contracts too. She'd want to talk with Eilfina, Meil and Dukal, but there was so little time left.

"You know," Jaitain said, wrapping Sola in his arms. "You can communicate with any of the participants of the Joining. The Joining established telepathic contracts for you."

"Really?" Sola asked. "You just read my mind! That's fantastic!"

She gave Jaitain a kiss. "I missed my morning wake-up kiss!"

"Then I'd better give you two to make up for the loss!" He kissed her for a long time.

"Too bad we can't kiss over those vacuous leagues of space!" Sola said.

"We can kiss in our minds!"

Meil walked up to them, clearing his throat as advance warning of his presence.

"I hate to break up a tender moment," he said, "but it's nearing noon for Colby, and I think we'd better head over to the Naia. I've decided on a location, just outside the ship, and have the coordinates. Nice hat, Jaitain! Glad to see you are protecting that brilliant brain of yours from the brilliant sun. I think I'll go find one of my own, a hat that is, not a brilliant brain. That's a lost cause. What about you Sola?"

"Sure, a hat would be great, though I think my brain is already fried."

Meil entered the house and returned with two more, wide brimmed, woven grass hats.

"Should we ask Ailva to join us?" Sola asked.

"Sounds like a good plan. Do you know where she is?" Meil asked Sola.

"I left her upstairs in her chamber," Sola said, "but I bet she's picked up on our request already and is on her way down."

No sooner had the words left her mouth, than Ailva appeared in the doorway, with a blue scarf in hand.

"Shall we go, then?" she said, swinging the scarf out with a gallant gesture and letting it rest over her pale green scalp.

They headed into the field.

"Has any one talked with Tjarlii this morning?" Sola asked.

Meil, touched his palm to his forehead. "I am remiss in my duties! I meant to tell you Tjarlii says the strike is unresolved. There won't be a run to the moon."

"Did you tell her we have another option now?" Jaitain asked.

"I did. She was pleased to hear it."

"I want to thank her in person before she goes," Sola said. "for her offer to help and for her attendance last night. She hasn't left yet has she?"

"She's got no reason to rush back. I think she's planning to stay another night."

"Good. I'll round her up later then."

They reached the Naia. It was stifling inside.

"We have an exceptionally warm day today," Meil said. "I'll run some cool air through here and things ought to be more bearable shortly."

He turned on the environmental system.

"Now, let's see if I can get Colby on the line."

"Colby," Sola said into the microphone. "Colby, do you copy?"

There was no reply.

"Hey, Space Cowboy, are you out there?"

Still no reply. Sola waited a few seconds and tried again.

"Colby Stanton. Colby Stanton, white courtesy telephone please," she said.

Colby's voice came through a crackle of static.

"Big howdy! Sorry, I was temporarily indisposed, if you know what I mean. Well, damn, woman! Is it high noon already? Lordy, we've got ourselves some nasty static today."

"It's these darned mountains screwing with our reception, but you should see 'em! Just like the Rockies! What a place."

"Well, I could sure use a change of view, I'll tell you that."

"I'll bet!"

"So, do you have some numbers for me?"

"Yes," Sola said. "We have the coordinates and we can pick a time. Do I need to do anything to prepare? Do I get to take luggage?"

"Sure! You can take as much luggage as you like. No extra charge!"

Sola looked over at Jaitain. She wondered if he might go with her if she asked.

"Everything's still on," she said to the crew, who were all looking at her with earnest expressions on their faces.

"Colby," Sola said. "What's our time frame? Has the Cousteau arrived?"

"Well," Colby said. He was leaning back in his chair. She could hear the familiar creak of metal stress as he pushed back too far. "I spoke with Jean Luc this morning. He said they ought to be in position at about, let me see now," he leaned forward in the chair, again the creak, audible even through the aura of static, "15:00 or 16:00. They want to do the transport no later than 22:00, because they'd like to get you back on board the Minerva by midnight. They can only transport you from the planet's surface to *their* ship, not from the planet directly here."

"I figured that, so how do I get onto the Minerva?"

"They have this nifty apparatus, sort of like a large hamster tube, that can lock onto the outer hatch of our decon chamber. It's got oxygen, but zero g. You get to maneuver through it and float on over to Minerva. Kind of like going through the birth canal and meeting the midwife on the other side!"

"I don't quite see you as the midwife type. Tell me it isn't translucent. I don't think I could handle the visual on that!"

"Ah, come on! Talk about one hell of a view, 360 degrees of awesome!"

"I don't think I'm up for that, Colby. Can't they just use MERT to transport me to Minerva?"

Jean Luc says their safety protocol won't allow it, unless you wait at least 8 hours."

"Glad to hear they respect their safety protocols. What about my luggage?"

"They can MERT that over here, no problem."

"Can I just wait the 8 hours? Are they in some sort of hurry? Hold on a minute. Colby, are you pulling my leg? I'm trying to visualize this hamster tube thing. There's no way! That's just crazy. Did you read that in some old sci fi novel?"

"Bingo. You've got it. No hamster tube. You're off your game today, Honey Pie, a little slow on the draw. You usually catch me in the act way sooner. I was beginning to run out of ammunition on this thing."

"That was a good one! You definitely had me going, but the having to wait 8 hours, is that for real?"

"Yup. But we do have another option, if les monsieurs are willing to go for it. They have a sizable shuttle bay. It's filled with tons of research equipment and their own shuttle, but it's large enough for Minerva, if they are willing to park their shuttle outside while I pull in and pick you up."

"But you haven't negotiated this yet?"

"Well, darlin', the problem is all five of them are dying to meet you! It's an all male crew. I can't blame them for wanting un peu de distraction féminine. So, the challenging question is, who gets to pick the short stick, pilot their shuttle out of the bay, and miss all the excitement?"

"The man with the greatest passion for chocolate!"

"What? I don't have any chocolate to offer, I'm afraid."

"Ah, but I do!"

"No kidding?"

"They make it here! It has the dark flavor of Godiva, the panache of Puccini Bomboni, and the punch of 80% pure cocoa. I'm bringing lots, so we'll still have plenty for ourselves if they take our bribe."

"I've never met a Frenchman who wasn't passionate for chocolate, and the good stuff is mighty hard to come by. I think you've just turned the tables on the situation. Now they will be fighting each other to take that shuttle run!"

"Are you saying I am trumped by dark chocolate?"

"I am saying nothing of the sort!"

"Nice diplomatic save. It's good to see you are still you!"

"Who the hell else would I be? Now, can I have those coordinates so we can get that chocolate over here?"

Sola turned to Meil.

"He needs the coordinates."

"I have set them for a small area about 25 meters from the ship, out in the field. Does that sound good to you?" Meil asked.

"That sounds fine," Sola said.

"Will Colby be able to translate our locator terminology?"

"Yes. He is a wiz with that sort of thing. He could probably get a lock on our radio signal and estimate from there," she added, "but they need more than a good estimate. I don't want to end up half-transferred," she said.

It occurred to her that in fact, she would be only half-transferred. A big chunk of her heart was staying here.

Meil looked into his computer screen. "The coordinates are: 23.4 ain by 36.1 tjan, and let us calculate a diameter of transference of 3 pars. Does that sound about right, Jaitain?" He asked, turning his seat to face Jaitain who stood behind Sola's chair.

"That will give you room for three or four cases or bags of supplies," Jaitain said. "Do you need more than that?"

"Enough room to add *you* to the transport," she whispered in his ear.

"Don't think I haven't considered it," he responded in kind.

She felt his warm, electric energy run along her neck, and down her spine. She sighed.

"But you have important work to do here," she said.

"Sola?" Colby's voice prompted. "Do you have those coordinates yet?"

"Yes, but they're in Caifanii, so Minerva will have to translate."

"No problem. Let's have 'em."

"23.45 ain by 36.12 tjan, with a diameter of transference of

3 pars."

"Okay. Got that. Now, we need to decide on an exact time when you will be ready to transfer within those coordinates."

"Right," Sola said. "Let me talk that one through with my comrades here. Hang on."

"No sweat."

"We need to choose the exact time for the transfer, after 16:00 today, but before 22:00.

"What about 21:59," Jaitain said, a pleading look in his eyes.

"Ha!" Sola said. "I'd go for that, but we probably ought to have a little bigger margin. What about 19:00, in case we encounter any technical difficulties?"

"Fine," Meil said. "We can have you in position at that time, right around sunset."

"Okay," Sola said, moving back to the transmitter. "Colby, 19:00 on the dot."

"We'll make it a date with fate. Now, I need to relay a few details to you, are you ready to copy?"

"Yes," Sola said.

"You need to wear absolutely nothing," he paused for dramatic effect.

"Yes, please continue," she said, waiting for him to get serious.

"Nothing made of silver, that is."

"I don't own anything silver, so that's not a problem."

"It's no biggie. They just said the process tarnishes silver irreversibly. You'll need to drink a lot of water prior to the transfer, a couple of tall glasses at least. The process causes dehydration, so it's best to load up. Oh, one more thing, if you can get hold of some copper, that would be helpful. A couple of copper bracelets, maybe," Colby said.

"Okay, do I also need the ear of a bat, the tail of a mouse, and a pinch of salt?"

"Hey, they're French. If you can't be stylish, why bother to show up? Okay, before you start riling on me for being such a wise ass, I'll be straight with you. There's a reason for the copper. You know the old wisdom about how wearing copper helps alleviate joint pain?"

"My grandmother swears by it."

"Well, les monsieurs have informed me that they have found their joints to be considerably less sore after transport if they wear copper. So, there you have it, for what it's worth. Not essential, but proactively therapeutic. Oh, and they'll need DNA and energy reads, but I can give them those from our data base."

"Colby, wait." Sola said, remembering that her body's resonant frequency was still higher than 8.7 MHz.

She wondered if that would make a difference. It was going to be a little complicated to explain, and it would not lower on its own until a couple of days after she left Caifanii.

Sola heard Ailva's voice in her mind saying not to worry, that it could be lowered before she left the planet.

"Never mind," she said.

Colby continued. "Here's what you will experience during the transport, just so you don't freak."

"I don't freak, Colby. I'm a professional."

"Yeah, but this is weird shit. First, you'll feel very warm for a moment, then very cold. Then you will feel a tingling sensation for a fraction of a second, very intense but not painful. Then your vision will blur, so they recommend you keep your eyes closed, unless you're up for a psychedelic trip."

"Sounds intriguing."

"Then you will feel, as they put it, like you are expanding very rapidly, like you're in a centrifuge. This will last another fraction of a second before you lose consciousness, at which point you will no longer be in physical form. In fact, they recommend your friends watch, it's supposed to be quite a show."

"Great!" Sola said, her trepidation about the process returning full force. "I get to *be* the fourth of July finale! Then what?"

"Then the next thing you know you're you again. You'll be tingly all over, and when you open your eyes you'll be facing five very self-pleased French scientists who will take one look at you and immediately swoon at your delightful molecular arrangements."

"What if something goes wrong?" Sola said.

"Then you're star dust! 'We are star dust, we are golden, and we've got to get back to the gaaaaarden,'" he sang, a little off key. "No, seriously, don't worry. Nothing will go wrong! They've all done this umpteen times and they say it's a routine procedure. Sometimes they do it just for fun!"

"Right!"

"No, for real. That's what Jean Luc said, 'Juste pour le plaisir! Avec les yeux overts!'"

"Well, I'm keeping *my* eyes closed! Anything else? What happens once I'm on board the Cousteau?"

"A little steel drum, a little limbo, a little rum. Who knows, you might get lucky," he teased.

She knew he was just trying to keep things light, to cheer her up, to reassure her, and himself that everything would go smoothly.

"More likely a little accordion, a little tango, and a little Champagne!"

"Touchée!"

"Not too much touchée, I hope! If the chocolate does the trick, I guess I'll be seeing you on the Cousteau for that Champagne!" she said with dramatic flair.

"Mais oui!" Colby said.

"Well, Space Cowboy, if that's all there is, then I guess I'll get myself packed and ready to disintegrate."

"I'm going back into my moon cave now."

"I'll be ready at 19:00," she said.

"Okay," he said. "Well, good luck with MERT. Take some pictures. It ought to be pretty cosmic!"

"No doubt."

"Bon voyage!"

"See you when the satellites come home!"

That was Colby's line, but he wouldn't mind her using it. Sola turned to face Jaitain.

"Sorry that took so long. Colby was being his usual wacky self, but we're all set."

"Then we'd best return to the house and make your preparations," Jaitain said. "What's chocolate?"

"Katidan!"

"Pjetri has given her an ample supply!" Ailva said.

"Ailva?" Sola said.

"No concerns, dear. There is no silver in the Olvino Saad."

"That's good news. I wouldn't want my long distance service to get permanently tarnished!"

They stepped out of the Naia and were hit by a blast of hot, moist air.

"We'll get rain out of this sky," Meil said. "We'd better hurry back if we want to stay dry!"

Halfway across the field, the rain began. It fell in thick drops, soaking their clothes.

"I hope Pjetri's hats will recover!" Jaitain said.

"Is anything on our world not used to rain?" Meil said.

"Good point!" Jaitain took Sola's hand.

They wanted to run, but the grass was too tall, and they didn't want to leave Ailva behind.

"Whoo wee!" Sola yelped, turning her face into the downpour for a moment.

The rain felt good. Her clothes grew heavy with it and they clung to her legs as she walked through the tall grasses, but there was a lightness in her gait.

She felt relieved that she no longer needed to weigh her choices. She did not want to leave, but she knew she would return someday.

Today, she was going home.

Chapter 35

Day Sixteen (evening)

Parting is such sweet sorrow

Romeo and Juliet
William Shakespeare

They were all in dry clothes, back in the farmhouse, sitting together by the fire. Sola watched the rain drip off the eaves as she sipped her tea. The downpour was over and a little sun was poking out between the clouds.

Jaitain was sitting close to her, his arm wrapped about her shoulders, the warmth of his body radiating into hers.

"I'm not letting you go until I absolutely have to," he said.

"Maybe you could just get energized along with her!" Eilfina said.

"I get energized just by *being* with her!" he replied.

His open affection toward her with everyone present in the room touched Sola. She'd miss the deep sense of community she enjoyed here.

"We need to retune your base frequency," Ailva said.

"Yes, thanks. I heard you say that was possible earlier, in my mind. That was helpful to know in that moment."

"It should be quite simple. Your body will adapt to the lowering more readily than it adapted to the increase.""When do we need to do it?" Sola asked.

"It will take just a few moments, so we can do it right before your departure."

"That's good," Sola said. "I'd like to stay high as long as I can!"

"When you return here in another season or two," Eilfina said, "you'll get to be high again!"

"You are a true optimist, Eilfina!"

"If Amnesty Interstellar and The United Planets Association support us," Eilfina said, "won't that speed things up?"

"Revolutions take time," Meil said. "Even strong external influences won't change things overnight."

"They will put pressure on Haikon, trade sanctions, that sort of thing," Sola said. "The United Planets will do everything it can to avoid direct confrontation, but will send on-planet support if needed. Negotiations will occupy the forefront, and those could last a number of seasons. I've seen negotiations drag on for years."

"No," Eilfina said. "I refuse to believe it will take years! I know it will be sooner. I can feel it here." She placed her hand over her heart. "You will be back in a few seasons. You'll see."

"I hope you're right!" Sola said. "I'll hardly have time to spend on Earth before I need to turn around and head back!"

"Then don't leave," Eilfina said, "just stay!"

For a moment, Sola was unsure of herself, suddenly confused as to why she was actually leaving.

"I am not making this any easier, am I?" Eilfina said. "We'll miss you so very, very much!"

"We will wait for you like we wait for the New Rain," Jaitain said.

"And I will miss you all terribly!" Sola said.

"Let's hope the New Rain comes sooner than expected!" Ailva said.

They all stood in silence.

Then there were some tears, then some light laughter, then some more silence.

"How much time do we have left before I transport?" Sola asked, though she really didn't want to face that knowledge.

"Another five dahn," Meil said.

"Okay, then I should think about what I need to take with me. The Olvino Saad, of course, and chocolate, I mean kaditan."

Ailva was looking intently at her. "You two need time together," she said. "Let us leave and give you some privacy."

"Everyone looks so comfortable here," Sola said, "and I'd love a little fresh air. Why don't all of you stay put, and we can go out on the veranda."

"Are you game for that?" Sola asked, looking at Jaitain. "I'd love to catch a view of the mountains peeking out from the clouds."

"I'd love that too," he said.

The two of them rose and walked out through the kitchen. They stepped into the cool, fresh air. Rays of sunlight filtered through the ashen clouds.

"I keep thinking I can find just the right words to make this easier," Sola said.

"They elude me as well," Jaitain said. "I keep believing that tomorrow you will still be here, that we can continue to enjoy being together. My mind refuses to grasp that tomorrow you'll be speeding through space, placing more and more distance between us."

Sola placed her fingertips over his lips. "Let's not talk about it. I just want to hold you."

He pulled her into a tight embrace.

Sola looked over his shoulder at the mountains, thinly veiled in mist.

"I feel as gray as the sky," she said.

"The sun is coming out," he said, "and look, over there!"

He pointed across the fields and she saw it, a rainbow. They could see the complete arc extending from one end of the valley to the other. As the sunlight increased, the spectrum of light intensified.

"It is a good omen," Jaitain said.

"It's beautiful," Sola said. "Perfect."

They stood wrapped around each other for a long while watching the bridge of reflected color hang across the sky.

"I've always been fascinated by rainbows. There are lots of them on Maui. When I used to visit my Grandparents, I would see one almost every day. When I was a little girl, I thought they existed. I didn't know that they are an optical effect created by refraction of light through moisture. I thought they existed exactly in the spot where I saw them, like a real bridge to a magical place. Sometimes, knowledge brings disillusion. I wish I could still believe the rainbow was a real bridge."

"I guess it is, in a way, a bridge to whatever magic you create in your own mind."

"That's true enough." She pulled his arms more tightly around her.

"I have a gift for you, Nulini," Jaitain whispered into her ear, kissing it lightly.

He reached into his jacket pocket, and pulled out a small red bag with a golden drawstring.

"This belonged to my grandmother," he said, and reached for Sola's hand. "I've kept it since her passing, hoping someday to give it to someone I love."

He placed the bag into Sola's palm. "I want you to have it."

She held the bag, feeling the gentle weight of his love invested in it.

"Go ahead," he urged, "open it."

She drew open the string and pulled out an exquisitely made bracelet. Two fine metals woven together in a spiral. One was a dark rose color, the other golden. On the inside, there was an ornate inscription.

"It's beautiful!" Sola said. "Thank you. Oh, this is so wonderful! Thank you!"

She slipped the bracelet onto her wrist. It fit her perfectly.

"Is this copper?" she asked, running her finger along the dark rose metal.

"Yes," Jaitain said.

"What is this other one? I don't recognize it."

"It is ulmine. It comes from a distant star system."

"It's gorgeous."

"My grandfather bought it from a traveler, and had it woven together with the copper as a wedding gift for my grandmother, to symbolize the weaving of their love in a strong bond."

"That's so touching and romantic!"

"I would like it to symbolize the same, for us."

She smiled at him and nodded. "What does the engraving say?" she asked.

"It says Nulini. It was my grandfather's term of endearment for her, just as it is mine for you."

"I will cherish this. I will wear it perpetually! Will water harm it? Can I wear it even while bathing?"

"Of course! We can't keep things on this planet which might be harmed by water!" he chuckled.

"Good point!" she said.

She noticed a few patches of pale blue sky.

"Look," she said. "The peaks are clearing."

The mountains had an iridescent, lavender glow over them.

"Hey," Sola said. "I don't remember telling you about the old joint pain remedy. How did you know about that?"

"I don't know what you mean," he responded, looking genuinely puzzled.

"Then it's pure serendipity! The MERT transport makes your joints ache. Wearing copper helps minimize that reaction!"

"I love it! I love you!" he said.

They stood for a long while together, breathing the fresh, cooled air and watching the sky clear to more and more patches of blue.

Sola placed her arms around Jaitain's waist and pulled him close to her.

"I want to give you something too, Jaitain. Something precious, like this bracelet, but I have nothing to give."

He took her hand and placed it palm to palm with his. She could feel the heat and energy flow into her, warming her entire body.

"You are my gift, Nulini," he said.

She smiled. "We sure are sounding mushy!" she proclaimed.

"Who can blame us? Shall we go back inside?"

"Sure," she said. "Let's eat! I'm hungry."

"You're always hungry!" he said, affectionately.

There was another banquet of a meal.

Sola was happy to again sit next to Tjarlii. She thanked the captain for her generous offer to assist them. She greatly enjoyed Tjarlii's stories of her odd adventures in the whirlwind world of waste disposal. Tjarlii was a colorful character to be sure. Sola regretted not having more time to spend with her.

She was secretly grateful, however, to be missing that garbage run to the moon, and the subsequent spacewalk rendezvous with the Minerva. That whole plan still seemed too wacky for words.

After the feast, Lena gave Sola various packages of food, including two loaves of her fresh bread, all neatly wrapped and tucked into an intricately woven basket. Pjetri had added so much kaditan to the basket, that Sola was tempted to call him the Easter Bunny.

Eilfina placed a garland of fresh flowers gently onto Sola's head, encouraging her to wear it during the transport.

Sola's eyes filled with tears. The garland was a lei of white plumeria blossoms. She embraced Eilfina, and then they were both crying.

Sola wiped away her tears and smiled.

The French scientists were going to think she was some sort of goddess, a bald, green one!

Dukal surprised her with a collection of his own poetry. He read two pieces aloud and impressed everyone with his vivid imagery and passionate style.

"Sola," Tjarlii said.

"Yes?"

Tjarlii wore an impish grin. "We do not know each other well, and I hope to change that in future. When you return, we must have an adventure together!"

"I heartily agree!" Sola said.

"I hear you lost your musical instrument in Haikon as a result of your abduction," Tjarlii continued. "Being a musician myself, I understand the impact of such a loss. Jaitain tells me the instrument you play is similar to one we use here, the himalina. I do not play the himalina myself, but Lena and Pjetri told me of a craftswoman here in the village who makes excellent himalinas! So, I hope you will accept this gift from me as a token of my respect for the work you have done in support of our cause, and as a small repayment for all that you have endured during your stay here on our unsettled world."

She gave Sola a package wrapped in brown paper. Beneath the paper was a handsome instrument made of smooth dark wood. Excellently crafted, it had a neck and fingerboard remarkably similar to a tenor ukelele, but a slightly rounder body, more like a lute. There was even a rosette with shell inlays.

"Tjarlii!" Sola said. "I am awestruck! You have outdone yourself."

"Will you play it for us?" Tjarlii asked.

"I will try. The tuning is likely quite different, so my chords may not translate, but if you are patient with me, I think I can figure it out."

She strummed the open strings. The sound was not unlike a uke. She tried a few chords. Some sounded good, some sounded Byzantine, a few sounded painful.

She laughed.

After a few minutes, she managed to find three chords that were close enough to uke tuning to use in a song.

She felt nervous with everyone looking at her so intently, but she played and sang the Hawaiian traditional song, *Henehene Kou.*

She captivated her small audience.

Eilfina looked enraptured. Jaitain beamed. Ailva was radiant, and Meil, Dukal, Lena, and Pjetri were smiling like Cheshire Cats! No one was more moved than Tjarlii, who looked like the mother of the lead in a pre-school play.

When she finished the song, Dukal cried out, "One more!"

Everyone nodded in agreement.

Sola felt so flustered it was hard to think of even one more song out of her large repertoire.

She finally decided on *I Kona*, her latest addition.

"Okay, I don't know this one all that well yet," she said, "but it's about a beautiful place that you love, so it's perfect."

Sola felt the song come straight from her heart, like never before. It floated into the room like the perfume of plumeria.

Everyone thanked her profusely and sighed with disappointment when she insisted that two songs were to be the sum total of her concert program for the evening.

Lena left the room and returned with yet another gift. It was a turquoise tjong. Sola held it up in front of her.

"Exquisite!" Eilfina said. "You have to wear it tonight."

"She's right," Jaitain said.

"You should put it on now!" Eilfina said.

Sola felt so loved, so pampered. How was she going to leave her generous new family behind?

"I don't want to leave all of you even for a few minutes! How am I going to go through with this tonight?"

She looked at each of their faces, trying to soak in all the love she saw there, and then she went upstairs with the tjong.

She removed what she was wearing and slipped on the elegant dress. The material felt like silk, as soft and as pleasantly cool to the touch. It flowed over her body like water and made her feel truly like a goddess. With the flower garland on her head and draped in this ocean of blue, she was going to give those French scientists and Colby, an eye full!

She had debated warning Colby about her temporary alterations in appearance, but was glad she'd decided against it. She wanted to see his surprised reaction!

When she walked back into the living area there was an audible awe.

Jaitain stood up and bowed to her in a chivalrous manner.

"We are most honored," he said.

He took her hand and led her back to the sofa seat as if she were the Queen of Sheba.

Ailva came to sit on her other side, and Eilfina came to sit on a thick cushion, by Sola's feet.

Dukal, Meil, Pjetri, and Tjarlii sat across the room.

Sola felt enveloped in love.

"What a feeling!" she said. "I am capturing an emotional imprint of this moment. I will think of it when I miss all of you, which will be every day!"

Lena came into the room bearing yet another package wrapped in thin, white paper.

"Sola, there will be a chill this evening. You can wrap yourself in this. She laid her package on Sola's lap.

Sola lifted the delicate paper, uncovering a shawl woven with sea green, pale silver, deep cobalt and sky blue yarns. The material was softer than any wool or even angora she had ever felt. She ran her fingers over its sumptuous texture.

"Oh, Lena!" she exclaimed.

"Lena is a true artist with textiles," Pjetri said, coming up behind his mate and giving her a strong hug around the waist.

"You made this?" Sola asked.

"Last cold season, yes," Lena said. "It is woven of the finest pikoli fur. It will give me the world of pleasure to know it travels with you!"

"Thank you!" Sola said, pulling the delightfully soft shawl about her shoulders and enjoying how perfectly its color scheme matched with the tjong.

"Now you are almost prepared for your journey home," Meil said, a sparkle in his eyes as he came over to her, his hand extended, a small box enclosed in his palm.

"This is something which will remind you of your time here," he said.

Inside, Sola found a rugged timepiece on a band of woven plant fibers.

"Mhalanai time!" she exclaimed. "How perfect!"

"It's not a new timepiece," Meil said, "but it has served me well, and should last many more seasons. If the power cell wears down, it has a back-up winding mechanism. I replaced the cell this morning, so I think it will last until your return."

"I will wear it with pride, my friend," Sola said, "as a gift from a Mhalanai hero!"

"Oh, I am no hero!" Meil said, looking sheepish, but obviously pleased by the compliment.

"I am honored," he added.

"If it were not for you," Sola said, in a more solemn tone, "we would all have drowned, or been taken captive by Loyalists."

"True enough!" Dukal said.

Sola looked at the timepiece with affection. Then with shock, as she registered the actual time.

"Oh, no!" she said. "I have so little time before I leave!"

"Then let's have a blessing for you now, Sola" Ailva said.

Everyone was suddenly very silent.

"This blessing," Ailva said, "is a song in an ancient form of the Mhalanai language. Its source is not documented, and we do not know how it came to be part of our legacy. The meaning of many of the words are now unclear to us, but the final line of the song appears in the opening of the Prophecy of the Great Day, so it is a song of great power."

Ailva gave a knowing smile to Sola, who understood.

That line from the Book of Ways was part of the second greeting she had heard while she was in those dreadful caves. That seemed like centuries ago to her now.

Ailva continued. "We use this song for many occasions: the celebration of a birth, a marriage, any great personal triumph. It is simple and we will repeat it many times, so please join in the singing once you become familiar enough with the sounds of the words."

Pjetri brought out a circular hand drum, and gave it to Ailva.

Ailva moved into the center of the room. She began to beat upon the drum with the tips of her fingers bringing forth a low, resonant drone, a heartbeat. She began to chant an open vowel sound, her voice filling the chamber with reverence.

Then she began the song, her voice caressing an open, fluid language.

Sola felt a surge of love and recognition. The language in which Ailva was singing sounded a lot like Mhalanai, but it was completely familiar to Sola. It was Hawaiian!

Not only that, Ailva was singing her grandmother's favorite song, the ancient Pule Ho'ao marriage prayer.

Eia loa`a maha
O haka moe
O haka i ka lani
Pili olua e, ho`ao e
Moku ka pawa o ke ao
Ke moakaka nei ka hikina
Ua hiki ho`i la nui

Sola stood with her eyes closed, tears streaming down her cheeks.

As the others began to include their voices, Sola joined in as well, the familiar words shining in her childhood memory like sweet pearls.

She was the only one present, however, who did know the meaning of all of the words.

Here is a place to rest,
A place to sleep,
A place in heaven.
Now two are becoming one,
The black night is scattered,
The eastern sky grows bright.
At last the great day has come.

Their singing continued, softly, prayerfully. The song became the central focus in all of their minds, like a mantra. It became the seed thought of a Joining.

With their hearts connected, and their minds joined, Sola shared the full meaning of the song with all of them. She felt their surprised amazement.

Ailva's drumming slowed and stopped.

The song went silent, but they all remained connected and quiet together for some time.

"Sola," Ailva's voice came into her mind. "What a gift you bestow on all of us! When you first heard my greeting, I spoke in ancient Mhalanai, but your mind interpreted my words in your own spiritual language."

"Hawaiian," Sola responded, with her thoughts. "And now we find this ancient, sacred song of yours is from an ancient culture on my home world!"

"There is certainly a profound significance to this discovery," Ailva continued. "There must be a connection in long ago history between our peoples."

The entire company of joined minds felt an electric buzz move through their beings.

"Wow!" Sola said, aloud. Then with her mind added, "What an amazing discovery, but what a mystery!"

"We will explore that mystery together!" Ailva said. "Let us release the connection of our minds. The Joining is completed."

Sola opened her eyes to see Ailva standing motionless in the center of the room, smiling.

Everyone appeared stunned, but joyously so. There was a sudden burst of talking from every corner of the room.

Questions abounded. Did the ancient Hawaiian people originate on Mhalanai eons ago, and somehow travel to Earth? Did the ancient Mhalanai originate on Earth eons ago, and somehow travel here? Did both peoples evolve from a mutual ancestry on a now forgotten world? Or were the similarities of language and customs between the two cultures merely an uncanny coincidence? That seemed unlikely, yet more logical than the other possibilities.

"My dear ones!" Ailva said, bringing the focus back. "There certainly is much to explore! But for now, as the time draws close to Sola's departure, let us assist her in gathering her gifts and personal belongings. It is time to go."

The sun was setting, and dusk was falling. With a lantern in one hand and something for Sola in the other, each member of their party walked across the golden field towards the Naia. Their procession must resemble a spiritual pilgrimage, Sola thought, and for her, it truly was one.

They arrived at the ship.

After a round of earnest embraces from her new extended family, and a few precious kisses from Jaitain, Sola stepped into her transport position.

They all gathered around her in a circle. Sola stood in the center, at the exact coordinates. Her many gifts, the box with the Olvino Saad, the basket with the food and katidan, were all tucked close to her feet. Lena's shawl was a practical gift as the air was cool and the silk tjong more whimsy than substance. Jaitain's bracelet was on her right wrist, Meil's watch on her left. The white plumeria lei adorned her head like a royal crown. Her heart filled with the bittersweet emotion of parting.

Only Meil was missing from the circle. He was inside the Naia verifying the coordinates.

Soon, he too stepped out into the field, joined the circle under a clear sky with remnants of a sorbet sunset, and gave Sola a nod to say all was in order.

"I will give you a ten point countdown, Sola," he said.

"But I have your timepiece, Meil!" Sola said.

"I have this one," Meil said, holding up a timer he had taken from the Naia.

"Okay, so we are set." Sola replied. "Meil, will you something for me?"

"Anything!" he said.

"After you reach zero, will you say, energize?"

"If you wish it, it is my command."

Sola was surprised she remembered to ask. Colby would be impressed, and delighted.

"I guess I am as ready as I am going to get," she said. "Good bye, my dear friends, I love you all! I trust I will see you again soon!"

"We love you!" They all responded.

Sola faced the mountains, which shone in pale alpenglow under the pair of rising full moons.

The view was so breathtaking that for a crystalline moment, it made her forget her anxiety.

The field was oddly still. There was no wind. No one spoke. There was only the resonance of loving hearts gathered, enclosing her.

Sola realized her hands were shaking and tears were streaming down her cheeks. She didn't stop them, or wipe them away.

Meil's voice drifted up from the circle. "Ten, nine, eight, seven..."

Sola breathed deeply into the night.

She felt a repose she knew came from the loving thoughts of her friends.

Meil's voice was steady and reassuring. "Six, five, four, three..."

It seemed like a million years ago, Sola thought, when she had stood in the airlock on Minerva, hearing that other countdown.

"Two, one, zero. Energize!"

Sola felt the transport begin.

Intense warmth flooded her body, followed by a shock of cold. She kept her eyes open. She wanted to stay present as long as possible.

Her entire body tingled, as if a mild electrical current ran through her.

She focused on Jaitain's face, directly in front of her in the circle, with the mountains behind him. Her vision started to blur.

Jaitain, the silent mountain peaks, the ethereal aura of the Caifanii sunset all washed away like watercolors in a downpour of rain. New Rain. Nulini.

There was a swirling of vibrant color, then dizziness, expansion, a cloud of energy rushing out in all directions.

She became the expansion. She was gone.

Chapter 36

Day Sixteen (19:00)

There's no place like home.

The Wonderful Wizard of Oz
L. Frank Baum

The void collapsed in on itself with a swirling of the light spectrum. Energy came crashing together under intense electromagnetic force.

Sola regained specific consciousness. She felt rapid pulses of heat and cold. A tingling sensation moved along her meridians in a rush of charged particles.

Then, abruptly, it was gone and she was standing on a raised platform under the harsh glare of artificial lights.

Facing her, were five men, none of them young, all of them with stunned expressions, none of them Colby.

"Mon Dieu! C'est la Madone!" said the one nearest her, his light blue eyes expressing a mixture of delight and perplexity.

His silver hair fell in a tangle over his high forehead and around his clean-shaven face.

Sola stood very still for a moment, unsure if she could move, or even reoccupy physical space.

She called to Ailva and Jaitain with her mind, letting them know she had arrived safely and in one piece.

She felt their love return like a wave. They received her message.

"Bienvenue," the silver-haired man said. "Welcome," he repeated, with a heavy French accent.

"Bon Jour," Sola said, surprised to remember the French greeting so easily. Her mind felt only marginally recollected after the state of non-form through which she just transferred.

"My name is Jean Luc," said the man, moving closer to the platform and extending his hand.

"I am Sola," she said. "Sola Alturas. Pleased to ... enchanteé." She shook his hand, finding it an unfamiliar gesture now.

"It is a unique experience, non?" said a short man in the back of the room, moving in to make his own introduction. "Phillipe," he said, a warm smile breaking across his round, red-cheeked face. "Enchanté!" He reached out to her.

Sola nodded, taking his extended hand and receiving an aggressive shake.

The sterile environment of the space transport, the harsh lights, the formalities, they all felt like a rude shock. Did she just wake up from a long dream? Was Caifanii a real world? Were her friends and Jaitain still standing in that field under that translucent moon glow? Were they still regarding the place that, just moments ago, had held her form, the place that now seemed strangely empty? It was unnerving.

"You gave us quite a surprise!" Jean Luc said, unabashed.

That didn't surprise Sola: the tjong; the garland on her bald head; her green skin; the various colorful packages strewn about her feet. She was quite the apparition.

"Gifts," she said, gesturing to the packages, "from my new friends."

"Ah!" Phillipe said, nodding in understanding.

All five Frenchmen stared openly at her, obviously unable to make sense of her appearance.

It was clear to her now that the promise of dark chocolate had not been enough to persuade any of them to draw the short stick and not be included in this welcoming committee. They were apparently making Colby wait until later to get a parking space in their shuttle bay.

"Let me introduce the rest of our team," Jean Luc said. He held out his arm and motioned for her to step down from the platform. She accepted his assistance gladly, unsure of her legs.

"This," Jean Luc said, leading her to a console in the rear of the room, is André."

"Enchanté, mademoiselle," André said with a respectful nod of his head.

"And this," Jean Luc continued, "is Yves."

"Pleased to meet you," Yves said, extending a pale, long fingered hand for her to shake.

"And this is Bernard," Jean Luc continued, taking her over to meet the final scientist.

"My pleasure," Bernard said, with a flirtatious glint in his eyes.

"We prepared a comfortable room for you," Jean Luc said. "It will be wise for you to rest prior to your friend's arrival."

Sola did not feel so much tired as confused. She smiled shyly. "That was quite a ride!"

"Oui! C'est vrais!" Jean Luc said. "Very true." The others chuckled. "You become used to it, but the first time, eh? That is something!"

"I have fresh bread, cheese, wine, and something akin to chocolate for all of you," Sola said, motioning to the large woven basket."

At the mention of chocolate, Sola noticed a slight hint of embarrassment on their faces, but none of them said anything.

"Merci, merci!" Jean Luc said. "We will bring everything to the salon and after you are rested, we will all have a lovely repast avec Monsieur Stanton, once he is also in our company, bonne idée?"

Sola found it odd to hear Colby referred to as Monsieur Stanton. "Bien sur!" she said, suddenly feeling so weak she could barely stand.

Jean Luc was on the ball and put his arm around her waist just as she felt her knees buckle. "It is catching up with you, eh?"

"Thank you for catching me!"

"You are doing quite well. The first time I transported, I passed out. I will help you to your room."

Sola was grateful for his courteous support. She had expected a crew of nerdy young scientists with minimal manners and awkward social skills. Instead, these more seasoned men, of her father's generation, treated her like royalty.

"I can't express how grateful I am to you for assisting Colby, Monsieur Stanton, and myself. We were out of options."

"This vessel is at your service," Jean Luc said. "It is nothing, a little detour only," he squeezed her arm briefly. "You are already making that service a tremendous pleasure! You are quite the sight, such a lovely young woman with your blue dress and flowers."

"And no hair and green skin!" she added.

"I am sure there is an interesting story behind that!"

"Mais oui!" she said, as they ambled down a corridor.

"The color is quite flattering on you. Very, how do you say it? Moderne y expressif! For a moment, we thought we had picked up a goddess from another dimension! We did not expect a sales representative of IDS-Interstellar to look like this. Je pense que ce ne est pas l'uniforme d'habitude."

"Not exactly," Sola agreed, "and, not exactly a routine assignment either," she added.

"Aventures fascinantes?" he asked.

"Indeed!"

"Here, we have arrived at your room."

They entered a small cabin with a wide bunk, a small metal desk, and its own bathroom.

"I will give you some privacy now. If you need anything, you may use the communications unit. It is just here." He tapped the unit, which sat on the desk. "When you are rested, just push this button and one of us will answer."

"When is Colby due to arrive?"

"Pierre is moving our shuttle out of the bay now, so Monsieur Stanton will be able to park your vessel. We will keep him entertained while you rest. It will not be wise to skip your recuperation. You will pay dearly for it later! Here is a glass of water. You need to drink it all before you lie down."

"I will," she said. "Can I ask a favor?"

"Bien sur!"

"I have not informed Monsieur Stanton about my temporary alterations in appearance."

"He knows not that you are green?"

"Correct, and I rather look forward to seeing the surprise on his face. Would you and the others keep it a secret for me, since you will see him before he sees me?"

Jean Luc had a sparkle in his eye. "I would not deprive your friend of the great joy of seeing you for the first time looking exactly as you do! I will make sure no one discloses your secret."

"I appreciate that."

"Pas de probléme. Rest well. We will see you in an hour or two." He left, closing the door behind him.

Sola wanted to see Colby now, but she could barely stand without assistance, so she dutifully followed Jean Luc's advice. She drank the water. She pulled off the tjong, not wanting to wrinkle it. She draped it over the chair by the desk, and then fell gratefully into the bunk. Within moments, she was sleeping like a mountain.

When Sola woke up, she felt much stronger and her mind was clear. She stayed in the bunk for a while filling her heart with love for Jaitain, hoping he would hear her telepathic call and answer, but there was no response, just her own random thoughts bouncing around in her head.

She got up, splashed some cool water on her face in the bathroom. Looked at her green reflection in the mirror and smiled. She pulled on the tjong, placed the flower garland back on her head and pushed the button on the communications unit.

"Bonjour," a voice said. "C'est Yves. Est-ce Sola?"

"Oui."

"Vous êtes prêt? Pardon. You are ready to join us?"

"Oui."

"Bon. Jean Luc will arrive shortly."

"Merci."

Jean Luc arrived and escorted Sola towards the salon.

"Colby has arrived?" she asked, feeling surprisingly nervous.

"Indeed, and we have not told him a thing! He will be as surprised as we were!"

"Excellent," she said. "Thanks again. How long did I sleep?"

"Almost two hours. That is trés bon. Your body needed the rest."

They continued down a long corridor, took a lift to the next higher level, walked down another corridor and stopped before a closed door.

"We are here," Jean Luc said. "Vous êtes prêt?"

"Ready!" Sola said.

Jean Luc pushed a button on the wall and the door opened automatically.

Sola stepped into the spacious room. Colby was facing away from her, engaged in a conversation with Pierre.

"Attention mes amie!" Jean Luc said. "Sola est arrivé!"

The look on Colby's face when he turned and saw her was priceless.

"Well throw my hat over the windmill!" he shouted.

Then he bounded across the room, picked her up off the floor and swung her around until she was dizzy.

The flower garland slipped from her head and flew across the room like an old-fashioned wedding bouquet.

Bernard jumped in the air to catch it with a gallant gesture.

Colby put her down, stood back and took another good look at her.

"You've gone seriously native, Pumpkin! This here's not permanent, is it?" he asked, running the palm of his hand lightly over the top of her head.

"It's already growing back in," she said. "I'll have an auburn five o'clock shadow by tomorrow!"

"Aren't you sweeter than stolen honey!"

Colby shook his head. "I can't get over this! Is that jade complexion temporary too?"

"Enjoy it while you can! I will only be a little green woman from Mars for another 24 hours or so."

"Well, I can't say I'm disappointed by that news, though you look remarkably stunning as a Caifanii!"

"I obviously owe you a story or two! More like a baker's dozen!" she said. "Speaking of which, I brought some fabulous bread and other goodies with me. Did you all get into them yet?"

"Are you kidding? These French dudes are tough nuts to crack. They wouldn't give me a single detail, except that you were fine and resting from the transport. Now, I understand why. You swore them to secrecy didn't you? You tricky little green devil. You didn't want to spoil your grand entrance."

"You got it."

"I'm glad," he confessed. "I was totally blown out of the water!" He leaned in close to her. "You trumped the chocolate, big time," he whispered.

"I noticed."

"There was no way I was going to convince any of these guys to take a hike into space and miss your arrival. That must have been some arrival!"

"I remember hearing a 'Mon Dieu!' I believe there was also a reference to 'la Madone,'" she whispered back.

"You are a Green Goddess!" he said. "Isn't that a salad dressing, or something?"

"Indeed it is! Let's find out where they stashed my big basket of culinary delights."

A long table was set up in the salon, and Sola arranged Lena and Pjetri's delicacies on plates provided from the galley.

Sola and Colby conversed with their hosts while everyone enjoyed the fresh bread, cheeses, wine, dried fruits, and chocolate.

The Frenchmen were enraptured with the food, having sustained themselves on routine rations for months. Apparently, French rations were hardly haute cuisine.

Sola watched with glee as they smacked their lips, uttered superlatives and all the while thanked her profusely between bites and sips. Pjetri's "chocolate" was, of course, the pièce de résistance!

Colby, who sat next to her, was savoring a piece of the katidan, letting it melt slowly in his mouth. Sola watched him. He looked like a contented kid. She felt like tousling his crazy blonde hair, but resisted the impulse.

"Hey," Colby said. "I have some nifty news."

"Do tell."

"I received a communiqué from IDS about three hours ago. They are giving both of us extended furloughs and extra compensatory pay for the 'inconveniences' of this assignment."

"Well, that's considerate of them! Guess we won't tell them we quit, just yet." Sola said.

"And," Colby said, raising his eyebrows for dramatic effect, "after Amnesty and the United Planets help straighten things out down there, they will maintain Caifanii as your exclusive territory, if and when the market re-opens. How do you like them apples?" he said, triumphant.

"That's mind boggling, considering my signed contract is lying on the bottom of the sea, and has probably been eaten by fish."

"They'll just have you get another one, with the newly appointed High Councilor of Trade and Commerce."

"Hopefully, the new High Councilor doesn't run a drug cartel on the side!"

"I doubt it. I hear rumors that he's a Mhalanai supporter."

"You're joshing with me."

"Yeah, but it's possible!"

"Right now, I feel anything is possible!"

Sola was going back! She could feel it in her bones!

She didn't have to go back as an IDS Representative. Their free ticket wasn't exactly free. She'd find a way. A rush of excitement raced through her. Deep inside her mind, she heard Jaitain's voice.

"Nulini," he said, "I am with you."

Sola smiled, and sent him a reply from deep within her heart, "and I am with you."

"So, when do I get to hear those stories?" Colby asked.

"We've got three weeks of travel time to fill," she said. "Let's get back on Minerva and start the long trek to Denver, shall we?"

"Hey, since 'All's well that ends well,'" Colby said, "this must be the end!"

Sola gave him a squeeze, filled with love for him, for Jaitain, for her new family left behind far below.

There were plenty of details to iron out, lots of questions to answer, some challenging conversations ahead, but Sola was sure everything was indeed well, though she was also sure that it was not yet the end!

Acknowledgments

I gratefully thank Elisabeth Appels, Patrick Markham, Anne Rainy Woods, Stephen Anderson, Michael Diamond, Jim Hampton, Fritz Knochenhauer, Sue Khosein, and Michael O'Neil for reading drafts, giving editing suggestions, expressing enthusiasm for the story, and believing in its success. Without their support, publishing *New Rain* would still be an unrealized dream.

Author's Note

I first wrote this story in Davis, California in 1989. I rewrote the story in a cabin in the Rocky Mountains of Colorado in 1997. I finished this revision in New Mexico. *New Rain* has lived in three states of the union and my dream of publishing this book has persisted over three decades. Thanks for reading this story. I hope you enjoyed it!

About the Author

Eve West Bessier lives in southern New Mexico. She was born in the Netherlands and at age seven immigrated to San Francisco with her mother. Eve is an award-winning author of poetry, fiction, and non-fiction. She is a Poet Laureate Emerita of Silver City, New Mexico and of Davis, California. Eve holds a Master of Education from the University of California, Davis. She has a Bachelor of Arts in English from San Francisco State University. Eve is a social scientist, educator, vocalist and voice coach, visual artist and nature enthusiast. You can find more information, including performance videos and recordings on her website.

www.jazzpoeteve.com

www.ingramcontent.com/pod-product-compliance
Lightning Source LLC
Chambersburg PA
CBHW032139270626
47172CB00009B/417